The Eleventh Hour

the Eleventh Hour

A Connor Hawthorne Mystery

LAUREN MADDISON

alyson books
los angeles

MANUFACTURED IN THE UNITED STATES OF AMERICA.

THIS TRADE PAPERBACK ORIGINAL IS PUBLISHED BY ALYSON PUBLICATIONS,
P.O. BOX 4371, LOS ANGELES, CALIFORNIA 90078-4371.
DISTRIBUTION IN THE UNITED KINGDOM BY TURNAROUND PUBLISHER SERVICES LTD.,
UNIT 3, OLYMPIA TRADING ESTATE, COBURG ROAD, WOOD GREEN,
LONDON N22 6TZ ENGLAND.

FIRST EDITION: NOVEMBER 2004

04 05 06 07 08 **a** 10 9 8 7 6 5 4 3 2 1

ISBN 1-55583-878-2

LIBRARY OF CONGRESS CATALOGING-IN-PUBLICATION DATA
MADDISON, LAUREN.
    THE ELEVENTH HOUR : A CONNOR HAWTHORNE MYSTERY / LAUREN MADDISON.—1ST ED.
    ISBN 1-55583-878-2 (TRADE PBK. : ALK. PAPER)
        1. HAWTHORNE, CONNOR (FICTITIOUS CHARACTER)—FICTION. 2. PALM SPRINGS
(CALIF.)—FICTION. 3. WOMEN NOVELISTS—FICTION. 4. LESBIANS—FICTION. I. TITLE.
PS3563.A33942E44 2004
813'.54—DC22   2004057075

CREDITS
COVER PHOTOGRAPHY BY HUW JONES/GETTY IMAGES TAXI COLLECTION.
COVER DESIGN BY MATT SAMS.

For my beloved Judy

It is the passion for life itself that you ignite in me as you cradle my heart in your immutable love. Our life together is filled with a joy I had never dared to imagine.

"Lady, I fain would tell how evermore
Thy soul I know not from thy body, nor
Thee from myself, neither our love from God."

—Dante Gabriel Rosetti

Acknowledgments

Nothing we do in life, even in the seemingly solitary act of writing, is accomplished in a vacuum. We find inspiration everywhere, especially in the lives of the people we know. If we are fortunate, we also receive the gift of encouragement. There are moments when others must have the faith in us that we don't have in ourselves. So, from the moment we begin to create a novel, our friends and loved ones move in and out of the frame, offering whatever help they can.

But in terms of constancy, I am immeasurably blessed by my profoundly loving and nurturing twenty-year friendship with my agent and onetime partner, Sandra Satterwhite, whose imagination, caring, and eye for detail saves me from many a silly or downright embarrassing error while I am plotting and scheming my way through these mysteries. She will even read my manuscripts more than once. Now, *that's* a friend who really loves me! And even though we are officially (and amicably) "divorced," we will *always* be connected at the heart.

As for other—shall we call it unseen?—help, there did come a time in years past when I realized that even in the quiet of my office, with no one but me in the house, I was never writing alone. Sometimes the words flowed so fast and furiously…as if someone else were typing. And you know what? Sometimes I think someone was.

Author's Note

As you turn the pages of this fictional adventure, I invite you to at least temporarily suspend your disbelief in the things you cannot see or touch or sense with the physical self. There is magic in the world—I guarantee it.

As Gwendolyn Broadhurst was fond of quoting to her skeptical granddaughter, Connor, "There are more things in heaven and Earth than are dreamt of in your philosophy."

Prologue

Oh cease! Must hate and death return?
Cease! Must men kill and die?
Cease! Drain not to its dregs the urn
Of bitter prophecy.
The world is weary of the past,
Oh, might it die or rest at last!
—Percy Bysshe Shelley, "Hellas"

AN ISLAND IN THE BERMUDA TRIANGLE

"This bloody well isn't science," growled Jake Fisher. "How the hell does he justify using a bulldozer to dig a trench on this site?"

Jenny Carpenter shrugged. As one of the least senior members of the archaeology team, she had no say in anything, least of all what the great Dr. Jürgen Pedersen decided. But she, too, knew that something was exceedingly wrong about all this. She'd joined the team only three weeks earlier, enduring the taunts of her fellow students about getting involved in a dig that had yielded no published results in over eighteen months. "Pedersen's Folly," some were already calling it, and there were more than a few who gloated to think the celebrated and thoroughly arrogant archaeologist had failed miserably. But Jenny had read every one of Pedersen's books, articles, and monographs. Even half-joking warnings about the dig site, nestled on a small island chain in the heart of the Bermuda Triangle, had not deterred her for a moment. She had felt drawn to that small island with something approaching obsession, and without having any idea why.

Now, however, she had her serious doubts. Other site workers were muttering about Pedersen, hinting that he'd gone complete bonkers over certain finds that he wouldn't let anyone see, nor would he reveal their existence to the foundation funding the dig. But he had somehow convinced them to keep up the flow of money. And he'd had heavy equipment brought in by freighter. But why? He'd laid out a complex grid of corridors with stakes and ropes and ordered the dozer operator to begin trenching within each corridor, precisely twelve inches below the surface. But the procedure made no sense. It was as if Pedersen had decided to use strip mining to find artifacts of ancient civilizations. It was perfectly insane, like using a

"Bastard actually thinks he's found Atlantis," muttered Fisher.

Jenny blinked at him for a moment. "What did you say?"

"Nobody knows…well, I know…but he's kept it from everyone else. But he's gone right round the bend, the poor sod. He's been whispering to people over the sat-phone, talking to complete nutters, not even genuine academics…conspiracy theorists, and psychics and some loony who calls himself a historian of Atlantean culture, Jesus! And the stuff Pedersen's found…crystals and such—a bunch of junk, if you ask me."

"Crystals?" asked Jenny, feeling incredibly dense.

Fisher sighed. "You know, quartz and such. Big ones, too. But not raw." He shook his head. "I admit that's a little weird, I've never seen anything like them, but so what if they're smoothed a bit. Who knows what aboriginal tribes lived on these islands? So they had some ritual or other that used sparkly rocks and glassy stones. What did they know from quartz?"

"But if they polished them somehow, that's evidence of a society of some sort, isn't it?"

"But there are no other artifacts," said Fisher, a rising impatience in his voice. "No signs of building, of hunting, of cooking, of burying the dead, of going to the bloody loo—no signs of *anything!* So why he's still got six people working on the site is anyone's guess."

They both looked up as a small plane, an executive jet by the looks of it, swept in low over the island and headed for the tiny airstrip on the seaward side. "Probably the Foundation people coming to have a look. Pedersen told 'em to stay away, but they're not spending another dime until they're briefed. And look at that." He swept his arm over the stripped corridors, and the bulldozer heading back up another adjoining row. "They'll think he really is mad."

Jenny said softly. "Is he?"

Fisher stared at her intently for a moment, then his expression softened ever so lightly. "Sorry to say, I believe he is. He's changed since we've been here. And I've worked with him for fifteen years, been the site boss on dozens of digs, and he's never…" His voice trailed off, but he recovered himself and suddenly grasped Jenny by the arm. "You get yourself on the first transport out of here. I mean it." He stood up and strode down the hill before she could recover from the shock of hearing him tell her to leave. But why would she do such a thing? This dig could be a jewel on her résumé—working for Jürgen Pedersen virtually assured you a certain cachet when you went looking for a job. Or at least it had. Jenny wasn't ready to give up quite yet. Still, it might not hurt to find out when the next boat would arrive.

She had just stood up and dusted off her pants when she heard an odd series of sounds. But surely it couldn't be…and yet her father and brothers had all been deer hunters, and her mother had been extremely competitive with a target pistol. Jenny knew gunshots when she heard them. The engine roar of the bulldozer on the flats below suddenly stopped. Apparently the operator had heard something. She saw him get down from his seat and start toward the nearest prefab building in which dig tools were stored. Another volley of shots and, to her horror, the man was flung backward into an adjacent trench. He didn't move. Jenny instinctively flung herself to the ground behind a boulder, her head buzzing with panic, a sheet of white noise in her ears. There were more shots, a woman's scream.

Someone must have been on that plane, she thought. *Maybe pirates or something.* She'd heard of modern-day criminals who roamed the oceans, stealing and plundering private yachts. Perhaps they'd moved on to attacking small islands. But why? What could be of much value here other than scientific equipment? She heard a shout, then after several minutes another scream. This time, though, she was sure it was a man's voice. Her heart thudded in her chest. She huddled down and waited, sure that any moment a shadow would fall across the ground beside her and she would die.

After more than an hour passed, Jenny peered over the top of the rock. She could detect no signs of movement below. She thought of Jake Fisher and wondered if he would come looking for her. An hour passed, then two. The sun was only forty degrees above the horizon and sinking quickly. Soon, unless someone started the main generators for the compound lighting, the island would be shrouded in deep darkness under a sliver of waning moon, and a sky where clouds were already forming. She waited until the last rays of light splashed across the expanse of sea, its fingers reaching onto the island and caressing the western faces of various buildings and machines until they sparkled. Jenny crept quietly down the path, trying to stay low, even as she realized the absurdity of thinking she could escape detection out in the open. Anyone looking up the slope would see movement. But she dared not wait until full dark.

Within minutes she was only fifty meters from the main lab, parts of which also served as Dr. Pedersen's residence and the storage facility for artifacts. Jenny stayed in the long shadows of one of the equipment sheds and watched for a minute or two. The utter silence was almost as unnerving as the gunshots had been. She knew if she moved perhaps twenty-five meters to the east, she would come upon the bulldozer operator. Her conscience prodded her to see if she could help him, but the image of bullets smacking into him was fresh in her mind. Someone had fired the weapon. Someone who was likely inside the main lab. She couldn't bring herself to move out into the open. She just couldn't. On the other hand, she couldn't stand there like a complete coward forever. Within minutes she would barely be able to see her hand in front of her face.

A sound finally bored through the heavy silence. She strained her ears. It was coming from the airstrip. Within seconds the small jet roared overhead and she instinctively pressed herself against the metal wall of the shed, trying to be as unobtrusive as the shovels that leaned against it. She needn't have worried. In the darkness she was invisible.

Jenny did everything she could to convince her feet to carry her to the main lab. But her heart quailed at the prospect of what she would find. On the other hand, the pirates, or whoever, had left. They'd taken whatever they came for, or more likely, they'd discovered there was hardly anything worth stealing. But had they killed everyone anyway? Jenny formed a compromise plan. She'd work her away around the perimeter of the modest site camp to the generator shed. If she'd still heard nothing by then, perhaps it would be safe to fire up the generator. Jake had shown her how in the first week. "Just in case," he'd told her.

But as she moved around the side of the shed, she heard a noise. All right, she thought she heard a noise. But her courage failed completely. She didn't want to die. She was entirely too young to die. Or so she hoped. Jenny slid into the equipment shed and hunkered down in the back corner, behind a crate of spare parts, and waited, sure that her fear would keep her wide awake. She was wrong. The adrenaline rush subsided, and her exhausted body eventually demanded rest. So it was that she awoke with a startled grunt and realized it was daylight again.

Tired of hiding, Jenny walked out in the middle of the compound. Then she saw Jake Fisher. He lay face down, his old Colt .45 automatic on the ground near his hand. She knew without going any closer that he was beyond help. The wide pool of blood spread beneath him told her that. But she knelt in the dirt and checked anyway, overcoming her revulsion when she realized how cold his skin was. He'd been dead for hours. She swept her eyes over the clearing and saw two more bodies, one of whom was the camp manager–cook. She could tell by the silly red bandanna he always wore around his neck. The other one had long hair, probably Celia Carter, a Ph.D. candidate finishing her dissertation under Pedersen's tutelage.

She got to her feet and stared at the wide-open door of the main lab building. With more courage than she'd ever imagined having, Jenny bent down and picked up Jake's gun. She didn't like guns, but she'd been taught how to use them by an insistent father anyway. She checked it. The safety was off.

Slowly, she advanced to the door. The interior, usually in a state of tidiness that reflected Pedersen's fanatical emphasis on order, looked as if a giant hand had swept through it. Every piece of lab equipment lay on the floor in broken hunks of metal, glass, and plastic. Every cupboard door stood open, even the ones that had housed the artifacts, and were kept locked at all times. Those cupboards were completely empty.

Jenny walked slowly across the floor, picking her away past a large microscope on its side, and a computer monitor lying face down. As she rounded the end of the long work table, she saw first a hand, then an arm, then the white shock of hair. Jürgen Pedersen's career had come to an unexpected and gruesome end. The back of his windbreaker was soaked in blood. But it was his hands that made Jenny clamp her hand over her mouth to keep from vomiting all over him. Several of his fingers were just…gone: chopped off, if the ragged stumps were any indication. Turning quickly toward the other end of the room, Jenny stumbled to a window and filled her lungs several times to overcome the nausea. Turning back into the lab area, she suddenly saw the point of the dismemberment of Pedersen's fingers. In yet another closet that had always been locked, stood a safe, what looked to her like an electronic one with no combination pad, but rather a small glass plate on the front. The door of the safe was ajar. And on the ground were scattered the missing fingers. Jenny was hardly a security expert, but she deduced at once that the safe opened by scanning fingerprints. And Pedersen must have resisted cooperating. But what sort of monster would do this?

Within half an hour, Jenny had confirmed that the other six inhabitants of the island were dead. She was alone with the bodies, the gathering flies, and the stench of death in her nostrils. When the supply boat came two days later, the ship's crew found her sitting on the end of the pier, her canvas backpack strapped to her back, the Colt gripped in both hands. She was rocking back and forth, back and forth, eyes devoid of recognition, and she didn't speak to anyone, even the psychiatrists, for more than seven weeks. When she left the hospital two months later, all she took with her was the old backpack, the clothes she wore, and what remained of her life savings. She had told none of the doctors about her dreams, and she knew exactly where she had to go, and the person she had to find. Unfortunately, she didn't know exactly why. But the person Jenny had become seemed to exist outside of herself, outside of her physical body, issuing directives and taking care of what survival required. For all practical purposes, Jenny was no longer Jenny, but she couldn't have explained whom she had become.

Chapter One

Fanatics have their dreams,
Wherewith they weave
A paradise for a sect.
—John Keats, *The Fall of Hyperion*

PALM SPRINGS, CALIFORNIA
OCTOBER

A shadow slid tentatively over page eighty-seven of the book Connor was reading and hoping she'd get to like before another chapter concluded. She sighed and flipped it shut. "Hi, sweetheart. I think I'll give up on this one and find something else to read."

"Excuse me. Um, I'm sorry to disturb you, but aren't you Connor Hawthorne?"

Connor sat quickly upright in the lounge chair, realizing with more than a little embarrassment that the person beside her wasn't Laura. Instead, she saw a diminutive, almost painfully thin young woman in tank top and shorts. "Yes, I am. Why?" Her embarrassment colored her response with an irritation that clearly unnerved the woman.

"I'm sorry. I shouldn't have bothered you." She started to back away, but Connor immediately regretted her sharp tone.

"No, that's all right, really. I was a little startled."

"I didn't mean to…but it's just…I recognized you from the cover of one of your books."

Connor found this unlikely since the publisher's insistence on a photo that verged on a glamour shot was a source of constant chagrin. Her thick mane of brunette hair was cut to frame her face in soft, natural waves, for the sake of convenience rather than fashion. Her chin was firm, though not overly prominent, as were the finely sculptured cheekbones. Crystal-blue eyes were set beneath dark, expressive eyebrows that contrasted sharply with a pale, creamy complexion. The sum total of Connor's features was both pleasing and compelling, bordering on the androgynous, but the book jacket photo was a little too 'feminizing' for her tastes.

The girl glanced nervously toward the small office at the front of the large courtyard where one of the owners of the women's bed-and-breakfast resort had just come out to tidy the pool area. "You probably came here to get some peace, not to have people bother you."

Connor swung her legs over the side of the chaise lounge. "You're not, so stop apologizing. Please sit down."

With another sidelong glance at the inn owner, the young woman sat. "Brenda's pretty protective of her guests' privacy. I work for her part-time, just to have something to do."

"Brenda's a good sort. That's one reason we like coming here."

"You play golf, then?"

Connor laughed. "Very badly. Just about everyone else comes to Palm Springs to chase little dimpled golf balls around with uncooperative clubs. We just like visiting the Coachella Valley now and then."

"You're here with someone, then?"

Connor felt a frown building from the inside out. Even though best-selling novelists were hardly superstar celebrities, she had her share of fans, groupies, come-ons, and proposals of every sort—some that occasionally made her retract the claim that she'd heard everything.

"Yes, I'm here with my partner."

"Then I really am making a nuisance of myself," the young woman replied. "It's just that I know you're a really smart lawyer."

Connor blinked. "Lawyer?"

"Aren't you?"

"Well, I was for several years. A prosecuting attorney in Washington. But—"

"I read that in the bio on one of your books. And there was an article in *The New York Times* that said you were especially hard on scam artists and people who cheated other people out of money and stuff like that."

Connor mentally shifted gears and chided herself for jumping to conclusions about her own irresistibility. "I suppose that's true. But I haven't practiced law for a long time."

"Oh, I'm not trying to, like, hire you or anything. But I thought maybe you could steer me in the right direction, or tell me if I'm way off base about something. The thing is, I'm worried about my sister and this guru she's gotten involved with."

Another shadow appeared over the end of the chaise lounge, but this time Connor didn't take any chances on guessing the shadow's identity it until she felt a familiar hand on her shoulder. "Connor's not big on gurus," said the voice behind her. "Hi, I'm Laura Nez."

"I'm Bettina Waters," replied the young woman, getting up to shake Laura's outstretched hand.

"Pleasure to meet you," said Laura. "So your sister is in some kind of trouble?"

"I think maybe she is, but it's hard to be sure. She doesn't think so."

Laura sat down beside Connor on the chaise, removed her sunglasses, and brushed her long, glistening black hair behind her shoulders. "Since none of us is doing anything else right at the moment, why don't you tell us about it?"

Connor stifled a small sigh. Laura was a magnet (Connor might even say sucker) for sob stories, but even that was something Connor loved about her, that instant empathy for those in trouble, and if ever she'd seen someone who looked like a lost puppy, this Bettina Waters was it.

Bettina glanced over her shoulder at Brenda, whose tidying

efforts were moving her ever closer to where the three of them sat. "My older sister, Carmen, used to live here in town. We shared the house our parents left us, and she worked at the Desert Palms Resort. But about a year ago, she met this group of women who were staying at the resort and she started acting really strange."

"Strange, how?"

"She dumped all her usual friends, barely talked to me at all. And she stayed in her room alone a lot or went to meet with those other women. Then one night I came home, and she was sitting out on the patio staring at a candle and saying all these weird things."

"Weird?" asked Laura.

Bettina frowned. "She didn't make any sense. It's like she didn't even know I was there. She was talking about the fire and the light and crystals and stuff. I don't know. And I think she was saying people's names, but no one I'd ever heard of. And it was as if there were people in the room—invisible people." Bettina shivered. "But then she sort of snapped out of it, and when I asked her what was going on, she acted like she didn't know what I was talking about, like I was the crazy one."

"Did it sound as if she were speaking in her own voice?" asked Laura, her head cocked to one side.

Bettina frowned. "Well, yes...I mean..." she paused. "Maybe not. Why?"

"Just wondered. Did it ever happen again?"

"Not like that. But she kept acting different, like she wasn't quite the same person I've known all my life. And then a few weeks after that, she sold everything she had and went to live in a commune in England."

"What kind of commune?" asked Laura.

"It's supposed to be a spiritual community called the Children of Artemis."

"Some sort of feminist group?"

"I thought that at first since my sister's gay, and what with the name 'Artemis' and all, but Carmen mentioned there being men in the community in her letters. So apparently it's not one of those separatist kind of places—you know, women only."

"And who is this guru you mentioned?" asked Connor.

"She calls herself Sister Sonia, and she claims to be the reincarnation of Artemis herself."

Connor shrugged. "Not exactly a new approach."

"Do you believe in that sort of thing?" asked Bettina earnestly.

"What sort of thing?" asked Connor, dissembling as she tried to keep from squirming. She could not in good conscience deny her solid belief in reincarnation or the existence of numerous other planes of existence, the details of which most humans remained blissfully unaware. She'd seen many manifestations of other realities up close and personal. Her own heritage was what was often referred to in certain circles as "high magic." And yet the entire subject still made her deeply and sometimes achingly uncomfortable. It could not find a restful home in her logical, rational lawyer's mind.

"Reincarnation. Magic stuff. Rituals and witches and things?"

Laura chose to intervene. "I think those are all different concepts. It's probably wise to not lump them all together. Spirituality is a broad subject."

"I thought spirituality was about God," said Bettina with a frown.

"God is a pretty broad subject, too," said Laura, a gentle smile in her voice. "People harbor a lot of different ideas about God. As long as there's no harm in them, then I think personal beliefs are okay."

"But I think this *is* doing harm."

"How so?" asked Connor, grateful to have dodged an explanation of her own belief system, which was still in a state of constant evolution, thanks to strange and inexplicable experiences that seemed to follow her everywhere.

"My sister used to be really outgoing, fun-loving, not exactly a party girl or anything, but she loved to camp and hike and did all kinds of sports. Not like me. I'm too fond of air-conditioning, soft beds, and golf cart transportation to spend much time outdoors. And I'm scared to death of snakes. Believe me, there are plenty of snakes around here, especially up in those canyons."

"Sounds a little like my friend here," said Laura with a smile. "She's not exactly the camping type either."

"Carmen was. And she loved having a lot of friends around her, sent tons of e-mails with funny stories and jokes. But since she went to England, she hardly communicates with anyone. She barely writes me at all. And we've been best friends, even though we're sisters." Tears welled up in Bettina's eyes. "The second-to-last thing I got was a postcard, and she told me to stop writing to her, that the members weren't allowed to receive 'negative' communications from the 'outside world.' It interferes with Sister Sonia's healing work." Bettina held up her index fingers to indicate the quote marks from her sister's actual words.

"What did you write that seemed negative?" asked Laura.

"That I was worried about her behavior. She quit her job without notice, which is totally out of character. She sold all her stuff, even some of my stuff without asking. She left me with the mortgage on our parents' house, and cleaned out her savings account, including her inheritance, the money she was saving to go back to school and get her graduate degree in psychology."

"How much money was involved?" inquired Connor, her inner alarm bells starting to whoop softly. She knew money was the primary motivator in most criminal activity—and certainly in every type of scam known to humankind. Predators had a talent for extracting money from the unwary.

"Over $100,000," replied Bettina.

"Hmm," said Connor. "You think she turned that over to this Sister Sonia's organization?"

"I don't know. But I bet she did. And then there's this." She reached into her pocket, pulled out a much-folded piece of white office paper, and handed it to Connor. Laura read over her shoulder after Connor flattened it out. In short, it was from a local attorney, informing Bettina that her sister, Carmen, wished to sell the home they jointly owned in as timely a manner as possible. The lawyer asked that the house be listed with a Realtor within ten days.

"Do I have to do that?" asked Bettina, clearly miserable at the thought.

Connor shook her head. "I can't advise you on that without knowing the details of your parents' bequest, how the house was left to you, and in what form of ownership it's held. My only advice is to consult your own local lawyer immediately, perhaps the one who handled your parents' estate. It isn't this guy, I take it?"

"No. I've never heard of him. But Geri Vale was my parents' lawyer. I'll call her."

"Bettina, I think Room 4 needs doing," said a voice behind them. Brenda, one of the inn's owners, was hovering nearby, the makings of scowl forming on her normally friendly face.

"Hi, Bren," said Laura breezily. "Sorry we're taking up Bettina's time. She was kind enough to stop and give us the run-down on what there is to do around here. I've been trying to talk Connor into a round of golf with me, and I found an ally in Bettina. Plus she knows everything there is to know about this town. I hope you don't mind us interrupting her work."

Brenda relaxed. "No. Of course not. I just thought… well…anyway. Take all the time you'd like. She patted Bettina's shoulder. "She's a good kid."

Once Brenda was out of earshot, Bettina relaxed. "Thanks for that. She'd be pissed if she thought I was spewing out my troubles to total strangers—and her guests, besides. She's got no patience with Carmen's weirdness. She told me to let other people live their lives and get on with my own."

"Not always bad advice," said Connor.

"I guess. But she's my sister. She's family."

"You're right, Bettina. I'd do the same thing in your shoes. And this Sister Sonia could be bad news all around. If she's after people's money, that's a pretty strong warning sign. But it's also next to impossible to get grown-up people to stop making asses of themselves, if that's what your sister's doing."

Bettina looked miserable, and Connor added, "Listen, if there's anything else I can do, or if you need someone to talk to, call us. We live in Santa Fe most of the time." Connor tore the blank end page out of the paperback she was reading. Laura suppressed a gasp. Connor smiled. "I really do hate this book. Otherwise I'd never deface it." She picked up a pen from the table beside the chaise and quickly jotted the information. "Here's our home phone and my e-mail. I check it all the time." She handed it to Bettina, along with the lawyer's letter.

"Thanks," said the young woman. "I'll only be in touch if I hear something else."

They watched Bettina Waters walk away, her shoulders slumped with worry. "Her sister sounds like one of those gullible ones," said Laura, moving to the neighboring chaise lounge. "But she's not alone. A lot of lonely, confused people fall for the blatant lies."

"I hate cults."

Laura raised an eyebrow. "And how would you define a cult? Do you know there are perfectly good churches out there— New Thought churches—that fundamentalists call cults?"

"Yes, I do. And that's the usual fundamentalist bullshit. But you know what I mean. Those groupie things, where there's one head honcho with all kinds of magnetism and a really convincing schtick that just caters to people's fear and angst. They're all about power, about wielding power over others."

"This Sister Sonia may be greedy, Connor, but that doesn't exactly mean she's another Jim Jones."

"No, but it still galls me. That kid may end up getting kicked out of her house, and losing contact with her sister completely because some egomaniac decides she's a tricked-up modern-day version of some Greek goddess."

Laura, whose nearly waist-length black hair was swept up into a casual chignon, smoothed some tanning lotion on her already tawny brown skin, the genetic legacy of her exotic Navajo and Asian parentage. She did her arms, face, legs and the modest amount of well-muscled midriff revealed by her two-piece suit. "This Children of Artemis group sounds vaguely familiar. I must have read something about it."

"In the papers, or one of those briefing sheets from my father's office you're so addicted to?" smiled Connor.

"Probably the latter. And it isn't an addiction, just keeping my hand in. Once an intelligence agent, always an intelligence agent."

"You hate the word 'spy' don't you?"

"It's so James Bond," replied Laura.

"Or worse, so Austin Powers."

"Oh, please," laughed Laura, tossing the bottle at Connor, who caught it deftly. "What are we doing for dinner?"

"Funny, I thought you'd be headed inside to fire up your laptop and check on Sister Sonia and the Children of Artemis."

"I'm not that obsessive. I'll look it up later."

"Suit yourself," said Connor, lying back on her chaise. "I'm going to treat myself to a short nap." She closed her eyes and waited, estimating that perhaps five minutes passed before she heard the neighboring chair squeak. "I knew you couldn't resist."

"Don't even start, sweetheart. You nap. I'll do a little research."

♦

When Connor returned to the room a half hour later, Laura was still tapping away at her laptop.

"Find anything interesting?" she asked, peering over Laura's shoulder.

"Not much on the public Web. Just a site for Children of Artemis with all sorts of vague statements about the merging of the divine feminine and the divine masculine and the power of women's spirituality, reemergence of Goddess energy in the world to balance the patriarchy—that sort of thing."

"And how does that strike you?"

"The principles are valid, as far as I'm concerned. Lord knows we need more of the Divine Feminine in this world, but it isn't exactly unusual for scam artists to gloss over their frauds with a veneer of truth."

"How about Sister Sonia?"

"She seems to have set herself up as some sort of miracle healer, on top of being the head priestess in this little group."

"What kind of healing?"

"Some of the more sensationalist rags call them pure miracles. Others talk about ancient herbal remedies, energy healing—you name it. She doesn't make any specific claims about where it comes from. But there have been some documented cases, apparently."

"And what about more accurate sources?" asked Connor, referring to Laura's connections to Connor's father, Benjamin Hawthorne, an ex-U.S. senator, presidential adviser, and former spymaster who still worked ex officio for the government.

"She's not on any high-priority watch lists, even in these paranoid times, but that's partly because she's chosen to base her operations outside U.S. borders. The Brits are a little concerned about her sudden acquisition of real estate for cash and an apparently plump bank account that has materialized rather quickly."

"Sounds more like a case for the Inland Revenue bureaucrats in England."

"But there is something odd about her."

"What's that?"

"I can't get a fix on who she really is."

Connor frowned. In a world where Big Brother was omnipresent, hiding one's actual identity had become increasingly impossible, particularly when someone with Laura's access to databases was doing the looking. "She's got to have a history somewhere."

"I'll find it," sighed Laura. "But it usually doesn't take me all that long. So far, I haven't even figured out her last stop before she got to this commune she's founded. And that ought to be easy enough."

"Why don't you just put some of my dad's supercomputers to work on the problem, and we'll see what's what after we come back from dinner."

Laura nodded and typed in a few instructions, which were then forwarded to another facility in Langley, Virginia. She shut down her machine and stood up. "You know, it's still early enough that we could work up an appetite before dinner."

Connor smiled. "And what did you have in mind?"

"Calisthenics," said Laura. "I think we're way behind on our calisthenics."

If Connor had a smart comeback for that, it was smothered by a deep and delicious kiss that defied words of any kind.

Chapter Two

It hath been often said, that it is not death, but dying,
which is terrible.
—Henry Fielding, *Amelia,* Book I

PALM SPRINGS, CALIFORNIA
THE NEXT AFTERNOON

"What's wrong, Brenda?" asked Laura, after she'd opened the door to a light knock. The innkeeper had arrived on their patio with a delivery of healthy snacks and juices for the in-room refrigerator. But her face was blotchy with traces of tears.

"I'm sorry," said Brenda. "I just wanted to drop these off." She shoved the tray into Laura's hands and backed away.

"No, wait," said Laura. "Please come inside. Sit down."

Connor rose from the chair by the fireplace and took the tray from Laura. "What's happened?" she asked.

Brenda took a deep breath, then another. "It's Bettina. I can't even believe it. The police were just here. They found her...Oh, God...they found her in a canyon around noon. She was...I mean, she's dead. I can't believe it, that poor kid is dead. They said she must have gone hiking yesterday and fallen and broken her neck."

Laura felt as if someone had kicked her in the stomach. She sat down on the edge of the king-size bed. "Bettina Waters—that girl we talked to yesterday?"

"Yes."

"But that doesn't make any sense at all. A hiking accident?"

Brenda looked at her with some puzzlement. "Well, she was young and fit, but freak accidents do happen. That's what they said, a freak accident. She fell off the edge of a trail, about a mile into the canyon."

"But Bettina told us yesterday that it was her sister, Carmen, who was the outdoorswoman. Bettina said she didn't like camping or hiking or anything remotely like it."

Connor nodded in agreement. "I remember that, too. Something about not liking to be too far from air-conditioning."

Brenda shrugged. "Maybe she just wanted to get away from town and do some thinking. She's been really upset about her sister leaving. Bettina's been moping around here for weeks."

Laura shook her head. "I'm sorry. I don't mean to sound like a know-it-all. I don't really know her, but something's not right about this. Going hiking seems completely out of character, especially when she was already upset about her sister."

"I guess," said Brenda, rising from the chair. "But the cops said it was just an unfortunate accident. I've got to finish making my rounds. Sorry to bring the news."

"I'm glad you told us in person, Brenda," said Connor. "And if there's anything at all we can do, please let us know."

"I know you ladies are supposed to be here for a week. I need to find someone to fill in with the cleaning and all, so if you wouldn't mind not having the room done today…"

"Of course not," said Laura. "I'll come over to the office later and pick up some fresh towels. Don't worry about it."

Brenda paused in the doorway. "Janet and I will try to plan some sort of memorial for Bettina, and we'll let you know when, if it's before you're scheduled to leave."

"Thanks. We'd certainly want to be there."

The door closed and Laura looked at Connor. The look between them spoke volumes. Laura went straight to her computer, Connor to her cell phone. She punched in a speed-dial number. "Malcolm, it's Connor. Do you know anybody on the Palm Springs Police?"

Three thousand miles way, Malcolm Jefferson, D.C. police

Captain and longtime friend of Connor Hawthorne, almost dropped the phone. "Please don't tell me you've been arrested."

"No, of course not!"

"Then please don't tell me you've been robbed or assaulted. Is Laura all right?"

"Yes, she's fine. And no, we have not been victims of crime. If you'd let me tell you what is going on, then you could stop worrying."

"Sorry. But with your track record, hon…"

"Gee, thanks. I just want to know if you know anyone who knows anyone. This girl we met at the resort here was just found dead in a canyon and—"

"Oh, great. I forgot to ask about 'found a dead body' on my list of things you sometimes do while on vacation."

"Sarcasm is unnecessary, thank you very much."

Malcolm took a deep breath. "I apologize. But you worry me."

"For the sake of accuracy, we did not find a dead body. We met a young woman yesterday here at the B and B where we're staying. She got to talking to us about some difficulties her sister is having—getting mixed up in some cult—and anyway, a few minutes ago we heard she was found dead in canyon near a hiking trail."

"And for some reason you don't think this is a simple accident."

"Call it a hunch."

"A Hawthorne hunch or a Laura Nez hunch?"

Connor asked Laura, "Malcolm wants to know which of us is having the hinky feeling about all this?"

"Both," said Laura shortly, her attention on the computer.

"You heard that?"

"Yes," he answered. "I did. And no, I don't know anyone in that neck of the woods, though I did get fairly friendly with that Orange County cop we worked with on the priest's murder in Santa Ana. I could give him a call."

"Thanks, I'd appreciate it. Oh, how's Ayalla?"

"Still in Boston," he said, without elaborating.

"I figured that much. I meant, how are things between the two of you?"

There was a long pause. "I think they're pretty good."

"Well, don't get all soft and sentimental on me."

Malcolm sighed. "She's just kind of hard to read. One minute I think we're completely in sync, and then she's off on some case and hardly talks to me."

"Sounds sort of like you."

"I'm not that bad," he protested.

"Oh, yes you are, and as far as I can tell, the woman really is crazy about you. How could she not be?"

"Thanks for the compliment. But it's been a long time since…"

"I know, sweetie, but Marie Louise has been gone for a lot of years now. It's okay to care about someone else, you know."

"I think I gave you that lecture at some point, too."

"Then I'm just returning the favor. I found out happiness can come back. I want that for you, too."

"Okay, this conversation is getting far too mushy," said Malcolm. "I'll see if my detective buddy is in the office today and call you back on your cell. By the way, I talked to your dad yesterday. He's getting settled in to his new office in London. Said he'd be in touch with you in the next few days and that Katy is impressing a lot of people at that architectural firm where she works."

"My daughter seems to be constitutionally incapable of being anything other than impressive. Thank God she doesn't take after her mother."

"Oh, for crying out loud. Enough with the modesty bullshit. I'll talk to you later." He clicked off.

Connor moved over to where Laura was hunched over the computer. "Anything?"

"Not yet. But I expect results soon. As long as we're going to hang around, I'll leave the wireless connection open. So how's Malcolm?"

"As far as I can tell, his same old slightly cantankerous self?"

"And the romance?" asked Laura.

"Prickly as ever, I guess. She's busy, he's busy."

"You think he's still hanging on to his wife's memory?" Malcolm's wife had been killed years earlier in a bank robbery. He would have followed her to the grave within days, had Connor not kept him from eating his own gun on a cold park bench by the Potomac. Later, he'd seen her through the investigation into the murder of her lover, Ariana, and a series of events so unexpected that Connor's own life would have been lost without his intervention. Theirs was a friendship of the deepest loyalty, forged in mutual respect and understanding of tragedy. And Laura had become part of the tight circle that included Connor's father, Benjamin. Now, a new element, FBI Special Agent Ayalla Franklin, was a part of Malcolm's life, but she didn't fit into the mix quite as easily, at least in part because of the friction that always seemed to arise between her and Connor.

"I think Ayalla's not sure what she wants, and neither is he. We'll just have to wait and see. He said he'd talk to that detective we met last year in Orange County. See if he knows anyone down here. I don't want to just go barging into the police station and start asking questions."

"You've been known to do that," smiled Laura.

"Yeah, but I'm getting mellow in my old age."

"Old age? You're not even fifty yet."

"Some days I feel older."

"Oh, good. I kept forgetting the names of two of the characters in my last book and started to think it was senility."

"Maybe just too little sleep and too much work," said Laura. "And I have just the cure for that."

"What?"

"You remember that writer's conference you were invited to, the one you declined because you had a deadline coming up."

Connor frowned. She received many such invitations. Then the light dawned. "The one in England. York to be exact."

"Yes," said Laura. "And I feel like finding out what has become of Carmen Waters. At the very least, we are going to make sure she knows what's happened to her little sister. I have a feeling no one else is going to tell her."

Connor snapped her fingers. "Do you remember what the name of that attorney was?"

"The one who wrote the letter?"

"No, the one she said was her parents' lawyer."

Laura thought for a moment. "Geri Vale. Hard to forget a name like that."

"Let's give Ms. Vale a call, and then I'll start making reservations. We'll need to cut short our week here and get back to Santa Fe."

◆

A couple of hours later, Connor and Laura knocked on the office door of Gerivina Vale, Attorney at Law. It turned out to be a one-woman operation, no reception area, no secretary, just a cozy, comfortable room with the usual Palm Springs décor in earth tones, a light ash desk, and matching rows of filing cabinets on one wall with glass-fronted bookshelves lining another. Ms. Vale was dark-skinned with white hair piled in an untidy bun. Connor guessed her to be of Polynesian descent, but her crisp, neutral accent upon greeting them gave no hint of where she might have grown up. Connor introduced herself and Laura.

"I'm not entirely clear on what your interest in this matter is," Geri Vale said, her tone neither challenging nor welcoming.

"Nor are we, to be honest," said Connor. "We only met Bettina Waters yesterday, and we're not trying to presume on such a brief acquaintance. But we do have some concerns about the manner of her death."

"And why is that?"

"She confided in us some concerns about her older sister, Carmen."

"Yes," the lawyer replied, still giving nothing away. Connor admired her discretion.

"Carmen Waters apparently joined some sort of organization. Bettina referred to it specifically as a cult. She moved to England, taking a significant amount of money with her that she had earmarked for graduate studies."

"People do change their minds," replied Ms. Vale.

"True. But Bettina apparently knew her sister well enough to find this extremely out of character. There were some rather unusual events before Carmen left Palm Springs as well. Then she recently received correspondence from a local attorney here indicating that Carmen wanted their parents' house sold immediately."

Geri Vale sat forward slightly. "She told you this yesterday?"

"Yes, she did. I told her that I wasn't qualified to advise her and suggested she contact someone immediately. She mentioned your name."

The lawyer appeared to unbend a little. "Bettina phoned me about it. She left me a message. Unfortunately, I was in court. But she did say she'd be in the rest of the afternoon and evening. I tried to return the call since she sounded so upset, and her parents were dear friends of mine. But no answer."

Connor and Laura exchanged a look. "That only adds to our concern about her death."

"Why? The police seem satisfied there was no suspicion of anything but an accident. It may have gotten too dark to see well. She slipped and fell."

Laura leaned forward in her chair. "Two things don't fit, at least so far. Bettina, in talking about her sister yesterday, made quite a point of the fact that they were so different in the types of activities they enjoyed. Carmen loved the outdoors; Bettina didn't. Carmen was the hiking and camping type. Bettina said she hated that stuff—was scared to death of snakes, especially in the canyons. It makes no sense that she'd suddenly get it into her head to go off hiking alone. And secondly, she told you in her message that she'd be home. We know how anxious she was to find out if she'd really have to sell the house. She would have waited by the phone."

Geri Vale sat back in her chair and gave both women a critical once-over. "Your suspicions may have some basis in fact. And I think they're worth reporting to the police. But I'm curious. What prompts this Good Samaritan urge on your part?"

Connor paused, then looked the lawyer squarely in the eye. "When I see something wrong, I don't turn around and walk the other way. If you knew me, then you'd understand. My friend here is the same way. We tend to get involved, even it appears to some as mere meddling."

"Actually, I do know of you, Ms. Hawthorne, just as I know of your father, Senator Hawthorne. I once followed your legal career with some interest, before you abandoned it to become a novelist. I can't say that I condone throwing away your obvious talent. Your argument before the appellate court in *Beronds v. District of Columbia* was, if I may so, brilliant. However, be that as it may, I sense that you are a crusader of sorts, so I'll take your interest as purely benevolent. And Ms. Nez I do not know, but she strikes me as a person of strong character. And her association with you is recommendation enough, at least for now. So what is it you are suggesting?"

"I don't have enough facts to form a theory as yet," said Connor. "However, I don't trust charlatans, and I definitely don't believe in coincidence. This group that has absorbed Carmen Waters bears looking into. I don't think there can be any doubt they, or its leader, this Sister Sonia, took control of Carmen's money, and that they are behind the attempt to liquidate her last asset—her parents' house."

"But if you suspect that Bettina's death was a homicide, why?"

"There we are in the area of pure conjecture. But there are at least two possibilities. One is that Bettina might have delayed the sale of the property for some time at least."

Geri Vale nodded. "Yes, she could have. The terms of the will were quite clear. The house could not be sold without the consent of both daughters."

"And is the property valuable, if I may ask?" said Connor

The lawyer nodded. "Conservatively, in this market, around a million and a half. The mortgage balance is nominal."

"Good motivation," said Laura. "And there is the added benefit of cutting Carmen off from her only remaining family."

"You really think this cult is that insidious, or that bent on achieving a stranglehold on its membership? Sounds a bit dramatic to me."

"Perhaps. But it's worth finding out," said Connor. "Laura and I are leaving for England next week."

"That seems a bit hasty," said Ms. Vale.

"I happen to have a legitimate reason for being in that part of the world. And no one needs to know that we have a more pressing interest than everyday professional concerns."

"Indeed," said the lawyer. "But there's one thing you might need to know before you get fully involved in all this. Bettina's message was quite long and rambling, and she specifically mentioned not only the contents of the messages she'd received from her sister and from that sorry excuse for a lawyer who sent her the letter, but she also recounted in some detail her conversation with the two of you, and she called you both by name. If there is a conspiracy here, your involvement is not a secret. If I were you, I'd take some precautions."

Connor smiled. "You may not believe this, Ms. Vale, but my friend here is about the best precaution anyone on earth could ever take. When I first met her, my father had assigned her as my bodyguard."

Ms. Vale's eyebrows rose as one unity across her forehead. "Really?"

"Yes, and she turned out to be very, very good at that. Which is one reason I'm here talking to you now." Connor stood up and Laura followed suit. "Thank you for your help. I think our next stop should be the police station."

Geri Vale stood also. "I know these locals, and you don't. This will be a lot easier if I go with you and back up your story. Otherwise, I'm afraid this one's going to go down in the books as nothing more than an accident."

"You realize, of course," said Laura, "that if this was a homicide, the person responsible is probably long gone."

"Yes. But at least the police need to be examining this from an entirely different angle. And that means a thorough investigation, including a full autopsy. As the executor of Bettina's will, I have some authority here, and I intend to exercise it."

"Good," said Connor. "Then maybe justice does stand a chance for a change."

"Ms. Hawthorne, don't tell me you really *are* as cynical as your books make you sound?"

"Actually, she's more so," said Laura with a smile. "But I'm working on that."

♦

The three women spent two and a half hours at the local police station. Geri Vale did indeed have a good rapport with one of the detectives, and although he wasn't inclined to buy the whole murder conspiracy theory, he did respect Geri Vale and he'd heard of Connor Hawthorne. A quick call to the Orange County detective confirmed that she and Laura were people whom the police could trust, and Malcolm had already been in touch with his colleague to call in a marker or two. That's the way it worked in the cop world, and for the most part, it worked to everyone's advantage. The fact that Connor had been a prosecutor and not a despised defense attorney always worked in her favor when she had to work with law enforcement. That was simply another fact of life. Cops—even the best ones, even the ones who understood the protections built into the American legal system—didn't like catching the perps only to see them walk away again because of smart lawyers.

Outside the station, the three women exchanged business cards and shook hands. Geri reminded them again to be careful. "I have an odd feeling you two are onto something that may be more malevolent than even you suspect." She paused. "And to be frank, I don't often use the word 'malevolent.'" She turned and walked away.

"Interesting character," said Laura. "You suppose she's right?"

Connor felt a series of tiny chills move up her spine. It was a sensation she was learning not to ignore. "Could be."

Laura's cell phone rang. Within a few seconds, Connor knew it was Benjamin calling. She checked her own phone and saw that it was turned off. No doubt he'd tried her first. "Hold on a minute, she's right here," Laura said, handing the phone over.

"Hi, Dad."

"I got an e-mail from Laura about a girl who died there in Palm Springs. She asked me if I'd look into some spiritual cult group here in England."

"Nothing really urgent, just a funny feeling I have about this Sister Sonia character. And I don't like seeing people taken advantage of. Besides, conning someone out of money's one thing. Murder's another."

"The police there think it's murder?" he asked.

"Not necessarily, but we're working on them," said Connor.

"Then I imagine they'll be on board shortly," said Benjamin. Connor could hear his smile from across the Atlantic. "If they don't know already that my daughter and her companion are women to be reckoned with, they will."

"My D.C. cop friend is already pushing from his end," said Connor. "Just to make it a little more interesting."

"Good. And Laura mentioned you'll be here before long."

"We'll stop in London to see you and Katy. Then I'll put in an appearance at the conference in York, just to keep up the cover story."

There was a long silence as Benjamin digested this, and Connor realized she'd already said more than she'd intended. Her father was very quick on the uptake.

"Any reason why someone should think you're there for something other than giving a speech?"

"Well...the young girl who was killed here—she apparently left a message for her lawyer, a long message, and she happened to mention that she had talked to me and Laura—mentioned us both by name. Now, there's no reason to assume that the killer, if there was a killer, actually heard her leave that message, but the lawyer thought it was worth mentioning."

"And presumably, this theoretical killer, who may have been present in the house when the girl made the call, didn't have time or opportunity to get into the lawyer's office and erase the message."

"True."

"So it's pure conjecture that anyone knows you're involved."

A recent memory suddenly flashed into Connor's mind: the end page of a paperback book with Connor's name, phone number, and e-mail address. Bettina Waters stuffed it into her pocket.

"Connor, are you there?"

"Yes, I'm here, and I really don't think there's anything to worry about. But we'll be careful, as usual."

"It's the 'as usual' that always worries me. Your version of normal risk is most people's idea of a worst-case scenario. I'll see you when you get here. Send me the details. Love you, honey."

"Love you, too, Dad." She flipped the phone shut and handed it back.

Laura was staring at her. "What is it? Your face went just a little pale. Was it something Benjamin said?"

"Sort of. We need to go back inside and ask to see Bettina's personal effects, whatever she had on her when was found."

"Why?" asked Laura. And then, with that uncanny ability she had to read Connor's mind, she suddenly understood. "The paper-back book page?"

"Exactly."

Chapter Three

Bell, book, and candle shall not drive me back,
When gold and silver becks me to come on.
—William Shakespeare, *King John,* act II, scene 3

ENGLAND

Carmen Waters didn't know whether to be frightened or flattered. The two emotions warred within her constantly. With very little explanation, she had been elevated from amongst the swelling ranks of Sister Sonia's slavish admirers to the inner circle of her acolytes. And even there, within the much smaller and more intimate group, she seemed the object of unusual attention from the great lady herself. While Carmen tended to be a gullible personality, she also possessed a highly intelligent mind and sharp perceptions. Little that went on around the community escaped her, and much of it made her uncomfortable in a way she couldn't quite identify. For one thing, she had to endure evening sessions with Sister Sonia, ostensibly for tea and spiritual discussion. But each evening she left with the sensation that she could remember very little of what had transpired.

While Sister Sonia seemed taken with Carmen, not everyone from the inner circle was quite so enthusiastic. They felt their numbers were sufficient (twelve in all), and their devotion sufficiently abject that a newcomer need not be admitted. Least subtle in his displeasure at Carmen's presence was Alan Durn, Sister Sonia's official consort. But even he did not let his annoyance show in front of their revered leader. Only in those moments when he caught Carmen alone—and fixed her with the frightening scowl that came naturally to his otherwise handsome features—did she feel a frisson of true fear.

Tonight the predinner ritual was proceeding as usual. Sister Sonia stood in her position at the head of the table with Alan on her right and Carmen on her left. This placement of Carmen, on the left hand of their earthly goddess, was yet another source of consternation among the disciples. The perfect number, they believed, was thirteen, not fourteen, and the lady's heart should be flowing to her left hand, toward her appointed consort, not some neophyte who, rumor had it, babbled about past lives whilst under hypnosis in the lady's presence. They only hoped that Carmen was some sort of seer or messenger who would soon fulfill her purpose and be sent away.

Karl Jensen was perhaps most determined that this should happen soon, for he, himself had been moved down the table to the other end to accommodate a fourteenth seat, and although he faced Sister Sonia, he felt his new position was one of being nearer to the door than nearer to the source of holy inspiration. Still, he knew better than to express his growing disillusionment with the apparent demotion. The only one with whom he shared his feelings was Alan. The two of them agreed on at least one thing—this obsession with the mousy little lesbian from Palm Springs must soon run its course. Karl personally had no patience with the gimmickry of it all. He was here for a purpose that had absolutely nothing to do with scamming a bunch of gullible New Age fanatics.

Sister Sonia was in perfect form. Her gleaming, blond, shoulder-length mane of hair swept back in symmetrical waves from her finely chiseled features. Her eyes glowed blue-green with hints of gold in the irises that reflected the dozens of candles in the room. If anyone could claim descent from a Greek goddess, Sonia had the looks for it. When she stood to offer the blessing, she was nearly as tall, at five foot ten, as most of the half-dozen men in the room. And she radiated power from every skin cell.

That was it, Carmen often thought, *the total package.* Without the inner power, Sonia was simply a remarkably beautiful woman, one for whom prospective lovers would no doubt compete fiercely. But here, surrounded by those who revered her and possessed of an almost unworldly energy that emanated from her in waves, she was much, much more. And Carmen had yet to understand just what that was. She'd had glimmers, odd dreams of people she knew she'd never met and places she had certainly never seen, but nothing that made sense. For that matter, her own emotions did not seem to make sense. One instant she'd experience unexpected elation that had no apparent foundation in the events around her, and then just as suddenly, she'd be engulfed in fear that arose without cause. Tonight, even as she watched Sonia deliver the blessing in an odd language that few professed to understand and, Carmen suspected, even fewer actually did, the emotion was fear. She was scheduled for an after-dinner session with Sonia, and Carmen didn't dare refuse, much as she wanted to retreat to her own room, or go and visit her friend, Jenny, who was assigned to one of the makeshift dormitories.

Carmen's housing was another bone of contention in the community. Although no one begrudged their leader comfortable, even fairly opulent quarters, everyone else was expected to lead a relatively Spartan existence. The disciples' accommodations, occupying the former servants' quarters in the ancient manor house, were not precisely monastic cells, but their comforts were limited to a twin bed, a tiny sitting area with desk and lamp, and a fitted carpet. The chief advantage was individual privacy. The lower echelons of community dwellers lived in dormitories converted from old outbuildings that would barely come up to the standards of youth hostels. Carmen, though still a relative newcomer, had been granted a room on the same corridor as the one shared by Sonia and Alan. Only Sonia's sizable and comfortably furnished sitting room separated the two bedrooms.

For her part, Carmen would just as soon have been relegated to the dormitory. She revered Sister Sonia, just as the others did.

But she'd come here with the idea of service to the world, and being part of Sister Sonia's healing work, not to be treated like some sort of oddity who wasn't required to pitch in and do all the scut work like everyone else. Yet neither was she treated like one of the disciples themselves. She wasn't included in the special meetings they held each day from noon until almost three o'clock. And she often wondered what could occupy their time for so long.

Carmen suddenly became aware that Sister Sonia had finished the rather lengthy blessing and everyone had begun to eat. Alan was staring at Carmen with the disdainful expression of a entomologist pondering a none-too-promising specimen. But then that was how he often looked at her. Ever since Sister Sonia had summoned Carmen to live in the main house, Alan's usual swagger, along with his slightly possessive demeanor, was rarely in evidence. He appeared to blame Carmen for a change in his fortunes, but she could not for the life of her imagine why. She wasn't competing for Sister Sonia's romantic affections, though the idea of being her lover had crossed Carmen's more than once. It seemed entirely absurd, though.

Thankfully, the dinner finally came to an end. Sonia leaned toward Carmen. "I'll meet with you a bit later than usual. Please come to my sitting room at nine." She left the table and went in the direction of her ground-floor office with Alan trailing behind.

◆

"Karl took care of everything," Alan said, slouching into the armchair across from Sonia's desk. She leaned back in her leather-covered, ergonomically correct executive chair.

"And the terms of the will?"

"As you predicted—"

She held up one hand. "I don't 'predict,' Alan, I know."

He started to argue, then appeared to think better of it. Why mess with her act? It was better she stay in character. Besides, she sometimes *did* seem to know things she shouldn't be able to know.

"Sorry. As you told us, the house will go directly to Carmen, along with her sister's trust fund. That's another $75,000 or $80,000."

"And the potential interference I warned you of?"

Alan frowned for a moment. "Oh, you mean the thing about there being two women who would try to save Bettina Waters. No, there wasn't anybody around when he got to her house."

"Are you quite sure?" said Sonia. "I'm not giving you this kind of information just as an exercise."

Alan straightened up in his seat. "Karl gave me a complete report. He took the girl up to the canyon, and he made sure it looked as if she slipped and fell. That's all there was to it. Then he got out of town within the hour."

"Then why is it I feel complications arising from the incident?"

Alan frowned. "Complications?"

"Yes, as if the streams of Bettina's destiny in this lifetime had not been completely cut off."

He sighed. Sometimes Sonia was impossible to understand. "There's nothing more to it than a simple accident. That's how it was reported in the local newspaper. I checked it myself online. No one has any interest in pursuing the matter." But even as he said this to Sonia, he was thinking uncomfortably of the piece of paper in his pocket, a tattered scrap that Karl had retrieved from the pocket of the young woman's shorts. The names Connor Hawthorne and Laura Nez had been neatly printed, along with a phone number and e-mail address. He'd looked them up on the Internet. Even he had to admit that these might the "two women" Sonia had warned them about, but the idea was so far-fetched. Bettina Waters could have gotten the names from strangers in a bar. No, it wasn't worth bringing up now, especially since he'd already denied it. He'd seen Sonia angry once or twice and it wasn't an experience he cared to repeat. Francine Halverson had almost appeared to be having a seizure when Sonia fixed her with a stare so filled with fury it seemed the room might catch fire. And that was over nothing more serious than a missing piece of correspondence from a potential financial backer in Australia.

Sonia continued to peer at him, but he kept his face impassive. When she finally reached into her desk for something, he relaxed, stood up and went around to stand by her chair. Placing his hands on her shoulders, he kneaded them gently. "Why don't we go to bed early tonight?"

"I have a session with Carmen," she responded, her attention fixed on the calendar in front of her.

"So skip the session. You work with her almost every day. We haven't been together...really together, in weeks." His kneading turned softer, more caressing. His fingers trailed along her neck as he brushed her back in preparation for kissing her just behind the ear. To his annoyance, she spun her chair around, nearly knocking him off balance. He had to grab the edge of the desk to avoid an ignominious landing on his derriere.

"I thought we had already discussed this, Alan. You have no claim on me and no right to expect any favors other than those I choose to grant you. You are my consort, not my master."

He scowled. "Look, Sonia. Aren't you taking this whole goddess thing just a little too far?"

Instantly, Alan knew he had made a grave error in judgment. He didn't realize just how far gone Sonia was into her fantasy world. She stood up to face him, and her irises grew large and black, with tiny rings of fiery orange at the edges. Instinctively, he backed away. Her hand shot toward him, and he stumbled backward. This time, he could not keep his footing and hit the floor hard; he was so stunned, it took him several seconds to realize that she had not actually touched him physically. She hadn't moved from her spot, and he'd been standing at least four feet from her. But still, he'd felt the impact in the center of his chest. Even now, it seemed as if there were pressure still being applied. He looked down at the front of his linen robe, his mind expecting to see some evidence of the blow he'd felt. He looked up at her. She stood, glowering at him, her anger filling the room.

"It is you who go too far, Alan. I should have foreseen your faithlessness. You have no idea of who I really am."

God, she's really lost it, thought Alan. *This is a disaster.* He scrambled to his feet, trying to retain some shred of dignity.

"Leave me," she commanded. He had no choice but to obey. He didn't want to risk another incident. He was to the door before she added, "Move your belongings to another room." His face burned with anger and humiliation, but he said nothing. He did allow himself to slam the door on the way out.

Alan stalked down the corridor, trying to get his emotions under control. No sense in everyone else knowing about this. Yet, they certainly would know when he moved out of Sonia's room. Then the talk would begin. On an impulse, when he reached the foyer, he turned toward the back of the house and let himself out into the garden. At the rear stood a run down gazebo. He stepped up on the creaking floorboards and had already sat down when he realized he wasn't alone. He should have noticed the scent of burning tobacco in the air. Karl's voice, soft and low-pitched, came from the direction of a glowing cigarette hovering on the other side of the dark enclosure. "Her highness giving you problems, my friend?"

Alan was silent. He wasn't long on scruples, but the ease with which Karl had apparently dispatched Carmen's sister made him a little leery of the man. There was something about the way Karl looked at people, as if judging whether they were worthy to exist in the world, that made Alan somewhat squeamish. On the other hand, he and Karl did have one attribute in common: greed. Before Sonia had started getting so damn weird, the whole Children of Artemis thing had seemed tailor-made for one of the most successful scams of all time. Alan himself had drafted Karl, a former university classmate, into the movement over drinks at a pub in London.

"It's perfect. The timing is just right. Sonia is a class act and about as convincing as Mother Teresa. I'm telling you, people are flocking to this."

"But does she actually heal anyone?"

"That's just it! Some of these people really do act like they're healed—not just the shills we plant here and there, but the real suckers, the ones who come limping in there with crutches and warts and what have you. It's probably just psychological, but to all the gawkers, Sister Sonia's done it, laid hands on them. It's like the second bloody coming of Jesus. And we're raking it in."

"So what do you need me for?"

"Take care of problems. Every now and then we get some asshole poking around, trying to discredit the Children of Artemis. And then there are some complaints now and then from the families of our members, wanting to know where all the money's got to."

"What, you think I'm some kind of enforcer?" Karl sneered.

"No, but you're smart. You know your way around databases. You can get information to keep the complainers in line, and you know all kinds of people, sort of in every 'field,' shall we say."

"So what do you figure is really going on with Sonia. She got some sort of mesmerizing thing going on?"

"She's a first-rate hypnotist, but…" Alan paused. He didn't want to come off sounding like one of the "marks" they were busy fleecing. "About a year ago, this girl showed up at the compound with something for Sonia, something she just had to give her in person. And she wouldn't go away. Forked over about five grand on the spot just to have a private audience with Sonia. I figured, what the hell."

"And?"

"I don't know exactly. They were alone for a couple of hours, and I guess Sonia took whatever the girl had in this bag she was carrying. And the girl looked kind of blank, really. Sonia told me to walk her to a dorm and find her a bed."

"And this all has to do with what?"

"That's just it," Alan replied, his eyes shifting away from Karl. "Ever since then, Sonia's been better than ever, and more people act healed."

Suddenly, Karl burst out laughing. "Get hold of yourself, mate. You're starting to take Sonia's press too seriously. Once a faker, always a faker. She just probably gets so into her role she spooks you a little. But all the really good ones do, don't ya know?"

♦

At the time of that conversation, they both understood what Alan wanted from Karl. Since graduating from university, Karl had dabbled in many different lines of work, few of them legal. His acquaintances ranged from the barely respectable to the downright criminal. Alan was indeed looking for some occasional strong-arm tactics, and he thought running into Karl must be a stroke of good fortune. Now, he wasn't so sure. Karl had been acting extremely independent and seemed to have been doing an awful lot of nosing around among the membership.

But Alan didn't have many allies at the compound, perhaps none besides Karl, with the possible exception of Helen Fiske, who had done everything to get his attention short of stripping naked and jumping on top of him. She, however, had so far shown herself incapable of intellectual pursuits beyond the trashiest of romance novels and the keeping of a personal journal that she vowed would someday become a best-seller, no doubt equally trashy.

Alan watched the cigarette flare up as Karl dragged on it, then saw the smoke arc away into the night. "Sonia's getting weirder," he finally admitted.

"Weirder than what? Than usual?"

"She's…I don't know…really buying into all this stuff we've been peddling."

Karl snorted softly. "Come on. She's too savvy for that. The woman's a born con artist. She's probably just having you on about it. And you're such a sucker, you would take it seriously."

Alan felt blood rush to his cheeks and was thankful for the thick dark of the moonless night. In an instant urge to take the smirk out of Karl's tone, he said, "She questioned your thoroughness on your recent trip."

"What the hell are you talking about? The job got done."

"But you didn't follow up on the two women she talked to in Palm Springs."

"I brought you their names, didn't I? You think I'm going to hang around there afterward just to stir up more trouble, make someone suspicious that it wasn't an accident. I'll talk to the good Sister and explain the facts of life."

Alan thought guiltily of the paper in his pocket, and the fact that he'd lied to Sonia about it. And yet, oddly, the very fact he'd gotten away with it made him feel better. If she was so fucking omniscient, why hadn't she known for sure that not only *were* there two women, but he had their names and contact information?

"Never mind. I'll deal with her highness myself. She's in a mood."

"Always is. Just don't start taking her too seriously." Karl paused. "Or this stupid little girl she's so keen on right now."

"Carmen." Alan's tone imbued the name with such disgust, Karl chuckled.

"What's the matter, mate? Think our fearless leader's dabbling in the Sapphic pleasures?"

Alan almost leaped to his feet. Now that his eyes had adjusted to the darkness, he could almost make out the grin on Karl's face. "Get your mind out of the gutter. She just wants to wring every penny out of the bitch."

"Sure that's all it is? Helen says those sessions are awfully long just for hypnotic healing, or the whaddya call it—past-life regression?"

"Sonia isn't doing past-life regression."

"You don't think so?"

"No! It's all just a game she's playing," snapped Alan.

"Then she's bloody good at it, because she's had me in there a couple of times, and I don't even remember what went on."

"You don't actually think she's…"

Karl laughed out loud. "Don't be an ass. That's her schtick, man. Every good con artist has to have at least one real talent. Great ones have an entire arsenal. Sonia, she's got hypnosis, she's a first-rate actress, and she's so fucking sexy she makes grown men drool. So she can put your lights out for a while. So what? I've seen those stage magicians make people quack like ducks. Big deal. She makes people walk out of here thinking they're healed. Same big deal. This bimbo is just a project for Sonia. Hell, she's probably trying to brainwash her or something. So leave it alone. If you piss Sonia off, you'll regret it."

Alan already did regret it. He figured he might as well admit to Karl what was going on. The news would be around soon enough. "She told me to sleep in one of the guest rooms."

"Oh, so that's the way the wind blows. Well, it happens to the best of us when the ladies get their knickers in a twist." Karl stood up and clapped Alan on the shoulder. It might have been meant as sympathy but it felt patronizing to Alan. "In the meantime, I believe the lovely Helen wouldn't mind paying you a visit."

"Don't even go there. I'm not cheating on Sonia. Talk about pissing her off!"

"Glad to hear you're being sensible about it. I'd rather not see any dissension in the ranks, know what I mean? We've all got a good thing going here. It'll run its course eventually, once enough people realize Sonia's a fraud. But in the meantime there's money to be made." He left the gazebo so quietly, Alan almost didn't realize he was gone.

◊

Upstairs in her private sitting room, Sister Sonia carefully locked all three doors that led into the room. Then she took the chain from around her neck, where it had hung concealed beneath her robes. From it dangled a small and unusual gold key with complicated wards. She walked to the antique gilt mirror that hung just to the right of the fireplace. She tugged at the side of the frame until it swung open on silent hinges. Behind the mirror the wall appeared entirely normal, a slightly darker patch of fine-grain mahogany paneling. Sonia pushed the precise center of the rectangle, and a section eighteen inches wide and twenty-four inches high popped out an inch or two. She pulled at it, then slid it to one side to reveal the door of a very old-fashioned safe, one that could only be opened with the key she held.

She inserted the key, turned it slowly to the left, then back to the right. The tumblers clicked into place, and the thick, lead-lined door swung open. As always, she was unprepared for the brilliance of the light within. She blinked rapidly, put her hand to her face, and looked through her slightly parted fingers for a few moments until her eyes adjusted. Then, as if sensing her presence, the powerful incandescence receded a little at a time, until she could see the outlines of the object, the source of all that multi-colored light.

On a velvet-lined cradle it lay, none of its dimensions more than seven or eight inches. It was neither square, nor round, nor oblong, but a melding of many shapes. Neither entirely transparent nor opaque, the large crystal shard pulsated with its own internal energy source. One large end was polished to a point, and there were other smaller points that radiated from various locations around its hourglass middle. At the other termination, the edges were jagged, glistening with razor-sharp edges, as if it had been torn from a much larger shape.

Sonia stared at it, felt its pulsations move into complete synchronicity with her own heartbeat. She reached out a hand to touch it—closer, centimeter by centimeter, the sensation almost painful, almost burning the skin of her palm. And yet she did not stop, nor did she draw her hand away. She closed her eyes—and closed the distance. The shock was both exquisitely painful and indescribably pleasurable. Her entire body trembled. Indecipherable images poured through her mind. Babbling voices, screams, laughter, shouts—all of it a cacophony she so longed to understand. Then she placed her left hand over her right, and she felt herself pulled into the crystal itself, into a dimension so indistinct she could not have described it to anyone. She only knew that when she returned, only minutes later in real time, it would seem to her as if days had passed. She desperately wanted to understand what was happening to her, what this object truly was. Sonia believed that the woman, Jenny, the one who had brought the crystal to her, had no idea of its importance but had been a tool of the gods in making sure it reached its rightful owner. Now she must decode it, decipher its meaning. And she begun to suspect that Carmen Waters might be the instrument through which this could be accomplished. In the meantime Sister Sonia had discovered something quite unexpected. She was no longer running a con game. She was actually healing people. She was becoming intermittently, though not reliably, clairvoyant. Her thoughts strayed to philosophical questions she'd never considered in her fifty years on the planet. And she had no idea how or why.

Chapter Four

Give all to love:
Obey thy heart;
Friends, kindred, days,
Estate, good fame,
Plans, credit, and the Muse—
Nothing refuse.
—Ralph Waldo Emerson, "Give All to Love"

WASHINGTON, D.C.

The plane touched down at Reagan National Airport only half an hour behind schedule, which would still give Laura and Connor plenty of time to catch a cab to Georgetown to meet Malcolm.

"He sounded awfully vague about why he wanted us to stop over on the way to London," said Laura. "What do you suppose is going on?"

"One guess…it's got something to do with Ayalla."

"You don't suppose she dumped him?"

"I hope not, but it wouldn't surprise me," said Connor. "I've never totally trusted her feelings for him. I think her career will always come first. And he's got his kids to think about."

"You're being overprotective and not giving him much credit," chided Laura. "He *is* a grown-up. And I seriously doubt he'd make any life decision that wasn't in the best interests of his children. They've always been his priority—first, last and always."

"I know." Connor sighed. "But I worry about him anyway, ever since Marie Louise died."

"He's waited a long time to find someone he could love, and I think he really loves Ayalla."

"As long as it runs both ways," said Connor.

The cab pulled up in front of the town house Connor had once lived in, years before. After Ariana was killed and an attempt had been made in that very house on Connor's life, she'd never been able to bear the thought of living there again. She'd insisted on Malcolm, his sister, Eve, and the kids moving in. Eventually, she had transferred the property to him, over his strenuous and extremely vocal objections. But she knew how much she owed him—not only her own life but Laura's as well. He had been there for them both in the worst of situations. The town house seemed to her a very small way to acknowledge such a friendship, no matter what Malcolm said.

The front door swung open, and there he was, all six and a half feet of him, with shoulders that almost filled the door frame. At 265 pounds, most of it solid, sculpted muscle, he was a formidable presence, a valuable asset when he'd been a street cop, and still useful when his subordinates showed any tendency to undermine him.

They both trotted up the steps toward their friend. He came to meet them halfway. His deep mahogany skin glowed in the soft light of the carriage lamps on either side of the front walk, and Connor noticed quite a bit more gray in his close-cropped hair as he swept her into a crushing hug.

"Someday you're going to break one of my ribs," she said, laughing as he released her and gave Laura the same treatment. "And what's with the mustache?"

He stroked it self-consciously. "I kind of like it."

"So do I," said Laura. "Definitely gives you a little extra something."

"Ayalla likes it, too," he admitted.

"Ah," said Connor.

"Now, don't start. She's inside waiting for us."

They preceded Malcolm into the handsome foyer of the town house, Connor in the lead. She ran right into the warm embrace of Eve, Malcolm's sister. Almost as tall as her brother, but, some insisted, twice as tough on "wanton sinfulness" (as she categorized all lapses in good behavior—from rudeness to criminality), Eve had been the mainstay of the family since the death of Malcolm's wife. She'd helped raise the children, watched them like a hawk, and kept even Malcolm's rebellious teenagers out of trouble. Her big heart encompassed others as well, especially Connor, whom she mothered unabashedly. Once Connor had fallen in love with Laura, Eve adopted her too and prayed for their safety and happiness every Sunday at the Cole Street Baptist Church. Eve Jefferson was the sort of woman whose spirituality was intensely practical, thoroughly sincere, and grounded in love. Anyone who knew Eve, knew she would protect her extended family with all the fierceness of a mama lion.

Unlike her brother, who'd consciously effaced the soft drawling accent of their childhood home in the Deep South, Eve's speech was all rounded vowels and eliding consonants and a comforting sibilance. "Lordy, it's good to see y'all." She held Laura at arm's length. "This gal's too skinny," she frowned at Connor over Laura's shoulder. "Ain't been feedin' her anythin' good a-tall. I can tell." She hugged Connor. "You just as bad, girl. Not enough meat on them bones to keep out the chill." She smiled and turned to her brother. "What is it with you always hangin' round with skinny girls. Ayalla could stand a few extra pounds, too."

"C'mon, Eve—" Malcolm began, looking as if he'd heard this about a thousand times.

"Don't worry, I'm done harpin'. Good thing I fixed a big dinner, though. I'll do what I can for these starvin' girls." She pointed toward them toward the living room. "I'll be in the kitchen. Got a pie comin' up done any minute." And off she went.

"She never changes," said Connor. "And I'm glad."

"Me, too," sighed Malcolm, "most of the time. Ayalla's waiting in the living room. She's kinda nervous, so be nice." He shot a warning glance at Connor.

Connor turned to Laura with a raised eyebrow, as if to say, "What did I do?" Laura smiled and gently pushed Connor into the room.

Eve had been busy. The large space, with its high ceilings and mahogany wainscoting, glowed warmly and invitingly. A fire burned brightly in the fireplace and several bouquets of flowers were arranged in vases throughout the room. The coffee table held plates of shrimp, cheese, bread and crackers, hot cocktail franks, and Malcolm's favorite—Swedish meatballs.

Connor, hungry as usual, was distracted by the food for a second before looking at Ayalla Franklin, who stood stiffly near the fireplace. Connor was once again struck by how formidable this woman could appear, though at this moment, Ayalla looked anything but confident. She seemed positively nervous. Near six feet tall, even in her low-heeled shoes, Special Agent Franklin was not wearing the FBI "uniform"—dark blazer and skirt, white silk blouse—with which Connor mostly associated her. Instead, she was casually dressed in a fawn-colored cashmere sweater and charcoal wool slacks. Ayalla's brown hair, flecked with blond highlights, was swept back from her face. Her skin was only a shade lighter than Malcolm's, but where his eyes were a soft brown, her eyes were a stunning crystal blue, and her high cheekbones subtly implied a more exotic heritage than his own. Hand-carved gold and bead earrings dangled from her ears, glittering in the firelight. Connor was for the first time truly aware of Ayalla as a gorgeous and very sensual woman. Perhaps Malcolm was not such a fool after all.

"Ayalla," she said, her smile not as warm as the one she lavished on Eve or Malcolm, but then she still suspected that the straitlaced "Feebie," as she called the FBI agent in private, was prejudiced against her for being a lesbian and only pretended to be accepting because Connor was Malcolm's dearest friend.

Laura gently brushed past Connor and strode immediately over to Ayalla, giving her a brief but firm hug. Ayalla's body relaxed ever so slightly, and she tried on a tiny smile when Laura said, "You look great. The last time I saw you I was worried you'd waste away to nothing."

"No chance of that with Eve's cooking," Ayalla replied, the usual resonance of her voice somewhat muted.

Connor looked behind her to see Malcolm, who still stood beaming just inside the door, while Eve, returning from the kitchen, peeked around his broad shoulder with a look of expectant glee. He looked back and forth between the women in the room as a huge grin spread over his face. "Connor, Laura, we have an announcement to make." Then, as if realizing he should be standing next to the other half of the "we" in his statement, he crossed the room in a few long strides and took Ayalla's hand.

A leaden feeling of dread filled Connor's chest. He had that look.

"Ayalla and I are going to be married—two weeks from Saturday! We want you to be there of course. Since Ayalla has no family and you're all my family too, we want you to be our witnesses."

There were several seconds of stunned silence. Then Laura, recovering first, reached out for the two of them, first taking their hands, then hugging them both in turn while saying "How wonderful! Congratulations. I'm so happy for you!"

Connor stood there blinking, wondering how it was that Laura always seemed to maintain her aplomb, whether offering her condolences or felicitations. In this case Connor would have preferred to the former, but she stepped forward and quickly hugged Malcolm and then took Ayalla's hand in hers and murmured something that she hoped sounded polite and positive, but she couldn't be sure. She of the quick-witted rejoinder was utterly tongue-tied. She prayed she didn't look as stunned as she felt, but she could feel two hot spots of red blotching her cheeks, and her hands were a little sweaty. She quickly wiped them on her jacket as though smoothing the lapels after the hug.

"Malcolm, where are you going to have the ceremony? Where are you going to live? When did all this happen? What do the children…"

Malcolm interrupted Laura with a hand in the air. "Slow

down, girl. We're going to give you all the details. Don't get your knickers in a twist! Let's sit down, have a meatball and a drink, and we'll fill in all the blanks. Eve, come sit down, too. You don't have to hover in the doorway. It's safe to come in. I told you no one would explode."

Connor wasn't on the verge of exploding exactly, but she did feel sort of gut-punched, as if she'd just lost her best friend. Her eyes met Ayalla's for the briefest of moments, but Connor's expression spoke volumes. *You'd better not be playing games with him.*

Chapter Five

Ah, Love! Could thou and I with Fate conspire
To Grasp this sorry Scheme of Things entire
Would not we shatter it to bits—and then
Re-mould it nearer to the Heart's Desire!
—Edward Fitzgerald, *Omar Khayyam,* ed. I, 1xiii

YORKSHIRE, ENGLAND

Carmen's head hurt worse than it ever had before. The sessions with Sister Sonia were getting longer and more arduous, and although she never admitted as much to her spiritual leader, Carmen remembered less and less of what transpired, at least in her conscious mind. On the other hand, the dreams were getting more and more vivid. These, too, Carmen kept to herself, though for reasons she couldn't quite define. She had begun to have doubts, serious doubts, about Sister Sonia's motivations for these late-night sessions.

For a brief few days since Alan had moved out of the small suite of rooms he'd shared with Sonia, Carmen had allowed herself the tiniest pinprick of hope that Sonia was romantically interested in her. The possibility seemed slim. Sonia was everything Carmen believed she, herself, was not—powerful, erotic, stunningly attractive, and shrewdly intelligent. When Carmen looked in her bedroom mirror, all she saw was the relative plainness of unremarkable features, certainly nothing that would attract someone like Sonia, who had always shown herself to be at least as concerned with appearance as with substance. Thus, Carmen realistically surmised that the attention she was getting was motivated by something else entirely. But what? She could not believe she possessed any talent, any special gift at all.

Tonight's meeting had lasted until well after midnight. Two hours later, however, Carmen was still wakeful, staring at the canopy over her bed. There were precisely sixty-one stripes in the wine-and-beige damask fabric, each stripe running from the head of the bed to the foot. Counting them over and over had become Carmen's way of shutting out the strange and unsettling images that populated her mind after the hours spent under the 'spell' of Sister Sonia's honeyed yet insistent voice. She didn't want to sleep, and she didn't want to dream. Of course, eventually she did both. But this time the dream was more than vivid, and Carmen was more than a spectator. She was part of everything that unfolded, though for a few brief moments she struggled to awaken, to make it all stop, but she was thoroughly trapped, and she was no longer Carmen Waters.

Lightning arced from tower to tower in the great walled city, and still Junela could not bring herself to admit the horrifying truth of what was happening. All the portents had been there; all the stern guidance from their guardians had flashed through her mind a thousand times, and her glimpses of the Akashic Records had presented her with evidence that could no longer be ignored. She'd deluded herself and those who trusted her guidance for far too long. Her inner dilemma had been painful. As with all such manifestations within the astral realms, the details of the Records were mutable under certain circumstances, but not when the actions of humans had finally turned into certain immutable channels that virtually sealed their fate. She had seen it, she had felt it. From the moment Arkan had died and Cantos had taken his place as senior minister, the governing of the great and powerful colony set like a jewel in the midst of this wild world had been in the wrong hands. And those blazing words in the Records had cooled to deeply engraved permanence. The end could no longer be changed.

The Lady Deirdre, consumed by her paralyzing grief at Arkan's death, had let Cantos have the run of the city. He was busily consolidating his own power base, dismantling within weeks the sacred rights and protections afforded all citizens. Prisons had been created where none had stood before. Where there had been harmony and civilization, now there was conflict. And in a society where a certain elite class held the power to control and even kill with their minds, chaos was inevitable.

Worst of all, the Lady had broken the seals to the inner temple. Junela knew now that the woman she'd once revered had passed into utter madness. Lady Deirdre sought the power of the great keys, the energetic vibrations of creation that lived and pulsated within the enormous and breathtaking crystals sunk deep into the planet itself. It was from these miraculous formations that all of their knowledge flowed, that all of their healing abilities were fueled, their enormous mental faculties powered. It was the connection with these crystalline record keepers and power conduits that united their entire culture under one ethos. For century upon century, the balance had been maintained. But somewhere darkness had crept in, and even Alandra was not sure of its source. Harmony had begun to waver, and she felt tiny echoes of dissonance tremble along the energy channels of her body, the lines that so closely mirrored the ley lines of the world on which they had chosen to dwell. She had gone to the Lady Deirdre, and her consort, Arkan. But they had chosen to ignore the subtle signs and she soon realized that they, too, had slowly begun to succumb to the temptations of absolute power. They had begun to believe themselves gods, and those who could be thought of as real gods would not tolerate such arrogance for long.

Junela watched the gathering storm. Brilliant bolts of forked lightning crisscrossed in the sky before touching down within the city, their combined force setting off a series of fiery explosions. This was not naturally occurring weather, she knew, but immense psychic energy gone berserk. Clearly, the inner temple had been opened—and not by one with pure intention or one seeking to act in love. Without purity of heart, the power of the keys would be unleashed as utter chaos, destructive in every way. But Lady Deirdre was acting in fear and grief and desperation. She thought only of her loss of Arkan.

It was said that anyone who dared to command these energies from the inner temple could not only alter the appearance of physical reality but also reverse linear time itself. Too, there was the possibility of crossing between the infinite planes of existence that ran alongside each other, close together but shielded from one another by the thinnest yet most potent of veils, barriers that would open only to those with sufficient power to pierce them. Junela greatly feared that the Lady was on the verge of breaking the one inviolable law of their species, of their civilization, a law so sacrosanct that none had ever dared to violate it. Deirdre would believe her personal power so great, and her loss so unbearable, that she would actually step into the matrix of energy within the inner temple and try to use her powerful mind and will to redirect the events of the past. Even Junela could not begin to imagine the dreadful consequences in the present of such an arrogant act.

She turned to Alandra—her lover, her friend, her life mate—and stroked her long, dark hair. "Stay close to me, darling. There is nothing more I can do."

Alandra's tears glistened in the brilliant flashes of light. "But you are the high priestess, and I am your second. Surely there's something—"

"No, my love, no. I've even spoken to Ishara, my old mother. She blessed me and sent me to you."

"We're finished, aren't we? All of us?"

"I'm afraid we are. We've all gone too far, you see. Too many of us have believed ourselves above the ethics of civilized beings, immune from the laws of the universe. We've held the power of life and death too casually in our hands, and the wheel must turn back to the beginning."

"Will we be together again?"

"Someday in another life, yes, we will, my darling. That I promise you."

Junela picked up the scrying mirror Alandra had been using, with little success, to discern what was happening elsewhere in the city. The skill to scry, however, was one of Junela's strongest. Within seconds, the *object of her search appeared in the slightly distorted reflection. And the psychic ability that was her birthright easily brought into her mind the thoughts and emotions of the woman she had once admired beyond all others. Junela could quite literally experience the world through another's eyes if she chose to do so, and this was certainly justifiable reason for the invasion of another's privacy.*

Far below them, in the chambers of the inner temple, the Lady Deirdre, Queen and Keeper of the Keys of Life, strode forward toward the column of light that swirled in the center of the chamber. There in its midst lay the core of cosmic consciousness, the innermost of all mysteries, the mind of not just the gods of their creation, but outward manifestation of the mind of the one God. It was the one place from which all beings of third-dimensional density were banned upon pain of utter destruction, not just destruction of body, but of soul and of mind.

In the light she saw it—the image of Arkan, her lover and her mate. He had taught her how to use her power, how to control others, how to remake the world into his vision of it. His voice drew her now. His soul called to her.

Her skin tingled, then burned, as she drew closer. She was at once repelled and drawn inexorably into the vortex. One step, then another. She reached out for him, still holding her crystal wand, and her hand pierced the final layer of energy.

The world around her exploded into fragmented light.

Above the ground, the golden walls of the city began not to crack, but to disintegrate, as if the very material from which they were made no longer could exist in the universe. A thousand thousand screams rent the air. The ground itself split and gaped open. And, as Alandra and Junela held each other close, the great island city of Atlantis and all the powers of its would-be gods and goddesses sank beneath the waves forever.

Carmen awoke, still absorbing empathically the utter confusion of terror-stricken people who had died even before the sound waves of their screams had reached the edges of the city. But where was Alandra? Carmen jerked upright in the bed, completely alone.

There was no Junela. There was no city. She fought to bring her consciousness back into this mundane room, a place so reassuringly real and solid. Yes, there was the canopy, and across the room stood the dresser, the wardrobe, and the slightly uncomfortable wingback chair upon which she'd draped her novice's robe. An impotent, watery daylight seeped through the cracks between the drapes so that most of the objects in the room were cast in deep, gloomy shadow, but at least the objects were real. Everything was the same. And yet, it wasn't.

Her heart still thudded in her chest, and the pain of so much death, the loss of Alandra, seared through her chest as if she had actually been there, done those things. But that was impossible.

Carmen had never been so afraid in her life, nor more alone. She began to sob, clutching the bedclothes around her as if they could protect her from this nightmare. But the nightmare originated somewhere inside herself, and from that there was no protection at all.

Chapter Six

Our deeds determine us,
as much as we determine our deeds.
—George Eliot (Mary Ann Cross), *Adam Bede*

Yorkshire, England

"I'm not satisfied with the preparations," Sonia declared to the assembled group, her tone particularly cold and sharp. "Have I not made it clear to you that this timetable cannot be altered?"

Alan was the first to speak, having tried for days to ingratiate himself with Sonia, and regain his coveted position as her closest disciple and lover. "Of course you've been clear. It's just that I, that is to say…we don't know exactly why…" He paled and didn't finish the sentence, realizing at once he'd made yet another tactical error. But before he could possibly try to repair by taking another approach, Sonia rose to her feet so quickly it startled them all.

"Why? You would fail to carry out my instructions because I haven't given you sufficient reason to do so? It is not enough that I gave them to you?"

"Er…no, I mean, yes," stammered Alan. "Not at all. It's just that if we had a better idea of the…um…total picture, then we could do a better job of getting the furnishings and the equipment into place."

Sonia glared at him for a several beats of his heart, then swiveled her head to include all of them in her displeasure. No one dared speak, cough, or even fidget. Such was the power that emanated from her. Alan, seated only inches away, could actually *feel* it, much as he would rather have denied the sensation. It both thrilled and frightened him. Sonia was becoming more attractive by the day, not just to him but to everyone in the compound. And she'd been a knockout when he first met her. Clearly, something had changed. And while the transformation rendered her ever more breathtaking, it also added a sharp, cruel edge to her personality and an unnerving menace to her expanding "powers." The word sounded puerile, he knew, but Alan didn't know what else to call them. Once upon a time, Sonia had been little more than a gifted and moderately successful charlatan. Alan had been the perfect foil for her act. Now she was utterly different, or had gone completely mad. Either way, Alan was woefully out of his element. He'd seriously considered making a run for it. Were it not for the fact that Sonia controlled all the bank accounts, he would have settled for a small nest egg and a new scam of his own somewhere else. But he couldn't stand the thought of missing out on his share. Besides, he still believed she'd want him back, and the energy that poured out of her made him ache with desire. His one consolation at this point was that Carmen wasn't permitted to attend these meetings of the inner circle.

Without warning, Sonia's entire demeanor changed. She closed her eyes for a few seconds, and when she reopened them she was smiling. Alan wasn't convinced the smile was any safer than the scowl, but he preferred it to the face of doom, as some of the disciples had taken to calling it…well, outside her hearing. Still, the swiftness of the transformation was alarming in and of itself.

"You're right, of course. It is time to share with you, my faithful disciples, the great truth that has been revealed to me." She paused for effect, consummate performer that she was. "A few months ago, I told you and the many followers of our path that I would one day soon deliver a message from the highest sources, from the pantheon of creator Gods who placed humans on this planet."

Alan shivered as he felt the word she'd skipped over—"you"

as in "you humans." As he suspected, Sonia no longer considered herself anything less than a demigod. He didn't think anything good could come out of that particular delusion.

"Some of you may have difficulty accepting this, but I assure you that if you do harbor any doubts, it is only because you have not yet achieved full rebirth of your consciousness, as I have. You do not see as I see. You do not hear as I hear." She smiled indulgently. "But that is why I am here, to guide you through this glorious transformation."

Alan looked down the table and caught Karl's eye. They were frowning in unison. What the hell did she mean by "transformation?" He shifted his gaze back to Sonia.

"You are all aware of the state of this world in which you exist—rife with violence, poverty, war, crime—and no doubt you have wondered how we might repair this damaged society. Many of you have tried. And many on this planet believe that it can be repaired, that the society of human beings can be salvaged and turned once more into a path of Light." She paused and closed her eyes for a moment, as if listening. "I have recently received a very different vision of the future, however: one that is rather more realistic."

The other disciples began to fidget. Clearly they, too, were utterly confused. *No more than I am,* thought Alan. *At least I know this is supposed to be a scam. These morons think she's some sort of freakin' goddess.*

Sonia drew herself up to an even more imposing height. If Alan didn't know better, he'd almost swear she'd gotten taller in the last couple of weeks. He glanced down to see if her shoes were visible under the hem of her robe. He could just make out the side of one…sandal. So it wasn't a question of wearing high heels for effect. He sighed, not wanting to think about it. He was just spooking himself.

"The future of most of this planet is not only bleak, but it is also entirely hopeless. This, my disciples, is the moment foretold by the ancient ones who came before us. We are approaching the end of time, the end of this world as you know it."

Alan now fully understood the meaning of the old saw, "could have heard a pin drop." Everyone in the room was frozen in place, their expressions ranging from puzzlement to shock. Sonia didn't seem to notice or care.

"The preparations I asked you to make with regard to our compound and the main hall are critical to our survival and transition into a very different world. So, please carry out every instruction as if your very life depended on it."

She smiled serenely and swept out of the room.

♦

Connor and Laura pushed their luggage carts down the tunnel labeled NOTHING TO DECLARE.

"Heathrow is crowded, but still more civilized about customs than any city in the States," said Laura. "I can't believe how long it took us to get checked in at Dulles."

"So how come you didn't throw your weight around a little?" teased Connor. "Pull out that security clearance of yours."

"Because I won't do that when it's just for personal convenience," replied Laura, seriously but not sententiously. "It doesn't seem quite fair unless I have an official reason."

"Always the Girl Scout," smiled Connor. "If we'd had to fly coach, I think I would have begged you to do it anyway. Did you see the length of that line for check-in?"

"Yes, and I thank my lucky stars and various angels that I'm attached to a famous writer who has the budget for business class."

"Attached?"

"Kind of hard to think of the right word."

Connor pondered that for a moment. "Why is it our lifestyle limits our word choices?"

Laura smiled. " 'Girlfriend' is innocuous and meaningless for all intents and purposes. 'Lover' is a little personal for social situations. 'Significant other' is just plain annoying. And 'partner' makes me think of contractual agreements."

"What's left?" asked Connor. "Wife?"

Laura looked at her sideways. "Aside from the fact that we're not married, sweetheart…"

"You know, I've been thinking about that."

"Thinking about what?"

Before Connor could answer, they emerged from the passageway and heard a familiar voice, "Mom, Laura, over here!"

They turned in the direction of the summons and saw Katy with an armful of flowers and a grin that so closely approximated her mother's it always startled Laura at first sight. Within millimeters the same height as Connor, Katy had also inherited her mother's pale, creamy complexion, the crystal-blue eyes with flecks of green, and truly black hair. But where Connor's was cut to frame her face in soft, natural waves reaching just to her collar, Katy wore hers in a tousled mane that fell well below her shoulders. Today she was dressed in a long cinnamon skirt, white wool sweater, tall leather boots, and a dark-brown raincoat with a silk muffler around her neck. All in all, Katy was very different from her mother, and yet, Laura thought, she, too, possessed that spark, that intangible radiance Laura had seen in Connor and in Gwendolyn Broadhurst, Connor's grandmother. Perhaps it was the Celtic blood that ran in them, the long line of powerful women from whom they were descended. Whatever it was, Laura knew it was potent and beautiful in each generation.

Mother and daughter hugged each other hard, crushing the flowers somewhat. Then it was Laura's turn, and Katy embraced her with a fervent welcome. The slender frame was deceiving, Laura realized. Katy was neither delicate nor weak. The girl was seriously fit, despite sharing her mother's penchant for junk food.

"Gramps is outside with a car," said Katy, leading the way through the crowds of arriving passengers occupied with their own reunions.

"You know he must hate you calling him that," said Connor.

"Apparently not. I've never known him not to speak his mind," said Katy with a grin at Laura who responded in kind.

"Benjamin always speaks his mind."

They wrestled their luggage trolleys through the door and out onto the sidewalk. Beyond the taxi queue lane, Benjamin Hawthorne stood beside a Rover estate wagon, chatting with a Heathrow security man. But the conversation appeared amiable, and unrelated to Benjamin's irregular parking, and the officer moved off with a nod as the three women approached.

After another round of hugs, and quick stowing of the luggage in the rear compartment, they took their places in the car, Katy in the front with Benjamin.

"I didn't even ask," said Connor. "But this is a workday. You never take time off, according to your great aunt Jessica."

Katy turned to look over the seat back. "I don't. Most weeks are sixty hours at least. But I've got so much vacation time saved up, I thought this was the perfect opportunity to use it. Besides, the project I've been working on is almost complete. Nothing left but the decorators coming in to finish the interior."

"I'm still amazed at how much of your design they incorporated," said Laura.

"Gee, thanks," laughed Katy.

Laura blushed. "You know what I mean. You're the youngest architect there. Your designs are brilliant, I've seen them, but who pays attention to junior staffers? I know what it's like to be the low man on the totem pole."

Benjamin snorted. "You were never that working for me."

"Plus I'd have to take issue with 'man,'" quipped Connor, "and I think totem pole is ethnically insensitive these days."

"As you might recall," Laura shot back with a laugh, "I'm a Native American! True, Navajos don't have totem poles, but I'm theoretically allowed to reference them. And I've had jobs where no one took me seriously, I can assure you."

"I find that hard to believe," replied Connor, smiling at her lover. "*Very* hard to believe."

"That's just because I've beaten Malcolm three times at the firing range."

"That, and your black belt, and a few other things."

"Details," said Laura. "Mere details. But we're off the subject. I want to see this building Katy designed."

"Not the entire building," said Katy with a shake of her head. "And not the overall design. I did some of the details, and they used my ideas for the atrium and the rooftop pavilion."

Connor patted Katy's shoulder. "That's my kid—talent *and* modesty."

Katy snorted. "Thanks, Mom. Not that you're biased or anything."

"Always."

Benjamin deftly steered them through the flow of traffic, exiting the ring road onto the motorway leading back toward the heart of London. Clearly, he was fully acclimated to the British system of driving on the left and circling roundabouts clockwise. "I'll drop you girls at the hotel," he said, glancing in the mirror, "and Katy at her flat. We'll all meet for dinner around 7:30." There's an excellent Indian restaurant just a couple of blocks from your hotel. I made a reservation."

"Sounds perfect," said Laura. "By the way, any results from the data runs I requested?"

"Yes, and I've got some files for you. I think you'll find the results fascinating. It took a lot of digging to get under Sister Sonia's camouflage, but I found enough that I think she warrants more attention from our people than she's been getting."

"Why? Is she anything more than a stellar con artist?"

"With homicidal associates," Connor reminded her. "Bettina Waters comes to mind."

"Yes," said Laura. "But none of that rises to the level of national security concerns…or does it?" she asked, eyeing Benjamin's reflection in the rearview mirror.

"Sister Sonia?" Katy interrupted just as Benjamin started to answer Laura's question. "Are you talking about that flake up in Yorkshire?"

"You've heard of her, then," said Connor.

"She's big news in the tabloids here. A couple of the more

sensationalist ones have a Sister Sonia watch going on. They report on her so-called healings and miracles every week."

"But how is she getting away with it?" asked Laura. "Surely by now her cures must have been exposed as frauds."

Katy shook her head. "That's what I can't figure out either. One of my friends from work, Ian Darcy, took his younger brother up there a few weeks ago. Philip's seventeen and has some form of multiple sclerosis. Anyway, they came back after a weekend, and Ian now insists that Philip is totally cured. He even let Philip go back to live at Sister Sonia's compound or retreat center or whatever the hell she calls it."

"How much did this so-called cure cost?" asked Connor, getting to the heart of the matter as always.

"Ian admitted to me that he wrote her a check for £10,000, just about every penny he had. But he says it's worth it."

"Has Ian heard from his brother lately?"

Katy frowned. "No, and I think that's beginning to worry him. He's mentioned taking a drive up there to find out what's going on. But I want to know what you're talking about. Where does 'homicidal' come into all this?"

Laura and Connor swiftly filled Katy in on the death of Bettina Waters and the activities of her sister, Carmen, who was apparently still resident at the Children of Artemis community.

"You think they actually sent someone to kill this woman in Palm Springs?"

Connor nodded. "There's absolutely no definitive proof. I grant you it's more of a hunch but —

"Your hunches are usually good. Still, murder seems a long way from being a con artist."

Benjamin, stopping for a traffic signal, reached down between the front seats and handed a bound accordion folder over the seat to Connor. "Something has changed in her pattern, it would seem. She's had numerous aliases and is a very convincing woman when she wants to be. She's scammed a number of wealthy individuals—men and women as well as banks, credit card companies, charitable organizations. Basically, she has no scruples whatsoever. The Children of Artemis is her latest undertaking, and it certainly qualifies as the biggest."

Laura peered at the file that Connor held between them as she turned the pages. "You know, I'm getting more than a little annoyed with the use of Artemis in all this. She was a perfectly venerable kick-ass sort of goddess figure. Personally, I like her. And if she had children," she continued, pointing at a photograph taken during a gathering, "it wouldn't be this bunch."

"Agreed," said Connor. "But perhaps we'd better focus on their crimes first, and later we can worry about their sacrilegious choice of brand name."

Chapter Seven

The mass of men lead lives of quiet desperation.
—Henry David Thoreau, *Walden*

The City of York

Alan sat at a table alone in the tea shop and waited for Sonia to do her weekly spending. Though she'd always been extravagant, she'd gotten more attached to finery than seemed possible. Between mail order and her shopping sprees in town and in London, he shuddered to think how much she was spending. At the moment, though, her wardrobe was the last of his worries. His stomach felt as if it were awash in acid, and it wasn't the tea. It was Sonia's bizarre announcement, and it made him want to crawl in a hole, or start running as far and as fast as he could. But he had no money. The few thousand dollars he had stashed away wouldn't last anywhere near long enough. Why had he let Sonia control everything? He slapped his hand down on the table, startling the two little old ladies next to him. His face reddened as they stared at him with that look of utter disapproval that only prim, aged ladies and Catholic school nuns can perfect through practice.

"Sorry," he muttered, as their gaze returned to their tea and scones. He took another sip of tea and glanced idly at the bulletin board near the cash register a few feet away. His gaze traveled over the handbills and notices, then to the people passing by outside the window. He was digging in his pocket for some pound coins to pay the check when he stopped with his hand still in his coat and suddenly stood up, knocking his chair over. One of the two women said something acerbic, but he didn't notice.

Alan strode to the bulletin board and stared at the boldly colorful handbill that had almost escaped his notice. There it was in exceedingly large, very bold print—a name that was unpleasantly familiar to him because he'd seen it handwritten on a piece of paper—Connor Hawthorne. The advertisement for the writer's conference and arts festival left no doubt that she was one of the star attractions. And there was no doubt in his mind that she was the very same Connor Hawthorne who'd met Bettina Waters in Palm Springs.

Son of a bitch! This cannot be a fucking coincidence. But how? This stupid event must have been scheduled months ago. Shit! If she starts poking around here... But then what? What's she going to find? Other people nosed around the place, and they didn't find anything to nail us on. But now Sonia's going right off the fucking deep end. Who knows what she'll say to people?

Alan tore the poster off the board, dropped far too much money on the table, and almost ran out of the tea shop. The only thing he could think to do was talk to Karl. Maybe the two of them could figure out a way to skip town with some cash before the roof fell in on the Children of Artemis.

♦

Karl was having concerns of his own. He, too, thought Sonia had crossed over into lunacy, and he wasn't about to stay long enough to witness her humiliation when the end of the world didn't show up on time. But he had no intention of leaving empty-handed, and he was more aggressive than Alan when it came to seeing that he got his share of the spoils. Thus he'd made a couple of covert attempts to open Sonia's office safe, which he'd discovered behind an antique mirror. The lock had confounded him, despite an antique design that Karl had thought would make cracking the safe a pushover. He'd had to go up to London, seeking old friends with various collections of specialized picklocks. He was sure he now had the right equipment.

And he reasoned that the safe was the logical place for Sonia to store her confidential information—ledgers, financials, account numbers, and possibly a nice hoard of cash as well. Either way, he'd take what he could get.

Karl slipped into Sonia's office with another quick look behind him. The Lady herself was in town buying out the stores again, with Alan in tow, and none of the other disciples would dare enter the leader's sanctum sanctorum without invitation. Karl figured he had at least an hour to see what he could find. With implements in hand, he quickly revealed the safe tucked into the wall and began working on the lock. It was the work of less than two minutes and a smile spread across his face as he heard the last tumbler fall. *Ah,* he thought, *having the right tools makes all the difference.*

His smile faded however when he opened the door and blinked against the light from within. "Bloody hell," he whispered to himself, as his stomach flipped over, not because there was obviously no money or paperwork in the safe, but because he instantly recognized what he did see—the crystal shard. Karl slammed the safe door shut with no thought of the noise it made. He didn't believe in coincidence, but it was impossible to explain this as anything else.

It had been months since the raid on the island, a job for which he'd been paid well by a former employer. He hadn't known the exact parameters of the task going in, and he hadn't been entirely comfortable with the murderous strategy his fellow team members had adopted to acquire the objective. But he'd kept his mouth shut and taken the money. All the crystals had been removed and shipped to the employer's research facilities in Europe. Karl still didn't know why they were so valuable. But he'd seen them up close and personal, and he knew in his gut that this was a piece of one of them. But how the hell did it get here—in this lunatic con artist's safe? Something floated into his mind, some event in the recent past, but it floated right back out before he could get a handle on it. What the hell was it?

Karl realized he was still standing in Sonia's office and risked discovery if she'd return. He quickly closed the panel and retreated into the corridor. He needed time to think. If those other pieces of crystal had been worth outfitting a killing team and taking out a bunch of innocent people, then surely this one shard had some significant monetary value. The question was how to cash in on it without ending up as dead as those poor bastards on the island. And could he be absolutely sure that this was the same kind of item? The others hadn't pulsated and lit up the way this one did. Why? And did it have anything to do with Sonia's bizarre behavior? The questions kept tumbling over and over in his mind so that he didn't see Carmen Waters before walking directly into her in the hall. She yelped as he trod heavily on her foot.

"What the hell!" he growled. "What are you doing sneaking around here?"

Carmen took a shaky step backward. "This...this is my room," she said, motioning toward the door to her bedroom. "I was...I was—"

"Never mind," he snapped, cutting off her stammering explanation. He stomped down the hall toward the stairs, not daring to look back and see her wondering why *he* was upstairs and so near to Sonia's office. He wondered if she'd mention it later. But Karl was pragmatic. He'd come up with an excuse if the question was asked. Carmen's startled face had triggered the memory he'd been chasing—a young woman showing up at the compound and insisting on an audience with Sister Sonia, a young woman clutching a battered backpack to her chest as if it contained the crown jewels.

He needed to get into town and make some calls from a local call box. He certainly wasn't going to let anyone know that the Children of Artemis compound was his current residence. Bad enough they'd be able to find out he was in the city of York when he telephoned.

Alan hung up and stood there in the call box, oblivious to an older woman who was waiting impatiently to use it. He leaned his aching head against one of the cold glass panes. It was the first thing that had felt good in a long time. Naturally, within fifteen seconds, someone had to spoil it. The old lady started tapping on the door. He sighed heavily, too depressed to muster so much as a snarl in her direction, and stepped out. She ignored him and took his place just as the thick, sodden clouds overheard opened up and drenched him in a spine-freezing deluge.

"Shit!" he said before starting in search of Sonia. He didn't actually want to find her, but at this point he had no choice. Until he could arrange something with Karl, he was stuck with the status quo. He knew he'd better put on a very different face. Sonia was getting really spooky with her mind-reading stuff. He felt the flyer wadded up in his pocket. *Would she know about that if he kept it? What if he couldn't keep his mind off it? And what would Karl say when he found out the woman who knew Bettina Waters was right here in York, or would be within a couple of days?* Alan recognized the pulse pounding in his head heralded a real fucker of a migraine. He plodded along the pavement, feeling the pain building up, much faster and more excruciating than ever before. If it got really bad, he wondered if he dared ask Sonia to heal it. Even he saw the irony in that because, for all intents and purposes, *she* was his biggest headache.

♦

Carmen Waters didn't go to her room after all. She waited a few moments until she was sure Karl was well out of sight, then took the back staircase down to the former servants hall and out to the rear courtyard. The encounter with him outside the door of her room had reminded her of how much she feared the idea of being alone with him, though she wasn't entirely sure why. But there was a menace about him. The others disliked her. That much she knew. And Alan just about hated her. But Karl didn't particularly care one way or the other whether she lived or died and that was more frightening. Instinctively, Carmen knew that Karl's personal interests came first, and anyone who threatened those interests would suffer for it.

She scurried out one of the French doors leading from the library into the garden. Though not particularly well-kept, she could still see the outlines of the careful tending it had once received.

She took the path along the side of what had once been a perfectly manicured maze, though its hedges were now overgrown and tangled. Getting lost inside was extremely unpleasant, as several of visitors had discovered once they'd escaped, scratched and bleeding. At the far end of the maze was a small hideaway of stone garden seats surrounded by low-growing shrubs. It was Carmen's only place of solitude. Thus she was both annoyed and surprised to find someone already there before her.

The young woman seated on one of the benches didn't immediately look up when Carmen stepped into the enclosure. When she finally turned her head toward Carmen, there was still little recognition or acknowledgment. Carmen was almost repulsed by the sheer blankness in the woman's eyes.

"It's Jenny, isn't it?" said Carmen, always one to remember names, even after brief encounters. She'd helped this particular individual get settled in the dormitory, though as she recalled, they'd shared little conversation. At the time, Carmen was occupying the other narrow twin bed in the tiny room to which Jenny had been assigned. But the girl had said so little, seemed so vacant, that Carmen had stopped trying after that day and evening. And two days later, Carmen had been invited to live in the main house. She hadn't seen Jenny since then.

"Are you all right?" asked Carmen quietly as she took a seat on the opposite bench.

For a moment or two, she thought Jenny wouldn't answer or didn't hear her, but the young woman took a deep breath, as if she'd forgotten to breathe for quite a while, and focused her gaze on Carmen. "What did you say?"

"I wondered if you were all right."

"Why wouldn't I be?" she replied with a decidedly defensive edge in her voice.

"It's just that you looked, well, kind of sad or lost in thought. I'm sorry, I didn't mean to intrude. I didn't think anyone would be here."

"Is this your place, then?"

"No, I mean, I do come here, but it isn't my private place or anything. Everyone is welcome to use the garden."

"But not everyone's welcome to live in the house. Or spend time with Sister Sonia."

Carmen blushed. "I…I'm not…I don't know why she asked me to stay up there. I'm not important, not like the disciples."

Jenny's expression hardened into a sneer. "Oh, yes, the disciples. They're mostly idiots, you know. They don't understand anything at all. They think Sonia's some sort of goddess."

Carmen hoped she didn't look as startled as she was at that statement. "But are you saying you don't think she's the reincarnation?"

"I didn't say she wasn't a reincarnation. But she's no goddess. The gods and goddesses haven't been around this part of the universe for a very long time. It's all clear if you have the sight."

"Sight?" echoed Carmen, feeling rather foolish. It began to dawn on her that she'd heard there was something not quite right about Jenny, as in not right in the head. But then, the sanity of everyone here was no doubt a question for many on the outside. For an instant she let her mind stray to her sister. But the moment she visualized Bettina, she felt a sharp, almost blinding pain streak through her head. She blinked away tears of pain and focused on Jenny, who was now looking curiously at her.

"I know you," she said."

Carmen tried to adopt a neutral expression. "Well, of course. We met the first day you got here, before I moved out of the room we shared."

Jenny snorted softly. "I know you. From before."

"Before when?" Carmen frowned. This woman really *was* a little off.

The young woman shook her head resignedly. "You already know. Sonia's made sure of that, hasn't she?"

Carmen felt a surge of panic in her head, in her chest. Involuntarily, one hand flew to her heart, as if protecting it or perhaps soothing it. "I don't know what you mean."

"Of course you do," said Jenny. "Just a few of us here now. I'm sort of surprised, really. There should be many more. Perhaps I'm not as good at recognizing them as I thought. But I knew you right away, naturally. And I knew Sonia from her photograph, before I came here."

Carmen was desperately trying to focus on the mundane details of the little garden nook: the shrubs, the sound of the birds in the oak trees, the hard and pitted surface of the benches. She needed to stay in the present, the very real present, not some bizarre and insane dream world. But Jenny's voice pierced through her mental barriers, sent her reeling backward as if she were falling, and yet the bench remained solid beneath her.

"You can't ignore it," said Jenny calmly, "no matter how hard you try."

"Ignore what?" Carmen snapped. "You aren't making any sense at all."

Jenny smiled. It spread slowly across her face in a way that was oddly and impossibly familiar to Carmen. "Junela," she said simply, "it's me—Alandra."

"Alandra?" she repeated, her voice a choked whisper. Images of faces and flames swam in front of her, and the roar in her head grew to such intensity that she could no longer hear anything at all. Carmen fainted.

♦

It only took Karl a few minutes to search the tiny room occupied by Jenny Carpenter. Clearly, she had brought little in the way of material possessions to the Children of Artemis compound. But now that he had her full name and enough information from her few pieces of identification, he could find out who she was and where she'd been. In the closet hung the old haversack he remembered her carrying into her meeting with Sonia, the one that had been limp and empty when she had come back out. His gut told him there was a connection. And he'd better nail it down before bringing himself to the notice of those powerful enough to stomp on him like an annoying insect. Corporations the size of Pantheon International did more to control current events than any government ever did. Only the most naive still believed that electing a prime minister or a president had much to do with the decisions that shaped the future of the world. *That,* thought Karl, *is why they're called suckers. Just like the ones who flocked to Sonia's fantasy world to find something better. They'd given up on the secular illusions and were substituting spiritual ones.* But not him. He had long since abandoned moral principles as risky and expensive, and there were few things left in which he believed other than his own abilities, things he could prove through his own senses, and the supremely satisfying power of money in large quantities.

With a last glance around the room, Karl left the dormitory and moved swiftly toward the car park near the outer perimeter of the compound. A quick drive into town, a few phone calls, a couple of hours killing time down at the local pub, and he should have some answers.

♦

It was fortunate Alan slowed down just as he approached the turnoff for the Children of Artemis community or he'd have been broadsided by a car coming out of the lane. To his surprise, it was Karl driving one of the community vehicles, a battered but serviceable Ford Mondeo. Alan almost swore in frustration. He needed to talk to Karl now. But he could hardly flag the man down with Sonia sitting right there in the passenger seat. Granted, she was apparently off in another one of her bizarre meditation states, but she generally emerged from these without warning and at the most inconvenient moments. He stared at Karl as he rounded the turn, but the man never even glanced over. Alan continued into the compound and thought once more of the wadded piece of paper that seemed to burn a hole in his pocket. The name Connor Hawthorne kept hammering in his head.

Chapter Eight

"Will you walk into my parlour?" said a spider to a fly:
'Tis the prettiest little parlour that ever you did spy."
—Mary Howitt, "The Spider and the Fly"

London

"This chicken korma is excellent," said Katy, helping herself to another sizable portion.

"Where do you put that much food?" asked Benjamin in awe, as she tore off a hunk of garlic nan and dipped it in a dish of fiery sauce.

"Didn't have time for lunch," she replied with a grin. "I miss a lot of meals, so I eat when the eating's good."

"My daughter has common sense," said Connor, taking the rest of the nan and scooping up the last remnants of her curry.

"You may not think so when I tell you what I have in mind," said Katy, wiping her mouth and draining the remains of her tall glass of sweet lhassi.

"Uh-oh," said Laura, one eyebrow raised.

Connor swallowed and focused her entire attention on her daughter. "You're quitting your job?"

Katy laughed. "Don't be absurd. I love my job. But I am taking some time off. I told you I've got a lot of vacation saved up. So I've decided to get out of the city and get some fresh air, take in the sights up north."

"North," said Connor, her intuition kicking in even more

quickly than usual. "This had better not have anything to do with the Children of Artemis."

"As a matter of fact, it does," said Katy, neatly folding her napkin beside the plate. "I've decided to see for myself just what this con artist has going up there and find out what's happened to Ian's brother."

"No," said Connor without hesitation.

Katy's expression went from defiant to unreadable. "I'm sorry, Mother. Did you actually say 'no?'"

"That's exactly what I said. If even half of what we suspect about these lunatics is true, they may be guilty of about a dozen felonies, including murder."

"Right now all I'm concerned about is Philip Darcy. You can investigate them all you want from the outside, but I doubt that will do Philip any good. He could be dying for all we know—and completely deluded into believing he's cured. No one is going to think twice about another groupie showing up. They arrive every day."

"You have no idea what the situation is there—what they might be doing, what they might be involving all these people in doing!"

Katy shrugged. "What? You're thinking human sacrifice? Wild orgies? Ceremonies in honor of pagan devils?"

"This isn't funny, Katy. I—"

Laura gently placed her hand over Connor's on the table. "We're not thinking quite so broadly," she said, fixing Katy with a look that said, *Now you're going too far.* "But there is at least some reason to believe that the leadership of this organization is relatively ruthless. If they are responsible for the death of that poor girl in Palm Springs, just for a chunk of money, then it seems logical to assume they wouldn't welcome anyone who came around prying into their affairs. I'd be willing to wager they run a background check on everyone who shows up wanting to stay there."

"I wasn't going to try and stay," snapped Katy. "Lots of people only go for the day for one of their bogus healing ceremonies. Sometimes they have over a hundred people show up. I seriously doubt they try to check everyone's identification."

"And what if they do?" asked Connor, her temper showing. "They could easily make a connection between you and me."

"From the name alone?" said Katy incredulously. "How does Katherine Jessica VanDevere add up to 'daughter of Connor Hawthorne?'"

"Anyone with access to the Internet could find out that we're related in about five minutes," snapped Connor.

"That assumes that this is some sort of high-tech spy operation where they run security screenings on every person who walks onto the estate for one of their healing gatherings. In all honesty, just how likely do you think that is?"

Connor started to open her mouth, then stopped and took a deep breath. "All right. Maybe, just maybe, I'm overreacting a little. Being a little overprotective."

"A *little?*" said Katy, looking as if she might continue the battle, but Laura shook her head slightly—willing the young woman to throttle back a bit. Katy took the hint.

Laura, as usual, offered an eminently practical assessment. "Connor, it's very unlikely that either of us can get near the place without sending up some red flags. We already know that Bettina Waters had our names and contact information, and that piece of paper wasn't found on her or in her house. So she either threw it away, which is unlikely, or someone removed it from her possession, which is much more likely. If that person happens to be the one who killed her, then we might be tops on the list of people they're looking out for."

Benjamin was nodding his agreement. "They aren't stupid, these people. If you've looked at the file, you'll see that they've had high-speed data transmission lines installed at the main house, along with a security system."

"I noticed," said Laura. "And how did you get so much information on this operation so quickly?"

"Turns out the local intelligence community isn't too happy about the sudden emergence of Sister Sonia. They already know it's a financial scam, but they're also concerned there might be some national security ramifications. A few relatively important people have ended up at the Children of Artemis compound, some of whom might be compromised if Sonia's up to her old hypnosis tricks."

"She was once a certified hypnotherapist," added Connor. "But I think that stuff's a bunch of bunk anyway."

"Spoken like a true lawyer and cynic," said Benjamin.

"Testimony obtained under hypnosis is never admissible," Connor reminded everyone at the table. "It's far too easy for the practitioner to plant suggestions in the witness's mind."

"But the technique might work just fine for Sonia's purposes," said Katy. "She wants to convince people of her 'powers' of healing and precognition. Hypnosis, even on a group scale, would go a long way toward furthering her agenda.."

"If it really worked," said Connor. "But it sounds more like group hysteria and the power of suggestion working on gullible, desperate people."

"Maybe," said Katy. "And in that case, there's even less risk. No one's going to hypnotize me, now, are they?"

"Still…" said Connor, obviously not in the least convinced of Katy's safety.

Benjamin raised his hands and made a time-out signal. "Look, Laura's right about it being impossible for either her or Connor to get into that compound as part of the crowd. At least it's highly unlikely. And if you're determined to find out about this girl who's supposed to be there—the sister of the dead woman in Palm Springs—then we don't have a lot of options. Besides, Katy has her own agenda, which is to locate and verify the well-being of her friend's brother. That being said, the only one of us who could get in there is Katy."

Connor looked positively mutinous, but Benjamin forged ahead anyway. "How about this? We'll give Katy a temporary change of identity."

"What?" said Connor and Katy in unison. Laura, however, simply nodded.

"We have a database of straw people—of every age group—who don't actually exist. When we need to give a protected witness or an agent a new face so to speak, we can do it fast because all the groundwork of inserting information into databases all over the world has already been done. It only takes a couple of hours to update them so the information is current up to today."

"But you'll burn an identity," said Laura. "They're pretty valuable assets."

Benjamin smiled. "True. But so is my granddaughter. And there's sufficient justification, especially since my British brethren are becoming so interested now in what sort of game Sister Sonia is playing."

Katy grinned. "Wow, I get a new name, an I.D.—I'll have the whole spy thing going. So, do I get one of those miniature cameras and some night-vision goggles?"

Laura burst out laughing. "Yes, along with the secret decoder ring. It's all in the secret agent starter kit."

Katy blushed. "Well, gee, I thought I'd get something cool out of it."

"You will," said Benjamin. "A couple of things. We'll install some tracking devices on your car, sewn into your handbag, and maybe even a piece of jewelry…just to keep my daughter from having a hissy fit over this," he said with a warning glance at Connor who looked as if she was about to come right out of her chair. "And we'll also give you an emergency signaler of some sort that you can activate if things get strange."

"Who's going to monitor the surveillance?" asked Laura. "Connor needs to put in her appearances at the conference now that she's committed to being there. It starts the day after tomorrow—Thursday."

"I'll send a couple of people to help," said Benjamin. "Until then, you can take the point."

Laura grinned. "Yes, sir."

"I don't like this at all," said Connor, scowling.

"I know, sweetheart, but would you actually want to have

raised a daughter who was afraid to take some risks on behalf of a friend?"

Caught between the proverbial rock and a hard place, Connor had little choice. "No, but that doesn't mean I have to like the idea of endangering her life."

"Mom, aren't you getting just a little melodramatic now? This isn't the Cold War, and I'm not slipping behind the Iron Curtain. I'm just visiting a spiritual retreat center that is less than spiritual and planted right in the heart of England. The worst they can do is try to hit me up for money. As long as I leave my checkbook at home, I think I'll be all right."

"Just don't get cocky," said Connor.

"Like my mother," said Katy with a sly smile.

"I am not cocky!"

Laura leaned over and whispered in her lover's ear. "Yes, sweetheart, sometimes you are, and you're looking in a mirror. So get used to it."

Connor sighed deeply and bitterly. "I'm clearly outnumbered and outvoted."

♦

The next day Connor, Laura, and Katy spent the afternoon at Benjamin's office in the city. He explained the ins and outs of the low-drain tracking devices. They would be operable for several days before their batteries failed. All could be identified and located via an uplink to a satellite, and the information downloaded to a ground GPS unit and signal receiver or a properly equipped laptop computer. Benjamin provided Laura with both.

As promised, for a few hours, Katy would become someone else entirely. He'd chosen a similar name so she wouldn't make the novice's mistake of not responding to it promptly. "Your alter ego is Kathleen Vance. And you, of course, prefer to be called Katy. You are an administrative assistant with a computer software company in Boston, Massachusetts. You were transferred to their London branch six months ago. This passport has the proper endorsements stamped when you arrived." He showed her the driver's license, passport, company photo I.D. and credit cards. Her picture appeared on all of them."

"You're going to have to be careful of your accent," said Laura.

"What accent?" asked Katy, frowning.

"You've lived here for years now, sweetie. An American isn't going to sound as vaguely British as you do after only a few months. Practice a little bit. I picked up a book on tape read by a Massachusetts author. Listen to it a lot before you get there. And say as little as possible."

"You guys really do think of everything."

"In my experience," said Connor, "no one ever thinks of *everything*."

"You'll take the train up from London," said Benjamin, and then pick up a hired car in York. It's already reserved in your name, that is, your new name. And this cell phone is also registered to Kathleen Vance. It has a GPS chip in it…one more layer of security."

"This really seems like a lot of trouble to go to, Gramps," said Katy. "Don't get me wrong. I appreciate it. But I still think I'm just going to be a face in the crowd at this place."

"That's what we're all hoping," said Benjamin. "But precautions won't hurt."

"No, they won't," added Connor. "Have you read the file on Sister Sonia?"

"All committed to memory," said Katy, tapping the side of her head. "Her known associates include one Alan Durn, who is either her boyfriend, flunky, or both."

"He could also be the brains behind the scam," said Benjamin. "There's very little information on him."

Laura tapped the cover of the report. "Even with all those aliases, you still haven't nailed down her birth name, who Sonia really was from day one."

Benjamin frowned. "I know, and that bothers me. It's virtually impossible nowadays for anyone to completely obscure their origins. But Sonia's just old enough, probably in her forties, that record-keeping was still slightly less than stellar in some parts of the world around the time when she was born. In the late 1950s, there were still some backwaters and small towns where births weren't very carefully recorded. I'm guessing she isn't an American, though. But even that's up in the air. Analysis of audiotapes of her speech has stumped our linguists, believe it or not, and these are people who can usually nail someone's birthplace within a hundred miles, often less, depending on the country or origin."

"You're starting to sound like you have Professor Henry Higgins on staff," said Connor.

"Close enough," smiled Benjamin, "and about as pompous. But even he's been stumped. Her accent, her diction, phrasing…it's a true hybrid of geographical influences, and she's apparently worked at that blend."

"Why all the secrecy for a basic con artist?" asked Laura. "It's almost as if she's been trying to keep a low profile since she was a child."

"Could be," said Benjamin. "There are still multigenerational criminal families who are adept at staying off the radar. Maybe she's the product of one of them. Or she was just born larcenous."

"That's pretty cynical," said Katy. "Even for you, Gramps."

"You don't believe in evil, then?" he asked, half serious, half amused.

Katy thought about that. "Considering some of the stuff Mom's gotten up to these past few years—along with you and Laura, and my great-grandmother—I guess I'd have to say the jury's still out on the whole good-versus-evil thing."

"As long as you keep an open mind. Then maybe you'll avoid getting complacent on this little investigative foray of yours, young lady. Greed is a powerful motivator, and I think Sister Sonia is as greedy as they come. That means she probably has no scruples whatsoever. And if she's willing to condone murder for profit…" He left the thought unfinished, but they all got the point.

"I don't suppose you'd give up on this idea," said Connor, still clutching at parental straws.

"And not get to use this cool stuff," replied Katy. "Not a chance."

"Good God, my daughter's a gadget junky, too."

"A girl after my own heart," said Laura. "And here's your most important gadget." She held up what looked like a run-of-the-mill personal digital assistant. "It's got some information programmed in, all numbers that will check out when called…answering machines and so forth. But, if you want immediate extraction—"

"Dental work?" asked Katy dubiously.

Laura chuckled. "Sorry. If you run into any problem and need help, or want to be picked up immediately, use this."

"What buttons do I press? Is there a secret code?"

"Uh, no. You just turn it off and hold the off button for more than three seconds."

"That's all?" Katy sounded rather disappointed.

"Sounds boring, I know. But this way no one else can possibly discover anything odd about the PDA, even by accidentally pressing a certain series of buttons. Once you turn it off, the screen will go blank, but there's an internal lithium battery that activates a silent signal. We'll be able to pick it up instantly. And you can turn it off by just reaching into your handbag. Nothing to fiddle with."

Katy took the PDA from Laura. "No built-in radio, tape recorder, nothing?"

"Sorry, hon. This is just an afternoon outing. We don't need Q for this mission."

Katy looked puzzled and Laura sighed. "So young. Q…as in James Bond, 007, his supplier of gadgets."

"Sorry, I never watched that stuff."

"An incomplete education," sighed Laura. "But no matter."

A sharp rapping sounded on the office door. Benjamin said, "Connor, would you get that? The other two operatives on the case have arrived."

Laura laughed. "I love it when you talk spy lingo…but operatives? Sounds like an episode of *Perry Mason*."

Connor swung the door open and, to her complete amazement, discovered a couple of dear friends standing in the hall—Lord William Carlisle and his wife, Ellen.

"What on earth!" exclaimed Connor. "Don't tell me Dad dragged you into this, too."

"Didn't have to drag us in the least," said William, taking Connor's hand in his strong, well-manicured grasp. "We're glad to be of service, especially where our Gwendolyn's great-granddaughter is concerned."

"I don't think you'll be needing your special skills," said Connor, giving Ellen Carlisle a quick hug. "This matter seems pretty down-to-earth."

Ellen smiled. "True, but you never know. So we're prepared for anything. And we both hate a con artist as much as you do, particularly when she's fleecing a number of our own more gullible countrymen."

"Not to mention giving magic a bad name," declared William. "Benjamin! Laura! So good to see you again."

They all exchanged a round of pleasantries. The Carlisles then listened to a brief recitation of the known facts about the Children of Artemis before launching into a lengthier discussion of what they guessed or hoped to discover. They assured Connor in no uncertain terms that they would take personal responsibility for Katy's safety. Having been through some death-defying moments with the two of them, Connor was more reassured than she'd been earlier. The Carlisles were two of her grandmother Gwendolyn Broadhurst's dearest friends and spiritual colleagues. She'd trust them with her life if need be.

"Laura and I will be leaving for York early in the morning," said Connor. "I need to be there before the first events of the conference to do some print interviews."

"I'll head up there in time to arrive for the healing gathering Thursday night," Katy announced. "Then I'll see what's going on. If it looks like a big weekend planned at the community, I'll book a room in town and go back again, as if I'm just enthralled."

"We talked about *one* visit," said Connor with genuine annoyance. "Not multiple visits."

"I'll have to play it by ear, Mom. If I don't find Philip the first time around, I'll have to go back. Besides, I'm sure they have some sort of marketing plan where they tantalize you into a return visit where you can get more healing."

"And donate more money, I imagine," said Lord Carlisle.

"Absolutely. And I'm playing the part of a gullible vacationer." She scooped up her packet of documents and handed her own genuine I.D. to her mother. "Hold onto these for me. Exit one Katherine VanDevere, architect...enter Kathleen Vance, administrative assistant and one of the proverbial suckers born every minute. I'll have to work on a sort of vacant, hopeful expression on my way to York. How's this?"

Her effort was far more comical than convincing, and she left the office to an outburst of laughter from her small audience.

"You'll stay close?" asked Connor, her eyes still on the door through which her only child had just exited.

Ellen Carlisle patted her arm. "As close as possible without arousing any suspicion that would endanger her. If necessary, though, we will march right in there and do a little playacting ourselves. We could probably pass for gullible dilettantes with more money than sense."

"I doubt it," said Laura. "But you'd give it a helluva good effort." She put her arm around Connor's waist. "Take a deep breath, sweetheart. Between the Carlisles and me, Katy is in excellent hands."

"But now she's talking about going back there more than once. When I agreed to this, it was for one quick visit."

"Cut her some slack. She's worried about her friend. We'll adjust the situation and the plan as we go. Now we need to get back to the hotel and pack." She turned to Ellen and William. "We're all having dinner, I take it."

"That sounds delightful," said Ellen. "Gives us a chance to catch up on all you've been doing."

"And gives you a little update on the doings of the Circle," said

William with a smile. "Perhaps you'll have time to join us in ceremony while you're here."

Connor winced slightly. "Maybe," she said. "Maybe."

Karl deeply regretted the impulse to call his contact at Pantheon
International. Rather than offering to make a few discreet and tentative
inquiries, the man he knew as Mickey had apparently hit the equiva-
lent of a panic button. Karl's mention of a possible crystal fragment
had already reached the highest levels. He was afraid he'd triggered
some sort of tactical response, and he already knew these people had
few scruples about how they carried out their assignments. Still, this
was no deserted Caribbean island. Whatever their plan, it would have
to be much more subtle than shooting everything that moved.

He'd spent the three hours the previous day alternating between
a public call box and his own cell phone. The latter he was using to
stay in touch with a researcher in London, someone who gleefully
tapped into just about any database in the world, without leaving
any footprints. It had taken him more than an hour, but he'd finally
nailed down Jenny Carpenter. There were a number of new stories
that hadn't been quite sensational enough to make the newspapers
in Britain. The information got Karl's adrenaline going. She'd been
an archaeology student who'd volunteered to join the Pedersen dig.
Apparently, the killing team had missed her completely. She'd been
found on the island in a state of shock and was unable to supply any
useful information about the murders. She'd spent a long time at
some sort of institution—a funny farm basically, or so his friend told
him. She'd eventually checked herself out and disappeared. Her
family had been unable to find her since.

She's not missing anymore, thought Karl. He was amazed that
Pantheon had left a loose end like the Carpenter woman. Perhaps
they'd held back because she didn't know anything, at least nothing she'd been willing or able to reveal. She'd probably been hiding
in a hole somewhere until it was all over. But Karl was fairly sure
Pantheon wouldn't leave that loose end much longer. And it was
likely he'd be called upon to take care of it. For the moment,
though, his instructions were to do nothing, which suited him fine.

◆

Mickey Dandridge, a.k.a. Michael Dardannes, a.k.a. Martin DeLong (and a host of other pseudonyms acquired over forty years of illicit, illegal, immoral, and generally repugnant activities on behalf of those who eschewed their own dirty work) was calmly but swiftly setting up a damage control strategy. Mickey didn't like surprises, and Karl's call was more in the nature of a shock. That there could be another piece of the matrix crystal lying around in some woman's wall safe was bad enough. That Jenny Carpenter had gotten out of the mental institution and eluded her watcher was also alarming. Added to that the growing notoriety of this scam artist, Sister Sonia, and the number of people involved in her community, and this had all the makings of a potential disaster. They could hardly swoop in and take what they wanted without drawing all sorts of attention from the local law. No, this had to be handled quietly. From what Karl said, the head guru kept the fragment a secret from everyone at the community. That was good. No one would know it was missing when he retrieved it. The only question was how and when…because the fragment might well be the key to everything. So far, the promise of the matrix crystal had proven to be much less than his superiors had anticipated. Their investment was substantial both in money and in human lives sacrificed, yet the reassembled pieces of the enormous formation simply lay there, lifeless and unproductive. Mickey had heard the rumors, that this thing was some relic of an ancient and powerful culture, but he had a low tolerance for bullshit. To him, it was a big, shiny, faceted rock that had been formed entirely by the simply explained processes of nature.

◆

"I can feel it," said Ellen Carlisle. "But I can't get a clear picture, even in meditation."

William nodded pensively, his hands thrust deep in his pockets. They were standing on the pavement outside the Italian restaurant waiting for Connor, Laura, and Benjamin to arrive. "I know, love. That's why I haven't broached the subject. Connor is already upset enough about Katy's amateur investigation. I don't think it would help for her to know that there might be anything more to this than a criminal conspiracy to defraud."

"And commit murder," added Ellen, "if the girls are right about the death of the young woman in Palm Springs."

"Still, the heir apparent to our Circle is still remarkably uncomfortable with the unseen. It frightens her a great deal more than thieves and murderers. Until we know more about this disturbance you feel in the energy patterns, let's keep it to ourselves."

"You're quite right, of course, but it's aggravating to sense something out of alignment and not be able to identify the source. It feels terribly old, much older than anything we've encountered before. And perhaps highly dangerous."

"This may be entirely outside our area of expertise, you know."

"I'm beginning to wonder," said Ellen. She sighed. "We'll see what happens. But I want to stay very close to Katy. She has some important role to play in all this, yet I also sense that she is leaping headfirst into something much deeper than she thinks. We must protect her."

"With our lives, darling," said William. "Our oath binds us to that path. Just as we protected Gwendolyn's granddaughter, so, too, will we watch over her great-granddaughter. The Light burns brightly in her as well."

"Do you think Connor understands that completely—that Katy is not simply her progeny but the eventual heir of the Circle of Light?"

William smiled. "Why don't we let Connor get used to the idea of being the leader herself before we start talking next generation. Besides, we're getting on in years, love. We won't outlast Connor. Then others will take our places before it is Katy's time to wear the white robes of her sacred office...ah, here are our guests."

◆

The rest of the evening was spent in pleasant and intelligent conversation. After a brief discussion of the death of Bettina Waters and speculation about the mental state of her sister, Carmen, the subject of Sister Sonia was shelved by tacit agreement. Instead, Ellen and William regaled the company with interesting anecdotes and legends about Celtic spirituality, the Druids and their rituals, and the speculation surrounding the existence of a living descendant of Mary Magdalene and Jesus of Nazareth. This last subject took them well past the coffee-and-dessert course, and they realized with some surprise that they were the last patrons left in the restaurant.

Before saying good night, they established a general protocol for checking in with each other. Cell phone numbers were exchanged. Benjamin handed William the small leather briefcase he'd been carrying. "Excellent walkie-talkies," he explained. "Long-range, powerful transmitters. There are four of them, just in case, and chargers, too. Just plug in the included earphones to disable the speaker. Keeps things quieter."

"Well done, old man," said William, clapping Benjamin on the shoulder. "You and your toys. Makes me jealous."

Benjamin smiled. "I'm more jealous that you and Ellen don't actually *need* walkie-talkies to communicate."

"Ah, but you will notice that we aren't turning down the offer of this most useful equipment. There are times when good old-fashioned circuits are more reliable than the human brain. Powerful emotion often clouds the mind's ability to send and receive. Using technology cuts down on ambiguity, believe me."

"Good, I'm going to go get the car." Benjamin shook hands and strode away.

Ellen took William's arm. "We'll pick up Katy's surveillance as soon as she leaves her hotel in York. That way Connor and Laura can check in together—give the outward appearance of business as usual."

"I'll relieve you tomorrow evening as soon as it's dark enough."

"Cheers," said William. And off they went at a brisk pace.

"I don't know when I've ever met people I liked more than those two," said Laura. "They just make me smile."

"Me, too."

"You think we'll be that totally in love when we've been together as long as they have?"

"Of course…not a doubt in my mind," said Connor, her eyes alight with reflections of the streetlamps. "You're my one true love…haven't I mentioned that?"

"Not in a few days," smiled Laura. "But you don't have to say it for me to know it."

"I'm glad. Sometimes when it comes to how I feel about you, words fail me."

"And you a big time author."

"The words I put in books don't matter anywhere near as much as the ones I say to you."

Laura leaned in to kiss Connor's cheek. "That's one of the reasons I love you so much. Care to sleep with me tonight?"

Connor grinned. "Oh, yes, I most definitely do."

Chapter Nine

I long to talk with some old lover's ghost,
Who died before the god of love was born.
—John Donne, "Love's Deity"

The City of York

Carmen woke up in her own bed. She had no idea how she'd gotten back to her room. The last thing she could remember was Jenny's face coming closer. But it wasn't Jenny. No...yes, of course it was Jenny. Who else could it have been? There was something pricking at the back of her mind, a memory that wanted to surface as badly as she wanted to avoid it. Her headache was worse than ever. The curtains were drawn back, and it was completely dark out. But that was impossible. It had been late morning when she'd gone out to the garden.

She turned her head far enough to see the clock beside the bed. The digital numbers were unmistakable—11:30. She'd lost almost twelve hours, missed dinner, missed her nightly appointment with Sister Sonia. Or had she? What if the session had been so intense it robbed her of memory? She began to tremble.

"You're awake."

The words were spoken very softly but still came as a shock to Carmen, who immediately sat up in bed and clutched the covers around her. "Who's there?" she tried to ask, but her throat had closed up and the words came out as an unintelligible croaking sound.

A figure rose from a chair near the window. "It's me. Jenny."

Carmen stared at her. "How…I mean, why are you here? What happened?"

"You fainted, I guess."

"But how did I get *here*?"

"When you came to, I walked you up here to your room. You told me where it was, which door in the corridor."

"I did?"

"Yes." Jenny sat down gingerly on the edge of the bed. "Do you know who you are?"

Carmen scowled. "What is this? Some sort of sanity test? Just because I fainted—I didn't eat yesterday or today. I got light-headed. That's all there is to it."

"I wasn't questioning your sanity. I know better. People who don't understand things always try to convince you you're crazy."

"What things?" asked Carmen suspiciously.

"Memories. Pictures. Sometimes you hear words."

"I really don't know *what* you're talking about."

Jenny's expression was shrewd but not unkind. "I think you do. Eventually you'll admit the truth."

"What truth? Who are you to sit here telling me you know what the truth is?"

"Oh, no one special." A tiny smile flitted across Jenny's face. "Just someone you promised to love forever and always."

Carmen's knee-jerk reaction was denial. She barely knew this odd, clearly emotionally unbalanced woman. She wanted to insist that Jenny leave immediately. But the words didn't come out. Her mouth opened, then closed. Another part of Carmen was inexplicably dumbfounded. That part of her recognized something in Jenny, something perfectly in alignment with a reality she couldn't bring into focus. It was old, so very old—a memory so distant, so difficult to grasp that it was but the merest shadow. *The dreams, she's in my dreams.*

Jenny laid a hand very gently on Carmen's arm. "It's coming back to you, I know. Just as it came back to me. It has something to do with the crystal fragment."

Carmen frowned. "What crystal?"

"Then you don't know about it. Sonia hasn't told you."

"Told me what?"

Jenny shook her head. "I should never have brought it here. I don't know why I felt as if I had to. But I did and maybe there's a reason for it."

"I have no idea what you're talking about," said Carmen. "And I don't think I want to."

"I'd say you didn't have a lot of choice in the matter," replied Jenny. "Just as I had no choice but to come here. But I found you, so maybe that's reason enough."

"You've never met me before now."

"Not in this lifetime, of course not."

The pain in Carmen's head throbbed to the rhythm of her pulse as it quickened. "Please, just stop. Everything is so confusing. And my head hurts."

Jenny touched her fingers to Carmen's left temple. "Just here, isn't it? You started getting these headaches when everything went into decline, when the sisterhood was breaking apart."

"Sisterhood?" echoed Carmen. She closed her eyes for a moment and focused on the sensation of Jenny's soft, cool fingertips. The throb subsided as Jenny's very touch drew the pain from her.

"The sisterhood of priestesses."

A surreal film was running through Carmen's mind—disjointed scenes too brief to fully grasp and without respect to chronology or place. Images of the place she'd only seen in her dreams melted into a glimpse of the walls around the Children of Artemis community and then the lush green grass of a Palm Springs golf course. Faces bled from male to female, from Jenny to Carmen's sister, Bettina, and Sister Sonia, and on and on. She couldn't hold tight to any one memory, any one image. She felt as if her mind was slipping away, her grasp on the present moment frighteningly tenuous.

"I'm so afraid," she whispered, afraid to open her eyes.

"I know," said Jenny softly. "So am I."

◆

Sonia knew something was wrong the moment she returned to her office after the trip into York. A subtle sensation of another person's presence lingered in the atmosphere, or at least that's the only way she could have described it. Not only had someone been here, a place expressly off-limits to *everyone,* but they'd stayed a while, and they'd been snooping. She rushed to the antique mirror and paused only a moment to examine her reflection. *I'm different every time. And better.*

She swung open the mirror and quickly unlocked the safe. Much to her relief, the crystal was still there, although its light was noticeably diminished. This, more than anything else, angered her. Someone had interfered with her beautiful stone in some way, drawn energy from it, or simply touched it. But she didn't know if that was actually true, any more than she knew how the mystifying object worked in the first place. But for some reason, her lack of certainty didn't really disturb her, as it once might have.

Sonia was no longer aware of herself as a cunning, moderately ruthless fraud. She had been altered by the crystal and had drifted away from her normal self-awareness. Everything in her life now was pure instinct, a series of thoughts, voices, ideas, coming to her unbidden, but not unwelcome. For Sonia felt more powerful than she'd ever thought possible, as if everything she'd ever coveted was almost within her grasp, and she had only to reach out and pluck it from the weaklings around her. Even their minds were increasingly open to her probing. Not entirely perhaps. She couldn't exactly read their every thought, but she could latch onto stray images or words she picked up, and she used her gift of blarney to weave those shreds of truth into an impression of omniscience. She smiled when she thought of how they had begun to fear her. That was something she *could* detect with enormous ease now—emotion of any kind, be it fear or anger or excitement or sorrow. All of them showed up for her—a rich palette of different colors drift-ing across people's faces—each signifying a strong emotion or state of mind. Sonia didn't know if it had anything to do with auras. She'd always thought that idea was absurd, and a perfect vehicle for scamming the gullible. But her opinion on the appearance of energy as a visible phenomenon was beginning to shift. It had to. Otherwise there was no explanation.

Sonia sat in the darkness of her office for a very long time, entertained by her thoughts and dreams and aspirations. More and more she found herself needing this solitude to contemplate the future. Hours could pass, and she barely noticed. Why should she, when there was all of eternity within her reach? She knew at least some of the others thought she was completely mad, but how could they think otherwise? Such limited imaginations they had. It occurred to her that she had not chosen all of her disciples wisely. But on the other hand, each would serve a purpose.

The end times…such a puerile notion, really. She knew that's what several of them thought she meant—the end of the world. But that was the stuff of fundamentalist boogeyman stories fed to the masses, and sensational books and films that catered to people's basic fear. No, the world would not end in an apocalypse led by a charge of four horsemen, the Book of Revelations notwithstanding. Sonia had recently read the Bible, along with a number of other scriptures—the Koran, the Talmud and the Torah, the Tibetan Book of the Dead, the Upanishads—and she absorbed them as if her brain were a sponge, soaking up and retaining every word. There were lit-tle nuggets of truth in each tradition, but, she thought with some amusement, not one of them really got it right; not one of them even barely grasped the nature of the universe in which this pathetic little planet existed. From her perspective, Sonia did.

A soft knock interrupted her train of thought, which angered her. Every time she bent her mind to integrating all of her newly acquired knowledge, a new revelation came to her. Intrusions interfered with that process.

"What!" she barked.

The door opened slowly, and Jenny Carpenter stood there on the threshold.

Sonia was mildly surprised and perhaps even a little bit alarmed. She had barely spoken to the girl since she'd arrived with the precious crystal in her knapsack and unhesitatingly turned it over to Sonia. Ignoring her was intentional. Sonia had no desire for Jenny to have even an inkling of how powerful the crystal was, or that all of Sonia's power originated in the heart of its pulsating energy. But she sensed the risk in alienating Jenny, so she throttled back her irritation.

"Is there something you need of me?" she asked in a controlled, vaguely maternal tone.

Jenny moved into the room until she was a few feet in front of the desk. "I need to know if you know the truth—and what you're going to do about it."

The line between Sonia's eyebrows furrowed slightly. "Know what truth, my daughter?"

Jenny's smile was brief and subtly expressed more knowledge than Sonia cared to observe in a mere minion. There was a certain brazen audacity to Jenny's expression and demeanor that troubled Sonia. Then it came to her. Jenny was no longer in awe of the supreme leader of the Children of Artemis, and she wasn't afraid either. That would *not* do.

"If you're going to come in and speak in riddles, then there is little I can do to help you."

"My apologies, Sister Sonia, I did not mean to confuse you."

Sonia's cheeks reddened. "Nothing confuses me. I simply wish to instruct you, and I see that I have neglected helping you to acquire the wisdom to know your purpose here. Perhaps now would be a good time to rectify that oversight. Why don't you join me by the fire, and we will talk." Sonia stood up and moved around her desk, and seated herself in one of the comfortable chairs facing the small, wood-burning fireplace.

To her complete discomfiture, Jenny didn't scurry after her. She didn't even move. Sonia, forced to turn in the chair to observe, saw that the girl was smiling again. "I think I won't," she said. "But thank you. I think it would be better if I stick to my own ideas of what my purpose is here. Everyone's revelations are important one way or the other. I know you've had quite a few lately. At least I assume you have, since we share the same source, don't we?"

Sonia quivered with anger. "I doubt that you are in the least able to access the flow of spiritual awareness that I tap into. It is an ability achieved only by the grace of the divine, a gift of sight that may only be wielded by very few of the chosen ones."

"Chosen?" echoed Jenny. "Chosen by whom?"

"By the gods."

"Which gods?"

Sonia stood up abruptly, her eyes sparking with anger. "Don't be impertinent, young woman. You have no idea the risk you take in speaking to me with such disrespect."

Maddeningly, Jenny smiled again. "Actually, I think I do. And I know who you are, or at least who you once were. But I don't believe that everything will happen as it did before. I won't let you make the same mistake again."

Sonia took a deep breath, her mind racing. *What did this stupid girl know about the past, the very past that was about to reemerge so that the truth could be known and the ultimate destiny of the players in its drama finally be fulfilled?* "I begin to see that you do not understand anything at all, and that you do not belong here in this community of loving believers. You may leave at once. I expect you to be gone from here first thing in the morning."

Jenny shook her head. "I don't care to leave. And I don't believe you'll do anything about it. Once I owed you my obedience and my allegiance. But not this time around. When you're ready to discuss what is really happening, send for me. You have no idea that what is going on has less to do with you than this place we are in, the sacred ground of this country.

"If you choose to ignore all the signs, disaster awaits you, and the laws of karma will trample you underfoot once more, but perhaps this time with fewer innocent bystanders as victims."

She turned toward the door, then stopped and looked back over her shoulder. "You needn't fear me unless you are determined to repeat the same mistakes. Which reminds me…Carmen won't be coming here to help you anymore."

"Help me? That's absurd. I've been helping *her.*"

"Really? Then why is she so frightened of who she really is? Good night, my Lady. I imagine we'll talk again fairly soon."

Chapter Ten

He was like a cock who thought the sun
had risen to hear him crow.
—George Eliot (Mary Ann Cross), *Adam Bede*

Mickey Dandridge sat at one of the tiny tables within the enclosure railing that vaguely separated the customers sipping Starbucks coffee from the throngs of passengers spilling out of the international arrivals tunnel in Terminal 5 at Heathrow. He sourly observed the line of suited drivers holding up signs bearing names of varying nationalities. There was something about those whose jobs forced them to dance attendance on the rich that particularly grated on his nerves, perhaps because he knew, without admitting it to himself, that his job was hardly much different. He got paid a great deal more than a chauffeur, and he lived a much more lavish lifestyle. Still, the pay scale was only because he demonstrated a willingness to do more than drive someone around in a car. Truth be told, most of the idiots with the signs would heave up their last meal at the sight of some of Mickey's accomplishments. Yet, in the end, what it came down to was that he still took orders from men with more money, more power, and even less conscience than Mickey.

The scrape of metal behind him drew his attention, followed by the creak of a man's weight being settled onto an insubstantial chair. Instinct told him that more orders were in store for him…and that he wasn't going to like them at all.

Twenty minutes later he was alone again. He finished his triple espresso and headed for the cab stand outside the terminal. His demands for more information had been met with contemptuous silence. But his instructions were clear: to obtain the crystal fragment by any means necessary with the least possible notoriety. And he'd been provided with a weapon, something he could hardly have smuggled into England in the current climate. How Matsumoto accomplished it remained a mystery. But when he went into the men's room and donned the holster and handgun, he felt significantly more secure.

According to Matsumoto, the scientists in the compound near Bern had deduced through a series of mathematical computations that there was one piece of the crystal column missing, just large enough to be important, and just small enough to be smuggled into England by a single individual. If the Children of Artemis compound was concealing a fragment, it might well the one they had been seeking. Mickey knew the island excavation had been searched repeatedly and with the best technology available once the authorities had given it up as a crime scene. Not a single shard of the column had come to light.

Self-regenerating energy supply, he mused: a fairy tale for greedy old men with visions of wielding even more power than they did already. Granted, if they were right, the potential applications were staggering—in laser weapons especially. And if you could make it work and launch that sucker into space, it would be possible to hold the entire world hostage in a sense. Mickey had no quarrel with power-mongering per se, but there was something about this particular project that bothered him at a gut level, and because he couldn't identify the problem, he chose to ignore it. But the uneasiness lingered, as if some part of him knew they were messing with something that not one of those egghead scientists understood in the least. But it had been Professor Pedersen who started it all, who convinced them not only that Atlantis must have existed, but had supplied the needs of its entire civilization with the use of the matrix locked within the crystal.

On the ride back to London, he quickly read through the thin dossier the man at the airport had slipped him, and then he weighed his options. He had one man inside, though how reliable Karl would prove remained a question. Still, it was a distinct advantage. He'd have the details of the security arrangements, and inside intelligence was worth more than guesswork based on outside surveillance any day of the week. He suspected Karl didn't particularly want to be involved with Pantheon anymore, but that was of no consequence to Mickey. Choices were the luxury of those who issued instructions, not those who followed them. Oddly, the irony of this statement as applied to himself didn't even register in his consciousness.

So, a quick in and out was the best idea he could come up with, timed to coincide with one of the mass gatherings held at the Children of Artemis compound. With everyone, especially the head wacko, Sister Sonia, otherwise engaged, it should prove easy enough to get the fragment and get out. If things got a little messy, Karl could clean it up once the item had been retrieved and Mickey was out of England.

The only real complication was the increasing attention being focused on the Children of Artemis. Pantheon might be one of the world's most powerful organizations, but it still preferred to fly under the radar where the intelligence services of various countries were concerned. Most were inept; some were exceedingly efficient. Nowadays, being on any agency's watch list could mean anything from minor inconvenience that could be safely ignored to a full-scale deployment of disinformation and resistance that cost time and money. The man at the airport had made it clear that the Brits were no longer simply content to keep a weather eye on Sister Sonia. She might not know it, but she was about to come under more scrutiny than any mere charlatan would have expected or feared. The question, of course, was why now? She'd been operating for a quite a while, fleecing people out of their life savings on a regular basis. So why MI5? And some American consultant named Hawthorne, according to the dossier, was asking questions, poking around in databases worldwide. He had some excellent connections, obviously. It might be wise to look into that, too, if he had time. If he got too curious, enough information could lead him to Pantheon.

But first things first. He looked at his watch. Just time enough to catch a few hours of necessary sleep, then hire a car and drive to York for a face-to-face with Karl.

◆

Having satisfied himself that Mickey Dandridge would do precisely as he was told, Yohiro Matsumoto boarded a plane that would take him directly to Tokyo, where his driver would be waiting patiently, no matter what the hour. This was an errand that required personal handling, and although he had used a go-between, a British local to pass on the necessary information, he had observed both visually and electronically the entire meeting. The time for the great change was approaching too rapidly to leave any detail, even the seemingly minor ones, in the hands of "foreigners."

In some ways, Matsumoto was an anachronism, a sheer throwback to another time. In others, he was well ahead of his own generation in his manner of thinking. He never wavered in his manner of dress—dark, perfectly tailored suit, crisp white shirt, subtle silk tie—or his personal habits of asceticism, or his commitment to the company he had founded. He was a traditionalist in the strongest sense. Business was business. Morality was relative to business successes. The Western businessman, for all of his profiteering motivations, rarely understood the strange juxtaposition of the Japanese code of honor and Matsumoto's willingness to countenance practices that would have made even the greediest of standard-issue entrepreneurs blanche. To protect the goals of the company, or, in this case, the conglomerate, no 'strategies' were out of bounds. Matsumoto played by a very different set of rules than his European and American counterparts, but few of them understood that sufficiently to detect their growing disadvantage in the sprawling organization that was Pantheon. Matsumoto had an entirely different agenda—he would say a more forward-thinking plan—than the central committee of Pantheon International.

His only divergence from the attitudes and behaviors of the men who would have been his peers twenty years earlier was an addiction to role-playing games, the sort that required donning a complex set of electronic gear composed of helmet, gloves, and body sensors that monitored his movements. And the one basic scenario programmed into the virtual reality unit, with almost infinite variations available—was similar in some ways to what the Christian born-agains would call Armageddon, the end times. He, on the other hand, liked to think of it as the restoration of the natural order. Somewhere between childhood and adolescence, Matsumoto had struck upon something he considered to be a sadly overlooked yet undeniable truth—that the Asian people in general, and the Japanese in particular, were superior in every sense to the *gwaijin,* the Westerners. The Asian culture was more ancient by far and had he been born a few centuries earlier, Matsumoto would undoubtedly have been a samurai, and a powerful one at that. He even liked to think that had he held a position of power during World War II—the outcome might have been somewhat different, though he was not quite arrogant enough to assume it as fact. But the fact remained that human history was replete with a series of pathetically bad decisions.

Quaint ideas of democracy and personal freedom were entirely alien to his way of thinking, as were communism, fascism, and everything in between. If he had to classify his perfect form of world government, it would likely be closer to oligarchy—government by a few. In his estimation, those few would be eminently suited to leading the world in the proper direction. Thus, his version of Armageddon was not about all-out destruction (why destroy the resources that one needed?), and it certainly was not Biblical in any sense. Though a practicing Zen Buddhist, Matsumoto devoutly followed no religion save one—the pursuit and acquisition of power and thus decision-making, world-altering authority over the billions of souls that inhabited the planet. Yet he did not covet the clichéd trappings of power—recognition, obeisance, envy. These were but the desires of the ego. He did not believe himself driven by personal ego but rather by a delayed destiny. His careful research had revealed a long succession of lifetimes in which he had failed to achieve the goals of his people. But the world had shifted enough—into apathy, conflict, greed, xenophobia, hatred, violence, and sheer chaos that the timing was perfect. And for him, the potential of the crystal was a signal. It had come from the Earth itself, left behind by a civilization greater than any other that had existed since on this planet. The signs and portents were shifting into position.

The traditional calendars of the all the great cultures—the Mayans, the Aztecs, and the Native Americans among them—were ending, signifying to him that a new beginning was at hand. This might even be the year and the month that his own Zen master had hinted at: the eleventh day of the eleventh month. Taking into account a very different sort of calendar, one that had been discovered by a few Pantheon divers who were exploring a closely guarded underwater site in what was known as the Bermuda Triangle, this could be reckoned the year 11,110. Few knew of Pantheon's discoveries, and few ever would. The executives of that company cared little for historical insights simply for the sake of knowledge—and certainly not for the betterment of humankind as a whole. Matsumoto, on the other hand, cared a great deal about history.

He settled himself more comfortably into his first-class seat and closed his eyes. For the next few hours, he played the game in his head, imagining the subtle twists and turns of each man's decisions and how they led inevitably to differing ends. This was his escape, for the conquest of the planet would never again be overt, would never be accomplished by armies and navies or even nuclear weaponry fired on unsuspecting civilian populations. Pantheon's war was suited to the modern age—its weapons were economic and political, all relatively subtle, yet devastatingly effective. But even that was not enough. Besides, such machinations lacked a certain sense of heroism and valor. Thus Matsumoto's one vice, one hobby—the virtual reality world. He smiled to himself. He had managed to combine the pleasures of a game of outright conquest with the strategies of a chess master moving pieces around a board. When the scientists brought the crystal online finally, he suspected the human perception of what was real and what wasn't might become rather difficult to nail down. To them, its effects were still largely guesswork. They suspected, or at least fervently hoped, that the crystal could set up the most powerful vibrational resonance imaginable. Such a resonance could have a number of different effects, and the Pantheon scientists were still arguing that point. Their focus, naturally, was on harnessing an inexhaustible power source that would fill the void left behind when fossil fuels were depleted or ruinously expensive and atomic energy waste threatened to irradiate the entire planet. They had theorized that the crystal they had mostly reconstructed was a surviving example of many that had once stood in a vast underwater chamber. The only evidence of their position were the broken foundations of glittering geodes that had formed the bases of a circle of crystalline formations.

For Matsumoto, all of this was about as significant as children arguing in a school yard. He had his own odd, and most would say, highly unlikely, agenda. But then he had spent years studying archaeological papers, unexplained artifacts, and thousands of pages of pure speculation, from absurd New Age fantasies about the lost civilization to scholarly, yet unproven, theoretical papers. He'd read every argument for and against, and yet most compelling to him were his dreams. He believed in omens and portents. And he believed in the power of dreaming. He deeply admired aboriginal shamans who could travel at will in places most humans could not even imagine.

Thus he had come to one conclusion. The crystal had not simply been used as a source of energy. Under the proper circumstances, Matsumoto believed that a human being could pierce the illusory barriers of linear time and travel back and forth at will, if he could control and stand in the energy field that a race of people had discovered millennia before his own birth. And he had a plan, both bizarre and bold, to have his own people steal the reconstructed crystal right from under the noses of the Pantheon scientists in Bern and take it to the one place where it might be activated, where it might actually work as it was intended to. The underwater site was impossible. It presented far too many technical barriers to accessibility. Matsumoto needed to get it right the first time. And that meant his day of reckoning would take place on dry land. But it would take place.

The discovery of one last piece of the crystal had come as no surprise to him. He knew it was only a matter of time, very little time. As the moment drew near, his carefully handpicked teams remained on twenty-four-hour standby. He had assembled a conventional force of operatives for the theft of the main body of the crystal. That was just a matter of brute force and lighting-fast execution. And Mickey Dandridge would take care of obtaining the piece from the lunatics at the place in York.

Matsumoto's other team was quite different. These men and women were not only skilled at combat of every sort, but they were also extraordinarily educated historians, each so thoroughly familiar with a particular period in human history, that they could recite chapter and verse every event, both major and minor that had managed to filter down through the ages of record-keeping. Best of all, they were his own offspring, all six of them.

Yes, they would do well, he thought, if his timing was impeccable, and the old monk was right. He slipped into his fantasy world and fell promptly asleep.

◆

Katy woke with a start as the train lurched into the station at York. She had that few seconds of disorientation that comes from too little sleep and an unexpected alteration to one's daily routine. She wasn't coming home on the Tube to her flat in London. She was, instead, about to infiltrate the enemy, though her mental choice of words made her chuckle quietly. If she weren't careful, she'd start taking this cloak-and-dagger stuff way too seriously. On impulse, she slipped her wallet out of her shoulder bag. There was a definite fascination in becoming someone else, even for a few days. She studied the name on the driving license—*Kathleen Vance*—and once more ran over the unfamiliar address and postal code. Benjamin had insisted it was too easy to check out an address and find out who was really living there. She'd been trying hard to tone down her habit of sounding much more British than a recently arrived American should. It helped that she'd listened to the book on tape on the way up. The vaguely Boston accent was still playing in her head. She'd finally decided that saying as little as possible was probably the best plan. She could perhaps adopt a vaguely awestruck demeanor that rendered her somewhat inarticulate.

As she disembarked from the train, she had to stop herself from glancing around for the surveillance she assumed was somewhere near the platform. No, she had to act the part of a distracted tourist type with but one mission in mind—getting to see the remarkable Sister Sonia and receive some sort of magical revelation or healing. She hadn't yet decided which she was looking for. A physical ailment couldn't be too specific or too serious. She had been wondering about something difficult to diagnose yet nonetheless debilitating to the sufferer—fibromyitis, for example, or perhaps chronic fatigue syndrome. But both of those conditions still had sets of symptoms, and Katy had a feeling she might have difficulty staying in character as a sufferer of something chronic. Migraines, perhaps. Those were common enough and certainly easy to fake. On the other hand, she could settle for professing a moderately sycophantic desire for "enlightenment." That certainly covered a lot of territory. For Katy, the only problem would be acting like a gullible fool. Her expression was one of intelligence and perception. Those who met her were never tempted to take her for an idiot. Unfortunately, she had never developed the skill of hiding her true self very well. For the most part, when Katy was angry, or sad, or joyful, or cocky, or in any other mood, it didn't take a psychic to figure it out. It was written all over her face.

Walking toward the taxi queue, she realize this might just be more difficult than she'd supposed. For Katy, still bound up with the thought of putting all the wrongs right, still secure in that false sense of invulnerability that youth wears so proudly, uncertainty was an unfamiliar and highly unwelcome state of mind.

◆

William and Ellen had taken it upon themselves to shadow Katy as soon as she got off the train, rather than picking up the surveillance from the hotel when she left for the Children of Artemis compound. That one moderately overprotective gesture netted them more than a sense of having acted zealously *in loco parentis*, though that would have been sufficient reason for rising well before dawn and making the journey up the M1 by car.

William spoke very softly. "Ellen, darling. That chap just getting down from the first-class carriage."

He didn't have to say anything more. Ellen heard the subtext in William's mind. Something about the man had caught his attention. Both of them had learned long ago not to ignore even the most subtle twinges of unease about strangers or events or anything they saw. Where most people gave short shrift to intuition, William and Ellen lived by it.

She took a deep breath and sent out what would be impossible to describe to someone who'd never done it. It was not a thought form per se, nor a probe into the man's mind. Instead, it was a kind of energy "ping" of the sort used by submarines—a signal that bounces off another object underwater, revealing the distance between source and reception. In this case, it slipped into the outer layers of the man's aura, took a quick spin around the circumference of his physical self, and returned to Ellen. Her immediate reaction was an involuntary shudder, which William rightly took as bad news.

"That bad, eh?"

"Nasty piece of work," she mouthed softly. "Violence is his stock in trade, I'd say. A sense of cruelty, an image of his hands and arms and chest covered in blood."

"Been in a war, perhaps?"

"Not a legitimate one. There's no inner light associated with valor or honor or camaraderie with one's troops, just a dark core of cruelty and determination. If his being here has anything to do with the Children of Artemis, we're up against something much worse than even Connor thought."

They strolled along twenty paces or so behind Katy. The other object of their interest had outdistanced every other passenger who'd gotten off the train. He was clearly not the sort to waste any time. Ellen breathed a little easier when the man bullied his way past Katy without appearing to notice her in the least. She pinged him again as he came within a foot or so of Connor's daughter. No, nothing about Katy registered for the man. That, at least, was good. But she knew that they had not crossed paths with him unless there were a reason. Once of the tenets of their spiritual path was that there really was no such thing as coincidence. The clues to surviving and even thriving in one's human lifetime were always available if one cared to keep an open mind. In the case of the Carlisles and their circle, this meant being more open than most.

"We'll have to split up," she said.

"I know," replied William, having followed her thoughts during their trip through the train station. Ellen was not willing to let the man disappear into the City of York. They needed to keep tabs on him. And without any emotional or personal connection to him, even Ellen could not simply find him on the astral plane and then pinpoint his location on the physical plane. She always said that if life were that easy, she'd have to risk the ridicule of being labeled a psychic and then have to dash around the world finding those who'd gone missing, especially children.

In this case the Carlisles had to keep an eye on the man until they ruled him in or out as a player in whatever was about to happen. But if Ellen had to go only on a gut reaction, he was not only dangerous, but a threat to someone within their circle of loved ones.

Without a word, William set off on an angular, parallel course with the man, careful to maintain a pace just quick enough to keep up without seeming to hurry. Ellen, meanwhile, kept her eyes, and every other sense of perception, fixed firmly on Katy. From station to car-hire office to hotel, Ellen never lost sight of her. She waited until Katy had plenty of time to check in and go to her room before entering the lobby. From there she went directly to their room on the second floor, just two doors down from the one reserved for Connor and Laura, who would be arriving shortly. She pondered how much to mention about their chance encounter with the stranger in the train station and decided that in this case Connor was probably worried enough. There's be time to reconsider once William reported back to the hotel.

♦

If there was one quality Mickey Dandridge used most without recognizing its source, it was his intuition. He, of course, would never call it that. That was a sissy word for something that was simply the product of years of experience. He had a gut feeling about things, and he knew he was being followed. His training was impeccable, though. He didn't stop and look around, didn't risk revealing his suspicions. He waited until he reached a point in the station where the glass wall provided a good reflection of everything behind him. Then he pretended to consult a timetable he pulled from his pocket. But his eyes were glued to the reflections. Someone would stop abruptly and pretend to be engaged in looking for an arriving friend, or they'd step behind a kiosk, or simply stay put, not bothering to pretend, assuming that Mickey didn't have eyes in the back of his head.

To his surprise (accompanied by an odd sense of disappointment that he might be wrong), none of those things happened. The crowd behind continued to flow steadily. No one was even looking his way. And yet he could feel it, feel the attention like breath on the back of his neck. Still, people walked by. No one paused for even a moment. Mickey looked through the glass doors. Perhaps the watcher had continued on by and was waiting outside. That would be a smarter move. His confidence restored, he moved swiftly to his left toward another exit door, hoping to panic the follower into reentering the train station or hurrying along the sidewalk outside, where Mickey would surely spot him. He scanned the outdoors through the glass until he emerged from the exit, then purposefully lost his grip on his briefcase and had to turn to pick it up. After all these maneuvers, he could not find one good candidate in the crowd. No one appeared to be even be alone. Grimacing with annoyance, Mickey began walking away from the station. To his satisfaction, he was on a one-way street and walking against traffic. No one could follow him in a car. He'd grab the first available cab that passed as soon as he was out of sight around the bend.

Though it was Ellen who was really the more powerful of the Carlisles, William had at least one special talent that the others in the circle could not quite match. If he wished for some people not to actually see him, they couldn't, even though they might be standing within a few feet. It wasn't magic precisely. Human perception isn't hard to manipulate, being purely subjective and based on much more than visual input. Stage magicians know as much. Yet this was no sleight of hand. William so effaced his own energy signature from the visual stimulation of the energy signatures surrounding him that someone could easily have walked right into him without knowing why they'd done so. He had to smile when he saw the look of puzzlement and then anger on the stranger's face. The man had sensed a—what was it the Americans called it? A tail? Now William was even more amused because the visitor, in frustration, had set off walking and was pausing every few minutes to hail a passing taxi. What he clearly didn't know was that one could not hail a taxi in York. It was against the law to stop for a passenger. All taxis were either on duty at the station or dispatched by request. It took the man almost twenty minutes of futile efforts before he stepped into the lobby of a small hotel and spoke to the clerk behind the desk. William stayed just inside the entry, out of sight of the clerk. He couldn't quite make out the words, but from the gesturing, William was pretty sure the man was complaining about the cabs that had ignored him.

The clerk picked up a phone, apparently to call a cab, but something the stranger said made him put it down again. The clerk nodded. The man pulled out his wallet.

Ah, thought William, *he's decided to just give up and stay at this hotel. I wonder where he was originally headed.* William waited to be sure his surmise was correct and was rewarded by the sight of the man headed for the lift at the back of the lobby. All that remained now was to find out who he was and whether there was any point at all to this surveillance.

Fortunately, given his somewhat amateur status as a sleuth, the hotel made this part easy. Unlike most hotels in York, which were fully computerized, this establishment hovered between being a hotel and a much more informal B and B. William stepped up to the desk and asked an innocuous question—directions to the train station—and saw that the hotel kept an old-fashioned registry book on the counter. And William was good at reading upside down. "M. Dandridge, " in a bold, furious scrawl that pressed hard into the paper. This was followed by an address in Switzerland, which somewhat surprised him. Everything about the man screamed "American," from the clothes to the demeanor.

Outside, William couldn't say he'd gotten any further along. But at least he had something to relay to Benjamin. Perhaps he could make something of the name, though it was hardly unusual. Still, he'd memorized the address as well. He walked back to the station where he'd left the car in the car park. As soon as he got in the driver's seat, he sat quietly and closed his eyes, checking the immediate area, then reaching out farther in an expanding circle. Nothing appeared to disturb the natural energy flow around him.

Within moments, he felt the touch of Ellen's consciousness, as always a gentle presence that warmed his heart. Her thought was simple and clear. Katy was safe. It was time to meet at their hotel. He smiled, sent a reassuring promise to be there soon, and started the car. He glanced at the walkie-talkies lying on the seat. He and Ellen had split up so unexpectedly, they hadn't had a chance to retrieve them from the car. Good thing there were forms of communication that electronics couldn't touch.

Chapter Eleven

La gloire et le repos sont choses qui
ne peuvent loger en même gîte.
(Fame and tranquility can never be bedfellows.)
—Michel Eyquem de Montaigne, *Essais*

THE CITY OF YORK

The lobby of the hotel where the authors were staying was teeming with activity—women checking in, women chatting, hugging, renewing old acquaintances. Connor and Laura waited patiently in line at the desk for their turn to check in. Connor spotted several authors she knew—Claire McNab and Katherine Forrest were comfortably ensconced in two of the comfy armchairs in a sitting area just off the lobby. Connor waved and they waved back.

"It's good to see them," said Laura, who had met them at previous author events. "Maybe we'll get a chance to have dinner."

"I'd like that," replied Connor. "Though right at the moment all I can think about is Katy."

"I know," said Laura, giving Connor's arm a reassuring squeeze. "But she's got a veritable army on her side, what with William and Ellen, you and me, and your dad. And you have to figure he's probably scraped up a couple of friends here and there to help out."

"True. I'm constantly amazed at the number of people in the world who seem to owe my father a favor."

"That's because he's a man who comes through for people

when they need help, and most of them have the good taste not to forget it. Then there's the whole other group of helpful types who only want to stay on his good side because of what he knows about them."

"Not terribly trustworthy, though."

"No, but occasionally useful. In this case, if Benjamin drafts a little extra help, it'll be from people he can trust absolutely. And he's got good friends in the intelligence services here."

Connor looked around her and smiled.

"What?"

"I was just thinking what an odd assortment we must look like, if any of the Brits are hanging around to keep an eye on things."

"At least this is the twenty-first century," Laura grinned. "Just think: A few decades ago, if we'd been gathered at a stateside hotel, we'd have had J. Edgar Hoover's little minions peering at us from behind every potted plant. And you're quite right. Lesbians come in all sizes and shapes and dress codes—a motley but brilliant crew.

"And that's got to be a good thing," chuckled Connor. "Thank God authors are nonconformists."

♦

An hour later Connor, Laura, and Katy, soon joined by Ellen and William, held a last briefing. Tomorrow, Connor would be fully engaged with her various commitments at the author's conference. She was on two panels and scheduled to give an interview as well. She would be tied up until at least six o'clock.

"I'll take the author's bus to the conference," she told Laura. "You keep the car so you can spell William and Ellen at their observation post. And I'll get the bus or a taxi back here afterward. Just don't set up too far away from that stupid compound."

"We can't exactly hang about the gate looking helplessly at a flat tire on our car all day," said Ellen, trying to lighten the mood. "Eventually, even the Children of Artemis would probably offer to change it for us. But you know we'll find someplace as close as possible without drawing attention."

Connor spoke quickly, trying to keep the fear out of her voice. "Yes, I know. I'm sorry. But I don't like this, and I can't shake the feeling that it isn't going to be a walk in the park. There's something building up, something that's making me..." She trailed off, unable to find the words to express her deepening sense of unease. No matter what she said, she came off sounding like any other worried mother. But there was more to this. If only she could figure out what that was.

Ellen's forehead creased with concern. She picked up on Connor's thoughts easily. As a member of the circle, they were closely joined in spirit. The very misgivings with which Ellen had struggled all day but kept to herself were obviously shared by Connor as well. But were they simply feeding off each other's worries, or was there a source of trouble and they were both tuning into it?

"I think you're both feeling the same kind of energy from the same source," said William.

Katy flinched a little. "I wish you guys wouldn't do that," she grumbled good-naturedly.

"Do what?" asked her mother.

"Answer questions that no one asked out loud."

William laughed. "Sorry. It's a habit."

"Oh, it's okay. The part that worries is sometimes I think I know what my mom is going to say before she says it."

"Most daughters do," smiled Ellen.

"True, but it happens when I'm around you and William, too." She paused. "And don't start exchanging *significant* glances. I'm not a complete idiot."

Ellen laughed merrily. "That's one thing I'd never accuse you of, my dear. You're one of the smartest young women I've ever known, and the most intuitive as well. Forgive me if I've given you any other impression."

Katy shrugged. "No, you haven't. But it's gotten to be a sore subject, and I'm not even sure why."

"For most people, not understanding something is a source of annoyance. Try not to worry about it too much. For the moment, let's keep our minds on Sister Sonia and her little band of New Age entrepreneurs."

A knock at the door startled them. "Did you order room service?" asked Laura.

"No," Connor shook her head. "I didn't. She got up from her chair and strode to the door. "Who is it?"

"Friend, not foe," came the flippant reply and Connor swung the door open.

"Dad. What are you doing here?"

"Thought the team could use a little extra personnel," he replied, but no one in the room took his offhanded reply quite seriously.

"There's news of something," said Ellen with instant conviction.

"I was already on my way up here when I got William's call about a Mr. Dandridge who apparently raised some hackles on the back of his neck at the train station"

Connor looked confused. "Dandridge? Train station?"

William scowled and Benjamin had the grace to look mildly chagrined. "Sorry. I guess you were going to keep quiet about that until I did some checking."

"Where does this Dandridge come in?" Connor demanded. "And I'm assuming you're talking about the train Katy came in on."

"It might be nothing," said Ellen calmly. We just got a negative sense of his presence."

"A bad vibe?" Katy interjected. "Might as well call it what it is."

"Your generation has bad vibes, my dear. Mine has negative psychic reactions."

"Whatever," Katy shrugged, a rebellious look on her face. "But if Gramps is here, there must be something to it."

"Yes," said Benjamin. "And tracing him wasn't anywhere as difficult as William assumed. The name might be common, but the person using it isn't. And this moniker is just one of many aliases he's used. He's definitely a mercenary type, but he's worked his way

116

up the corporate ladder. He's the security chief for a mammoth multinational conglomerate called Pantheon International."

"Sounds as if he's got nothing to do with our situation," said William, with a trace of puzzlement. "Wonder why we were drawn to him."

"Don't jump to any conclusions yet," said Benjamin. "Pantheon isn't your run-of-the-mill multinational. And this isn't the first time their name has come up in security files. They're closely held, no public ownership or traded stock. They have tentacles out just about everywhere in the world. Their main headquarters is reputedly in Switzerland, but they have lavish and very well-secured offices in most major international capital cities. Most intelligence services are convinced that Pantheon's hands are anything but clean, but damning evidence of any kind is pretty much nonexistent. When investigations do get started, they inevitably run out of steam. They get called off by high-ranking officials, or investigators meet with entirely indisputable "accidents" that seem to dampen enthusiasm for pursuing the matter."

"All very interesting," said William, drily. "But I still don't see much connection with the Children of Artemis."

"Nor do I," admitted Benjamin, "but let's ask ourselves some questions. What brings a man like that to York? Right now all we have is the women's arts festival, the authors' conference, and the Children of Artemis compound."

"I don't expect he's planning to attend the women's arts festival," said Connor, raising an eyebrow. "Talk about standing out in a crowd."

Benjamin smiled. "Precisely. And we're entirely out of tourist season, besides which Mickey Dandridge doesn't strike me as a tourist. He gets off the same train as Katy. From what William reported, he acted as if he suspected he was being followed—also not the mark of a tourist. He has no family here as far we know. What does that leave us in terms of anomalous conditions here in the ancient city of York and its environs?"

"The Children of Artemis," Laura and Connor said in unison.

"Which is one more reason this idea of Katy's isn't a good one," added Connor. "If this place has attracted the attention of some octopus like Pantheon, then there's more to it than separating people from their money."

"However," said Benjamin. "What if Dandridge is in the same boat as your friend Ian. Maybe some relative of his is caught up in the Artemis scam. He might be on the same sort of mission we are. So let's keep an eye on him while I do some more checking. By the way," he reached into his briefcase, "I had the office fax me a photograph while I was driving. This the guy?" He handed the photo to Ellen, who passed it on to William with a nod.

"Yes, that's the chap I followed," said William. "And we know where he's staying."

"I already asked someone local to keep an eye on him. And I'm expecting a full report on Pantheon by the morning. We need to find out if there's any connection between them and the Artemis people...other than Greek mythology."

Ellen looked as if she were going to speak, then closed her mouth again, but Connor had caught the gesture.

"What is it?"

"It's hardly enough to mention. More of an inner alarm. But I keep getting the idea that Sister Sonia is in more trouble than she thinks."

"She is if she's running a complete scam," said Connor.

"No, I mean something more than that. It's as if she's trying to get out on the astral planes—I mean, really trying. And she doesn't know what she's doing. She's had no training, no initiation, and yet she's familiar with some of it. She's almost acting as if she has power there. And she may."

"How is that possible for a noninitiate?" asked Laura, whose own background in Navajo spirituality had taught her that it was a fairly long road of study, practice, and dedication before one was permitted to journey in the Dreamtime at will.

"It's only possible, I think, if she is a reincarnation of someone who's been involved in a similar situation in the past."

"You're not saying she actually is Artemis?" asked Katy with a frown.

"No, not at all. But she is someone of importance, or she was, from a time even earlier than our Celtic traditions reckon time. And that means it's as much a mystery to us as it would be to almost anyone. She could come from a spiritual tradition many thousands of years before our own, and you know yourself ours dates back well before Christianity."

Laura's face was a study in puzzlement. "Granted my math isn't all that good, but you're talking about the possibility of a civilization that is supposed to have flourished more than 10,000 years ago. That just hasn't been proven in any meaningful way."

Katy's eyebrow went up in an eerie reminder of her mother's trademark look of skepticism. "You're talking about what? Atlantis? Lemuria? One of those mythical continents that sank under the sea?"

Ellen shook her head. "I'm merely guessing, and all of it is based on odd spikes of intuition. So don't press me on details. I don't know anything more about those ancient civilizations than you do."

"But you believe in them?" asked Katy incredulously.

"And why not?" responded Ellen. "Do you believe in our Celtic civilization, although almost every history book extant in the world pretends it did not exist? That the tribes were mere flocks of barbarians. Do you believe in our Circle of Light, even though only a handful of people on the planet know of it?"

"Well, yes," admitted Katy. "But that's different?"

"Why?"

"Because you're here. You exist. You're doing the work of the Circle, and you have the history of your spiritual tradition."

"It's been said," interjected William, "that the history of even older traditions is stored somewhere on the planet."

"Like the Nag Hammadi manuscripts?" asked Katy.

"Not exactly written history," he smiled. "I'm thinking more in terms information recorded in shall we say a somewhat unusual medium."

"Such as?"

"Natural formations of minerals—crystals. Haven't you ever heard of "record-keeper" crystals?"

"Only in New Age bookshops," Katy frowned. "And I thought that was just a sales pitch. None of the ones I picked up every offered to let me in on some ancient secrets."

"I'm pretty sure they don't just up and start talking," smiled William. "And you're right. There are those who don't know any better who will call a crystal anything just to sell it. But we use minerals and gemstones in our ceremonials. They are part of the earth, and we also believe that they have a memory of some sort, even if we don't know exactly how it works."

Connor interrupted. "Aren't we getting a little far afield here? Not that I ever mind getting a history lesson."

"Perhaps," said William. "But the point Ellen is trying to make is that we might be encountering something rather more significant than a venal charlatan. So we need to see her up close. I'm beginning to think that Ellen and I need to visit the compound. Perhaps the day after tomorrow, once we get an initial report from Katy. The healing event is supposed to continue throughout the weekend."

"Very well," said Ellen. "That sounds like a plan. But for tomorrow we shall take up our observation post and be well within range if Katy needs us. We'll be able to track her GPS device easily enough, so she can't wander off without us knowing about it."

Connor was looking particularly glum. Laura laid a hand over Connor's. "What's the matter, sweetheart? You feel like you're being left out?"

"Look, I don't want to sound ridiculously ungrateful., I just feel like it's my job to protect my daughter."

Katy favored her mother with a withering look. "Actually, since I turned eighteen, it's pretty much been my job…parental angst notwithstanding."

Connor started to protest, then apparently thought better of it. "Okay. No matter what I say, I'm offending someone."

"You're just worried, darling," said Laura, "and that's perfectly natural. And we're all tired besides. I suggest we split up for dinner. No sense in all of us being seen together."

"I'm ordering room service," said Katy. "I'm supposed to be here on my own."

Benjamin reminded her to have another look at the dossier he'd given her with photos of Carmen Waters. "I'd like to find out if she's still alive and well."

"Probably not if she's made out a new will," said Connor sourly. "Her usefulness would definitely be at an end."

Katy looked at the others somberly. "I hope you're wrong."

William and Ellen invited Benjamin to join them at a nearby pub that served reasonable pub grub. Laura and Connor opted to mingle with other the authors at a buffet in one of the hotel's function rooms.

Katy left first, then Benjamin and the Carlisles. When they were alone, Laura turned to Connor and put her arms around her. "I know this is awfully hard, sweetheart. But she really isn't a little girl anymore. By the time you were her age—"

"I know, I was married and had a baby. But that was…"

"Different?" Laura laughed softly. "It always is, honey. Now get your mind off all the things that *could* happen—that most likely *won't* happen—and kiss me."

"That's the sort of distraction I can hardly pass up, now is it?"

"It had better be a genuine crisis before you decline such a request," said Laura, her face tilted up just a bit to compensate for Connor's extra couple of inches in height.

"No crisis," said Connor. "But lots of reasons to kiss a beautiful woman in my arms," she added, matching her actions to her words.

Chapter Twelve

In life's small things be resolute and great
To keep thy muscle trained: know'st thou when Fate
Thy measure takes, or when she'll say to thee,
'I find thee worthy; do this deed for me'?
—James Russell Lowell, "Epigram"

"The end of times," intoned Sonia, her voice rising and falling in waves over the assembled crowd. "What does it matter that we heal every minor illness, every inconvenience of the physical body when all is going to change, to shift, into what I would christen a brave new world."

Katy, wedged into the crowd a mere twenty feet away from the makeshift platform, noted with wry amusement that Sonia apparently had no qualms about plagiarizing Shakespeare. But then the image of a tempest at sea appeared vividly full blown in her mind, and she was startled into wondering whether Sonia's voice carried a hypnotic quality after all. Katy hadn't read the play since prep school.

"Sadly, most of you will not make the transition," Sonia declared, ignoring the looks of dismay in the audience. "That depends entirely on the will of the gods, and the will of those who speak for them."

Meaning Sonia herself, thought Katy, *but she's making the reference suitably oblique. Somehow I doubt it's because she's incredibly modest.*

A woman moving through the crowd slowly but deliberately drew Katy's attention. She was clearly not the least bit mesmerized by the great Sister Sonia, although she wore the white linen robe and gold-dyed rope belt of an acolyte of the movement.. If anything, she appeared to pay no attention at all to Sonia's speech. Instead, she was scanning all around her, as if looking for someone. For a moment, Katy's pulse quickened, wondering if she herself was the quarry. But no, the woman's eyes passed directly over Katy and then veered off. Without knowing precisely why, Katy was instantly more interested in where the woman was going than in what Sister Sonia was saying. She carefully edged her way back so as not to draw attention to herself. After all, most people in there were listening with rapt attention. The last thing Katy needed was to be noticed as someone not buying into the Children of Artemis mystique.

Once she'd wriggled her way to the rear, she visually panned the area for the woman, and found her almost instantly, standing right next to someone who could only be Carmen Waters. Katy heaved a sigh of genuine relief. Whatever the Artemisians had in mind for the future, Carmen was still alive and kicking. Well, not kicking perhaps. She seemed disoriented, her eyes darting to the other woman, then back to the stage where Sonia's voice was reaching a crescendo.

"It's time, my sisters and brothers, to face up to the terrible ravages that humans have perpetrated here on this planet, to take responsibility for your own diseases, your own failings, your own lack of faith in the gods who created you. If you do this, if you demonstrate your regret, your obedience, your faith, then you still have a chance to see this new world that will materialize around us as the old one is utterly destroyed. No one who is not within the protective embrace of the Children of Artemis will survive."

"But how long do we have?" shouted a terrified voice in the crowd. A murmur began to build. Katy took a quick survey of facial expressions in the audience—fear, disbelief, skepticism, anger, confusion. Sonia had them all riled up now. But she let the wave of sound build…and then stopped it cold with one upraised hand.

How the heck does she do that? thought Katy. *That's one trick I wouldn't mind learning.*

"It will not be long now," she said with a sad, yet somehow superior smile. "In fact, only a matter of days remain to this world."

Those last few words fell into the agitated crowd like cold rain, and had the same effect—as if someone had poured water on a fire. Shoulders sagged, people who had looked simply confused now appeared terrified. A few were even smugly resigned, as if they'd expected as much all along.

This is such bullshit, thought Katy, figuring there must be others in the crowd who shared her opinion, even if she couldn't pick them out quite yet.

"She isn't entirely wrong, you know," said a voice quite close to her right ear, startling her into minor heart palpitations.

"What?" said Katy. "I didn't…I mean, I don't really…"

It was the woman in the white robe, with Carmen Waters in tow. "I'm Jenny Carpenter, and I apologize if I startled you. It's just that I could tell from your expression you aren't really buying into all this. Why did you come here?"

Although it was a question for which Katy had rehearsed an answer, the way it was asked threw her off a little. She'd expected it from someone at the gate or the registration table (where she'd been highly grateful for the false I.D. Benjamin had provided). But there was something in Jenny Carpenter's expression that made Katy want very much to tell the truth. Jenny was neither threatening nor prying, and she seemed to already know that Katy was not there for her own healing or, even less so to join an Armageddon prep group.

Trying to keep her attention away from Carmen Waters, whom Katy knew she had no business knowing or recognizing, she decided that half the truth was better than nothing. "I was just curious. A friend of mine is getting a cure here. And I wondered if it was, you know, really working."

Jenny's smile transformed her face completely. Plainness gave way to radiance. "It depends on when your friend came here. Cures seem to be working much better these days. What is your friend's name?"

Katy could have sworn she detected a certain cynicism in the woman's voice, yet she was clearly being given the message that real cures were feasible.

"Um, his name's Philip Darcy."

"Oh, yes. As a matter of fact, I helped him myself."

"But I thought—"

"That it was Sister Sonia alone who worked miracles?"

Katy blushed. "Sorry. I really don't know a lot about all this."

"You probably know much more than you think," said Jenny with unaccountable conviction. "But you'll find Philip in the dormitory. He's in Room B on the first floor. And doing much better these past couple of days. He'll probably be ready to go home today or tomorrow."

Katy gestured toward the stage. "But what about the…the transition thing? Surely he'd want to stay for that."

"I don't think he'll be involved at all," said Jenny with a smile no less beautiful but far more enigmatic than anything Katy had seen Sonia muster onstage. "On the other hand, I think perhaps you and I will have more to talk about. Find me later. I'll be at the healing tent."

With that, she went off, Carmen beside her. Katy was concerned about the lack of animation in Carmen's expression, but it was obvious, too, that Carmen trusted Jenny. Inexplicably, Katy had a strong intuition that Jenny could indeed be trusted. But she had her doubts about some of the other Artemis people she'd seen milling about. The ones at the registration desk seemed both a little too friendly and a little too officious. They wanted every blank on the registration form filled in. Katy had assumed they wanted to keep padding their mailing list, looking for donations, but it could easily have a more sinister purpose, if only she knew what that might be. She strolled around the side of the main house and found herself momentarily unobserved and within easy reach of a door. On impulse, one that would have no doubt given her friends and family heart failure, she darted to the door, tried the handle and found it open. Katy slipped inside and quietly closed the door behind her.

Heart beating rapidly, she quickly surveyed her surroundings.

She was in a little mud room off the kitchen of the manor house. She stood completely still, listening for sounds of movement nearby. But all the sounds were muted, coming from outside, not in. And she could still hear Sonia's voice over the loudspeaker. The speech wasn't over yet. This would be the perfect time for a very fast reconnoiter.

She moved quickly and quietly through the kitchen, every sense on the alert. Her first thought was to find some sort of office and rifle through a few file drawers, perhaps find something at least mildly incriminating. It occurred to her, of course, that this was far from the original purpose of her visit. She'd insisted on this adventure out of concern for her friend, and that was how she'd sold everyone else, her mother especially, on supporting her efforts. But now she was taking the mission to a much more dangerous level. She almost laughed when she heard herself thinking about a "mission." Obviously, a few techie toys and a backup team had gone right to her head. She'd never taken a close interest in the clandestine side of her grandfather's career, but now she was beginning to see the attraction—at least the adrenaline-rush part.

Most of the doors along the main corridor of the wing she'd entered were closed. Opening them was the next big risk. She decided to fall back on the time-tested ploy of pretending to search for a bathroom, and practiced an anxious, I've-got-my-legs-crossed look just in case one of the doors she opened revealed staff who were not out on the grounds listening to their fearless leader. She found, in order: an ample storage closet for supplies; a largish library that looked as if it had probably been sold right along with the house, so at home did all the leather bindings look lined up with military precision on the built-in shelves; a room furnished with two-meter folding tables, metal folding chairs, and rows of telephones—some sort of boiler-room phone-solicitation operation, she imagined; and finally another closet.

Passing through the foyer, with a quick glance through the leaded panes on either side of the main entrance door, she zipped along into the other wing. Here, more doors stood open. The dining room was enormous, even by eighteenth-century standards, although the long table was set for fewer than twenty people. She also discovered the billiard room and study (de rigueur in any manor house worth its name), and was just beginning to consider abandoning the ground floor in favor of a riskier assault on the upper floor, which might or might not be devoted entirely to residential purposes, when she hit pay dirt. The second-to-last door swung open to reveal a traditional office, complete with half a dozen computers, a copier, a fax machine, and three printers, including a large and expensive color laser model. Apparently, the Children of Artemis did their P.R. materials in house. She stopped to glance at a stack of completed flyers, which were the same as the ones being distributed outside, though she hadn't bothered to read her copy when it was handed it to her.

The face of Sister Sonia stared out at her, an expression of smug satisfaction and ersatz wisdom defining the beautifully sculpted features. Katy had to admit that any reincarnated goddess would certainly not object to that body or that face. She moved among the desks, looking first for anything in plain sight. She was admittedly daunted at the prospect of opening any of the tall file cabinets ranged along one wall, all of which were probably locked anyway. One particularly large corner desk was furnished with no less than four pillars of stack trays. That must belong to the organization freak in the office staff, she supposed, since most of the other desks more closely resembled her own—moderately neat stacks of papers lumped here and there. Katy knew where everything was in her own stacks of documents. She assumed these people probably did, too. So she was exceedingly careful not to rearrange the order of papers as she rapidly flipped through the various folders. She had better luck on the desk filled with stack trays. The owner had conveniently labeled each tray—another anal-compulsive habit to her way of thinking. But it suited her purposes admirably. Financial reports, donation lists, internal memoranda, directives from Sister Sonia—a veritable gold mine. But how could she learn anything from it, or better yet, take it with her. She could hardly fill up a few Sainesbury's bags from the kitchen and carry them out of the house. She probably should have

one of those tiny cameras, although that, too, struck as her melo-
dramatically silly.

Then her eyes lit on the copy machine, all warmed up and ready
to go. Dare she? It would certainly make some noise, but perhaps
there was enough going on outside to muffle the sound. Just a few
copies, but of what? She only had minutes at the most. She grabbed
the financial reports for the current quarter. Surely that would yield
something of use. Yanking the top folder clip open, she shoved the
entire stack of twenty-five or thirty pages into the automatic feed on
top of the machine and spent a few precious seconds figuring out the
little icons on the LCD control panel—one set only, collated—and hit
the copy button. It roared to life with rather more audible enthusiasm
than she would have liked. But she refused to stop it. Instead, she
went to the door and peered out. There was no one in sight. And the
windows in this office were heavily draped.

Quickly, she thumbed through the other stack trays. At least the
copier was high-speed. Her first batch was done. She hurriedly
returned the originals to their folder and chose one marked "Internal
Memoranda." That was quite a bit thicker, but she couldn't resist it
when she glanced at the most recent memo, which was entitled
"Facilities Planning for the Transition. Target Date: November 11."

It went into the copier next, though she had to stand there and
feed it in two sections as the whole stack was too large to fit the
automatic feeder. Katy began to feel that her head was going to
explode from the tension, and yet the rest of her remained
relatively calm. Within two minutes, the file was completely dupli-
cated. Now she realized she had to draw the line somewhere. Even
if she had another hour to copy material, which she certainly did-
n't, she'd have no way to get it out of the house and off the
grounds. One last choice, then. She scanned the remaining trays of
files and there it was—the obvious choice—a set of membership
lists bound in heavy cardboard covers. There were five of them and
a quick glance confirmed that they were probably all identical. The
run date was only two days previous so they were current. She had
no time to disassemble the covers and make another copy. Instead

she decided to trust in the fate to help her out with this and simply commandeered one of the five. She shoved the others back in the tray, hoping it would be at least a little while before the owner of the desk noticed a shortage.

Instinct told her that her luck was probably nearing the end of its run. Grateful for the large shoulder bag she always carried, Katy slipped her sets of copies inside. Now it was considerably heavier, and sagged a bit, but she experimented by carrying it looped over her shoulder, with one hand sort of tucked beneath it. With a last look around the office for any obvious traces of her search, she carefully opened the door just a crack and peered out. To her immediate dismay, two men were walking down the corridor toward her: one a sort of faux Adonis type, whom she recognized as the man who'd been standing directly behind Sonia on the platform; the other a dark-featured, powerfully built gentleman, whom she'd wager was no gentleman. His face, even from a distance, was set into a mask of barely controlled fury. She knew any bullshit about looking for a bathroom was not going to fool this man for even a second. Quickly shutting the door and letting the handle slowly slip back into place, she searched frantically for a place to hide. The only possibility was at the end of the row of filing cabinets where they had not been shoved up against the outside windows. She could fit there. Otherwise, she could crouch under a desk. But if they chose to sit at one, the odds were too much against her that they'd choose hers. She opted for the narrow space and squeezed herself and her bag into it. As an afterthought, she reached in and found the PDA and kept it clutched in her hand. For all the careful instruction, she'd still treated the entire situation as more or less a lark. Not anymore. She was genuinely frightened and found herself deeply regretting her impulses.

◆

Scanning the crowd from an excellent observation point he and Ellen had discovered after a little bit of a search, William grew more and more frustrated over not being able to pick out Katy among the audience members. He'd caught sight of her only once through his high-powered binoculars, talking to two women he assumed were members of the community. Then they'd split up and Katy had gone round to the other side of the house, completely beyond his field of vision. His immediate fear was that she'd been lured inside the house or somewhere else on the grounds, and yet he hesitated to raise the alarm quite yet. Instead, he consulted his wife.

"I still can't find her," he frowned. "What are you getting?"

Ellen, whose face was frozen in deep concentration, took her time answering, but he waited patiently. The sorts of information she could gather were sometimes not easily translated into third-dimensional reality, and mere words.

"She's definitely inside a building, probably the manor house."

"Bloody hell!" muttered William. "Why on earth would she risk something so foolish?" She was only supposed to observe and try to find her friend's brother."

"Katy's her mother's daughter, I'm afraid…or I'm glad. Depends on how one looks at it. But…wait…"

William stared at Ellen, fearing the worst.

"Katy's frightened, badly frightened. But I don't sense anyone around her, not within range of her auric field. But still…"

"Time to call in the cavalry?"

"We are the cavalry, darling," said Ellen. "But she hasn't activated her PDA yet. So the situation is threatening but not critical. I don't think she's going to call for help if there's the least chance she can get out of whatever it is on her own. What I sense is that she needs some sort of a diversion."

"But what?"

Ellen thought for a moment, then grabbed the walkie-talkie and pressed the send button. "Laura, are you there?"

The voice came back immediately in both of their earpieces. "Yes, is anything wrong?"

"I'm not sure, but Katy is inside the house, and she might be trapped somehow. Maybe there are people nearby. Her fear level is increasing. I get the strongest sense that we need a diversion of some sort to draw attention away from her presence, but I don't know what."

There was a moment's pause. "Consider it done. One diversion coming right up." The connection went silent again.

"What do you suppose she has in mind?" said William. Ellen smiled. "I'm starting to have an inkling."

◆

Laura didn't panic in the least. Years of training kicked in during any crisis, even one that involved Katy, the daughter of the woman she loved. It was harder to be objective sometimes, but not when action was called for. Then it was pure instinct, just as it had been from the moment Laura had first saved Connor's life in a shoot-out to the death in the lonely reaches of the Navajo reservation. From that moment on, Laura's and Connor's lives were inextricably linked. And Katy was part of Connor.

Laura had spent the past hour working closer to the entrance of the main gate, past the lines of parked cars. She'd been subtle so as not to draw attention from the Artemis parking control people who'd kept trying to wave her back. "I'm collecting a friend in a wheelchair," she'd called out. "Can't really negotiate these narrow roads with the chair and not end up blocking traffic. And she called on my cell to say she's having some trouble breathing."

Clearly, anyone with life-or-death illnesses could be a liability to the Children of Artemis, so they continued to let her pass until she was only yards from the entrance gate, which had finally cleared out once everyone had registered and moved up to the speaker's platform. *Okay,* thought Laura, *there's nothing like being totally obnoxious to get people's attention.*

◆

Inside the house and still wedged into her hiding place, Katy heard the office door open. Her heart almost stopped when she heard two men's voices. Her finger hovered over the on/off switch to the PDA. Her panic, however, did not affect her sense of hearing and she listened with rapt attention. Obviously, the two men were not there to do office work but to argue. She didn't dare peek out.

"She's completely, utterly mad," said one voice.

"So what else is new? Surely Her Ladyship's consort has figured that out by now." There was a pause. "Oh, but that's right. You've taken up separate quarters since Sonia found a new play toy."

"Fuck you, Karl!" the other voice snarled. "She's done pumping that little moron for information. And that's all it was. You've got a filthy mind to go along with that filthy temper of yours."

Katy heard a rustling sound of cloth. "Don't piss me off, Alan, or you'll find out just how filthy my temper is."

"Let go of me!"

A chair scraped and slid as if someone had fallen against it. "That better? Now I'm telling you for the last time, this little scam is over. She's building up all those people out there for a big letdown and that includes our own disciples. The eleventh is just a few days away. You think she's actually going to produce Armageddon, or whatever her version of it is? I, for one, am getting out of here. But first I'm going to eliminate every trace of my presence from these files and these computers before the police end up raiding the place."

Katy stopped breathing. *Oh, shit. He's going to stay in here.*

"You do that, but you're not taking the crystal."

Katy heard a sharp intake of breath. "What the fuck do you know about that?" said the voice she'd identified as Karl.

"I'm not a complete idiot. I figured it out a while ago. That girl Jenny must have brought it to her. It's why she's changed so much. I walked in on her one night when she didn't lock the door. She was staring at that thing, had it out on her desk, and I swear to God she was talking to it."

Karl laughed. "And was it talking back, you idiot? It's just a rock. It's all part of her delusion. I could care less what she does with it. If you're smart, you'll clear out now, before this all gets ugly and the police and Inland Revenue pencil pushers are all over this place. Now I'm going to start doing a little erasing. And you're going to help. Start with that last file cabinet and look for anything on the disciples and the membership."

Katy heard footsteps coming closer. Her finger began to press the switch on the PDA. And then all hell broke loose outside the window. She hard the screech of tires, some scattered screams, and then a car horn blaring repeatedly.

Alan ran to a window, and yanked back the curtain, completely concealing Katy in her hiding place.

Karl followed him. "What's going on?"

"I don't know, but we'd better get out there now."

The office door slammed open. A breathless woman's voice shrilled at the two men. "Thank God I finally found you. Sonia wants you both…quickly. There's some madwoman starting a riot out there." The hand Katy could see dropped the edge of the drape and for a moment she glimpsed a profile of one of the men.

◆

Laura's timing was impeccable. She put her car in gear and shot through the gate, stopping only a meter or two from the edge of the crowd. People scattered. Some screamed, thinking they were about to be run down. Laura laid on the car horn with all her might, over and over, drowning out Sister Sonia completely. Then she leaped out of the car and scrambled onto the roof and began using the intriguingly compelling voice of command her Grandmother Klah had taught her.

"Listen to me, all of you. This is nothing but a scam. My brother came here to be healed, and she didn't do anything for him. She even tried to pay him off to pretend his cancer was gone, be one of her poster boys. But she's just taking your money. My brother died yesterday. And the world isn't ending either, not this week or this year or anytime soon. It's just another trick to get you to sign over everything you own to her. Check it out. I'll bet you didn't even look at the stuff you signed when you came in." Laura, of course, was only guessing at this last part. They'd probably only put their names to standard liability forms promising not to sue or acknowledging that cures were not guaranteed, but sure enough, dozens of people in the crowd started scrambling for the registration table to see if what Laura said were true. Sister Sonia tried in vain to stop the disruption.

"My children, listen to me. Listen. This poor woman is clearly very ill and overcome with grief. Don't let her fears disrupt the mission of the Children of Artemis. Don't let your own fear overtake you. If I could not save her brother, it is because the gods ordained it."

But very few were listening. Many were shouting questions at her. Laura saw her turn quickly to a disciple, who picked up the hem of her robe and ran for the house. *Excellent,* thought Laura. *That ought to empty the place out.* By now, of course, her car was surrounded by Artemis devotees, trying to get at Laura, but she kept dancing out of their reach, and their efforts were hampered by the crowd now surging around Laura, trying to hear what she was saying.

Laura kept one eye on the Artemis people trying to pull her down, and one eye on the house, willing Katy to appear from some direction.

◆

William began to laugh. "You're not going to believe this," he said, handing Ellen the binoculars.

"Why, what's going on down there?" she asked, as they were far enough away that she could only make out a commotion centered around a car that had just entered the Children of Artemis compound.

"When our friend says diversion, she means it," said William. He sobered a bit, though. "Now how the hell is she going to get out of there?"

"Perhaps it's time we moved closer," said Ellen. "Just in case."

"I don't know what we could do," replied William, "but improvisation is our strong suit."

◆

Inside the manor house, Katy could hear the uproar but couldn't imagine what was going on. Still, the only thing that mattered was that the two men who had been standing mere inches from her, who would have discovered her cowering—*No,* she thought, *not cowering, hiding*—dashed out of the room behind the woman who had summoned them. Katy released her death grip on the PDA signaling device, waited to a count of five and headed for the door. The departees hadn't even bothered to close the door. She quickly checked the corridor and then half ran down the hall back the way she'd come. She reached the side door in under thirty seconds, and after assuring herself there was no one in the immediate vicinity to see her exit, she slipped out and walked briskly along the side of the house.

When she rounded the corner, to her amazement she saw Laura Nez standing on the roof of her car, haranguing the crowd like a revival-tent minister bent on saving their souls. To Katy's left, on the platform, Sister Sonia was standing rigid with fury, still trying to regain the attention of her acolytes, both current and future. The man running the sound system was fiddling frantically with the volume controls, trying to make Sister Sonia audible above the uproar. But it was in vain. Everyone was milling about, and many were already headed for the gate. Katy was tempted to simply stand and stare at Laura making an absolute spectacle of herself. Instead, she moved directly into the milling throng.

◆

Out of the corner of her eye, Laura saw Katy appear from the side of the house and immediately blend into the crowd. From the front door, two men came running, one of whom gave her the distinct impression he'd have dealt with her a lot more directly and harshly than the floundering Artemisian disciples. With an immense flood of relief, Laura saw that it was time to make her exit before the throng made it impossible for her to move the car away. With a parting shot at the scam artists and charlatans, she slid down the right side of the car, flung the door open, threw herself into the driver's seat and was in reverse in seconds. Katy would be safe. She would simply flee with the rest of the would-be sheep. She would, thought Laura, in a moment of giddy relief, "get the flock out of there." She had little doubt that someone would note her license plate, and that her anonymity was burned, along with Connor's. The car registration would lead right back to them if these people had the resources to track it down, and she was beginning to think they probably did. Something about the operation itself spoke of a slick preparation for a big killing disguised in a veneer of amateurism.

♦

Katy saw Laura's hasty departure and stuck with a large group of people who clearly leaned toward believing the angry woman on top of the car, and were decamping rapidly from the gathering. She stuck close to the center of that group until they were well past the gate, clutching her bag and nodding vigorously in agreement with their various and sundry statements of utter outrage that they'd been duped by a charlatan like Sister Sonia. Looking back, however, Katy saw that Sonia was swiftly regaining control of those who'd stayed behind, either true believers or the still undecided. There were many, and she realized that Sonia's talents as a manipulator were not to be dismissed. There was an emanation of power from her that even Katy, with no training in such things, could feel. She had no doubt that given enough time, she could have probably kept almost everyone on her side. But Laura's entrance and exit were so precipitous and her outrage so powerfully disruptive that the hypnotic energy field had collapsed temporarily.

Katy regretted she'd had no chance to meet up with Jenny Carpenter at the healing tent, or to find Ian's brother and see his improvement with her own eyes. But there was always tomorrow.

She'd come back for the Sunday session. With Laura having drawn every speck of attention to herself, Katy had gotten off scot-free. *Well,* she thought sourly, *at least until my mother hears about this.*

♦

One person had seen Katy leave the manor house by the side door—another visitor with absolutely no illusions about Sister Sonia and no intention of listening to her line of crap. Mickey Dandridge, using yet another alias, had been in the very act of casing the joint, as his American ancestors might have said, when the ruckus started. The way the disciples and acolytes and community residents reacted, he realized that everyone would be in a state of high alert. This was hardly the best time to slip in and out unobserved. He was just finishing his circuit of the house when he saw the young woman come out, look around in what his practiced eye deemed a furtive and frightened way, and scurry off toward the front. His concern, of course, was the shoulder bag she carried, but it was not big enough and entirely flat. If he had to guess, he'd wager she was some sort of tabloid reporter trying to get the goods on the holier-than-thou Sister Sonia. But she'd bear watching if he saw her around here again. He was pondering whether or not there was sufficient time for him to make one quick survey of the inside of the house when a woman in Artemis dress came down the walk from the garden and entered the side door. Within moments, another one followed. No, the house was definitely not a welcome place for the likes of Mickey Dandridge. And although he'd seen Karl from a distance, he knew better than to be seen talking to him here and now. That would have to wait. He was already annoyed that Karl had not appeared at their scheduled meeting in town that morning. Obviously, some discipline was in order.

Chapter Thirteen

The inquiry of truth, which is the love-making,
or the wooing of it,
the knowledge of truth, which is the presence of it,
and the belief of truth, which is the enjoying of it,
is the sovereign good of human nature.
—Francis Bacon, *Of Truth*

"You did what?"

"Is that question addressed to me or Katy?" asked Laura with just the correct degree of feigned innocence. Too much and Connor would explode. Just enough and perhaps she could actually cajole a smile out of her. But judging from Connor's expression, the attempt was in vain.

"Either of you! But mostly Katy. What were you thinking, going into that house without telling anyone?"

Katy stiffened. Her face was set in the same angry lines as Connor's, though to be honest, she was feeling a little foolish for having taken such a risk. But she'd be boiled in oil before admitting that to her mother. "The opportunity was there. And don't try and tell me that you or Laura or the Carlisles or Gramps wouldn't have done exactly the same thing."

"That isn't the point at all. Any of us might have, but we've got more experience."

"In what? You're a novelist for God's sake. And just because you once prosecuted a few hundred criminals doesn't mean you're an investigator."

"Well, neither are you."

"Then I don't suppose you'll be at all interested in what I found out, or the files I brought back with me."

"Files? What files?"

Katy reached into her bag and dragged out the photocopies and the membership list she'd purloined. "Just the financial records for the Children of Artemis for the last quarter, and the entire membership list."

Laura watched the exchange with some degree of amusement and certainly compassion for both of them. Growing up was hard. Katy wanted to prove herself an equal to her accomplished and brilliant mother. Connor wanted to protect her child at all costs without stopping to think that Katy had inherited her intelligence, courage, and, not surprisingly, her temper. The advantage of having a balanced perspective at the moment wouldn't really help either of them until they both settled down, so Laura wisely kept her mouth shut and avoided the deadly error of appearing to take sides.

Katy slammed the paperwork down on the coffee table. She'd come to Connor and Laura's suite as soon as she'd navigated her way back through York to the hotel. Delaying the inevitable wasn't going to make it any easier. She figured Laura would have felt obliged to tell the truth about what happened, and she didn't blame her. But she was firmly on the defensive, and it wasn't a place she liked to be.

"But they'll miss this stuff immediately," argued Connor. "They'll know someone was rifling through their offices."

Katy's expression drifted toward smugness. "These are photocopies. I made them myself. There were half a dozen membership lists just lying around. No one will wonder who borrowed one of them."

"You…you photocopied all this—with people right outside? You just made yourself right at home?" Connor dropped into a chair, shaking her head. She was obviously torn between being totally outraged with her offspring and rather proud of her, too.

"Yes, and I was on my way out of there when these two guys came down the hall and I had to hide. Then they walked into the office and started arguing and—"

"And Ellen caught on that you were in danger and let Laura know." Connor turned to face her lover. "And you found it necessary to put on a stage show on top of your car? In the middle of the compound? Are you both utterly insane?"

Laura could see that the edge had gone out of Connor's anger. That's how it worked with her. A flare-up, and then her normal, sensible approach, along with her sense of humor, rose to the surface once more.

"Actually, she looked and sounded pretty impressive," said Katy. "If I didn't know better, I would have sworn she was a furious grieving relative out for blood."

Connor just buried her face in her hands and stayed that way until a knock at the door signified the arrival of the rest of their little group.

Benjamin came right to Katy. "Are you all right, sweetheart?"

"I was until Mom threatened to send me to my room without supper."

Connor started to open her mouth but then thought better of it.

"You did go a little further than we planned," said Benjamin with just a hint of reproof. "You got off lucky, my dear granddaughter."

Katy relented. "I know I did. If it weren't for Ellen's psychic radar, I'd be cooked."

"Nothing to it, love," said Ellen. "Glad I could help. And I wouldn't have missed Laura's diversionary performance for the world."

"I'm almost sorry I did," said Connor. "Almost but not actually."

William piped up. "I must say it was the last thing I expected, but perhaps the best idea she could possibly have had. It completely shattered the mystique of the moment. I'd never have thought of it myself."

Ellen smiled. "That's because William would as soon be presented to the Queen in his knickers as make a public spectacle of himself."

He grimaced. "I do hope that in case of life or death, I'd go anywhere in my knickers, with or without Her Majesty's approval."

"And what is all this?" said Benjamin, gesturing to the stack of papers on the table.

Connor answered first. "Our young Mata Hari helped herself to the photocopy machine and brought back a whole sheaf of financial records, along with a membership list she lifted from the office." Despite the sarcasm, there was a detectable note of pride in her voice and Katy's vaguely sullen expression lightened perceptibly.

"Sounds as if we have a tale to hear," said William, settling into a chair. "Why not start from the beginning?"

Katy, now the center of attention, gave a full and detailed report, from her meeting with Jenny Carpenter and Carmen Waters, whom they were all relieved to know was still among the living, to the moment in the office when she'd been trapped listening to the argument between two men, one called Alan, the other Karl. When she got to the part about the crystal, Benjamin sat up in his chair. "What crystal?"

"I don't know. They just talked about some crystal that they thought was making Sonia act crazy. Someone named Jenny brought it to her a while back. Maybe it was the same Jenny I was talking to. Why?"

"Something rings a bell here. Give me a minute. Laura, do you have your laptop here?"

"Of course, it's in the bedroom. I'll get it."

"No, there's a connection in there. I need to access some data files from my office. You all keep talking. Why don't we order some dinner up here?"

◆

An hour later, dinner was delivered, and shortly thereafter Benjamin emerged with a sheaf of notes written on hotel stationery. "There's a weird connection here, but I don't know what it means quite yet. There was something about the name Jenny Carpenter that struck a chord, but that's not uncommon. It wasn't until you mentioned something about a crystal that it started coming together."

"So explain already," said Connor impatiently.

"Okay. The details of this didn't make the public press, but a while back some archaeologists on an island in the Bermuda Triangle were all murdered, all except one who somehow survived, probably because she was well hidden enough, or the people who raided the island didn't know she was there. Her name was Jenny Carpenter. She was found completely incoherent when the next supply boat arrived. She was institutionalized for months and then just disappeared."

"So she probably ended up at the Children of Artemis," said Connor. "Hardly surprising since the place is probably chock full of complete head cases. But what has that got to do with—"

"Patience, daughter," said Benjamin with a smile. "The part that definitely didn't make the news is what was most likely taken from the island by whoever flew in and killed the people there. The dig was being run by an eminent archaeologist, Dr. Jürgen Pedersen. But during the last few weeks of the dig, his reports became more and more bizarre. A friend of mine at the Smithsonian got in touch with me on the outside chance there was something to what he considered pure raving on Pedersen's part. He claimed to have found the remnants of a giant natural formation, a quartz-like crystal obelisk or pillar. And he swore it had qualities that no one had ever documented."

"What qualities was he talking about?" asked Laura.

"That's just it. He refused to elaborate, except that he did use the phrase 'infinite energy source.' Then he started acting as if what he was doing were top secret. Finally, he actually tried to get in touch with the President."

"Of the United States?" asked Ellen incredulously.

"Yes, that president. And whoever fielded his calls kicked it down to some flunky in one of the NSA offices. Eventually, I did get a memo about it, but it all seemed so absurd, I didn't give it any more thought. Then Pedersen and his whole group were murdered except for Jenny Carpenter, and NSA sent a team to take a look around. All they found were empty trenches dug by a bulldozer, a lot of bloodstains, and the remnants of a dig site. That's it. Whatever the pirates or whoever came for—it was gone."

"Except Jenny must have found or kept a piece of that crystal he was talking about, and she brought it here."

"Which means that someone will want it, too. If they were willing to kill half a dozen people in cold blood for the other pieces."

"But what possible value could it have?" asked Connor. "We're talking about a big, shiny rock."

"Maybe not," said Ellen cryptically.

"Hmm," added William.

Laura looked thoughtful.

"You want to tell us what the 'hmm' is about?" said Katy impatiently.

"Remember what we were talking about last night? That Sister Sonia might have tapped into some kind of energy that was very ancient, that she might be a reincarnation of a powerful person from the very distant past?"

"Yes, but I thought you were just sort of speculating."

"We were. But legend has it that those ancient cultures did have sources of energy we wouldn't even begin to understand. And they might have been crystal formations. Besides, if any of those shards contained information, that could be what's energizing Sister Sonia. That could be why those two men you overhead think she's lost her marbles."

Connor sighed. "You know, you too are constantly trying to stretch my imagination to include more of the unknown, but this just seems beyond the pale."

Ellen smiled at her warmly. "But don't you see? This isn't a great deal different than the sorts of things you've already experienced yourself. It's just, well a different kind of…I hate to say technology in the same breath with spiritual tradition, but that's the only way I can think to explain it. By all reports, Sister Sonia was no more than a moderately successful scam artist, probably using shills in her healing scams. And then suddenly there are reports of actual healing and a few other strange occurrences. One possible explanation is that she's using or more likely misusing remnants of power from a very ancient source. That in itself could be dangerous."

"But she's completely obsessed with the end of times," interjected Katy. "That's what her speech was about, at least the part I listened to. Is she getting *that* from the crystal?"

"I doubt it," said William. "Armageddon end-of-the-world stories are as common as peas. They're in every culture. It seems more likely that she's latched onto it as a new angle for fleecing people while she's using the power she's gained to do some actual healing."

"I never did get to see Philip," said Katy. "But Jenny assured me he was actually doing well, that he'd be going home."

"Apparently she's not buying into the end-times scenario," said Connor.

"No, I guess not. But I'm going to find Philip tomorrow and make him go home, one way or the other."

"You're not thinking of going back there!" said Connor, slamming her fork down on the plate so hard it startled everyone.

"And why not? No one caught me doing anything. Laura's the one who made a spectacle of herself."

"Yes, and you talked to two people and admitted you weren't there for healing or curiosity but for a specific reason—to find Philip. What makes you think Jenny Carpenter hasn't already reported that to Sonia or someone else in charge there?"

"Just because of the way she acted when Sonia was speaking. It's almost as if she were laughing at it or something. Maybe not that overt, but definitely not taking it seriously or showing any deference to the goddess on the stage."

"It's too dangerous now."

"I'm going back. I want to talk to Carmen Waters and get her out of there, too."

"This is going too far," said Connor. "Carmen's probably totally brainwashed. She'll rat you out in a heartbeat."

"Then we'll just have to go along with her," said William firmly. "This time we're going to keep her within arm's reach."

"But…"

"But what, Mother? You can't go there because you think they may have your name. And if they didn't and they check the car registration, they definitely will know you're involved somehow. Laura certainly can't go there after the stunt she pulled today. Benjamin's got to keep a low profile in England or his security consulting is pointless. That just leaves me and the Carlisles."

Benjamin was uncharacteristically silent and eventually they all ended up looking at him, wondering why. He finally pursed his lips and sighed. "I do think you're forgetting about one thing."

"What's that?" asked William.

"Dandridge. The man you followed from the train station. Remember we were speculating about what he could possibly be after in York. It might just be the very thing we're all talking about—the crystal."

"But why? What connection could he have to that?"

Before he could answer, Laura said, "So you're thinking what I'm thinking."

"Our minds run in the same channels when it comes to international conniving."

Laura shrugged. Everything she knew about intelligence, counterintelligence, and conspiracy she'd learned from her former boss and mentor. Benjamin's mind found and integrated unlikely connections that others simply overlooked. He had a gift for seeing the pieces of a puzzle and fitting them together intuitively, as if the picture sprang fully formed from his mind.

"Okay, Dad, we're sufficiently in the dark," said Connor. "Perhaps you two spymasters would like to share."

"I could be completely off base, honey. But I don't like the way this is shaping up." He began ticking off the points on his fingers. "First, Mickey Dandridge is tied to Pantheon, an organization every intelligence service in the world tends to view with utmost suspicion, and he shows up in York. Pantheon controls a great many energy sources on this planet and they're always looking to acquire more. Second, according to satellite data gathered as routine surveillance, Pantheon has had a small fleet of ships keeping station at specific coordinates in the Bermuda Triangle for months. Third, the murders of Dr. Pedersen's group took place less than a hundred miles from those coordinates. Fourth, if you'd gone to the trouble of stealing something like these crystal artifacts, and you suddenly discovered you'd missed a piece, what would you do?"

"Send someone to get it," said Laura without hesitation. "And I'd send someone like Dandridge. His file indicates a definite tendency toward being successful in his assignments."

"Ten to one he was involved in that raid on Dr. Pedersen," said Benjamin

"That really might be a stretch, Dad. You've put together a case out of some potentially unrelated facts and speculation."

"Spoken like a true lawyer," he smiled. "But I told you that it was only a theory. It still, however, bears keeping in mind. Better to be too cautious than unprepared."

"True," sighed Connor. "I once thought machine guns were overkill. This woman taught me otherwise." She reached for Laura's hand, silently sharing their memories of life and death and survival. "So we'll take all the precautions necessary, even if this turns out to be what I suspect: a nest of thieves and murderers, not a target of some international conspiracy to control the world through crystal power."

They all laughed, and the tension in the room abated a little.

♦

There was no laughter in the precincts of Yohiro Matsumoto's ascetic but spacious home. The children had gathered with him and sat in silent respect until he was prepared to speak. He observed each of them in turn, but he didn't acknowledge them personally or by name. Although he loved his offspring after his own fashion, sentimentality was entirely foreign to his nature. As such, he rarely addressed them as individuals. They were parts of his personal vision, each critical in its own way yet honor-bound to an old concept of self-effacement so direly antithetical to the human soul's need for self-expression that none of them ventured the least shred of individuality beyond their own historical specialties. If Matsumoto could have created clones bereft of personal will, he could not have produced servants any more subservient to his will than these six who knelt before him on the tatami mats. This might have given him great pride, had he allowed himself the emotion. But, as his master had taught him, emotion was a waste of vital energy.

Finally, he took a last sip from the delicate teacup that had been set before him with greatest ceremony.

"The time is nearly at hand. The old monk has spoken to me at length. He does not approve of my plan and has grave doubts about the outcome. He insists that what I undertake is nothing more than arrogance of will, yet he is ignorant of destiny in some ways. He continues to live only because he has assured me he will not interfere. Such decisions, he says, are not his to make."

Matsumoto could feel the both relief and satisfaction wash over his children. He knew they were anxious to proceed. They shared his vision of changing the world, of righting the injustices engendered by humankind's general cupidity and self-interest. They had absorbed his ultimate pragmatism, which called for order, regimentation, and above all, homogeneity—all that would be vital for any society to prove successful.

He stood and walked to a drape that hung suspended from the ceiling behind where he had sat. "You have seen this before," he said, "but now, as we embark upon the final phase of our project, look upon it again and understand once more why the tasks that have been set you are so important." Carefully, he drew back the curtain and once more he was overcome with the sense of history reclaimed. It was portrait of sorts, a fresco removed from the underwater excavation that Pantheon had been conducting.

Matsumoto had claimed it for himself. For here was the picture of a warrior, an ancient warrior of more than ten millennia past. He was clad in a gold breastplate, over a white tunic, and carried a sword with a jewel-encrusted hilt. But the most significant aspects of this image were these: the immensely tall crystal pillars behind him ranged in a semicircle and the man's facial features. The jawbone, the cheeks, and the eyes—unmistakably Asian. Here perhaps, was the ancestor of those who stood before the painting. At the very least, Matsumoto knew that a once-powerful civilization had been defined by its culture, one closely matching his own. And from the first time he had seen the painting, he had also grasped his destiny and the reasons for his deep yearnings that had not yet been fulfilled in this world.

"My children, the world will belong to us again. Not because we have the power of arms, the brute force of weapons of mass destruction. These are but the playthings of mere children. The gods themselves will return to this planet, will walk the paths they once walked, and they will restore what has been lost. We are their strong arms, their eyes, their very will working in this dimension of time and space. But now we have been granted the opportunity to extend that service to other places, even to other times, and that is exactly what we will do.

"The crystal will be liberated from its current hiding place within forty-eight hours. The remaining shard will join its mother as soon as the crystal reaches England. We have but a few days left before the appointed and correct time for action is upon us. Prepare yourselves in every way. Pray daily at your shrines. And continue your studies until the last possible moment."

He dismissed them with a nod. They rose, bowed deeply, and withdrew, leaving him with his dreams, his hopes, and his obsessions.

♦

Alan might not have known the precise, clinical definition of obsessed, but he was relatively clear on the phrase "completely bonkers," and as far as he could tell, that was an utterly apt description of his former lover, former partner in crime, and former good-natured grifter. At the moment, however, he was only concerned with dodging breakable and not-so-breakable objects that Sonia was hurling about her rooms with dangerous abandon. Many of them were unmistakably aimed at his head.

"How dare she! How dare that woman disturb the sanctity of my gathering, the delivering of divine guidance to all those people in need. She ruined it for me! She insulted me! Me—a goddess actually incarnate on the planet, walking the earth among common people just to bring solace and save a few of their miserable lives for a future most of them don't even deserve!"

Alan ducked a Royal Doulton cup and saucer, though the cold tea splashed him on the way by. "But she didn't ruin it, darling. She was only there a few minutes. The disciples made her leave. And you got everything under control again. We only lost a few, a few malcontents who wouldn't have stayed anyway."

She glared at him. "How would you know? How would you know anything? Obviously I'm under attack. There's some evil at work here. That woman didn't show up to be outraged about a dead relative. I could see it in her…the calculation, the intent the…" She stopped because she'd been about to say, "the power." But she had no intention of acknowledging any power but her own. That in turn, reminded her of another worrisome puzzle. She asked, "Where's Jenny Carpenter?"

Alan made a brief attempt to seem only vaguely familiar with the name. "Uh, that girl who came here a while back, the skinny, depressed-looking one."

"She doesn't look depressed anymore, does she?" said Sonia. "And you know why? Because she's challenging me. She's actually daring to challenge my authority. She has even interfered with my healing work with Carmen."

"What do you mean, interfered?" Alan was baffled. He wasn't aware anyone defied Sonia these days for any reason.

"She's kept Carmen away from me."

Alan's jaw almost dropped. This was unbelievable. No wonder Sonia was so angry. She was probably afraid she was losing her iron grip on the Children of Artemis. And maybe she was, which could only be a good thing as far as he was concerned. He'd actually started to believe that getting away from her would be impossible, that her "powers" were real and dangerous, too. But if some wimpy acolyte like Jenny Carpenter could defy Sonia, then anyone could. Still, he wasn't quite ready to test this theory…not while she was within reach of so many pointed, heavy objects that could seriously damage his still-handsome face.

"Do you want me to find Carmen?" he asked, with the air of someone willing to do her every bidding.

She turned her back on him and stared at the mirror on the wall, the one that concealed her safe and the hidden treasure within. "No. She's useless to me now. I have everything I need from her. If she chooses to refuse my help, let that be her loss. She won't be making the transition with us, I assure you."

She looked back at Alan. "Find Karl and send him to me. I have an errand for him to run."

"Karl isn't here right now. He went into town."

The look on her face made Alan flinch involuntarily. "Call his cell phone. I want him back here right now."

◆

Fortunately for Karl, his cell phone was turned off. Otherwise, he would have been caught between a rock and a hard place—and he wasn't even sure which was which, just that either one of them could do him some degree of injury. Right now he was focused on the angry countenance of Mickey Dandridge.

"You haven't done squat to get hold of that damn crystal. You could have done something while she was occupied with the crowd. You've already been into the damn safe. It would have taken minutes."

Karl squirmed on his barstool. They'd taken a table away from the other patrons and spoke in low voices. But the menace in Mickey's voice was enough to give Karl several million second thoughts about ever having gotten involved in all this. How could he possibly explain to this man that he hadn't dared remove the crystal from the compound while Sonia was there? That somehow he was quite sure Sonia would *know* the moment he opened the safe and touched the damn thing. He was convinced that his only shot was taking it while she was in town, far enough way to give him a window of escape. Then he could turn it over to Mickey and take off for parts known only to himself, along with every dime of the cash contributions from the weekend.

"Well?"

"The timing wasn't right. There was too much going on. She could have gone right back into the house, and I'd have been out-numbered about twenty to one if she'd caught me stealing it. Once all the commotion started, I didn't know what she might do."

"And, speaking of commotion, did you find out anything about that woman who drove into the compound?"

"Not yet."

Mickey shook his head in disgust. "Figures. I ran the plate immediately. It was a rental car hired by someone named Connor Hawthorne. That name sound familiar?"

Karl swallowed hard. It did. But he wasn't about to admit why. The paper with the two names on it, the paper he'd given Alan, wasn't going to exactly fade out of his memory. "No, why? Was that the woman on top of the car?"

"I doubt it. If you did your research...takes about ten minutes on the Internet...you'd see this." He pulled a few folded sheets of A4 paper from his pocket and handed them to Karl. "She's an author, a relatively famous one. And there's her picture, so she wasn't the one who caused the scene. But I'd be willing to bet it was her girlfriend, Laura Nez. Seems Ms. Hawthorne is a lesbian."

"So. The Nez woman said something about her brother hav-ing died."

"That remains to be discovered. But I doubt it's true. You see, this Hawthorne woman is the daughter of someone a lot more important than you might guess—an American ex-senator, presidential adviser, and, if the stories are true, a player in international intelligence circles. He could cause us a great deal of trouble. And Ms. Hawthorne herself is a former attorney and a prosecutor—and may have a deplorable tendency not to mind her own business. I don't suppose you'd have any idea of why people like that would be interested in some two-bit phony religious scam like you and your cronies have got going?"

Karl was speechless. Everything was going to hell. The Children of Artemis, and Pantheon might be running right into a buzz saw. What if the Americans or the Brits were onto them? Maybe they had a wild hair about what Pantheon had been up to, or maybe they just wanted to nail the Artemis people. Either way, it wasn't good, not good at all. And if he'd had any doubts before about sharing the details of the incident in Palm Springs with Mickey Dandridge, he quelled them permanently. He himself could have led the law right to their doorstep. He should have killed those other two women as soon as he realized Bettina Waters had talked to them. On the other hand, if this woman was such a fucking celebrity and her father some government big shot, that would have been even worse. He'd have had half the security people in the world looking for him. Apparently his silent contemplation was irritating his companion.

Mickey leaned forward and slapped Karl's face none too gently. "Get a grip, you stupid bastard. Now let's discuss exactly how you are going to get that crystal out of the safe and into my hands within the next twenty-four hours. And don't tell me you can't, or that this raving lunatic bitch has some sixth sense as to its constant whereabouts. If you have to put a bullet in her head, do it. But don't waste any more of my time. The people I work for are not known for their patience, and the man who is specifically overseeing this recovery would just as soon pull one of your eyeballs out of its socket and make you look at it with your other one. Or feed you your balls after they've been sautéed in a nice sesame ginger sauce. Do you begin to get my drift?"

◆

Jenny Carpenter and Carmen Waters, unaware that they were currently chief among the targets of Sister Sonia's ire, were sitting in a tiny copse of trees, as far from the house as possible without actually leaving the grounds. For some reason, Jenny insisted that they could not simply leave the Children of Artemis compound.

Carmen, whose headaches had abated considerably in only a couple of days, thanks to the healing ministrations of her new or perhaps (if Jenny were to be believed) her very old friend, was still coping with extended bouts of déjà vu. Jenny explained that they were memories, but for Carmen, the jury was still out on that question. Instead, she preferred not to think about it. She found herself doing something she'd always thought was the subject of fairy tales, not real life. Carmen was falling in love. The relationships she'd had prior to this had been very few, and once or twice she'd categorized them as love…until now. Nothing compared to the way she felt about Jenny. The odd thing was that it didn't feel like a new relationship, like a new adventure. It felt like the continuation of something ancient and miraculous and completely embedded in her heart and soul. She said nothing of this to Jenny, not because she feared ridicule, but because she feared that Jenny would not only agree but tell her why. And Carmen wasn't sure she could take any more of the "memories" that had filled her dreams and her grueling sessions with Sister Sonia.

But these very thoughts were racing through her mind when Jenny took her hand and moved closer to her. "You're always remembering."

Carmen closed her eyes and tears flowed down her cheeks. "Yes. But I still don't know why."

"Because you are mine and I am yours."

"I know those words, I've heard them."

"From me," Jenny smiled. "But then you were called Junela, and my name was Alandra. We were lovers, quite wonderful lovers. But we were separated painfully by death and destruction all around us. And each time we've reincarnated, and managed to find each other, something else has happened to ruin our happiness, to prevent us from coming once more into the union of hearts and souls that is our true birthright."

"But why? If what you say is true, why would each lifetime end with us apart and not together?"

"I don't have all those answers, even though I once served as a high priestess and you were my second in the temple. Perhaps we and others of our kind have long been tied to the wheel of karma that we set in motion thousands of years ago. But one thing I do know, my darling Junela, if you don't mind me calling you that, is that this lifetime is different. This is the one where all the pieces come into balance again, not just for us as soul mates but for many other people, too. Balance is universal. It doesn't happen for isolated instances or individual. The current of love flows from us into everything around us. So we must act together in concert, as we were always meant to."

"But how?"

"By stopping Sister Sonia for one thing. Or at least keeping her from misusing the crystal. And there are some other aspects to it as well, although I am not entirely clear. I must meditate further on it. I do know that others are near who will help us, even though they may not know why."

"Others of the Children?"

Jenny smiled. "No, sweetheart, they are mostly just lost souls or, in some cases, greedy and venal human beings. We need help from those who are truly powerful, and I have sensed the presence of others in the vicinity—like that young woman we met this morning in the courtyard."

Carmen was puzzled. "The one who was looking for Philip. But how can she help us?"

"She's more than she appears, and there are those around her who are much, much more than they appear. They'll be here when the need is greatest. And that Indian woman who came in her car and put on a show for everyone."

"What? She was acting crazy."

"But her energy signature wasn't the least bit crazy. She knew exactly what she was doing, although I don't know what reason she had. But she did disrupt Sister Sonia's act, and that in itself must be part of the plan."

"Whose plan? A plan for what?"

"I'm not being patronizing, sweetheart. But you'll have to come to the understanding a little at a time and in your own way, in your own memories. For now, just know that we must put right something very terrible that happened long ago. We did not cause it, but we also did not act soon enough to stop it. This time we shall succeed, not only in the big karmic scheme of things, but you and I will be as one for the rest of this lifetime. That much I promise you. It is our time. The Goddess herself has granted a miracle, and it is our miracle, Junela."

Slowly and carefully, Jenny leaned forward and kissed Carmen on the lips. Their arms slipped about each other's waist, and the kiss continued, moving from tentative exploration of lips and tongues to hungry feasting as the heat of passion built steadily between them. Carmen almost felt as if she were sinking, and she finally submerged, not in a way that threatened her life but merely bathed her in the most unimaginable joy. She felt Jenny's hands stroke her cheeks, her neck, and then gently pull her closer. Carmen wanted exactly that— to be closer, to merge with her, blend their energies, their chi, their very souls. *Just as it always happened before*, came the unexpected thought. But she did not reject it this time, did not let it interrupt the flow of love between them. For it was perfectly, beautifully (if inexplicably) right in every way.

♦

Inside the manor house of the Children of Artemis community, Sister Sonia opened her wall safe and stood mutely before her treasure. It was once again glowing with its full light, and she could see into the depths of the colors, the movements of people, flashes of gold and white robes, and a face—the face of a man she now saw in every dream. She had even learned his name—Arkan. He was her mate, her other half. She didn't know how or why, but she would return to him. She would restore something that had been taken from them both. The crystal began to pulsate ever more powerfully and she was drawn into the dream again—into the sumptuous halls of her great palace, into the chamber—and for a moment she touched a vast void from which she recoiled in terror, a place familiar and yet so ominous and profoundly frightening she could not imagine ever having survived it. And yet she had been there. This much she knew. But it could not be allowed to happen again. And it would not. Her intuition was strong now. The transition was close. And she would be restored, she the goddess would be restored to all of her glory, all of her power. And the world itself would be transformed into a very different place, all thanks to her power and beneficence.

Finally, no longer able to stand the sensation of giddy anticipation at what would soon transpire, she gently closed the safe, shutting off the light from her view, even though the auric field of energy around her still pulsed at the same rate as the crystal, as if they shared one heartbeat. She no longer actually had to look at it to know the history it contained, the wisdom it had held, the power it conferred upon its keeper. And she was that keeper. She was bonded to this strange object as if they were symbiotic twins. That is how she had known someone else had opened that safe, had seen the object, had at least inadvertently drawn energy from it. And it only stood to reason that such a person had been an agent of evil—for Sonia at least, or more appropriately, the Lady Deirdre, incarnation of the goddess Artemis, whose consort would soon emerge from the crystal itself whole and alive. November 11: Over and over she reminded herself: the eleventh hour of the eleventh day of the eleventh month.

Chapter Fourteen

The One remains, the many change and pass;
Heaven's light forever shines, Earth's shadows fly;
Life, like a dome of many-coloured glass,
Stains the white radiance of Eternity.
—Percy Bysshe Shelley, "Adonais"

Benjamin Hawthorne was pursuing one of his favorite activities—synthesizing disparate information into a coherent picture, if indeed there were a coherent picture to be found. He was beginning to succeed. Alone in his suite, with two laptops running, one hooked up to a satellite phone for security reasons, the other linked to the hotel's modem jack, he swiveled back and forth between them. At the same time, he wore a hands-free earpiece and microphone hooked to yet another satellite phone while he "made the round" in a manner of speaking. One by one, he speed-dialed old friends and colleagues in various corners of the world, looking not so much for hard facts as speculation, guesswork, instincts. The men and women he spoke to were experienced, some might say hard-core, professionals who rarely overlooked even minor anomalies in the ebb and flow of activity in their areas of responsibility. That explained why they'd survived in a field where the failure rate was high, the political ramifications always hanging over them like the Sword of Damocles, and the risks of making fatal mistakes higher than they'd been in decades. No longer did a few agents' lives hang in the balance.

Now bad intelligence could cost hundreds of lives, or thousands, whereas good intelligence could save even more.

Slowly but surely, he limned out a vague but reasonably accurate sketch of Pantheon International. Its advantage in terms of maintaining a low profile was its image as a loose formation, more of an alliance of business interests, or so it looked upon superficial investigation. Someone at the heart of the organization knew that demonstrating an obviously centralized or rigidly structured hierarchy was almost guaranteed to draw more scrutiny than an informal sort of energy cartel with apparently divergent individual interests that would keep them from acting effectively in concert. But all of this, Benjamin had discovered, or at last surmised, was more illusion than fact. His assistant in his D.C. office, and the two staffers in the London office had worked all night pulling electronic files on all the major figures involved in Pantheon, along with as much of their business dealings as could be discovered. This was not easy. In a world where shell corporations proliferated like colonies of rabbits, the most important maneuvers were veiled by layers of bureaucracy and legal filings. Benjamin knew that finding every thread was an impossible task in terms of the time he had for research, so he needed to drill down quickly.

The fax machine beeped quietly and began to spit out paper. He kept working until it had finished, then picked up the stack and leafed through it. The file was from a friend at MI5 who kept him up-to-date on "interesting" developments or findings that might bear fruit, if not now then in the future. He found little of interest as he skimmed through it and was about to shove all of it back into a folder when he reached the second-to-last page—a photograph of two men sitting back-to-back at two tables. The caption identified the location as the Starbucks at Heathrow's international terminal two days previous. A jotted note in the margin said simply: "Don't know the chap with the reddish hair, but the Asian fellow is a big shot with Pantheon. Doesn't get out much either. First time we've caught him on camera on our patch. Name's Matsumoto. Odd thing is, he got right back on a plane to Japan. Didn't get to see much, did he?"

Benjamin smiled. He did know the other chap—Mickey Dandridge. And now things might be coming together just a little. He could think of only two plausible reasons a man like Yohiro Matsumoto would waste that many hours flying from Tokyo to London for a meeting that lasted fewer than thirty minutes. Either he had been delegated to oversee Dandridge because of some internal difficulty, or Matsumoto had a very personal stake in the outcome of Dandridge's activities. Either way, he now had place to focus—Matsumoto. He started another round of calls and sent new instructions to his researchers. When he stood up and stretched, he once again felt his age, several years past the usual retirement point. Still fit and strong, he couldn't deny that a lifetime of stress and a not-insignificant number of field missions had taken their toll on his body. Much as he'd rather still be in the field, he knew those days were behind him. He wasn't exactly a desk jockey, perhaps, but the sensation was too close for comfort. With a sigh, he sat down again. This was where he could be most useful, and this was where he would stay. There was a time when he would have been far too anxious about protecting his family to sit here compiling information. But he had every faith in Laura Nez. He'd trained her himself, and between that and her unerring devotion to Connor and, by extension, to Katy, he knew they were in good hands. The Carlisles, even if Benjamin never quite understood their talents, which could hardly be explained by rational means, were the icing on the cake. He was well aware that their loyalty to the Broadhurst women, beginning with Connor's grandmother, was absolute. Their tradition and the basic tenets of belief of their Circle made it incumbent upon each member to protect, with their lives if necessary, the high priestess and her heirs. Connor might shy away from that title as if she'd put her hand on a hot stove, but there was no getting around it. Nor for Katy either, even if she had yet to discover that truth.

The Carlisles, true to their word, did not let Katy out of their sight. They took turns being in her vicinity so as not to draw attention, and William was rather foolishly proud of his slightly baffled, yet nonetheless hearty country-squire demeanor. "Came with the wife," he'd said. "She loves all this magical stuff. Don't see much in it myself, but if it does anything for all those...er...women's complaints, you know, then all the better." After a few encounters with his bluff, good-natured skepticism, most of the disciples had stopped bothering him, which is to say, sounding him out for donation potential. He left just enough of an impression that he might write a check that they were appeased.

William tried not to fiddle with his tie since Benjamin had given him a marvelously ingenious miniature camera fitted into a rather gaudy tie clip. On an ordinary day, Lord Carlisle would not be caught dead wearing such a thing, but it was all in a good cause for now. He also doubted he'd encounter anyone he knew. He only had to remember to keep moving around so that the images Laura was capturing and taping wouldn't end up consisting of ten minutes of William choosing a scone from the tea table. The exercise was rather like having someone looking over one's shoulder every second, he thought uncomfortably. A second device was fitted under his lapel—a powerful microphone attached to a transmitter that fitted under his jacket in the small of his back. He only hoped he'd pick up something more useful than his own vague blatherings, and the inane reassurances of the Artemis disciples that Sister Sonia's work here was both miraculous and worthy of financial support.

♦

Katy felt a touch on her shoulder. Half expecting Ellen, she turned around with a ready smile. However, it was Jenny Carpenter, who took Katy's hand and squeezed it gently. "I missed you yesterday at the healing tent."

"Sorry. I was going looking for you when all that commotion

started, and it made me rather nervous. I decided I'd better come back today and look for Philip."

"He just left in good spirits. I imagine you'll see him back in London when you get there. You're an American, aren't you?"

"Yes, I am."

"But you've worked in England for a while."

"Not too long," said Katy, reverting to her cover story. "It's only temporary."

"Hmm. But we all tend to end up where we're supposed to be at any given time, don't you think?"

"I suppose so," said Katy cautiously. "How did you end up here, if you don't mind my asking?" She knew a great deal more about Jenny Carpenter than she cared to admit, but it would be interesting to hear the story from Jenny.

"I was confused and rather pathetic when I first showed up at the community," said Jenny without a trace of self-pity.

"And Sister Sonia helped you?"

Jenny smiled. "Not in quite the way you might think. But yes, she's part of the reason I've found myself, so to speak."

"You must be one of the inner circle then," said Katy, deciding to delve a little. "I heard people talking about the disciples."

Jenny laughed out loud. "Oh, not at all. I'm hardly on Sister Sonia's list of favorites."

"Then why does she let you stay."

"It isn't really a question of 'letting' me stay—more a question of not knowing what else to do about it."

"You don't sound like a believer in the goddess omniscience thing."

"No one is omniscient, Katy. But some of us do have access to more information than others."

"You mean about the Children of Artemis?"

"No," said Jenny, cocking her head to one side and looking at Katy appraisingly. "About people, about life, about events both past and future."

Katy frowned. This was beginning to sound a little far-fetched.

But she stayed with it. "You mean the transition Sister Sonia's talking about, the end of times."

"There's no such thing, really. It's just another of the illusions people like to grab onto so they have something to be afraid of."

"That seems a rather odd comment coming from someone at this community."

"I'm not here to further anyone's delusions," said Jenny. "But I am here for a reason. Just as I suspect you are."

Katy felt her heart quake slightly at the insinuation that she might be there under false pretenses. "I only came here as a favor to a friend."

"That, my friend, is true. But not the one you've told me and not for any reasons you chose to give the gatekeepers."

Katy didn't know quite what to say. There was no menace in Jenny, no challenge, no sense of being interrogated. "But I—"

Jenny took her hand. "Please...don't worry about it. Everything becomes clear at the precise moment it needs to be so. You certainly don't owe *me* any explanations. But my intuition tells me that we will be meeting again very soon and under somewhat different circumstances, not altogether pleasant perhaps, but in the long run it will be all right."

"In this 'brave new world' of Sister Sonia's?" said Katy with an edge of mockery.

"There is no other world but this one, or more precisely, there is only one universe driven by one Source. But that does not mean that the universe is actually limited to what we can comprehend from our narrow human perspective. This experience we're having right here, right now, is like looking through a tiny peephole in a door. We can't possibly begin to grasp the size and shape of the room as it actually is. It's the same way with the world. Almost no one sees the infinite variations layered one on top of the other so that in essence we all live in different worlds, unaware that the past, the present, and the future lie together along a single multidimensional and infinite spiral."

Katy raised both eyebrows. "I'm afraid you've lost me completely."

"No, I haven't really lost you. What I'm saying is simply something you're not accustomed to hearing. And it does require some thought. It might help if you were to consult someone close to you—someone with experience in these matter, like that distinguished gentleman in the tweed jacket and the lady in the elegant hat who never stray out of sight of you. You're fortunate to have such powerful friends because you're likely going to need them. But don't worry. Your reasons for being here are quite safe with me. If anything, I welcome it because it's a sign that events are unfolding as I saw they might."

Before Katy could even react to this astounding display of perception on Jenny's part, she added yet another bombshell. "You'll need your mother, too, by the way."

Katy almost let her jaw drop. "You don't know my mother."

"Not personally. I don't even know precisely who she is. But I sense her presence near you, and it's a powerful one. She must have some role to play in what's about to happen."

"But how…?" Katy's words were drowned out by the squawk of feedback from a loudspeaker and in an instant Jenny had melted into the crowd.

With the news that Philip Darcy had already left the compound, Katy was left not knowing what to do. If Jenny were to be believed, and instinct told her she could, then Katy had no excuse for being here. And if Jenny could pick out the connection between Katy and the Carlisles, then perhaps someone else could as well, particularly Sister Sonia. She was turning to leave, not wanting to sit through another tirade when she saw him—the man William had followed from the train station. And worst of all, he was looking directly at her, appraisingly, even arrogantly, as though he did not care whether she knew. The trill of anxiety that flooded through her showed up instantly in Ellen's awareness. She sent a mental message to William that something was wrong, and at the same time tried an old magic technique of trying to see through the eyes of another person with whom one was closely connected. But it wasn't working. Ellen's primary psychic connection was with

Connor and the others of the Circle. Though Katy was of the same bloodline, she was far from being an initiate in any sense. Thus, parts of her mind and awareness, pathways that would be opened through study and spiritual discipline, remained closed and unused. She scanned the crowd near Katy, trying to discern the source of the girl's trepidation. William, too, had moved closer and was the first to spot Dandridge, even though the man had turned away. There was something unmistakable about someone's back, their way of walking. And having followed him some distance, William was very familiar with that particular physique. He relayed this information to Ellen, who responded instantly. *If he's here now, then something's going to happen, something to do with the crystal. And I don't think Katy is simply afraid because she saw him. I think he saw her and recognizes her from yesterday. He must have been here then, too. Maybe he even saw her near the house.*

Stay close, let's see what happens, thought William. *But at the first hint of trouble for Katy, we're getting her out of here.* He stepped aside from the crowd, letting Ellen stay close to Katy, and called Laura with his cell phone. "Dandridge is here on the grounds," he said tersely. "He's bound to be up to no good. And Katy saw him too."

"It's time to get her out of there."

"My thoughts precisely." After a pause, he said, "Now where the hell have they got to?

♦

With her usual disregard for common precautions, Katy had decided to ignore the presence of Mickey Dandridge and go in search of Jenny Carpenter. She had a lot of questions and hated cryptic answers as much as her mother did. Thus, it was purely by chance that she was passing the side of the healing tent when she heard a familiar voice, one she'd listened to less then twenty-four hours before in the office inside the manor house. She didn't know which man was speaking, but if she had to guess, she'd say it was the dark-haired man. Something about the voice seemed to fit the face she'd seen. She stopped where she was and folded herself up against the drape of canvas that formed a sort of foyer into the healing tent.

"You still don't have it, do you?"

"She's in her office, for God's sake."

"So when is she due out here for her big speech?"

"Twenty minutes ago. But for some reason she's locked herself in and keeps saying that everyone will just have to wait on the timing of the gods."

"Fucking loony tune," snarled the other voice. "I've got a deadline. I can't wait around here much longer. There's something fishy going on. Someone else is nosing around, too. I can feel it in my bones."

"Look, as soon as she clears out, I'll just nip in and grab the damn thing. But you'd better be ready to take it. I'm heading straight for the back of the garden where the shrubs are tall enough to hide us. I'm not going to risk getting caught by Sonia."

"Oh, what now? You're afraid of the big, bad goddess?"

There was a long pause. "You'd be afraid, too, if you knew her, and if you'd seen some of the things she can do."

"I'm not afraid of some two-bit bimbo in a costume. Just get your ass in gear. The minute she hits the stage, you get the damn crystal."

Katy flinched back as a figure came striding out of the tent. Fortunately, he didn't look back. It was Dandridge. A moment later, the dark-haired disciple of Sister Sonia left, much less quickly and much more reluctantly.

"What are you doing here?" a voice whispered, startling the daylights out of her.

"Eavesdropping," she replied, relieved to see Ellen at her elbow.

"It's time to leave," said Ellen. "William and I have a sense something is going to happen, something much more disruptive than our friend Laura's performance yesterday."

"You bet there is," said Katy, before she quickly relayed the gist of the conversation she'd overheard.

"All the more reason why we need to leave."

"No, I have to find Jenny Carpenter."

"The girl you talked to yesterday, the one who was with Carmen Waters?"

"Yes, and I have to warn her."

"Warn her? Good heavens, child, what for?" asked Ellen.

"We know she brought the crystal here, and...I can't explain it. I just have to tell her. What if those men are the ones who killed the people on that island? They must have found out she survived. They might hurt her before they leave with the crystal. They might even abduct her or something."

"I'm more concerned with you not getting hurt," replied Ellen, as she felt William's energy approaching behind her. When he joined them, she gave an even briefer résumé of the current situation. To her utter surprise, William agreed with Katy.

"The Carpenter girl's got to be warned. No way around it. But I'll find her. You get Katy out of here."

"No," said Katy, more firmly entrenched than ever. "She's my friend, sort of. We can do this together. She already told me she knew you guys were with me, looking out for me."

"She what?!" exclaimed Ellen.

"It's a long story. I'll tell you later."

William quickly informed Laura by phone of the latest development. She in turn called Benjamin, who had stationed a couple of backup people near the turnoff from the main road to narrow lane leading to the compound. "If Dandridge tries get out that way, they'll stop him. I want you to work your way closer to a spot down the hill from your observation post. But don't get too near. You are definitely persona non grata at the Children of Artemis headquarters."

"Yes, and they've beefed up security today. They even have movable barricades across the entrance."

"Don't try to sneak in, but if anything goes down that William and Ellen can't handle..." He left the sentence unfinished, but Laura didn't need any more explanation. Sometimes crises had to be tackled on the good old third-dimensional earth plane. And that would be Laura's specialty. She didn't carry a gun. Even working under Benjamin's aegis, it would take some maneuvering to get approval for a carry permit in England. And they hadn't yet thought it necessary to go to such lengths. She regretted that decision at the moment, but she did have a wickedly sharp K-Bar knife in a sheath in her boot. It was extremely effective at close range, though she had no desire to see any situation arise that would call for violence. Still, if any blood were shed today, it would not be Katy's or the Carlisles' either.

♦

It took Katy, William, and Ellen surprisingly few minutes to locate Jenny Carpenter, and that may well have been because Jenny was looking for Katy. They had just traversed the lawn and walked around the right wing of the manor house when Jenny appeared at the end of a garden path leading away from the house.

At the same moment, Katy and Jenny both said, "Someone's trying to steal the crystal."

They looked at each other in amazement. "But how would you know that?" said Katy.

"I just sort of saw it happening—and something much worse." She nodded to Ellen and William. "Introductions later perhaps. We have to get—"

The rest of her words were drowned out by a roar from the burgeoning crowd. Then they heard the familiar voice. "Greetings, my beloved children of Artemis."

"Damn," said Katy. "She's not in her office. That guy who works here said he'd get it as soon as she was outside."

"What guy that works here?"

Katy quickly described him.

Jenny nodded grimly. "Karl. He's bad news. More of an enforcer, I'd say, than a disciple. I think he may be the one who went to Palm Springs and killed Carmen's sister."

"Does Carmen know?" asked Katy in disbelief.

"Not yet. It's too much for her right now. And I'm only guessing from things I've overheard and things I've…seen, sort of."

"I know…seeing and not seeing. Whatever. The magic stuff can wait, too. Where's her office?"

"On the second floor at the other end of the house. Come on."

William grabbed Katy's arm. "You can't just go barging in there. We have no idea whether this man is armed. And we know he's working with Dandridge. According to your grandfather, he's as dangerous as they come."

Jenny paused. "Dandridge?"

"Someone who is determined to get that crystal. He's probably paying Karl to steal it."

"But why?"

The words were out of Katy's mouth before she realized the significance they might have for Jenny. "He works for some big multinational company that may have stolen the rest of the crystal from where it was originally found." She stopped as she watched Jenny turn pale. "I'm sorry. You know about that—I mean, you were there on that island where it happened."

Jenny's face turned rigid. "Yes, I was. And if this man is one of the murderers, then he's going to get what's coming to him." She ran into the house before they could stop her, and Katy was right on her heels.

"Bloody hell!" said William, running after them, with Ellen at his shoulder. He tossed the phone to Ellen. "Call Laura. We need her *now*."

♦

Laura's phone earpiece chirped. It was Ellen, breathless and frightened. "Katy's followed Jenny Carpenter into the house. Jenny's determined to stop Karl, and Dandridge has got to be close by. We need help. They're headed upstairs."

Laura's sixth sense was already in full operation. Ignoring Benjamin's instructions to simply get *near* the compound, she had already worked her way around the perimeter fence to a spot not easily observed by the crowd or the disciples and acolytes milling about. The fence was a formidable one, but Laura was sufficiently athletic enough, and certainly terrified enough for her friends' safety that she was over it in seconds, and running between out-buildings to get to the house. When Ellen's call came, she was close, very close with only a last few yards of open ground to cover. She didn't care who noticed her now. She flew, her feet barely touching the ground. Reaching the house, she entered the same door Katy had used the day before and dashed down the corridor looking for a way up.

◆

Mickey Dandridge, having little to no faith in Karl's commit-ment to this mission, had elected not to wait quite so far away. He was only a hundred yards or so from the rear of the house, con-cealed behind some boxwood hedges when he saw the woman come racing around the back and into the door. Even at that dis-tance, he knew immediately it was the same woman from the pre-vious day, the one who'd caused the disturbance in the courtyard. He was right! This was all some sort of setup and someone else was after the crystal. He took off toward the house, reaching for the gun holstered in the small of his back. It had been thoughtful of Matsumoto to pass it to him before they parted company at Heathrow.

◆

Karl was absurdly nervous. He'd stolen, robbed, cheated, and strong-armed people his while life. The first time he'd come snoop-ing into this office, it had seemed so much easier. He was just watch-ing out for number one: himself. And he'd figured there had to be something valuable that should by all rights end up in his pocket. But once he'd seen the crystal, once he'd felt its effect—and much more important, seen what it had done to transform good old Sonia—his normal acquisitiveness had turned to dread. There was no rational explanation for it either. And now he was trapped. Dandridge would have no qualms whatsoever about killing him or maiming him for life, and this boss of his sounded like the devil incarnate. So even if he somehow got past Mickey, there was always some other terror waiting in the shadows. Then there was Sister Sonia. She was beyond spooky now, and he had this weird feeling, probably left over from one of those sick fairy tales his mum used to tell him, that the would-be goddess could strike him dead on the spot with just one hard look, or maybe a lightning bolt thrown in for dramatic effect. As if that wasn't enough to give him a first-class case of heebie-jeebies, there was the crystal itself. He'd have to touch it to get it out of the safe. He didn't have a fanciful enough imagination to think it might turn him into some sort of god-like superman in a matter of minutes. After all, Sonia had changed over time; it had taken weeks and the transformation was so subtle at first that no one really noticed.

As Karl stood in front of the safe, the only thing he really wanted to do was run far and fast, money or no money. Instead, with the attitude of a man whose life was going rapidly down the flusher, he took out his tools and quickly got to work. This time it was only a matter of a couple of minutes before he had the door unlocked. He put down the bits of wire and metal and reached for the handle. Slowly, he opened it, this time prepared to squint. The light was as brilliant as ever and he reached behind him for a scarf Sonia had draped over a chair. Gingerly covering the crystal, he grasped it in both hands and pulled it from its resting place.

◆

Outside, surrounded by several hundred enthralled believers, Sonia suddenly screamed bloody murder. The crowd shrank back in fear. Her entire demeanor changed. No longer was she the radiant, lovely goddess. Her face contorted with an ugly rage—blinding, murderous, insane fury. Someone had violated the crystal. She knew the moment it was touched. Without another word, she spun around and ran toward the front door of the house leaving the crowd gaping in stunned silence.

♦

Anyone who was not deaf as post and within a mile of the Children of Artemis compound could hardly have missed the horrible sound of Sonia's outcry since she had been standing directly in front of the microphone, and the speakers for the sound system were easily powerful enough for an outdoor rock concert. Everyone in the house was momentarily frozen in shock. Jenny, William, Ellen, and Katy had just reached the top of the stairs and started down the corridor toward Sonia's private quarters. Laura was at the bottom of the stairs staring up. Dandridge had entered the house and was loping down the hallway.

Karl, for his part, had nearly dropped the crystal when he'd heard the horrible sound. For a brief and terrifying moment, he thought the sound had come from the crystal itself. Then he realized not only that it must be Sonia, but that somehow she knew...in that very instant he'd touched it, she'd felt it. And nothing would stop her retribution. He dropped the crystal on the desk and ran...right into four people headed straight at him. Jenny, in the lead, was the only one he recognized. "What are you doing here?" he shouted. "Get out of my way!"

"Where's the crystal?" she demanded, refusing to budge.

"In there," he panted. "In the office. I don't want the goddamn thing. Let me out of here." He shoved past them, only to encounter someone else he recognized—the crazy Indian woman from the day before. "You? What the fuck is going on?"

"Yes," said a voice behind them. "What the fuck *is* going on?"

♦

Laura whirled and found herself facing Mickey Dandridge. He apparently had no qualms about gun laws in England for clutched in his massive hand was a 9-mm automatic, its little eye pointed right at Laura's chest. Her mind automatically calculated the distance between them. Too far. She had no chance to disarm him. Her only thought was still of Katy and the Carlisles. Even if she took a round, she still might be able to take out Dandridge before she died, if she didn't take a direct head shot or one to the heart. In the split second between thinking and moving, Sister Sonia provided the perfect distraction. She hadn't made a sound coming up the stairs and she was right behind Dandridge before he heard her. He turned, startled, and fired. In the same instant, Laura, her instincts honed from years of training, was on him, knocking him flat. The gun flew out of his hand and beyond his reach. He sprang to his feet, but Laura's roundhouse kick completely surprised him. Had he been standing anyplace else, he would have just gone down hard. Instead, out of position on the landing, he went downstairs, headfirst.

The first thing Laura did was to secure the gun; the second was to look over the banister for Dandridge. She expected to see him lying in a crumpled heap. But the hallway was empty. He had somehow survived both the kick to the head and the fall. He was gone.

She turned to find Jenny hunched over Sonia's inert form. William was on the phone to the police. Katy, backed against a wall, watched the entire scene with utter horror. Ellen reached for Katy's hand and held it tight. They watched as flecks of red foam bubbled up between Sonia's lips as if she were determined to speak. Jenny leaned closer.

"Not…time…yet" was all she could make out.

"What's happened?" came a quiet, small voice behind Ellen. Carmen Waters appeared in the hall, having just emerged from her own room. "Oh, my God," she said, looking down at the blood that had stained the entire front of Sister Sonia's pristine white goddess ensemble. "Is she…?"

Jenny looked up at her, a strange and unreadable expression

on her face. "She's dead, Junela. The Lady Deirdre is dead."

"But I thought you said she was going to try to make history repeat itself, that she had something she had to do in all this, and that's why we had to stay."

"Apparently, she did have a part in this," said Jenny, tears flooding down her cheeks. "But this time it was to die before she could repeat a mistake that cost so many people their lives. She's paid for that now with her own."

"So then it's over."

"No, I'm afraid not. It means there's someone else out there we have to worry about now, someone else who has the same idea—and no scruples about following through on it."

Laura looked down at Jenny. "Would you mind telling me just what's going on here, and what you two are talking about?"

"I will, soon enough. You have my word. But first, we have to put away the crystal, and I have to ask all of you to please not discuss it with the police. This has to be seen as a robbery or a personal attack on Sonia, or something like that. If they were to confiscate the crystal, there's no telling what sort of damage could be done. It has to stay where we, where all of us can protect it."

Laura looked to Ellen for guidance. She was out of her depth on this crystal thing. Ellen nodded. "I think Jenny is right. The police are never going to understand the potential ramifications. They would just think of it as some item worth stealing, but not know why."

Suddenly, Jenny looked around. "Where's Karl?"

"Karl who?" said Laura.

"The one who was helping Dandridge. He broke into Sonia's safe."

But Karl was nowhere to be seen. Since he couldn't have gone past them, he'd taken the servant's stairs at the end of the hall. Immediately, Jenny leaped to her feet and dashed to Sonia's office. To her relief, the crystal lay right where Karl had left it on the desk. She whisked it up in its wrapping and thrust it into the safe, but before she swung the door closed William stopped her.

"Apparently, this Karl fellow knew how to break in. But does anyone else have a key to the safe?"

This had not occurred to Jenny. "No, not even Alan—her consort, I guess you'd call him, or at least she called him that."

"And where is old Alan?"

"Probably miles from here," said Carmen. "He hasn't been particularly happy these days. And I would imagine he took whatever cash he could lay his hands on and hit the road."

"I suggest we remove the crystal from the premises," said William. "The police won't allow us to stay here, or to come back in. The Scene of Crime officers will be swarming all over the place."

Jenny thought for a moment, then turned to Katy and Laura. "We need to get you two out of here. William already called the police, so they know he's here, and it's natural his wife would stay with him. I'm going to say that I was giving them a tour of the house when Sister Sonia came rushing up the stairs followed by a man with a gun. He shot her, and I shoved him and struggled for the gun. He dropped it and then fell down the stairs but got up and ran away. Here," she said to Laura, "give me the gun." Laura handed it to her and watched with some degree of admiration for Jenny's clearheadedness as she wiped it with the hem of her robe to remove Laura's prints and substitute her own. "They'll be angry that I've smudged away his fingerprints by handling the gun, but I'll just act shocked and stupid."

"You're anything but that," said Ellen warmly. "And you're right that there's no need to have Laura and Katy involved in this."

William held out his hand for the weapon. "Let's confuse it a little further, and I'll take charge and act like the lord of the manor looking after the dangerous implements."

In the distance, the distinctive wail of the British police siren could be heard approaching the manor house. With the lanes so congested, they had a little time left. Jenny took the crystal shard from the safe and handed it to Katy. "Put this in your bag and just walk out the back door. There's a gate in the fence directly east of the house. That way you can get to your car and be out of here before they start setting up barricades. There should be one incredible traffic snarl by now."

Katy looked at her dubiously. "You want *me* to keep this?"

"For now. All of you are good people. I can tell, believe me. And you're all part of whatever is playing out here in this time. Remember what I said, too. Your mother is important in this, and she can help. Where are you staying in York?"

William quickly scribbled down the name of the hotel and their suite number. "Call as soon as you can. We'll come and get you and Carmen if you'd like, or you can come to us. It doesn't matter what time." He handed it to her and Carmen slipped it into the pocket of her gown. "Now we'll have to act more like strangers," he said to Jenny, "at least until later. We'd better get back into the hallway. Someone's bound to come up here any minute."

Oddly, none of the loyal disciples had dared to investigate the commotion on the upper floor. Most of them were huddled in the dining room on the ground floor instead. And when they heard the police sirens, most of them wished to be anywhere but the home of the Children of Artemis.

Laura and Katy made good their escape, mingling with the milling crowd and then making their way casually toward the path that led to the gate Jenny had told them about. Laura slipped her knife out of her boot sheath and up her sleeve, just on the off chance Mr. Dandridge not only had nine lives but enough determination to risk arrest by hanging around after murdering someone.

"So do you have any idea what Jenny's talking about?" asked Laura as they half-trotted down the path.

"Not really. But I do feel as if I've known her for a long time, which is kind of odd. And ever since I first met her, which was only yesterday, though it seems longer, I knew I could trust her."

"Are you nervous about carrying that thing?" Laura said, pointing to Katy's shoulder bag.

"Kind of. It feels strange—heavy but alive...I know that sounds ridiculous."

"Everything about this is slightly absurd," said Laura. "But so is life. We'll need to circle around this lane to get to my car. It's okay if they find yours still parked there in the morning. You can just say someone offered you a ride because you were too nervous to drive back. But Connor's rental will lead them right to me and to her and to Benjamin. I think we need to brief him before all this hits the fan, and he can decide how much to tell the locals about Sister Sonia, and the rest of it."

"Hard to believe she's really dead."

"Why? You didn't actually suspect she might be immortal did you?" Laura smiled.

Katy gave her a look that was worth a thousand words. "No, of course not. I'm not quite that naive. But she had so much life in her, so much moxy, I guess you'd call it. Hard to imagine anyone getting the better of her. And I think she believed it, all of it. That's the weird part. I think she really thought she was someone else."

Laura pondered that for a moment just as they came in sight of the gate. "Who knows? Maybe she was."

Chapter Fifteen

For death and life, in ceaseless strife,
Beat wild on this world's shore,
And all our calm is in that balm—
Not lost but gone before.
—Caroline Elizabeth Sarah Norton,
"Not Lost But Gone Before"

YORKSHIRE

Chief Inspector Reginald Lindstrom knew he had stepped into an enormous mess when he arrived at the Children of Artemis compound. The local constabulary had been only partially successful in restoring some semblance of order to the scene, and the sergeant had sheepishly admitted that perhaps dozens of people who had been present when the crime was committed were now long gone. After receiving a report of a shooting, they had responded as quickly as possible, but just as Jenny Carpenter had predicted, the traffic choking the lanes had delayed their arrival considerably. Then they were faced with an onslaught of fleeing visitors whom they'd had to restrain somewhat forcibly. And, by the time they'd reached the actual scene of crime and viewed the body, they barely knew where to begin the investigation. This was highly irregular.

York, despite a colorfully violent history in terms of being conquered through the centuries by various political factions, was not exactly a hotbed of violence. Yes, there had been complaints from neighbors about the Children of Artemis, about their occasionally loud gatherings and their suspected immorality. But never had there been a hint of anything particularly criminal. But the stakes had escalated from mere nuisance to outright murder. He was actually deeply relieved in some way that it was just a murder. When he'd first heard the reports of panic coming over the radio, he'd had horrifying visions of some Jonestown debacle with dozens or even hundreds of people trying to hurry along the end of the world by quaffing down spiked Kool-Aid.

Two Artemis disciples had been discovered in the office shredding documents as fast as they could, and although the police had put a stop to it the moment they were found, there was no way of knowing what had been destroyed. Lindstrom expected that the first to go had been the files on the disciples themselves and certainly the membership rosters. One distraught female disciple reported that the safe where cash was kept had been opened and virtually emptied. She had no precise figures, but the income from the previous week, held in abeyance until a deposit could be made on the following Monday, was in excess of £20,000, mostly in cash. The checks had been left behind, presumably useless to whoever had cleaned out the safe.

Robbery seemed the likely motive here, but Lindstrom withheld his opinions for the time being. There was also the possibility of some personal grudge against the victim. The same woman mentioned that two of the disciples were missing—Alan Durn (Sister Sonia's 'consort,' whatever that meant) and a man named Karl Jensen. All this would have pointed to an 'inside job' of some sort, perhaps a conspiracy between the two (who certainly would be found before they could leave England), except for the testimony of the witnesses to the shooting, who were even now being held in the office of the now deceased Sister Sonia, under the watchful eye of a constable who would brook no conversation among them.

The witnesses presented yet another headache. Among them were Lord William Carlisle and Her Ladyship Ellen Carlisle. Chief Inspector Williams was of the old school, unlike some of his younger colleagues. While he did not overtly favor the word of a "gentleman" over that of a commoner (he'd seen murder in every social class), he still could not help but show a certain deference to the titled nobility of his country as long as they behaved as such. His brief discussion with Lord Carlisle had already eliminated any doubts he might have had about the man's honesty. Call it pure instinct, but there it was. And Lady Ellen had been not only cooperative but seemingly sympathetic to the Herculean task of sorting all this out. Neither of them had objected to being sequestered in the office. Neither had tried in any way to pull rank or threaten to call the Chief Constable, or any of the things they might easily have done, since it appeared they were truly innocent bystanders who were most definitely in the wrong place at the wrong time. In stark contrast, the flock of visitors, acolytes, and commune dwellers were all clamoring to be allowed to leave. He would leave the exit interviews and the collection of their personal particulars (names, addresses and so forth) to the detective constables who were now arriving on the scene.

The two Artemis women bothered him a bit, not because he was fairly sure from their demeanor that they were lovers, or at least fast friends, but because he was convinced they knew more about this than they had already let on. Once he finished his tour of the house and grounds, he would sit them all down separately and see whose stories conformed and whose did not.

At the moment, he had one very dead would-be cult leader, one 9-mm handgun surrendered by Lord Carlisle immediately to the first officer on the scene, and one escaped perpetrator who might or might not be injured.

He decided to begin with the Carlisles. At least he could spare them any more hours of confinement.

◆

"No, can't say as I'd ever seen the chap," said William, drawing on his pipe in his most avuncular fashion. He had decided to tone down but still retain the country squire image, sensing that it would be reassuring to Chief Inspector Lindstrom, who struck him as a man who wanted both people and events to fit into his life view. "But it did happen so quickly. One moment were walking along behind that young lady, the Carpenter girl, when we heard feet running up the main staircase. It was Sister Sonia, quite beside herself about something—thieves, I think—but it was hard to make out. She was positively wild-eyed, to be honest. And just as Miss Carpenter tried to stop her and get some idea of what was going on, this fellow came up the stairs behind Sister Sonia. She turned around and confronted him when he tried to get past her. Then he shot her."

Lindstrom looked up from his notes. "He didn't say anything at all—threaten her, demand something, express some outrage?"

"No, that's the curious thing. He just shot her, as if he had intended to do it all along. Does that make sense?"

"In a way, perhaps," said Lindstrom. "And then what happened?"

Miss Carpenter acted rather courageously, I must say. She was between us and the chap with the gun and within a few feet of him once Sonia fell. She charged right at him. I think it rather caught him off-guard, don't you know. He was expecting us all to cower back, but she leaped at him and the gun was waving about in the air. I shoved my wife behind me, and started toward them, but that's when the man caught his foot on something or tripped. I'm not sure. But he let go of the gun and toppled backward. Since he was very near the head of the stairs, down he went. Of course, I expected he'd break his neck, but a few seconds later I looked over and there was no sign of him."

"What happened to the gun then?"

"Miss Carpenter picked it up—just in case he came back, I think—and then she handed it to me for safekeeping. I don't believe she felt particularly comfortable having it."

"But you're familiar with firearms, Your Lordship?"

"Heavens yes, ever since I was a lad. Though we don't keep much in the way of revolvers or automatic handguns—not really the thing you know, except for an old World War II piece of my father's. Only hunting rifles and the odd double-barrel for the annual shooting party down our way."

Lindstrom, having obtained a detailed description of the shooter, politely dismissed Lord Carlisle and asked to see his wife.

She told much the same story with little variation, although she neglected to mention that her husband had thrust her into the background. Lindstrom suspected that had been a touch of masculine vanity on Lord Carlisle's part and welcomed the discrepancy. Identical stories of eyewitnesses always raised red flags. It spoke of conspiracy or coaching, neither of which would speak well for those involved. She also thought the man had caught his jacket on the newel post, which had then caused his fall, and that he had let go of the gun as he fell because he was trying to grab on to something. Lastly, she could not be absolutely certain that the man was clean-shaven. She'd had the impression of a mustache, or perhaps just more than a day's growth of facial hair. She called him red-haired, and William had used sandy-blond. All in all, though, it was still close enough to employ a sketch artist and Lindstrom politely asked if they would be willing to help in that regard. To his surprise, Ellen drew forth a sketch she'd been making while they waited. "I know your people are experts, but I fancy myself a bit of an artist. Perhaps you could see if the others concur with my observations. It might help."

Lindstrom was impressed with the work. It was a precisely rendered pencil drawing, and if this did indeed accurately represent the man they'd seen, then his job had just grown immensely easier. Of course, what Ellen didn't tell him what that she'd seen this man on more than one occasion and his features were engraved in her memory. The tiny discrepancies she'd thrown in as to hair length and such were merely window dressing to maintain the fiction that they'd all been distracted by the horrible shooting of Sister Sonia.

Lindstrom invited them to leave and had a constable escort them to their car after obtaining their local address.

Jenny Carpenter was hard to read. She was calm but not too

calm, distraught over the death of Sister Sonia, but clearly not heartbroken about it. She freely admitted that she had begun to see that the Children of Artemis was not all it purported to be and had intended to leave there before long, as soon as she made arrangements to travel. Her version of the events again differed only slightly. She added a touch of verisimilitude to the hand-to-hand struggle by describing the man's horribly bad breath, as if he were a smoker and a coffee drinker who was lacking in the oral hygiene department, and the overpowering scent of cheap cologne, which she could not identify but seemed to remind her of a male relative from long ago. She was also convinced that the man was an American, although she maintained he hadn't said anything other than to hiss, "Let go of me, you stupid bitch."

She expressed some degree of remorse, however, that she might have been responsible for shoving him down the stairs and admitted she was both disappointed and relieved to discover that he was able to leave under his own power. "I know he shot Sister Sonia in cold blood, Chief Inspector, but still, to cause someone's death. It's very bad karma, you know."

Lindstrom sighed. He'd probably hear a great deal more about karma today than he'd ever care to know. He told her he would have to ask for the robe she wore as evidence, even though the bloodstains would no doubt turn out to match the blood type of the victim. Jenny had knelt beside her and attempted some sort of emergency treatment. But the SOC officers had already advised him that their preliminary examination indicated she was shot through the heart and would have died almost instantly, certainly within very few minutes.

She asked if she might go and change. Lindstrom was tempted to send a female constable with her, but there was something so earnest, so honest and clear about Jenny Carpenter that he couldn't quite bring himself to treat her shabbily, as if she were a suspect who must be strip-searched. He compromised by asking if there were some place on this floor she could find additional clothing since her sleeping quarters were in one of the dormitories.

"Yes, she replied. "I can borrow something from my friend, Carmen. Her room is on this corridor."

"Well then, that will be all right. First, I'm going to ask one of the SOC officers to take samples from your hands. Then the constable will conduct you to the room and, er…ask—Miss Waters, is it?—to come in here and be interviewed."

Jenny patiently permitted the technician to swab the blood stains on her hands, then waited in the corridor while the constable showed Carmen into Sister Sonia's office where Lindstrom was conducting the interviews. Jenny was immensely relieved that the crystal was beyond police search. She'd left the safe open, lending more credence to the idea that there had been a conspiracy to rob Sonia and the Children of Artemis. Carmen cast her nervous glance as they passed in the hall. Jenny smiled a little and sent her a mental sensation of well-being.

In Carmen's room, Jenny quickly stripped off the blood-stained robe and placed it, her underwear, rope belt, and sandals in the paper sack the constable had given her and passed it through a crack in the door to him. "I'm just going to have a quick wash and a change, and then I'll be right out," she said."

"Yes, ma'am," he said, having received no instructions to the contrary, but he waited directly outside the door for the next twenty minutes until she emerged, dressed rather differently. She'd borrowed 'civilian' clothing from Carmen's closet—a pair of jeans, a sweatshirt, and some sneakers. They were a little tight on her, owing to Carmen's more slender figure.

"Don't want to be one o' them anymore?" said the burly constable with surprising sensitivity.

"No," said Jenny simply, "I don't."

♦

Of all the individuals involved, Carmen had the least to contribute, as she'd come out into the corridor from her room after Sister Sonia was already down and the gunman had disappeared.

Thus, she had no knowledge of the events leading up to the murder, except that she'd heard quiet voices in the hall a few moments earlier and assumed it was Jenny showing the Carlisles around. Lindstrom, however, got the distinct impression that she was being too careful with choosing her words. His conversations with the others had flowed more naturally. He wondered if she were just timid, or if she were hiding something at which the others had been more adept at concealing.

She described her relationship with Sonia as being a student and hypnosis subject, although she didn't appear very pleased with the arrangement, as if Sonia had done something not quite right or had not lived up to expectations. *Maybe put the moves on her,* thought Lindstrom. *No telling what these cult leaders will do to their flock, given half a chance.*

He finally found himself growing frustrated with Carmen Waters. She didn't volunteer anything, answered every question with an economy of words that would have made him suspicious under other circumstances. But the testimony of the others supported the same version of events. Were it not for the Carlisles, and had this only involved Artemis people, he would have been considerably skeptical about the disappearing gunman. But besides the reputation of the couple, word had reached him that a visitor had seen a man matching the gunman's description limping hurriedly away from the house, straight toward the rear of the property. Additional constables had been assigned to follow up that trail.

"You may go now, Miss Waters. If I may ask, what are your plans?"

For the first time, she looked slightly animated. "As soon as I can, I want to go home to the States, back to California."

"We'll let you know," said Lindstrom. "And in the meantime."

"I wouldn't really want to stay here, even if the police allowed it. So I imagine I'll move to some hotel in town."

"Please keep us informed," he said sententiously and nodded to the constable to show her out.

Lindstrom sat back in his chair. What a bloody stupid mess this was.

◆

The six of them sat around the coffee table in Connor and Laura's suite, contemplating the crystal. "So it was all about this?" asked Connor, shaking her head. "Sister Sonia got murdered, and my daughter could have been shot, all because of some stupid rock."

Ellen cleared her throat meaningfully. "I think 'stupid rock' may be not only an understatement but an insult."

"You're saying it's possible to insult an inanimate object?"

Ellen chuckled. "Not exactly, but I think it best to withhold judgment until we understand more about it."

"It certainly isn't doing much glowing or pulsating," said Connor. "And I thought that was the whole idea."

Ellen, who had been studying the crystal said simply, "I don't think it has a connection with anyone in this room. But somehow it had one with Sonia. It responded to her. And it certainly changed her."

"Not for the better, however, I might point out," said Connor. "She got to be more of a megalomaniac than she'd ever been."

"Power does strange things to people, my dear. Depends on the state of their hearts and souls. Sonia was probably a broken soul with a deadened heart. The only parts of her that were energized by the crystal were the parts that made her want power and control over others. And she also got a somewhat warped picture of the future from it, though I can't say just how warped. But I'm willing to wager that it was during her exposure to the crystal that she came up with the whole doomsday end-of-times scenario that got to be her main obsession."

"But what does that all mean for us?" asked Laura. "If she had a warped impression, that's one thing. But could it still mean there is some shred of truth to it, some threat to the world itself? Or is that just too far-fetched for words?"

William knocked out his pipe in the ashtray. "I wouldn't call it far-fetched, necessarily. But perception is a funny thing. I do have the sense that Sonia was tuning into something. And I also believe that we're seeing a replay, or at least a partial replay, of some extremely significant event from a very long-ago past. Not all of you may understand the wheel of karma…I can't even say that I do completely. But it always continues to turn, and human beings are thus invited to create different outcomes to other life lessons and experiences. Usually, they are small, personal types of experiences that may impact on the world, only in more subtle ways. Sonia has somehow, because of who she once was, set into motion a sequence of events that touched thousands of lives, maybe tens of thousands. I think that's what Jenny is trying to tell us. And, speak of the devil, I think our two Artemis friends have arrived."

Jenny and Carmen were indeed standing outside the door. Laura, closest to the door, admitted them. When they entered, Benjamin and William stood up, as did Connor. Introductions were exchanged all around for those who had not met before, and more chairs pulled up to the informal circle.

"How are you two doing?" asked Laura. "I hated skipping out on that whole scene, but at the time it seemed the right thing to do. Still, it left you holding the bag."

"It was really all right," said Jenny. "The chief inspector wasn't the least bit discourteous, though he is clearly suspicious of just about everyone there." She smiled at the Carlisles. "Except you two, of course."

"Rank hath its privilege sometimes," grinned William. "Especially if you're very careful not to try and take advantage of it."

"I guess he's satisfied for the moment, because he let Carmen and me go. And I found out that someone saw that man getting away, limping badly anyway."

Benjamin scowled. "I had a feeling he was a survivor type. He got past the two men who were watching for him, which means he spotted them first. And now he's probably very angry and perhaps frightened and/or desperate. If he's working directly for Yohiro Matsumoto, he's in deep trouble for having failed to carry out his instructions. But I've got people looking for Dandridge, and the police are on full alert. He'll have a helluva time trying to get out of England."

Laura looked at Jenny. "Would you tell me something first?"

"If I can."

"Why did you call Sonia the Lady Deirdre?"

"It's a long story," said Jenny, "but if you're willing to hear it—"

Connor suddenly sat forward on the couch. "Look!" She was pointing at the crystal, which had slowly but quite noticeably begun to pulsate with a colorful play of lights twinkling inside its many facets. The effect was both beautiful and mesmerizing. "Ellen, you said it wasn't responding to anyone but Sonia."

"No, I said to it wasn't responding to anyone in this room at the time. But our complement has increased by two." She looked from Jenny to Carmen.

Jenny pondered the crystal for a moment. "So it's really true," she whispered. Then, in a more audible tone, "I said it's a long story, and you may not even believe it. First, perhaps I had better reintroduce myself. Once upon a time, my name was Alandra. And this," she said, indicating Carmen, "was Junela. We were priestesses of the temple until the day the Lady Deirdre destroyed us all."

The others listened with rapt attention, though perhaps varying degrees of skepticism, as Jenny Carpenter described in great detail a life she and Carmen had lived more than 10,000 years earlier in a civilization some would eventually come to call Atlantis. "That wasn't its actual name in our language," she told them. "But it's the same place some of your seers and psychics have glimpsed as little by little the veils of separation between streams of time grow thin."

"Streams of time?" asked Connor, the first to speak once the story was complete.

"Some of your scientists know that time is simply another dimension, that it is neither fixed nor linear. They do not truly understand its dynamics, but they suspect much more than they can prove, and believe me, there is much more to it than they even suspect. I know you and your partner, Laura, and the Carlisles are aware of more than the three dimensions most human beings perceive or wish to believe in. You have traveled in other 'places' than this planet seems to contain."

Connor nodded reluctantly. "Yes, that's true. I've been other places, I suppose you could say, though I don't have much of an explanation for it. But that still doesn't explain to me how a civilization such as you described could exist here that long ago. Humankind was still extraordinarily primitive."

"Yes," Alandra said slowly. "And this part you won't really like at all. But we weren't precisely humans, at least not homo sapiens. But we also weren't that different, except that we used a great more of our brain than other similar species. For that matter, even compared with today's modern standards, we used much of the brain that most humans still do not access, at least not consciously. But the point is, we settled here on a barely developed yet beautiful planet. And we chose to build our society out of reach of the main continents for the very reason that we did not want to interfere with the evolution of other species that had been created to flourish on the planet. It was part of our code of ethics, if you will, that we keep to ourselves. We only wished to expand our consciousness of Source that created us. We wished to study and learn and worship and live a life of peace and tranquility."

Connor took a deep breath. "This sounds as if you're saying you came from someplace else entirely."

"We did," said Alandra simply. "Rather far away, as a matter of fact." She watched Connor's expressions move from puzzlement to disbelief to confusion to outright refusal. "I apologize if this is too outlandish for you, but it's what I believe happened—no, let me put that a bit differently. It's what I remember happening. Perhaps if Carmen, that is, Junela, were to explain her part in this."

The other young woman had been silent during the telling of the history of Atlantis, only nodding occasionally in agreement but otherwise remaining impassive, even when Alandra reached the part about Lady Deirdre's treachery, her violation of the inner sanctum that was not only the power source for their city, but the gateway as well.

"I didn't remember any of this only because Jenny... Alandra...told me what my dreams meant. It all started with

Sister Sonia. And now I know it was because of the crystal. She used her skills with hypnosis to probe my dreams, to find out what I remembered. At first I was terrified that I was losing my mind. Eventually, I felt as if I couldn't discern the difference between waking and sleeping, between what was real and what wasn't."

Ellen patted her hand. "*Real* is an extremely *relative* term, my dear. We try not to use it at all if possible."

Carmen smiled. "Thank you. It's taken me quite a while to figure that out. I think Sister Sonia pushed so hard that it was affecting me physically. I had actual fainting spells where I blacked out completely. Jenny found me in the garden in that state and sat me with all one night, through the dreams and the terrors of not understanding. But once she explained it to me, everything actually made sense in a weird sort of way.

"Sonia was inadvertently reactivating portions of Junela's memories and accessing parts of the humanoid brain I was talking about, the parts all your scientists keep puzzling over."

Carmen continued. "After that, I wasn't afraid anymore, not of my dreams, not of Sister Sonia. I was ready to leave that place, but Jenny said we had to stick around because Sonia was going to try repeat the same mistake, try and change the course of time so that she could bring her lover Arkan back."

Now, is that this Alan character we keep hearing about?" asked Laura.

"He was the guy I saw run out to Sonia yesterday, wasn't he?" inquired Katy. "In the office, the other man, Karl, called him Alan."

"He was her chosen consort, but something she learned from Carmen must have made her doubt whether he was the reincarnation she sought. She must have assumed Arkan was dead in this lifetime, or had not been born into it, and she would actually find him by using the crystal to shift an entire stream of time into another channel."

"But could she actually do something like that?" asked William. "I can't imagine anyone wielding that sort of power, especially someone like Sonia, with no training or discipline or spiritual path."

"She didn't need that training or discipline, if she became the personification of Lady Deirdre. But I don't see how she'd have done it in any event," said Jenny. "Without the entire crystal matrix, I think it would be impossible. And even if she had the one crystal obelisk from which this shard must have come, I doubt that would be enough to accomplish what Lady Deirdre tried to do."

"So what was her plan?" asked Benjamin.

"She was convinced that the shard would be sufficient to shift this particular time stream into another one, a parallel but different one. But only if it were accomplished on a particular day."

"Some high holy day?" said Connor with a hint of sarcasm.

"To us, yes," replied Jenny quietly and Connor instantly regretted her impulse.

"I apologize," she said.

Jenny smiled softly. "No need. Even I know how outlandish it all sounds, like a sci-fi fantasy plot run amok. But I can't help that. The universe is a lot bigger and a lot more complicated than 99.9 percent of human beings believe. They have a remarkably narrow perspective, but it protects them in a way. Keeps them tied to their carefully framed lives. Most people hate the unknown and the unknowable."

Connor blushed slightly and Laura patted her hand. "My lover isn't all too fond of what she can't explain, but she manages to soldier on in the astral when need be."

"Indeed," added Ellen. "Connor is the leader of our Circle. She inherited the post, so to speak, from her Grandmother Gwendolyn Broadhurst, who is by the way, still out there somewhere fighting the good fight."

Jenny looked at Katy. "I knew your mother was someone of importance, someone who could help us—and all these people, besides. It's a miracle."

"But what are we supposed to help you with?" asked Connor. "You've got the crystal shard back, and we know you aren't going to try and misuse it. Sister Sonia is dead, and though I hate to say it, a lot of people are probably better off for it."

Jenny sat up straighter. "That may be true. But I haven't explained enough, I guess. If the center of this karmic 'adjustment' isn't Sister Sonia, then it's someone else. Someone will try to use the power of my...maybe I'll just call them ancestors...to do something very similar, to shift this particular time out of its natural course. And if that's true, then it will have to happen soon, according to the prophecies."

"You said something about a particular time or date," prompted Laura.

Jenny was silent for several seconds. "The eleventh hour of the eleventh day of the eleventh month."

Connor frowned. "Okay, so eleven A.M. on the eleventh of November. That's three days from now. But that rolls around every year. Why this year? It isn't 2011 or anything like that."

"Not on your calendar perhaps," said Jenny. "But ours would still be running. Even though the entire city and all its people were destroyed, that wouldn't have stopped our time stream running."

"Then what year is it for you, or for them...whatever?"

Jenny turned to Carmen. "Junela was the keeper of records. She knows."

Carmen closed her eyes. "I've tried to figure it out, but I can't. All I know is that it could be the right year for the gateway to be fragile enough to be breached. For the Atlanteans, it would be the twelfth millennium, somewhere in the 11,000s, but I can't be sure."

"Sonia was sure," said Jenny firmly. "And she was the one communing with the energy and knowledge held in the crystal."

"Wouldn't that knowledge be limited because she had only a piece of it?" asked Connor. "A fragment."

"That's more three-dimensional thinking, I'm afraid," said Jenny. "Do you know anything about fractals?"

"Um, not much. I've read some but never really understood it."

"It's...well, simply put, the natural definition is that every part of a fractal has the same form and structure as the whole. Every individual part of it contains the whole. Or you can look at it in a different way, that everything, at the subatomic level, is completely connected."

"Science was never my strong point," Connor scowled, "but I'm starting to get the idea. You're saying that any part of the crystal can provide all of the information that was stored in the entire piece." She shook her head disconsolately. "I can't even believe I'm saying this."

"Want an aspirin for that headache, sweetheart," said Laura with just enough sugary solicitousness to make them all laugh.

"No, thank you. I'll cope. And I apologize again for letting my own prejudices color my judgment. To be honest, I'm fond of the idea that we've only had one hominid species hanging out on the planet evolving and learning. The kinds of things you're talking about we've barely even theorized."

"We just started a whole lot earlier than you did," said Jenny. "That's one of the reasons my people came here, to find a different way of life than the one they'd known. But they still brought their knowledge with them and, in the end, it couldn't keep them from making very 'human' mistakes. Our spiritual enlightenment was the goal, but it never caught up with our abilities to manipulate or at least bend the natural laws of the universe to our own use."

"Was there anyone else at the compound who was familiar to you?" asked Ellen. "In the sense that they, too, might have lived in that time frame 11,000 years ago?"

"No one but Carmen and Sonia," said Jenny. "At least they are the only ones I could identify. Everyone else was very much tied to the Children of Artemis phenomenon. As a matter of fact, a lot of them were starting to talk about leaving when Sonia got derailed from the healing and started talking about the end of the world."

"People generally hate that sort of thing," said Connor drily. "End-of-world scenarios aren't exactly the stuff of feel-good, cult guru scams that want to stay in business for very long. Pretty soon they start sounding like those Heaven's Gate suicides."

"Doom doesn't sell well," added Laura.

"Sonia didn't care. And the disciples, the inner circle, they didn't dare complain too much. The money was still pretty good, I think, but they were sure she was going to ruin it with her new…focus."

"But you still haven't told us why you think that someone else is going to take up where Sonia left off."

"It's the strongest intuition I've ever had about something. That's all I can say. But I was shocked that Lady Deirdre, or Sonia, died. But while I was waiting for the police to do their interview, the sense came over me that we were running out of time. I just don't have a reasonable explanation for it."

"Intuition doesn't have reasonable explanations, dear," Ellen reassured her. "But the question is where do we go from here?"

Connor, who had been observing Carmen for quite some time, sat forward on the couch, "I think before we tackle the unknown, we'd better deal with the known. Jenny, you haven't told Carmen anything about Bettina, have you?"

Jenny's eyes brimmed with tears. "No, because I wasn't sure. But you are, aren't you?"

Connor hesitated, and Laura took it as her cue. "We were in Palm Springs and met your sister there."

Carmen's face crumbled. "I wrote such stupid mean things to her all because Sister Sonia kept telling me I had to. But now I see it was all about money. Those women who came to Palm Springs—they made the Children of Artemis sound so exciting and wonderful. I thought everything would be different in my life if I just came here. And then everything started getting so weird. I wanted to call Bettina, even ask her to come and get me. But then a lot started happening, and thank God Jenny was there for me. I need to apologize to my sister."

She was looking right at Laura, who was struggling to find the right words, words that wouldn't hit this woman like a tidal wave. She'd never get a chance to apologize to Bettina.

Ellen got up from her seat and went and knelt in front of Carmen, taking both of Carmen's hands in her own. "I'm so sorry, child, but your sister is dead. That's the main reason we all ended up right here in York in this room together. Laura and Connor spoke to her the day she died and suspected that someone had killed her. They couldn't let it alone, so they came here to investigate and, if need be, to rescue you before anything happened to you as well. We believe that Sister Sonia sent someone to eliminate your sister so she couldn't influence you to leave, or at the very least she wanted your inheritance."

It seemed an eternity before Carmen reacted. She stared down at Ellen, and they all watched the emotions come and go across her pale countenance—like one of those moving pictures you can create by flipping cards of different images very quickly. Finally, all she said was "No!" And she began to sob, leaning forward on Ellen's shoulder. The rest of them sat in silence, patiently and lovingly waiting for the storm to subside. Of all of them, Jenny looked the most pained. But she let Ellen do her work, and clearly it was a particular sort of work.

Laura could detect an energy field around Ellen that was also embracing Carmen. And as red and orange flowed from Carmen, it was absorbed and transformed by Ellen's golden aura, as if drawing out the worst of the pain and neutralizing its worst effects. After several minutes, Ellen released Carmen, who sat back in her chair and looked at Ellen with some wonderment. "Who are you?" she asked.

"A friend, always," said Ellen. "Now perhaps you and Jenny need some time to be alone and absorb this all." She turned to Connor. "Perhaps they could use the other room for a while to talk about all this. And Connor and Laura can answer your questions later. You're bound to have questions."

"Of course they can have some privacy," said Connor, still a bit ashamed that she hadn't been able to break the news herself. But there was something so fragile about the girl, so vulnerable. Connor had simply lost her nerve. She felt Laura's hand on hers and knew she understood.

Once the other two women had left the room, at first no one seemed to know what to say. It was Benjamin, with his usual practicality, who got the ball rolling.

"We don't have to necessarily agree with Jenny that someone wants to use the crystal for the same purpose as Sister Sonia. And we don't even have to assume that her beliefs in this particular past life are valid. But the fact remains that someone went to a great deal of trouble to steal the original crystal fragments and to obtain this last piece that was somehow overlooked during that raid on the archaeology dig site. Whatever the purpose, the conspiracy itself certainly exists and may prove a threat to a great many people, whether supernatural or otherwise." He picked up a fat file folder. "While you all were out getting yourselves involved in mayhem and murder, I've acquired some new information about Mr. Dandridge and Pantheon and, most interestingly, a Mr. Yohiro Matsumoto who met with Dandridge at Heathrow airport only yesterday and appears to have a very personal interest in the crystal. And I think it's time we find out why."

Chapter Sixteen

Action is transitory—a step, a blow,
The motion of a muscle, this way or that—
'Tis done, and in the after-vacancy
We wonder at ourselves like men betrayed:
Suffering is permanent, obscure and dark,
And shares the nature of infinity.
—William Wordsworth, "The Borderers"

SWITZERLAND

Twelve stories beneath the surface, the chief security officer of Pantheon International's Bern, Switzerland, research facility found himself on the losing end of an argument with a particularly intransigent member of the management. He had long since grown tired of Mr. Matsumoto's surprise visits—usually replete with suspicious inquiries about the level of security at the lab in general, and, more specifically, the storage facility for the crystal, code-named "rock garden." The name was as silly as the man's questions, Grumman thought. But his job was not only to safeguard the facility but also to placate those who could get him fired with a single phone call. He was wise enough to know that security grunts didn't rate much in an organization the size of Pantheon, and he was only a year and a half from a very comfortable retirement, so long as he didn't piss anybody off, at least not anybody important. Francis Grumman wanted to blend into the background, do his job, and go back to his home in Austerlitz, where he would find a suitably accommodating, slightly younger, and moderately well-padded wife to cook his meals and keep him company.

Again, he demonstrated the controls for the series of electronic locking mechanisms that provided four barriers between the main corridor of the underground facility, and the enormous lab in which the crystal was kept. The only means of egress were the main double doors and a freight elevator platform large enough to hold more than four semitrucks or a full-size military transport helicopter, three of which were stored on another level of the facility. It was designed along the same lines as the elevators aboard aircraft carriers that lifted the planes to the deck to be launched and then returned them to the hangar decks below when they returned.

Tonight Matsumoto was accompanied on his inspection tour by one of his sons, though introductions were so terse, Grumman barely caught the connection. The family resemblance, however, was eerie, so he needn't have been told the two men were related. Other than Matsumoto's graying hair, and the fine lines around his eyes and mouth, the men might have been identical twins.

The son sneered at Grumman after the minilecture on the alarms, the knockout-gas release valves, and the panic button for sealing off the entire facility. "But you've added nothing since our last visit. You haven't upgraded a single system. What about the laser beams across the doorways and in the hallways? They'd allow you to track the progress of any intruder."

Grumman sighed and attempted to keep his tone polite. "I sent a request to Mr. Dandridge's office immediately after your last visit. I asked him about installing the additional security measures. He said it wasn't a necessary expense and we could add more guard patrols for much less."

"So you consider Mr. Dandridge's authority and judgment greater than mine?" asked Matsumoto Sr.

"No, sir, of course not." Grumman could feel a tiny trickle of sweat under the brim of his cap. "It's just I don't personally have the authority to requisition that kind of equipment or approve the purchase orders for installation. I assumed he would follow through based on your recommendations, and I was surprised when he denied it."

Matsumoto smiled grimly, and Grumman mistook it for a sign that Dandridge was in for a serious encounter with the Matsumoto contingent. In truth, this was precisely the attitude Matsumoto would have expected from Dandridge, who took himself and his position far too seriously. And he was pleased, of course. This entire charade had but one purpose, to be sure that nothing about the security arrangements had changed since he had laid his plans to take crystal.

Grumman turned toward a detailed diagram and mock-up of the facility embedded in the wall, complete with status lights for all the doors, both interior and exterior. "You see, I was thinking that we could install those lasers of yours here, near the first hatch that seals off the lab. Then every few feet at different horizontals down the corridor."

Matsumoto nodded at his son, who swiftly drew a pistol from a shoulder holster, a bulge beneath the coat that Grumman had noticed but chosen to ignore. The younger Matsumoto stepped a bit closer, as if to follow the security chief's explanation, and in one blur of movement, shoved the man to his knees, and shot him in the back of the head. Grumman went down face first on the polished linoleum.

"Now it begins, my son," said Yohiro Matsumoto, nudging the body with his toe. "Shut down the security system to the elevator and disable the override on this panel. Cut off the internal alarm system and the power to the electric fences. Then give the signal to the assault team."

Within minutes, the giant elevator was on its way to the top level. Matsumoto's commandos were well rehearsed and among the best mercenaries in the world. For the amount of money they were being paid, they would happily stage a raid on Fort Knox itself. This, in comparison, was absurdly simple. They had impeccable intelligence and the perfect 'inside man' for the job. The moment the warning lights on the fence went out, the cutters went to work with their torches, slicing through the fence in seconds rather than wasting time cutting strands. Their position was out of sight of the guard shack near the gate, and within only a few hundred yards of the helipad and the elevator platform. The logistics were a dream for a determined set of thieves such as this team. They could not only get at their objective easily enough, and get it quickly onto a transport, but they also didn't have to haul it away in a truck and risk roadblocks or border checkpoints.

The eight-man team was through the fence and across the open ground in less than two minutes. According to plan, they split up and found the outside guards precisely where they were supposed to be. Eight guards, eight corpses, and back to the rendezvous point. Another four minutes gone. The team leader heard the sound he'd been waiting for—the grinding of the enormous horizontal hatch doors sliding back into their recesses. Within a minute, the platform would appear and they would start the slow ride twelve stories down.

◆

The father and son walked quickly to the main lab where the crystal had been reassembled, or at least as reassembled as it could be with the use of newly developed glass/polymer blends that promised to have the same degree of conductivity as the crystal itself. It wasn't glue, but in essence, it served that very purpose. There was still a gap on one side, a small gash that could only be filled by one object in the world, and it gave Matsumoto a deep satisfaction to know that he would have it in his hands within twenty-four hours. He would accomplish what none of the others could. He would restore the crystal completely. But he certainly wouldn't be foolish enough to limit its potential to something as irrelevant as producing commercial energy.

With deft maneuvers, they swung the straps of an enormous lifting crane underneath the stationary cradle that held the crystal. Matsumoto never failed to be awed by its size and magnificence, and even his son had to pause for a moment and drink it in. "It's truly beautiful, my father."

"Indeed, and it is ours, or will be the moment we lift it from this prison in which it lies dormant."

Matsumoto could not have been more pleased with the timing of Pantheon's research team. In preparation for testing the crystal in an open environment, they had spent weeks constructing a stout rolling trolley that could support its several tons of solid weight and more than twenty-foot length. While he operated the controls of the crane, his son carefully manipulated ratchet-controlled guiding lines to position the crystal over the trolley. When the crystal was aligned, he signaled his father to lower it gently onto the padding. Then it was only a question of using the motor-driven trolley's guidance mechanism to move it close to the opening where the platform would come to rest.

Matsumoto checked his watch and motioned to his son. "Set the charges quickly. The elevator will return within two minutes and thirty-five seconds."

His son opened the attaché case he'd brought with him. Lying inside were half a dozen bricks of what resembled modeling clay—the irony of course being that these little lumps were for destruction and required little in the way of creative imagination, simply a good working knowledge of how to shape them to produce the desired direction of force and effect. Having rehearsed this in virtual reality more than a hundred times, it took Matsumoto Jr. less than the allotted time. When the platform's edge appeared below the high ceiling, and they could make out the combat boots of the mercenaries, all six charges were placed, wired, and the detonator-receiver's antenna raised to the optimum level. Its frequency matched the transmitter in his father's coat pocket.

The assault team rushed off the platform before it had even reached floor level.

"Quickly," ordered Matsumoto. "Take up your positions. We will take the crystal up to the helicopter. You will protect this area until I send the elevator back for you. Since the security chief has missed his fifteen-minute reset on the security system, the backup security force will have been automatically deployed. They are due here in four minutes, but I have no doubt you can handle them. The electric door circuits have been disabled and they'll have to manually override. If they come through, take them all out."

"Yes, sir. I summoned the transport as soon as we started down," said the team leader.

While Matsumoto delivered his orders, his son had already steered the multiwheeled trolley onto the lift platform and waited for his father to step on. The lift began to rise, and the assault team fanned out around the lab, taking up defensive positions out of sight of the thick Plexiglas windows that permitted a view into the corridor. They waited, listening to the slow hiss of the enormous hydraulic jacks that lifted the weight of the elevator.

Two minutes passed and the noise stopped. The cargo had reached ground level. If they could move it quickly enough, there was the possibility the assault team could leave before the backup security detachment even arrived. The team leader glanced toward the empty shaft, He didn't mind killing, but avoiding a firefight rated high on his list of preferences. The seconds ticked away and the elevator showed no signs of returning. Perhaps they were having trouble with the mechanical trolley. It was then that he saw it, the little lump of gray wrapped around the base of one of the square columns supporting the ceiling. His eyes followed the wires that led from it along the wall, ten feet, then twenty, then he spotted the next one. His stomach lurched and his heart began to hammer in his chest. Cold hard fact was staring him right in the face. The elevator wasn't coming back down, and they weren't supposed to leave the building alive.

He leaped to his feet, slinging his rifle over his shoulder. "We're outta here," he shouted. "Out the door."

But Matsumoto had told the truth about one thing: the heavy, bulletproof, fireproof, assault-proof door really was sealed, its circuits fried. The leader stepped back and in a frenzy opened fire on the Plexiglas viewing hatches. They spidered ever so slightly, but didn't come even close to breaking. His men looked at him as if he had lost his mind, but he didn't even bother to explain. And he wouldn't have had time anyway. Far above, Matsumoto watched with satisfaction as the crystal was finally winched completely into the belly of the transport. He and his son boarded the craft, piloted by his favorite daughter. And as they lifted off the helipad, he reached into his pocket, took out the transmitter, raised its antenna, and pressed a single button. Thanks to the remarkable advances in technology engineered by Matsumoto Electronics, the signal reached its destination more than one hundred feet below him. He couldn't feel the ground tremble, or hear the rumble of collapsing walls or the screams of eight dying men, but he knew what it was like—what it would look like and feel like. He'd experienced it all in virtual reality. For the mercenaries left behind, it was rather more painful and more permanent. But then that was the whole point. There were to be no witnesses, no loose ends. In a few hours, satellite phones around the world would be ringing off their hooks as news of the disaster at Bern had reached the principals of Pantheon. But it would be days before they could even dig their way into the lab. And by then it would be far too late. Pantheon would no longer even exist.

Matsumoto donned his headphones so that he could communicate with the pilot. "The first phase is complete. Now we are almost ready."

As soon as they touched down at the private airstrip in France to refuel, he would contact Dandridge and arrange a meeting place in England to collect the final piece. Then Mr. Dandridge would also become a piece of history—unpleasant history.

♦

Marginally unaware that his future was being measured in smaller increments than even he had hoped, Mickey Dandridge, given his innate skepticism, was holed up in a safe house of sorts a few miles from York. He had an old friend there, someone he'd worked with in the past, in the bad old days of spying for whoever's pockets were the deepest. Since he'd taken over at Pantheon, he'd had to be vague about his current employment, but he still managed to keep in touch with those who might prove useful in the future. Gerry Basington was one of those people, and although Gerry had eyed his injured mate with some trepidation, he'd allowed him the use of a bedroom, and obtained the services of an unlicensed but willing physician to treat Dandridge's injuries. Considering the fall he'd taken, he'd actually come out rather well: a concussion, a probable hairline fracture of the ulna or radius in his right arm, and one or two cracked ribs. His ankle was swollen as well, but the doctor concluded it was a bad sprain, not a break, and wrapped it firmly after taping his ribs and giving him a temporary splint for the arm. A bottle of painkillers concluded the surreptitious treatment.

The doctor received a nice wad of cash for his services, but Dandridge handed it over without complaint. Basington already had reluctantly agreed that the quack wouldn't get a chance to spend it anywhere. Minutes later, it was removed from his body, along with every shred of identification (including facial features and fingers) before the carcass was hastily buried in the floor of a rarely used outbuilding on Gerry's tiny farm. The addition of lime and other some other farm chemical all but assured that neighborhood dogs would not come sniffing around.

"I say, old man, "said Basington as they sat in front of the electric fire the next morning "What the bloody hell have you gotten yourself into?" The papers Gerry had picked up in town all carried news of the murder at the Children of Artemis compound, each different in its lurid details. The more sensational tabloids had of course delved into wild speculation about the true circumstances surrounding Sister Sonia's untimely death, though there was sorely little of substance in terms of her real background. The newshound researchers had discovered even less than Laura's more thorough and detailed searches…and neither she nor Benjamin had turned up much of significance. Dandridge was grateful for the confusion. Nowhere was the crystal mentioned, although more legitimate presses carried news of the disappearance of certain members of the Artemis inner circle, among them Karl Jensen and Alan Durn.

Worst of all, however, was a sketch carried by nearly every paper of the suspected killer, and Dandridge—used to the consistent inaccuracy of eyewitnesses in a crisis—was purely shocked at the accuracy of the rendering. It was almost as if he'd stood still long enough to have his picture drawn. That, of course, was impossible. *But how did they get the image?*

"You're a hot commodity," said Gerry. "I suggest you stay well out of sight until things cool down considerably."

Nothing would have pleased Mickey more than to do just that, but the threat of Matsumoto loomed over him. And besides, his pride was severely wounded. A mere woman had dealt him a near deathblow and had cost him the accomplishment of a vital mission. She was now "on his list," so to speak, along with the cowardly Karl. He hadn't the luxury of hiding out. Besides, if the investigative services were as efficient and focused as he suspected, it wouldn't take them long to find out that he'd once been arrested along with Gerry Basington, and the geographical proximity of Basington's house to York would bring them down on him like flies to honey. No, he had to move on—and soon. His first, and highly unpleasant task, of course, was to contact Matsumoto and apprise him of the state of things here in England.

♦

Matsumoto, however, was already in England, and only by exercising his iron-willed discipline could he control (though certainly not quell) his fury at the sight of Dandridge's face peering at him from every newsstand. Although he retained a small hope that the retrieval of the crystal shard had at least been accomplished, he tended to doubt it. There had certainly been no mention of it in any of the news accounts. Already, he had laid plans for having his own people carry out the retrieval if Dandridge had failed.

Predictably, there was very little in the media about his raid on Pantheon's laboratory. They were a closemouthed bunch anyway, and the extent of that particular facility was not a matter of public record. Pantheon would hardly allow itself be become fodder for the press. Its goal was a low profile, not becoming the center of a media circus. Matsumoto had already received the obligatory telephone calls from the managing partner of Pantheon who described with almost laughable horror the destruction that had been wrought at the Bern laboratory. Not only were tens of millions of dollars in equipment destroyed, but they were worried about the condition of the crystal once they found it amidst the rubble. Matsumoto demonstrated the expected amalgam of outrage, disappointment, anger, and disapproval over lax security arrangements. His tirade on the latter was enough to ensure that his discussion with Herr Grindel did not last long. No one likes being chastised, least of all smug billionaires.

Matsumoto turned his attention to more important matters. Dandridge must be found, but he suspected that the man would come to him. Every law enforcement officer in England was on the lookout for him, along with the millions of people who had seen his likeness. Mickey had nowhere to go and few alternatives but to seek Matsumoto's protection.

A couple of hours later, his prediction was proved correct when his satellite phone rang.

"Things went badly at the site," said Dandridge cautiously. Satellite transmissions, even with the encryptions Pantheon used, were much less vulnerable to eavesdropping but not entirely invulnerable.

"That is moderately obvious from what I read. But despite the complications, did you achieve the objective?"

Dandridge hesitated long enough to make the answer plain enough. He had failed. "It was all I could do to get away from the compound before the authorities arrived."

"What stopped you?"

"Some woman, a visitor."

"A woman stopped you?" Matsumoto's tone was both derisive and incredulous.

Dandridge was immediately on the defensive. "She must have had martial arts training or something. She was on me before I knew what was happening. Knocked me down the fucking staircase. As it is, I've got cracked ribs and a concussion."

"And what of your supposed inside man? Where was he in all this?"

"I never saw him after he went into the house."

"So it's possible he has the object?"

"It's possible, but I can't believe he's stupid enough to keep it. He knows that others want it very badly."

"He knows about me?" asked Matsumoto, an angry edge in his voice.

"No," said Dandridge hastily. "I'd never mention names. But I made it clear that he had to answer to people a lot more dangerous to his health than he could imagine."

"Then perhaps he will be in touch shortly."

"He will. He has this number to call."

"Where are you now?"

Dandridge hesitated again, and Matsumoto smiled a little. The man was not a complete idiot. He would much prefer to clean up the situation himself, if only to save is own skin. "I'm on the move right now," he lied. "I'll contact you the moment I hear from…from my colleague."

"That had best be very soon, Mr. Dandridge. Time is, shall we say, very much of the essence."

◆

Dandridge was literally sweating when he pressed the end key on his telephone. *For God's sake, Karl, where the fuck are you?* He had to leave this place soon. If anything, he'd been here too long. And he had no clue as to how good Matsumoto's people might be at triangulating satellite signals. He went back into the house where his old friend Gerry sat before the fire, wondering whether he ought to give old Mickey the boot. He wasn't particularly keen on the idea of the coppers sniffing about his place, not with a freshly buried corpse in the storage shed. But as long as there was no evidence of Mickey, they'd never get a search warrant.

He heard the front door open and shut. Now was as good a time as any to suggest a swift departure for his unwelcome guest. "I say, Mickey, old pal, might be a good idea for you to clear out pretty quick."

"You're right, Ger. I think you're right." Mickey shot him through the back of the old, tattered wing chair in which he sat. Gerry's head slumped to one side, and Mickey put another slug through his brain just to be on the safe side.

"Sorry, 'old pal,'" he muttered. "Just business."

He briefly considered trying to eliminate all traces of his presence, but he'd touched too many things in the house. He'd never catch every fingerprint. And besides, the bullets in Gerry would match the bullet in Sister Sonia. The connection was painfully obvious. He'd only killed Gerry because he couldn't be sure of what he might have babbled under the influence of the doctor's painkilling injections.

There was no getting around these murders—and that his relatively legitimate life was over and he would no doubt be taking an early retirement, or perhaps availing himself of some plastic surgery and living out his days working at some other Pantheon project far from scrutiny. Either way, Mickey Dandridge was going to disappear once this stupid exercise in futility was finally over. The only way he could redeem himself now was to find Karl—and the damn rock.

◆

Running for his life, Karl had basically the same idea about the value of the crystal. He could trade it to Mickey or Mickey's bosses for his life. He needed to get out of England. And he needed to avoid being connected with the murder in Palm Springs. He reasoned that the police would not have been any more likely to take the crystal into evidence than they'd assume there was any importance to the dozens of other New Age paraphernalia in Sonia's office, which was replete with wands, candles, crystals, medallions, ceremonial objects like athames, and figurines of various gods and goddesses. He'd left the safe empty and open. They'd assume money had been stolen, not a shiny rock." The odds were in his favor that it was still right where he had left it on the desk. Getting back into the house was hard but not impossible. He'd explored it thoroughly for bolt holes in the event of a hasty departure. And he'd found the perfect solution—an old priest's hole from the days of Henry VIII, when Catholic priests were highly unpopular with the authorities and Catholic families arranged means of entrance and egress for priests to come and say mass, and then escape again without detection. One of these passages led directly to the sitting room next to Sonia's office. Despite her supposed clairvoyance, she herself had never found it as far as he knew.

The passageway led to a trap door concealed in the garden seat of an arbor in the garden. His challenge was to get that far without being detected. The grounds were still be patrolled by constables with dogs. He would just have to wait as near as possible and spot his chance. His maneuvers were complicated by a lack of transportation. He'd driven away in one of the Artemis vehicles and then abandoned it at the train station in York. Once he'd established from a painstaking perusal of the newspapers that neither his face nor his name were immediately associated with the murder, he used a phony set of credentials he kept for emergencies to rent a tiny economy-class car—a smelly, slightly battered Renault that had the advantage of being nondescript but not entirely disreputable. Just in case, he picked up some camera gear at a secondhand store so he could pretend to be a curiosity seeker trying to sell photos to the press if he were caught inside the fence.

He waited almost an hour before the sweeps of the area veered away from the back of the house and then carefully let himself in through a decrepit wooden gate that made entirely too much noise.

He ducked and looked around. The squeak had not attracted any attention. Karl took a deep breath and adjusted the camera strap around his neck. Moving slowly from one clump of shrubs to another, he worked his way to the enclosure where the garden seat stood. Once inside, he actually began to feel a little of his old confidence return. Even Mickey would have to forgive him when he learned to what lengths Karl had gone to get the crystal shard.

He quickly climbed down the once-rickety but now marginally reinforced ladder into the passageway, which was only partly lined with stone. There were many gaps where dirt showed through, and stones littered the floor under his feet. Flashlight pointed downward to avoid tripping, he carefully made his way to the end of the passage and shone the light up the ladder. It was a long climb—two stories. But he hadn't much choice. Still, he took it slowly. If he fell and broke a leg, no one would ever find him.

After the arduous ascent, he stood at the top on a little platform, waiting to get his breath back under control. It was then that he heard the voices. He knew them both—Carmen Waters and Jenny Carpenter. He was almost overcome with fury, with a barely controllable urge to break both their necks. Irrationally, he blamed them for all this, particularly Carmen. If she'd never come here, he'd never have carried out that stupid murder in California, and other than a possible charge of fraud for his connection with Artemis, he wouldn't be in this mess. Jenny, too, though was on his "list." She'd brought that damn thing here, that stupid crystal. And from that moment on, everything had deteriorated. A perfectly good scam had gone right down the tubes.

He leaned his ear against the door to listen.

"I don't see how we can really make any kind of inventory," said Carmen. "I never really paid that much attention to the stuff in here. She always wanted to get started on the hypnosis right away."

"But the police asked," said Jenny. "And Laura and Katy and her mom thought it wouldn't hurt to have a chance to see if we could find anything else related to the history of the crystal."

Karl's ears pricked up at the world 'crystal.' He didn't like that they were talking about it, focusing on it.

"You know Connor thinks the whole crystal thing is nonsense," replied Carmen.

From his hiding place, Karl felt his optimism dissolve. Connor could only be one person—Connor Hawthorne. And if she were involved, then his odds of survival were probably dropping fast. She would have told the police about the murder of Carmen's sister. They'd easily make the connection and who knew what sort of damning evidence that stupid Sonia might have kept, if only for blackmail purposes. And then there was Alan, another fool. He actually knew what Karl had done. If he started talking…Karl could feel his bowels churning with anxiety.

"Yes, but you notice she didn't want to touch it."

"True. But Katy didn't mind. She even held it," Carmen remind her.

"But she did get kind of a funny look on her face until Connor told her she'd better put it down."

"Mother's are like that," said Carmen. "I remember how protective my mother was. And Connor is obviously worried about having Katy involved in all of this."

"Do you think the crystal is safe enough at the hotel?"

"Why not?" said Jenny. "Only we know it's there—and know it's important."

There was silence for a few moments, and then Carmen said, "Can we just get out of here? This place has a lot of bad associations for me."

"I'm sorry, love. Of course. We'll tell the chief inspector we haven't found anything valuable missing as far as we know."

Karl, whose leg was going to sleep, shifted his weight slightly. To his dismay, the floorboard creaked.

"Did you hear something? asked Jenny.

"Probably just the house settling. It's a stupid, creaky old place anyway. Let's go."

Karl waited until he heard the outer door close and debated

going inside to see if there really was anything of value he could easily sell. But even his instinctive cupidity couldn't override his sense of survival. Instead, he made his way laboriously back down the ladder, through the passage, and back up through the hatch in the garden seat. He peered around until he was certain no searchers were nearby. His only thought was to get in touch with Mickey. Karl had no intention of tackling a hotel full of people on his own.

♦

Just about the time Mickey Dandridge was ready to give up on Karl and assume he'd run as far and as fast as he could, the phone beside him chirped.

"I know where it is," came the breathless voice.

"You're supposed to *have* it," he said coldly, without bothering to acknowledge Karl or even ask where he'd been.

"I went back to the house, figuring it would still be there since no one would think it was important. But I overheard these two women—"

"Which two women?"

"Jenny Carpenter and Carmen Waters,"

"Shit!" Dandridge winced. The damn woman who'd somehow survived the raid on the island. They should have killed her while she was at the mental institution. That had been a stupid oversight, although on second thought, if that had happened, they might never have known what became of the crystal if it had been shipped back to her parents with her personal effects. So perhaps fate had a hand in all this, and maybe his luck was shifting.

"So what did you hear, and where is the crystal?"

"It's at some hotel in town. They've hooked up with this woman, Connor Hawthorne, and her daughter, Katy."

"I told you the Hawthorne woman was going to mean trouble, Karl."

"Um, there's something else you should probably know. Sonia sent me to California to take out Carmen Waters's sister so she could claim a fat inheritance. It was Connor Hawthorne who got the police onto thinking it wasn't an accident, as I had arranged it to look. She convinced them it was a murder."

Mickey swore. "The Americans are looking for you, then."

"No, not me specifically but someone from the cult."

"Once they go over the files, you'll be tops on their list, Karl. Are you sure these women have the crystal?"

"Yes, it's in one of their rooms, probably Hawthorne's. We just have to get it."

"There's no "we," Karl. You just stay the fuck out of sight until I contact you."

"You got me into this, Mickey, and you'd better get me the fuck out of it."

Mickey hung up and checked his reflection in the rearview mirror. He'd done a fairly good job of altering his appearance. He'd shaved his hair close to the skull so as to downplay the sandy red color and exchanged his suit for some of Gerry's more outdated garments—jeans, a beat-up leather jacket, a black T-shirt with the name of some obscure band, and a heavy silver chain with an iron cross on it. The addition of a bushy mustache from Gerry's old costume kit for 'jobs' finished the effect. And it worked. He looked nothing like the man in the police sketch. And besides, they were no doubt watching ports of entry and exit, not the streets of York. What kind of idiot would hang around there after committing a murder? *This idiot*, he thought to himself, but what choice did he have?

It didn't take him long to discover that the authors for the book festival were all staying at the same hotel. He had the creased photograph of Connor Hawthorne, and after calling the hotel and asking to be connected to her room, knew that she was out. Of course, this didn't give him the room number. No reputable hotel was giving those out these days. He was considering different strategies when fate once again handed him a victory.

◆

Katy, Connor, and Laura stopped for a quick lunch near the hotel and then walked back. None of them had any reason to notice an aging hippie-type sitting in the window of a coffee shop across from the entrance to their hotel. But he certainly noticed them. Connor was tall and athletic and a good-looking woman. Not easy to miss. Beside her was the Native American woman who'd caused the commotion at the compound. And to his amazement, the third member of their party was the very person he'd seen come out the side door of the house. *That must be the daughter, Katy, that Karl was talking about.*

He'd already paid his check so he'd be ready to move if need be. He was across the street and moving into the lobby as they boarded the lift. He moved quickly to the stairwell that ran right alongside the elevator shaft. Once there, he ran up the steps to the upper floor and peered out. The elevator stopped, and he ducked his head back in. Sure enough, all three women got off. He waited until they were around corner before stepping out of the stairwell. The two older women went down one branch, the younger one headed left instead.

"I'll come down to your room in a minute," the younger said.

"Okay. I'm expecting Dad's already there," said Connor. "Don't be long."

"Yes, Mother," came the slightly acerbic reply as the two other women unlocked a door halfway down the hall. All of them had their backs to him. In a moment of inspiration, a plan came to Mickey: a way to get the crystal back and maybe even eliminate everyone who knew about it and wasn't supposed to.

With swift, silent steps, he rushed down the hall in the direction the younger woman had taken and smiled to see her door just about to swing shut. With one huge stride, he caught it just before the latch clicked. Then he just waited. Sure enough, he felt a slight push on the other side. She was trying to close it completely. In that instant he threw his considerable weight into the door and it flew inward, knocking Katy flat. He was on her in a moment, and with a move perfected through long practice, subdued her quickly by temporarily cutting off the flow of blood to the brain. It was in knowing just the right spot, and Mickey knew them all, including the ones that killed rather than immobilized. But he wanted this girl alive. She was about to be his bargaining chip, and the bait for a trap. With Matsumoto's help, this would all come right in the end. All he had to do was get her quickly out of the hotel and into his newly acquired vehicle. Unlike Karl, he'd found a less traceable solution. He'd followed an old lady home the previous night, assured himself that she lived alone, and strangled her in her bed. After stuffing her body in a closet and carefully locking all her doors and windows, he took the keys to her hatchback and drove away. He had at last twelve to twenty-four hours. Even if someone came looking for her, with her car gone, they had to assume she was out somewhere.

There wasn't anything in the room large enough to conceal a full-grown woman, and he could hardly sling her over his shoulder and walk downstairs. But then he remembered the left-luggage shelves in the little area at the bottom of the stairwell. Departing guests could store their bags between checking out and catching their trains or doing their last-minute shopping. Mickey, whose brain registered every detail, thought he'd seen a fairly large duffel bag. A quick peek into the corridor, and taking Katy's room key with him, he strode quickly back to the stairs and down. He grabbed the long duffel and ran back up the stairs.

In the room, he dumped its contents. This would be a tight fit, but doable. Given Mickey's determination at that moment, it was hardly surprising that in less than five minutes, he had packed Katy into the bag, added her handbag for good measure, and exited the room and the hotel. He slipped away from the curb, observing the traffic carefully, and drove out of York. Beneath the hatchback cover, Katy lay unconscious. Once he'd reached the A___, Mickey picked up his satellite phone and dialed Matsumoto.

"I'm assuming you have welcome news for me," said the icy, cold voice.

"I have a way to kill several birds with one stone," said Dandridge. "*The* stone. I need a safe place somewhere not far from

York. I have a passenger I need to keep in a quiet place until her usefulness is depleted."

He heard a muffled conversation. Apparently, Matsumoto had his hand over the mouthpiece. "My son will meet you at this location," he said when he finally came back on the line. "I will be there soon after. And you will provide an explanation of this plan of yours at that time." He gave Dandridge explicit directions, which he scribbled on an old envelope lying on the seat.

"Believe me, you're going to like what I've planned," said Dandridge. "You'll get what you want, and we'll eliminate some very untidy loose ends at the same time."

♦

Once the connection was severed, Matsumoto turned to his children. "I don't necessarily trust Dandridge, but the man is no fool. If he believes he has a plan to accomplish our objectives, then we will consider it." He looked at his eldest son. "But once that objective is acquired, Mr. Dandridge will pay the full price for his bungling."

♦

The next call Dandridge made was to Karl. "Your information was valuable after all. Meet me at this location." He repeated the directions. At first, Mickey had considered just leaving Karl dangling out there. But when a man had a possible murder charge hanging over him, his lips were liable to get very loose, very fast, even with the threat of Pantheon as an incentive to keep quiet. No, he wouldn't take any chances. Besides, this was one more way of placating Matsumoto. Mickey really would tie up all the loose ends. The other two women would be easy enough. Getting rid of Karl would be like shooting ducks in a barrel. And he already had the daughter. Who else was there? He almost smiled. He was a little embarrassed at having nearly panicked.

Chapter Seventeen

It is the curse of Kings to be attended
By slaves that take their humours for a warrant
To break within the bloody house of life.
—William Shakespeare, *King John*, act IV, scene 2

"I thought Katy was just going to freshen up a little," groused Connor. "I swear, sometimes that girl is—"

A knock cut of her complaint. "There she is."

Instead, Jenny and Carmen were at the door. They had just returned from a very quick shopping trip to acquire some serviceable clothing. There hadn't been any call for civilian clothing while living at the compound. Jenny had shown up with basically the clothes on her back, and Carmen's wardrobe had been donated to charity without anyone having actually consulted her.

Laura noticed how much happier the two of them were looking today. Some of the stress had gone out of their faces, and they had a distinct tendency to touch each other casually and hold hands unself-consciously. She suspected their love affair would last for a very long time, a lifetime at least. "Any news from the police?" she asked.

"They were asking, not telling," said Jenny. "And there really wasn't much we could do to help in terms of inventory. I hadn't spent much time in Sister Sonia's private quarters, and Carmen was usually under Sonia's influence when she was allowed into the inner sanctum. From some of what Carmen's described, I have a feeling Sonia was also drugging her to help the effects of the hypnosis along."

Another knock but still no Katy. This time it was Benjamin, briefcase in hand, with a look on his face that said he had more news to share.

"Come on in, Dad," said Connor. "We're still waiting on Katy, as usual."

He grinned. "It seems I used to say that about you when you were young. You had a positive knack for keeping people waiting."

"Another inherited trait then," said Connor with a grimace. "Did I pass along any of her good characteristics, or did she get those from her father?"

Laura punched her in the arm. "Don't be absurd. She gets all her good traits from you. I think you only learned punctuality later in life."

"How much do you want to bet the Carlisles show up before she does?"

"No bet," said Laura, answering the next knock at the door. She greeted William and Ellen with hugs. "I'll just run down to her room and see what's keeping her."

While they waited, Connor brought the crystal out from the bedroom bureau where she'd put it, and they once again puzzled over its inexplicable habit of coming to life around Jenny and/or Carmen. They hadn't yet tested to see which woman it reacted to most enthusiastically, but Ellen was already convinced it was the both of them, so empirical research seemed like a waste of time under the circumstances.

Ellen mentioned that she'd had some extraordinarily odd dreams the night before, but would hold off on giving an account until everyone was present. She was fairly sure, however, that the dreams constituted a message that was related to the situation. And she would welcome their theories about the content.

Connor began to pace, her usual impatience showing. "Now what's keeping both of them?"

In the meantime, Laura had been surprised to get no answer when she knocked at Katy's door. She waited, and knocked again, more loudly, thinking perhaps Katy was in the bathroom with the water running. But when Laura put her ear to the door, she heard nothing. Something in the pit of her stomach flipped over. It was a feeling she dreaded, because it invariably meant bad news. Her Grandmother Klah had warned her never to ignore that little feeling or, sometimes, that little voice. Laura walked quickly back down the hall, her mind racing, searching for some benign explanation. *Katy needed something from a shop. She'd gone downstairs to…what?* That didn't even make sense. The expression on her face must have been utterly transparent when she opened the door to the suite she and Connor shared, for all eyes turned to her instantly, and Connor asked, "What's wrong?"

"Well, she doesn't seem to be in her room. Maybe she had to go out for a minute."

Laura knew how lame that sounded before the words were entirely out of her mouth. And then she looked Ellen Carlisle, whose face had gone completely pale. "Get a key to her room right now," she insisted, rising from the couch.

Connor stood rooted to the carpet for a split second, then ran for the door. She didn't bother with the lift, but took the stairs down two at a time. Her name and reputation and outright panic got her a key to her daughter's room, despite the resentment of the harassed desk clerk who was arguing with a man who insisted his duffel bag had been stolen from the left-luggage shelves and was determined to describe it in detail. Connor didn't give a damn about his luggage—and told him so. She met them all outside Katy's door, key in hand, within only a couple of minutes.

The moment they stepped inside, they knew something had happened. The desk chair was tipped over, and in the middle of the floor lay a pile of unfamiliar clothing and personal belongings.

"What the hell is all this?" said Connor kicking it aside. "This isn't Katy's stuff."

"Be quiet," commanded Ellen. "William, take my hands for a

moment. Concentrate with me. Whatever happened is recent. Try to get a mental picture before the energy is completely faded."

They all waited, Connor's panicked expression the only thing Laura could focus on. Carmen and Jenny looked both confused and alarmed, as much by Katy's absence as by whatever Ellen and William were doing.

The interval seemed to last forever, but in reality less than a minute passed before Ellen turned to Connor and said, "I'm sorry. I can't get anything clear, but Katy didn't leave here alone. And it doesn't seem she was, that is to say, she was awake."

"You don't mean..." Connor could not bring herself to finish the sentence.

"No, no, my dear," said Ellen gripping Connor's hands in her own. "I didn't mean that at all. But it's as if she was completely unaware, in a deep sleep or something."

"A trance, hypnosis? What?"

"Just not conscious."

"But then someone would have had to carry her out of here, and that would be noticed, for God's sake," said Benjamin, who was as distraught as Connor but trying to maintain at least some level of calmness in a crisis. "It isn't as if you just carry an unconscious woman through the lobby—"

"The bag!" shouted Connor. "There's a man in the lobby who said his duffel bag is missing." She was about to race back out the door when Benjamin caught her by the arm. "Stop a minute. You may be right. That may be how they did it. But if you go downstairs and start shouting, you'll get too many people involved, including the police. If Katy's been taken, there's a reason and we have to find out what it is."

"But we have to look for her," said Connor, her voice breaking. "We have to find my daughter." Tears were sliding down her cheeks, and she angrily wiped them away.

"And we will," said Benjamin. "But not if we panic and get nuts about it. Let's leave this as it is and go back to your room. If someone tries to make contact, it's going to be with you directly."

"Contact?" asked Laura, looking at Benjamin with an unreadable expression. "You're thinking this is about some sort of ransom."

"I am," he replied quietly, his voice barely steady. "I can't think of any other reason."

"But that means her cover is blown," said Laura. "They, whoever they are, would have to know that she's Connor's daughter."

"I told you it wouldn't be hard to figure out," snapped Connor, her fury all but boiling over.

"Come on, there's not time to argue about this. Let's go," said Benjamin before he closed the door behind them.

◆

The next few hours passed with agonizing slowness, little relieved by Connor's rage, a sentiment so strong, coming as it was from her own spiritually powerful life force, that it affected them all to the depths of their souls. Ellen tried her best to shield them, but it was an uphill battle, so she spent most of her time focusing her awareness in an ever-increasing circle around the hotel, as if throwing out a psychic net to see what she might catch that was a little bit "off" in the flow of events. But she found nothing and kept to herself for the moment the conclusion that Katy was probably no longer in the city of York.

◆

The son of Yohiro Matsumoto, called Yoshi by his siblings, was not impressed with Mickey Dandridge, or the 'cargo' he'd snatched from the hotel in York.

"You think involving important people like the Hawthornes in our affairs is a smart strategy?" he said scathingly. "You might was well kidnap the prime minister's daughter. My father has looked into these people."

"I've done my research," said Mickey, on the defensive and

hating that some wet-behind-the-ears kid was telling him how to manage a crisis situation.

"Then you no doubt will be aware that Connor Hawthorne's father, this girl's grandfather, has many resources he can call upon, many people who will rush to his aid, including every high-level security officer in this country."

Mickey pursed his lips. He hadn't perhaps thought it out quite that far. All he wanted was a simple exchange: the girl for the crystal. He figured that as long as he didn't do the kid any harm, he could avoid any major wrath from the Hawthorne family.

"And you've allowed this moronic Karl person to become involved, even brought him here to a place that was to be known only to you and my family"

"I couldn't have him wandering around out there. He'd get picked up eventually."

"You should have killed him already," said Yoshi, who had sent Karl outside to keep watch.

"I'll take care of him. I thought I might need some help for a few hours until we make the switch."

"How much do these people know about the crystal?"

"I don't see how they can know anything. I think the Carpenter girl brought it to Sonia and then took it back once Sonia was dead. The only reason the Hawthornes are involved is because of Karl. Sonia put out a contract on the sister of one of her disciples, or whatever they're called. And he went to California and did the sister, trying to make it look like an accident. But the Hawthorne woman and her girlfriend caught on somehow. They don't know who did it. They just figure it was someone in the Children of Artemis crowd, trying to get their hands on more money."

"And you're quite sure that's the only reason they became involved? Because they're investigating a murder?"

"Yes!" said Mickey. "That kid in there was even using phony I.D. She was playing detective."

"She had no weapons, no electronic devices of any kind?"

"No. I checked her bag, for fuck's sake. She's got keys to a rental car, a wallet with the fake I.D., some makeup and crap, and a PDA."

Yoshi's eyes narrowed. "Let me see it."

"What?"

"The personal digital assistant: Let me see it."

"The stupid thing is just a PDA."

"Get it."

Mickey grumbled his way to the bedroom where Katy was still out cold and securely tied to a chair. He rifled through her bag and brought the device back to the living room.

Yoshi studied it carefully, then turned it on and tried the various functions. All of them appeared normal. He even pressed different combinations of keys and accessed the wireless function to see if it was trying to transmit. He wished he had some of his own equipment to test it and take it apart, but it did indeed look as if Dandridge was right for once. But just to be on the safe side, he opened the battery compartment and took out the cells. Then he tossed it on the table, unaware that his precaution had just activated the GPS homing device concealed within. "So your grand idea is to suggest a trade—this girl for the crystal shard?"

"Yes, and why not?"

"And what do you suppose they will think if you ask for it in exchange for the young woman in there?"

"What do you mean? Why would they care?"

"Do you not suppose they will *then* attach some great significance or value to the crystal, if you are willing to commit such a crime simply to get it?"

Again, Mickey was on the losing end of the argument. That hadn't exactly occurred to him either, so anxious was he to retrieve what Mr. Matsumoto wanted. He valued his life and all of his body parts a great deal. "But then what's the point of trying to make a trade?"

Yoshi shook his head in disgust. "Small wonder that people like you do not succeed. We will simply ask them for money, you fool. That is a motive people can understand. And from what my father has learned of the great Benjamin Hawthorne, he will not make any move against us until his granddaughter is safe." He went to the window and looked out at Karl. His expression was thoughtful. "And I retract my former dis-agreement about your colleague. He is going to prove useful because he is going to be…what do you Americans call it, the patsy?"

It was Laura who suggested turning on the tracking monitor for Katy's PDA. Connor immediately went back to Katy's room and took some tiny comfort in the fact that she did not find Katy's handbag. Now there was at least a chance she would be able to acti-vate the GPS homing unit. If Katy were conscious, if she could get at the PDA, if—Connor tried desperately to avoid the worst ques-tion: if she were alive. For a few moments, Connor stood there in her daughter's room, looking at her things scattered about, fighting back tears. The mere thought of losing her sweet, wonderful Katy was too painful to bear. There'd been so much death in her life—her former lover, Ariana; her beloved grandmother; and her own mother, Amanda. *Where did it stop?* And how could she have let her own child be put at risk? Connor sank onto the be and began to sob.

Laura found her there a few minutes later when Connor had not returned with a report on whether the PDA was at the hotel or with Katy.

"Oh, sweetheart," she said, gently taking Connor in her arms. "Don't think the worst. She's okay. I know she's okay."

Connor raised her eyes to Laura's. "Are you just guessing, hoping like I am?"

"I'd know. The same way I knew in Massachusetts that you were still alive, even when the others were losing hope. Ellen knows, too. She's even more in tune with the universal flow than I am. She can feel Katy's life force out there somewhere."

Connor wiped her eyes. "And you'll tell me when, I mean…if you know something has…changed." He voice failed her com-pletely and she couldn't go on. Just to say the words seemed like inviting the worst to happen.

Laura took Connor's face in her hands and looked her square in the eye. "If I think anything has changed, for better or worse, I'll tell you. I promise you, darling."

Connor laid her head on Laura's shoulder and cried.

Dear Mother Goddess, Laura prayed silently. *Watch over this child Katy and keep her safe until we find her. I ask this in the name of all that is good and holy and pure in this world.* She took a deep breath. *And, Gwendolyn, I know you're out there somewhere. We need you, too.*

♦

The call came only minutes after Laura and Connor returned from Katy's room with the news that the PDA was indeed missing and could well be with her. Benjamin, a ghost of a smile on his face, said he already knew that. He'd been paying close attention to the monitoring equipment. He'd arranged a full-time satellite uplink and had done something incomprehensible to the others to boost the strength of the receiver itself. Ten minutes earlier, just after Laura had left the room, Benjamin had identified the signal of Katy's GPS transmitter. He knew her location, or at least the location of the PDA within ten meters. They were all feeling a surge of hope when the phone rang.

Benjamin waved Connor off, to her obvious annoyance, and answered, having already set the unit on speakerphone. "This is Benjamin Hawthorne," he firmly announced. His gut was churning and his instincts told him that this was the call.

"I have your granddaughter," said a male voice. Jenny and Carmen immediately reacted. Jenny grabbed a pad of paper and pencil and scribbled, "It's Karl."

Benjamin nodded. "How do I know that's true?"

The voice described Katy and what she was wearing in detail.

"That's hardly convincing evidence that you actually have abducted my granddaughter," said Benjamin harshly, as if prepared to argue every point.

"Fine," the voice snarled. "Then perhaps if we send you a finger or two, perhaps an ear. Would that be more convincing to you?"

Benjamin quickly allowed his voice to change tenor, playing

the part of a frightened old man. "No, no, please don't harm her. What do you want?"

To their utter surprise, he said, "A hundred thousand pounds in cash tonight."

"But…" Benjamin was caught momentarily off-guard, then quickly recovered. "Where am I supposed to get that kind of money now, tonight?"

"You figure it out. And then you and your daughter and her girlfriend will all bring the money."

"Why all of us?"

"I don't want any trouble from them. I want you all where I can see you. I'll call back in an hour. You'd better be ready with the money." The line went dead.

They all stared at each other. "He didn't say a thing about the crystal?" said William.

"And how does he know I'm Katy's grandfather? That's something worth wondering about."

"He's got sources of information way beyond his capabilities," replied Laura. "Dandridge has to be in on this."

"But why money?"

"Maybe it's just something as simple as wanting to get out of town," said Connor. "I told you we were making way too much out of this crystal nonsense."

Ellen looked as if she would argue, but thought better of it under the circumstances.

"So when do we stop talking and go get Katy?" Connor pressed. "We know where she is."

"We know where the PDA is," corrected Benjamin, "and I have every hope that she's right with it. But we have to be careful." He consulted his pocket diary and dialed a number on his satellite phone.

"James, I need a favor, a very fast favor… No, it doesn't involve any of your manpower, just a little loan—about £100,000 in small denominations… Yes, but you know I'm good for it… No, if I tell you why, then you'll be duty-bound to interfere, and I can't let you, not this time. But when this part of it is taken care of, you'll be the first to know, and you'll have some interesting arrests to make... I need it now, like within the hour. Can you get in touch with a York banker? Good. Thanks, James... Yes, I know."

"But why bother with the money if we know where Katy is, Dad?"

William spoke up. "I could have handled that part of it, old man. Just a quick call to my own banker."

Benjamin looked at each of them in turn. "Strategy. This is a chess game, and if I'm right, the person on the other side of the board is not Karl, or Mickey Dandridge for that matter. They're third-rate players. You see, I do believe this about the crystal, and I also believe that Yohiro Matsumoto and Pantheon are behind all of it. They have the resources to detect whether I'm trying to raise this money. They already know who I am. Otherwise, their demands would make no sense. The average person, even a wealthy American, couldn't pull off a transaction like that at this time of day. But someone with sufficiently powerful connections could. And as for you, William, I'm saving you for the endgame. I doubt they have any notion of your connection to us, and I want to keep it that way. I appreciate the offer, but if you started moving a large sum of money, there's a slight chance they'd know that, too, simply by monitoring electronic transactions tonight." He paused. "Lastly, if I'm wrong, and this is only about money, then we need to have the goods in hand just in case."

"Now we need a rescue plan."

◆

Katy had already figured out that it would be in her best interests to feign unconsciousness for as long as possible. Whatever drug her abductor had administered had either been too little a dose or had simply worn off sooner than he'd calculated. She could clearly hear conversation in the other room. Only one voice was familiar because she'd heard it at the Artemis compound—Karl. She suspected one of the others might be the man who had shot Sister Sonia, which didn't exactly raise her hopes of survival, because he obviously didn't have any compunction about killing people. But he'd kept her alive, so she must be intended to serve some purpose. The third voice was oddly accented, but not in any way she could identify. The man's words had the cadence and pronunciation of someone for whom English was not a native language, yet he had learned to speak it flawlessly and with an utterly neutral accent. The grammar and diction were exceedingly formal: no slang, no profanity, unlike the other two. But if she were any judge, she'd say the educated-sounding one was in charge of whatever this was. When he spoke, they listened. And she heard plenty. The crystal was a constant topic, that and something about ransom money, which didn't make much sense. But it definitely was the crystal that the neutral-voiced man wanted. And several times he mentioned his father, that his father would want this or that, and was on his way to England. She heard Karl make a second phone call and rattle off directions to the a farmhouse north of the city. She doubted it was this particular farmhouse.

She heard footsteps in the hall and the door opened; instantly Katy's head was on her chest in the same position as before. She barely breathed. The door closed.

"Still out cold."

"Good, then it's time we leave," said neutral voice. "You'll stay here to keep an eye on her while we meet the Hawthornes and collect the money."

"What, and then Mickey and you take off and leave me holding the bag?"

"Not at all," said the voice. "Clearly, it would not be in our best interests to leave you behind. You might be tempted to speak of matters that are confidential. It would be more logical to keep you on the team, so to speak. I don't imagine you will mind working for us now, will you?"

"No, I guess not."

"Good, then if you would be kind enough to extinguish the light and check through the windows to make sure we are still quite alone."

Katy, whose room was growing darker by the minute, saw the light under the doorsill go out. Then she heard something that struck terror into her heart. A single gunshot and the sound of something heavy falling.

An instant later she heard the neutral voice. "Apparently, Karl experienced the misery of a falling-out amongst thieves. When the authorities find him, I believe that is what they will conclude. Now we have work to do while the Hawthornes enjoy their wild-goose chase."

She heard the front door close, and everything went completely quiet. She continued working at the ropes. She'd gotten one knot free and stretched out the loops around her wrists. The last thing she wanted to do was end up starving to death tied to a stupid chair, or worse, wait for the men to come back and hasten her manner of death.

◆

The Hawthornes weren't exactly on a wild-goose chase. Thanks to Benjamin's flair for technology, the phone call to Connor's suite giving the location of the money drop was instantly and undetectably forwarded to his regular cell phone. He knew the occasional echo on the satellite device might give them away, so he'd chosen a local cell instead. He'd also placed a powerful booster antenna atop the car to avoid static or interference. It wasn't perfect, but he'd hoped Karl wasn't all that bright and that no one who was more perceptive would be listening to it. When he took the call, they were parked on a shadowy lay-by less than 500 meters from the location blinking on the GPS tracking receiver. Connor and Laura were already out of the car, along with William and Ellen. All four were crouched behind hedges near the stone farmhouse and waiting for a signal from Benjamin. As soon as he hung up from his conversation with Karl, he sent a beep to the earpieces of their walkie-talkies. Now all they could do was wait in the cold silence.

Thus it was that all of them heard the shot, and it was all the other three could do to restrain Connor from rushing headlong inside to rescue her daughter.

"Stop!" hissed Laura. "I told you. She's alive. She's all right. And that shot wasn't for her, I promise."

Ellen nodded in agreement. "I'd feel it, Connor. I swear to you. That girl is very dear to me." Connor nearly wept with frustration, but she hunkered back down. Moments later, two men came out of the farmhouse and got into one of the cars parked behind it. To their immense relief, they were not dragging Katy with them, assuming of course that she was inside.

They ducked lower as the headlights swept over the hedges, and within moments the sound of the car had died away. Now it was a question of speed. Find Katy. If she was not there, then they needed to race to the money-drop location and complete the ransom demand. If she were there, three men loaned to Benjamin by his friend, James, would greet the kidnappers instead.

Connor was the first through the door, showing no caution whatsoever. The house was dark and she fell over something, then switched on her flashlight and found the body of a man stretched out in front of her. William and Ellen were silently coming through the back door, and Laura was right behind Connor. "That would be Karl," whispered Laura, shining her light on his face. "And that explains the gunshot."

Connor crept down the hall to the first door and carefully began to open it. An instant later, the door came back at her, sending her reeling against the opposite wall. "What the hell!" she exclaimed, completely forgetting the need for stealth.

"Mom?" came a tentative voice from the other side of the door.

"Katy!" Connor yelled, picking herself up and rushing the door. This time, however, it did not fight back, and to Connor's eternal thankfulness, there stood her daughter, standing in the middle of the room, still half tied to a chair. And Connor hugged her, chair and all.

"I'm sorry, Mom," said Katy once Laura had helped extricate her from the tangle of rope. I thought you were one of those guys coming back, and I felt like dishing out a little payback."

Connor rubbed her forehead, where a lump was coming up rapidly. "Don't apologize, sweetheart. I'll take a full-scale skull fracture just to see you safe and sound."

William had immediately radioed Benjamin that Katy was safe. He whipped the car into the driveway and directly up to the front door, left the motor running and ran into the house. It was his turn to hug Katy and he could hardly stop doing it.

"Hey, Gramps," she mumbled "I can't breathe. You're pretty strong for an old guy."

This made them all laugh with relief and sheer joy. Connor couldn't take her eyes off her daughter. "I swear I'm never letting you out of my sight again."

"Oh, yes, you are, mother," said Katy drily. "Don't get all dramatic. But what happened? I could hear them talking out there for hours. And then something about £100,000. But most of it was about the crystal. Isn't that what they wanted, the crystal?"

They all looked at each other. Ellen was particularly grim. "I think, Benjamin, that you were right all along. Those two men who left aren't going to walk into any kind trap tonight, certainly not the one we set. All of this was nothing more than a diversion. They had no way of knowing we could find Katy because of the tracking device, but they didn't care when we found her or if we did. This was just to get us out of the way."

"But the crystal's at the hotel and Carmen and Jenny are standing watch over it with the door locked and chained," said Benjamin. "These people can't be rash enough to simply try and take it from such a public place."

Ellen shook her heard. "I think they'd do anything to get it."

As if of one mind, they all headed for the door and squeezed into the car. There was no way to call the room and warn the two women to be especially careful because of the way Benjamin had rigged the forwarded telephone line. Instead, all they could was drive, and Benjamin set a record in getting back to the heart of York. But by then it was far too little, too late.

◆

Jenny and Carmen had waited anxiously for the return of their friends. For her part, Jenny was as certain as Ellen and Laura that Katy was still very much alive. But she had little clairvoyance beyond that. She couldn't even tell if the rest of them would be safe on their rescue mission. As their worries mounted, so did their tension. They began to expect the worst. When the knock came and a voice announced, "Please open the door Ms. Hawthorne, it's the police," Carmen simply didn't think; she reacted. And she paid painfully for the mistake because the first man through the door punched her hard in the jaw. Jenny, outraged at the sight of her lover topping backward over an end table, charged at them head-long. But Mickey Dandridge treated her with the same cruelty. He grabbed her by the hair, slapped her hard, then used the same pressure point with which he'd rendered Katy unconscious. Yoshi was already holding the crystal shard reverently in his hands. But just as Jenny slumped to the floor, the pulsating lights within the brilliant fragment went out almost completely.

"What happened to it?" said Mickey. "Why did it stop?"

"I don't know," snapped Yoshi, looking from Jenny to the crystal and back again at her inert form. "Maybe it has something to do with her."

"Hey, I'm not trying to get another body out of this fucking hotel."

Yoshi shrugged. "If we need her, we can get her later. For now, this is what we came for."

They were long gone before the Hawthornes, Laura, and the Carlisles unlocked the door and came bursting into the room.

Carmen was already coming around and immediately saw Jenny lying there. "Oh God, Oh God, is she all right?"

Laura had already checked her pulse. "She's alive. Just knocked out."

Katy rubbed her own neck. "I'll bet the son of a bitch used the same trick on her as he did on me. Puts you out like a light."

Ellen put an arm around Carmen. "Calm down, child. It's all right now. Everyone is safe."

"Yes," said Connor, pointing toward the coffee table. "But the crystal is gone."

"We must get it back," Ellen said quite firmly.

"But we don't even know where to begin looking," replied Connor. "And to be honest, all I care about is that my daughter is alive and well, and Jenny and Carmen are alive and well, and Dad isn't even out £100,000 sterling. So why can't we just let this go? If this Matsumoto character wants the damn thing so badly, let him have it."

"Because he may do something with it that's much worse for the state of the world than anything Sister Sonia was about to dream up," insisted Ellen.

Connor looked at her. "You're serious, aren't you?

"Yes, I am. And once Jenny comes around, I think she will agree with me wholeheartedly. We must discover what can be done with this artifact, and who can do it."

"You know what, Ellen? I really hate these doomsday scenario things."

"I'm not crazy about them either, my Lady," said Ellen, countering Connor's moderate sarcasm with a serious use of Connor's spiritual title. "But we have to deal with whatever shows up. That's part of the job description."

Chapter Eighteen

The abode of God, too, is wherever is earth and
sea and air and sky and virtue.
Why further do we seek the Gods of heaven?
Whatever thou dost behold, and whatever thou
does touch, that is God.
—Lucan, *Works*

On the ninth of November, Connor, Laura, Benjamin, and the Carlisles, along with Jenny Carpenter and Carmen Waters had returned to London and dispersed to various destinations. There was nothing more to be done in York, and the police continued their investigation of the murder of Sister Sonia, though the case was slated for closure since the bodies of Karl Jensen and Mickey Dandridge had been found in separate locations on the outskirts of York. That, in itself, was a puzzle to the local authorities because now they had additional murders to solve that seemed related to Sister Sonia's death, and yet both of the current victims were the two most likely suspects in the original murder. This frustrated Lindstrom enormously, as one could not in all good conscience arrest a corpse.

The Children of Artemis, now leaderless, or perhaps more precisely, parentless, began to wander away as soon as they were given permission to do so by the local police. Some stayed, figuring on free lodgings until someone came along to kick them out. Soon, the legal wrangling would begin over the assets of the community, all of which appeared to be in Sonia's name, a woman with no past, no current confirmed identity, and obviously no future. The only member of the community unaccounted for was Alan Durn, the infamous consort of the late great goddess herself.

Back home once more, Ellen and William settled down to some serious research, both in the generally accepted sense of the word, meaning they consulted books, rather archaic and esoteric ones at that, and also in the not so common sense of exploring the astral plane for access to some very old sections of what some called the Akashic Records. These were not records by any traditional definition. Depending on one's level of understanding, they could just as easily contain records of what, to humans on planet Earth, had not even happened yet. But because the streams of time and probability could conceivably shift, nothing was engraved in stone, so to speak. Humans occasionally made entirely unpredictable choices, and thus records would themselves shift to reflect this. How can something be and not be? Such conundrums remained in the realm of multidimensional thinking, and few human beings were ready to tackle that mountain. Some few did. Among them were a few mystics, even a handful of scientists, spiritual practitioners, and guardians like those of the Circle of Light. They had been among those who had joined forces with other powerful spiritual groups both on the physical planes and the astral planes to keep Hitler himself from reaching England. So, in a sense, they had already altered the course of history, for it could have turned out quite differently. As far as William and Ellen were concerned, that topic almost inevitably led them into an unending and insoluble debate about ideas such as destiny and fate, so they generally steered away from that conversation.

Today, however, they were locked in an unusually heated argument, heated for them anyway, though it would have seemed a mild disagreement to a bystander. For they were not only gentle by nature but British by birth.

"Ellen, what you're proposing simply isn't possible given the circumstances."

"And why not?" she asked, a definite edge to her voice.

"If what Jenny remembers when she was Alandra is true, or at least is a valid part of one particular reality or time stream, then we know that Lady Deirdre's attempts to pervert the power of the crystal formations ended in disaster and complete destruction."

"True."

"Then how could anyone like this Matsumoto character, by simply fooling around with one arguably damaged obelisk, accomplish anything that would adversely affect this particular world as whole?"

Ellen's face took on the stubborn set he had learned to recognize and avoid when possible. "I don't know any of this for certain, but there is some risk. I feel it in my bones, in my heart. He is going to try to 'fool around' with that crystal, as you put it so lightly. And my point is that anything is possible."

"But he has no knowledge, no skill, no circle like ours to direct energy and force."

"How can you be sure of that?"

"Benjamin's research indicates he's nothing more than a greedy, arrogant businessman. He may be completely convinced that he can somehow control a source of energy that could prove invaluable."

"Or he could think he has the power to control people with it, William—or worse, alter the course of the future."

William regarded her thoughtfully. "But he could only do that if…"

"Exactly," she said, nodding vigorously. "Now you're beginning to see my point."

◆

Katy had returned to her office, even though it was the weekend, and was delighted to see Philip visiting his Uncle Ian. She decided to forego mentioning anything about her adventures in York, and simply congratulated Philip on his astoundingly good health. At least she hoped it would last. But her skepticism was as strong as her mother's when it came to such things, so she would reserve judgment. She was simply more than grateful to be back to a life that was quite comfortingly sane. She'd offered to let Carmen and Jenny stay with her in her small flat, but they'd chosen instead to accompany Laura and Connor to Rosewood Cottage in the small village of St. Giles on Wyndle, a beautiful old thatched "cottage" of handsome proportions that had once belonged to Connor's grandmother Gwendolyn Broadhurst. Connor had inherited the house, along with the more burdensome role of high priestess of the Circle of Light. But as she did not work in that capacity very often, only when absolutely necessary, she didn't grumble too much about it.

Jenny and Carmen found the house enchanting and had immediately settled into one of the guest rooms. They all slept soundly and arose surrounded by clean air and pure normality. Connor and Laura opted for a walk in the garden Sunday afternoon, beautifully kept up by Mrs. Broadhurst's loyal horticultural expert, the gruff but efficient Ferguson. Though in his seventies now, he brought his nephews every week to prune and trim and weed. Connor knew it was well worth the modest fees he charged.

"So what do you suppose we're going to do about the crystal?" asked Laura.

Connor looked at her with some surprise. "I wasn't aware we definitely needed to do anything. I haven't heard a peep out of Ellen."

"It's only been a day since she and William started investigating from their end," said Laura. "And you know as well as I do that this isn't over."

"Sweetheart, I don't even know what 'this' is!" said Connor in exasperation.

"You had a dream last night, didn't you?"

"How did you know?"

Laura smiled and linked her arm through Connor's. "Some nights the Dreamtime is like Grand Central Station. I thought I caught of a glimpse of our Gwendolyn."

Connor sighed softly. "Yes, she was out and about. Funny, I haven't even felt her presence in a while, and all of a sudden there she was."

"And what did she have to say?"

They sat down on a wicker settee. "Not much really, but I have a feeling she'll be back. She just said something about how impossible people are when they take up human form."

"She didn't mean you, did she?" asked Laura with a soft chuckle.

"Probably. Well, at least partly. But no, she sounded rather irritated with someone or something."

"So Ellen's right. There's an amateur out there messing with something he shouldn't."

"Gwendolyn did use the term 'mucking about' in what's none of their business, or something to that effect."

"Tonight's conversation should be interesting. Wish I could be there."

"Why can't you?"

"You don't show up to such occasions uninvited, darling," said Laura. "It's against the rules to drop in unless your higher self is asked by that other person's higher self."

"Can't my good old everyday lower self just ask you now?" asked Connor.

"To join you and Gwendolyn in the Dreamtime?"

"Yes," said Connor. "Sort of like an advance invitation."

"It doesn't quite work that way, but you're welcome to try from wherever you find yourself later."

"I intend to find myself in bed with you."

"That sounds perfectly fine to me," grinned Laura.

"Which reminds me," said Connor, "now that we're talking about asking things."

"Yes?"

"You know the other day, and it seems like forever ago, when were getting off the plane and I said—"

"Hi, guys," came a voice from behind them. Connor swore

softly under her breath at being interrupted, and almost turned to greet the intruder with a scowl until she realized the voice was not some stranger's but Katy's.

"What on earth?" said Connor. "I thought you were tucked into your nice cozy flat in London and dearly glad to be shut of your meddlesome old mother."

Katy grinned. "Well, part of that's true, but Ellen called and suggested we all gather down here tonight. So I hopped in the car."

"Funny she hasn't mentioned it to me," said Connor.

"She said she sent you a message last night."

Connor looked puzzled for a brief moment. "You know, now that I think about it, you're right. I seem to recall a little buzzing in my ear, so to speak."

"So what do you have to eat? I'm starved."

"We didn't get much food in yesterday, but there are some crackers and cheese and…wait a minute…which part of that is true? About your cozy flat or your meddlesome mother?"

"I'll never tell," said Katy.

♦

Carmen and Jenny weren't in the house, but there was a brief note explaining that they'd gone for a walk in the village. While Katy raided the larder and munched on handfuls of whatever she could find, Connor called Ellen the old-fashioned way, by telephone and confirmed that they'd be having a meeting of the minds, so to speak, at about eight. Ellen said she was bringing dinner for everyone so not to worry. She knew the village shops were closed in St. Giles, and the local pub would hardly suit the occasion.

Connor went back to the kitchen. "I guess we're on. And I'm going to go and check on the other guest rooms. For once I'm glad this is a big house. We can put everyone up for the night. I guess Dad is coming down, too."

The sound of tires on gravel confirmed that supposition, and once again Connor wished her life contained somewhat fewer coincidences, except that in her heart she knew there was no such thing as coincidence. That, as usual, annoyed her, though not in a hugely pissed-off sort of way; it was more like the way a mosquito can buzz in your ear at night so you can't sleep. It's there and you can't avoid it.

Benjamin took the long way around and appeared outside the kitchen door, an overnighter slung over his shoulder and his arms full of grocery bags. "I didn't think you'd have time to shop yesterday afternoon, and the shops here are closed on Sunday, aren't they?"

He dumped the bags on the long oak table. "I recall that my granddaughter is an eating machine, so I've brought plenty."

"Gee thanks, Gramps. You make me sound like a side-show attraction. Besides, Ellen's bringing something for dinner. Oh, look, you got shortbread!"

Connor choked back the maternal impulse to utter the infamous phrase "no sweets before dinner" — a rule that had gone out with bedtimes and curfews some years earlier. "I suppose we could put together some hors d'oeuvres for Carmen and Jenny when they get back."

"Then we'll go sit in the library," said Katy. "I do love that room."

"It has been the scene of some interesting family history," said Connor wryly. "But then you love that sort of thing."

"Actually, I do," said Katy, after politely swallowing her shortbread cookie. "Family history is big these days—you know, finding your roots."

"Honey, you already know about your roots, and you know that in some cases they are exceedingly odd."

"Odd but fascinating. And Dad's side of the family is exceedingly boring, so thank God for the Broadhurst women."

Connor winced ever so slightly at the mention of her ex-husband of long, long ago, to whom she had been married ever so briefly. She was only grateful that he'd had so little interest in his offspring that he hadn't had a chance to imbue Katy with his innate pomposity. Fortunately, his subsequent wife was happy to worship at his feet with all due respect, as were Katy's half sisters. Thus, he was not troubled about his first daughter's utter lack of devotion. He was scrupulous in sending birthday gifts and Christmas cards and had attended her prep school graduation. That was about it and, for Connor, more than enough.

She and Laura quickly arranged some trays of cheese, crackers, and other delicacies that Benjamin had brought and adjourned to the library where they were soon joined by Carmen and Jenny. "This is the most beautiful village," said Carmen. "I can't believe it. I don't even care about going back to Palm Springs." She suddenly fell quiet. "Although now that Bettina's gone, I guess I'll have to go and take care of things."

They were all quiet, not knowing exactly what to say. The loss was still quite fresh for Carmen, and a lot had happened to her in a very short time. Finally, Laura made a practical suggestion. "That attorney of yours, she seems pretty competent. You could get in touch with her and ask her what needs to be done. Maybe you don't even have to be there. It might be kind of hard going back right now."

"And you're welcome to stay here, both of you, for as long as you like," added Connor. "This place gets so little use as it is."

Carmen's eyes glistened. "Thank you. All of you have been so incredibly kind. To even care so much about my sister, someone you met just once."

"She was a nice woman," said Laura. "We could tell she loved you a lot even from our brief conversation with her."

Before the sadness overtook them even further, Jenny stood and walked over to the bookshelves that lined much of the walls of the spacious room from floor to ceiling. In this room Gwendolyn Broadhurst had gathered not only the history of the world, but also an exhaustive array of books on every conceivable religious and spiritual tradition. The selections were often esoteric in the extreme and rare beyond description.

"Did your grandmother read all of these?" asked Jenny. "All these languages? Look, this is in Latin."

"Yes, she read Latin. As well as Greek, French, Italian, and German." A warmth of remembering illuminated her face. She smiled. "Her pronunciation of all the romance languages was atrocious, but she understood every written word. And her command of the classics, the so-called dead languages, was impressive."

Benjamin rose from the old overstuffed and well-worn leather wing chair where Gwendolyn had loved to sit and read. "Why don't I get the fireplace going?"

"Excellent!" said Katy. "There's always been something special about this room, and maybe it's because I can picture my great-grandmother sitting here with her toes near the fire, reading a book, or getting up to go over and consult that old globe. She loved picking out the most exotic places to study. And when we're here together, I just get the feeling she's here, too."

"That would hardly surprise me," said Laura, looking around her speculatively. "As a matter of fact, I think that we can probably assume she's not far away."

Jenny and Carmen looked at each other quizzically, as if trying to figure out if their new friends were serious or just having a little joke. Laura took pity on them.

"We actually are serious about Gwendolyn," she explained. "Connor's grandmother left this earthly plane in a rather unusual manner—sort of stepped through a portal. I know, it's hard to explain. But for whatever reason, she still seems very much in evidence from time to time. And we're glad to have her."

"I miss her," said Katy. "She doesn't talk to me that much. Not like she does to Mom."

"Believe me," said Connor, with more than a trace of irony, "she mostly lectures me. You probably wouldn't enjoy it all that much."

"Your dead grandmother lectures you?" asked Carmen, clearly unable to disguise her incredulity.

"And you thought the Artemis people were nuts?" chuckled Laura. "You haven't seen anything yet."

"Well, at least you folks are for real," said Jenny, staunchly defensive of her newly acquired allies.

"Remember what Ellen said," Connor reminded them. "Reality is relative around here."

"The relative being Gwendolyn Broadhurst," said Laura, unable to resist laughing at her own joke, which raised the energy in the room considerably.

"I think she heard that," said Connor.

"Probably," replied Laura. "Thank the Goddess she has a good sense of humor."

The chime of the doorbell announced the arrival of the Carlisles with armloads of bags and picnic baskets. "We are blessed with the cook of all cooks," said Ellen, "even though I don't mind taking a turn in the kitchen when she'll let me. But she insisted on putting together a movable feast for all of us. I personally can't wait to see what it is."

They all settled down in the kitchen, preferring the informal friendliness of it to the ornate formal dining room with its enormous mahogany Chippendale dining table expansive enough to seat twenty without any guest knocking elbows with another. But it had always struck Connor as a place that should be reserved for affairs of state, though she had certainly eaten enough dinners there as a youngster with her grandmother keeping a watchful eye on such things as table manners and appropriate topics of conversation. Unlike others of her generation, Mrs. Broadhurst had felt children should be seen *and* heard, but only if the children in question made honest attempts at reasonably interesting, or at last polite conversation, and observed a level of decorum appropriate to the setting. She was not in the least opposed to high-spirited childlike games in the out of door or in the playroom, but in the house civility ruled. Of course, in Connor's case it had been more a question of getting her to spend time doing something other than sitting with her nose in a book. And the child's choices of Nancy Drew over literary classics was something of a trial for Gwendolyn. But she managed to introduce a few of the more exciting ones over the years, and Connor had thus developed a remarkably Catholic taste in literature, though mysteries remained her first love.

The feast proved to be sumptuous indeed—including mostly items that did not need to be heated. Carmen and Jenny had their first taste of a few English delicacies like cold roast pheasant, a delicately seasoned turbot, fresh vegetables, locally produced cheeses and homemade breads. There were smoked oysters, which William claimed to be his favorite, and ample supplies of wine to accompany each course. Still, not even eight hungry people could consume the surfeit of goodies, so with a groan of satisfaction, they packed up the remains and adjourned to the library.

After several minutes, the small talk about the dinner and the joys of village life died away and silence reigned. Each of them appeared lost in thought, and it was several minutes before Ellen spoke, her voice filtering softly into the tranquility produced by the ambiance of Gwendolyn's onetime sanctuary, the tiny pops and hisses of the fire, and the general gastronomic contentment of the group.

"We have some news," she said. "William stumbled across it quite by accident in a book that I don't recall ever seeing in our library, though I have no doubt that if we searched here, we'd probably find it. After skimming through it, I recalled some odd things Gwendolyn said a long time ago. At the time, I didn't pay much attention because I thought she was simply theorizing, as she often liked to do."

From her voluminous bag, Ellen produced an ancient leather-bound book. "This was written several thousand years ago," she explained. "Not this particular version, of course. But the author whose name does not appear anywhere, undertook to translate an ancient Greek text found in a walled-up niche not too many miles from where the great library of Alexandria once stood. And that manuscript claimed to be a translation of some much older language, the name of which is not mentioned, at least not by this author. Of course, without the original, we must rely upon the skills of the translator, but in any event, the possibilities are intriguing. This particular book was written in Latin."

"Was it some sort of religious text?" asked Laura.

"No, and that surprised me a bit, because the opening chapters are about religious subjects, mostly comparative discourse, but the bulk of the material appears to have been written by a scientist."

Connor looked askance. "I don't think there was much in the way of scientific inquiry in the time frame you describe."

"Apparently, it wasn't inquiry. It was more in the nature of a history of the loss of knowledge and a prophesied return to the Dark Ages, at least intellectually. I won't bore you with all of the details, but there are certain passages you may find intriguing, assuming my own translation skills aren't too rusty. This is one of those times I'd like to have Gwendolyn here to rattle it off for us."

"We were talking about that earlier," said Connor. "Her incredible facility with languages."

"It's one of the skills that made her such an effective leader," said William. "And she even had an intuitive understanding of spoken communications in languages that were never written down, languages we heard on the astral and didn't understand. She was completely conversant with the most ancient Celtic dialects spoken by not only the wild tribes, but our ancestral spiritual forebears who wrote almost nothing down at all. But I'm sorry. I digress as usual." He motioned for his wife to continue.

"We might never have found this," she said, "or much of the other information we've gathered, except for William's foresight in cataloging our entire library and having much of it carefully scanned into computer databases so that word searches are possible. We were looking for key words like 'Atlantis,' 'crystals,' 'time travel,' and of course the date in question—'November 11.'"

Jenny sat forward on her seat eagerly. "And did you find anything to corroborate my own memories and Carmen's?"

Ellen pursed her lips slightly. "Yes and no. There is, of course, so much wild speculation about an ancient civilization that it's difficult to separate that from what could be actual history. But this book itself has convinced me beyond any doubt that there is a factual basis. And it wasn't the text that was most compelling. It was the diagrams. The translator indicated that he'd made true renderings of the originals. Here, we've made copies of some of them."

She opened a file folder and handed it around so that each of them might take a set of copies. Jenny was the first to react. It was a gasp of recognition, really. The first page was a carefully detailed sketch of a ceremonial chamber lined with tall, not entirely identical obelisks. Even in black and white, she knew they were the crystals of the inner chamber. And in her mind the entire scene took on color and depth.

"Here," she said excitedly, holding up the drawing. "These draperies were of a deep royal-blue color, and the bases of the columns were clad in the purest gold. The entire floor was a geometric pattern in dozens of different colors, leading in pathways from the outer circle surrounding the obelisks to the outer-facing side of each crystal. And the obelisks themselves stood in a complete circle with a star pattern in the very center of the floor. Only the Lord and the Lady were permitted to pass beyond the ring and into the center. You can't really see that from this perspective, though. I'm afraid you'll have to take my word for it."

Ellen smiled. "Turn to the next page, my dear."

When she did, Jenny actually fell back in her seat. This drawing had been executed from an entirely different perspective, as if the artist hung suspended over the chamber. And it was precisely as Jenny had described. The crystals stood in a ring, joined by rays of patterns in the floor, and there in the center was the symbology she'd described—a star pattern very much akin to the pentacle of modern-day Wiccans. And in the center of the star was the clearly drawn figure of a woman, naked and heavy breasted, holding in one hand a sword and in the other a branch of leaves.

"The Mother," Jenny whispered. "She was the keeper of all mysteries. This was the image of our Creator." Her eyes closed, and she slumped in the chair. Carmen started to get up and go to her, but Ellen restrained her with a gesture. After a few moments, Jenny began to speak, but none of them understood what she said. Still, the cadence of the words was entrancing, the sound of the language musical, as if Mother Nature herself had found a voice. Each of them heard something different—the trill of a sparkling brook of water tumbling over rocks; birdsong in the early hours of the morning; the rustling of a gentle breeze through the treetops; and, if such could be described in words, the heartbeat of the entire cosmos unifying with its steady rhythm all the parts of creation into one indivisible whole. For a few brief moments, every person in the room felt connected to every particle of creative energy extant in the universe.

And then it ended, cycling down to a single word, a single note, a single sound until there was silence. After a few moments, the everyday noises of the world filtered back into consciousness—the fire, the first spatterings of rain on the flagstones outside the library windows, the creak of the old house itself. Jenny opened her eyes to find the others staring at her in wonder and bewilderment.

"What happened?"

Ellen looked around at the others and finding them as speechless as she herself felt, tried nonetheless to explain. "We're not sure, my dear. But you spoke in another language, one so unlike anything we've ever heard that we could not repeat any of it if we tried. But it had a profound effect on all of us, at a heart level, a spiritual level. It didn't seem to matter that our minds, our intellects could not grasp the meaning. I don't think this kind of communication is supposed to work that way anyhow. It was more of a..."

"It was a prayer," said Carmen firmly. "And I've heard it before."

"Yes," Jenny said softly. "It was a praise to the Mother of us all."

Clearly, no one wanted to let go of the feelings they'd had during those moments, and yet they were already fading. They had shared in something so remarkable they couldn't categorize it. Ellen was correct. This wasn't about what one could discern with the mind, but only with the heart and spirit.

"Clearly, there was something beautifully sacred about that civilization," said Ellen.

"There was. We honored love and beauty and truth. We honored our human form as well as our spiritual selves. There was no qualitative distinction drawn between physical expressions of love between humans and spiritual expressions of love for the Mother and all the beings in the universe. It was all one, and it was all good."

"But something happened to change all that?" asked Ellen.

"The Lady Deirdre came to believe that she could cheat death itself, that she could put herself above the Mother."

Jenny lowered her head and absently paged through the remaining diagrams. "It's all so incredibly familiar," she said. Even this rough sketch of the city itself. There, on the fourth level of the central temple. That's where Junela and I lived until...until the end."

Carmen who had also been studying the drawings, lifted her eyes to Jenny. In them was more recognition than ever before. "Yes, you're right. I can see it, too."

"I'm curious about something," said Connor. "Well, actually a lot of different things, But this is more personal I suppose. Were all of the priestesses lovers of women?"

Jenny smiled. "No, of course not. But in our society, gender wasn't the primary basis for forming relationships. The energy of love between souls was the driving force. I can't give you percentages about how many of us loved those of our own physical gender, because one's choices need not remain the same. We had the ability to recognize our spiritual mates in whatever form they had taken on. So no one was limited to one...nowadays I suppose they call it a lifestyle. But, for us, love was simply a way of life. We extended it not only to those with whom we were physically intimate but to all beings. Yes, some mated for life because they happened upon the incarnation of a twin flame, or a Goddess-granted gift of extraordinary passion. That existed between Junela and me, and of course between Lady Deirdre and Lord Arkan.

So when he died, she refused to accept it."

"Exactly, and that was a complete denial of everything we believed. Death had never been a permanent separation—a cause for grief, for mourning, and perhaps even a reason to decide not to choose another intimate relationship in that lifetime. But we believed that each person's time was chosen, either by their own decision before incarnation, or by their choices in life, or perhaps even with the guidance of the Mother Herself. It was our custom to celebrate the lives of those whose physical forms had ended, not wallow endlessly in anger over the loss."

"Whatever happened that your leader would abandon a lifetime of faith, then?" asked Ellen.

"I don't know. She seemed possessed, and I sometimes wonder if it wasn't partly Arkan himself, wanting to return to her as much as she wanted him back. That's only a supposition, but the love between them was a powerful force." She paused. "That's the real secret you know, and I have no idea if it's there in that book you found. But it's the pure energy of love that brings the crystals to life because that energy invokes the Mother."

"I notice you speak only of the Mother," said William, his intellectual curiosity piqued. "Most ancient civilizations allow for a male deity as well."

"Yes, of course. The universe itself is driven by and hangs within the balance of duality, of complementary energies that can be called male and female. Unlike your current mainstream religions, which have been reduced to a sad parody of spirituality with but one patriarchal pronoun of a god, we acknowledged both. However, for us, life emerged from the womb of the Mother. Thus, our worship of her was more overt perhaps. Yet the Father existed as well. That energy, for lack of a better word, 'fertilized' the engine of creation. What you see here is the temple of the Mother. The temple of the Father was maintained by acolytes and priests. The priests came to our temple each month on the night of the full moon and entered into the sacred circle to perform their rites of devotion. There were eleven of them and eleven of us. Our twelfth was Lady Deirdre, and the thirteenth of course was the Mother. It worked the same for them. Arkan was their twelfth and the Father their thirteenth. But the sacred number of priestesses matched the number of crystal pillars—eleven."

Laura, having studied the drawings carefully, put them aside. "You told us briefly before of the destruction, and yet I'm not sure I understand what this Lady Deirdre did exactly."

Jenny sighed. "Again, it is so difficult to put into words, but she entered the temple on the full moon and ordered the priests away. This, in itself, was a major disturbance in the ebb and flow of life energy that sustained us. But that was also the one night when she was not permitted to enter the circle. She also entered with arrogance and anger directed at creation itself. I've told you already that the crystals are energized by pure love. She loved Arkan, but that was not her foremost thought when she entered the chamber. And somehow she set up such a dissonance that it literally set up a field that began to shatter the great crystals into pieces. Such power was released, such an intense vibration, that it had the force of an atomic bomb, sending energy out in wave upon wave, crumbling buildings, causing heart attacks, making people so frightened they literally dropped dead in the streets. And the vibrations extended deep into the earth. That is why, I think, that the island began to sink." Jenny paused. "But I can't blame all of this on Lady Deirdre. Something had already begun to deteriorate in our society. Perhaps it was her bitterness poisoning the energy field that sustained Atlantis, and it spread like a disease, but things right before the end were no longer idyllic by any means. Much of what we cherished as a people was being lost. Greed and arrogance were showing up. Basic rights that had belonged to every citizen were being curtailed. And there were some who were clearly bent on accumulating personal power and control over others. It was sickening to see.

"I don't mean to insult you, but it was beginning to show signs of the same ills that plague your society now. So perhaps it was not meant to survive and Lady Deirdre was only the tool by which its demise was accomplished."

"That may be," said Benjamin quietly, "and I'm not offended. The world we live in now is plagued with all of the things you've mentioned and more. But we have to work with what is. And what I'm wondering if whether there's anything in all this that can help us figure out what Pantheon actually wants with the crystal, or perhaps it's only Yohiro Matsumoto. I'm not sure. But he certainly was the driving force behind Katy's kidnapping and the theft of the remaining fragment, and perhaps even the raid on the island that resulted in so much death." He regarded Jenny with deep compassion when he said this, knowing that she still must be suffering the effects of that experience. She was certainly a candidate for post-traumatic stress syndrome. He only hoped it wouldn't affect her judgment now, when they needed her knowledge.

"Why did Lady Deirdre think she could reverse the fact of Arkan's death?" asked Katy with her usual practicality.

"Because time is fluid," said Jenny simply. "We talked about this a little bit when we were in York. And it runs in infinite parallel streams. There could be a different reality operating right next to us, sort of—the same people sitting in the same room, but with an entirely different purpose. And their actions could lead in completely different directions than ours. That's just one example. If you take the idea back to the very beginning of creation itself, can you imagine how many different time streams have branched off from that first moment of life? Every single choice made by every single being creates an entirely new set of possibilities and outcomes."

"That sort of boggles the mind," said Connor.

"Which is why the human mind nowadays is limited to third-dimensional thinking with linear time as its framework. And it's why we access only that tiny little portion of our brains. If we were able to access all of our capabilities, we could grasp this without actually going insane. For that matter, some of your schizophrenics probably do grasp it, but you lock them up. Deirdre used an enormous proportion of her physical brain. She could actually see other time streams as they developed. While Arkan was alive, she simply observed them, taught us about them, helped us to see lessons in the choices of others. But when he died, she somehow came to believe that she could either enter another time stream in which he survived, or she could manipulate events that led to his death in her own time stream. Either way, she was tinkering with the mechanics of the cosmos, and that's a mistake beyond reckoning. But I could not dissuade her from it."

"Do you think Sonia was developing the same sorts of powers or consciousness that Lady Deirdre had?" asked Katy. "Is that why she began to seem much more powerful, or actually was more powerful. You know my friend's brother really appears to have been healed,"

"Healing was part of our society. The laying on of hands was sacred work because it channeled energy into any sort of disease that had developed in the physical body."

"Then wouldn't everyone in your culture have been virtually immortal?" asked Connor.

"I suppose that would have been possible. But no one lusted after immortality. We all knew this was but one life in many. Why prolong it past the point of one's destiny, one's useful time of growth and learning and service to others? Immortality simply for the sake of hanging around longer just didn't seem a worthy goal. We were not acquisitive by nature or temperament. Almost everything was communally owned, other than a few personal possessions. Everyone had enough."

"It does sound idyllic," said Katy.

"But it wasn't. Like every piece of creation, it grew, it thrived, it died. With all of our wisdom, corruption of the heart and mind still crept in."

"What do you suppose our world would be like if Atlantis had survived?"

Jenny shook her head. "I have no idea. How could we ever have integrated primitive humans into our society? We truly were more like visitors to this planet. Your forebears were meant to develop here. And so they have."

"Not all that successfully by the look of things," commented Connor.

"Oh, now you're being too cynical," said Ellen. "Look at how much good has been accomplished. Look at how much good is done in the world today."

"Mass murder, genocide, religious wars, mushroom clouds, napalm, deforestation, persecution, hatred and prejudice, ethnocentrism, public stoning of women and children, pollution, species eliminated by the hundreds every day—need I go on?"

"Gee, sweetheart, you really know how to bring down a room," said Laura. "I'm glad you're not the person writing the history of the world. You might leave out all the good parts."

"Yes," said Jenny. "I don't mean to sound like some stupid slogan of the sixties, but love really is the most powerful force in the universe, and it can save even what we think we've lost."

"Hmm," muttered Connor in polite disagreement.

"I actually tend to agree with Jenny," said Benjamin, "despite my experience of man's worst inhumanities to man, and I hate to be a wet blanket when the discussion is getting so interesting, but we're getting pretty far afield. Perhaps we could table the state of the world discussion and focus on one particular part of it."

"The crystal," said Ellen. "Yes, we must get back on track here. And my first supposition is that someone, probably this Matsumoto character, has an intention of using the crystal for entirely personal, and primarily esoteric purposes."

"You mean like Lady Deirdre?" asked Carmen.,

"That would explain part of it," said Jenny.

"Which part?" asked Laura.

"That she died. At first that really caught me off-guard, made me doubt my sanity even. I had become completely convinced that she was trying to lead people down the same destructive path, and when she was killed, that obviously wasn't going to happen. Then I realized that it had to be someone else who would attempt the impossible. She had simply returned to work out a karmic debt."

"And did she?"

"I can't tell," said Jenny. "I'm nowhere near wise enough to figure that out."

"But what could this man possibly do with one crystal obelisk? It took eleven of them to maintain the energy field that protected and vitalized Atlantis. And it certainly took the entire circle in a state of disruption to destroy it," said Carmen.

"But that's just it," said Ellen with a shade of triumph in her voice. "He can create a circle right here in England. At least that's my theory."

"But where would be get ten more of these two-story crystals?" asked Connor. "He had to resort to murder and kidnapping to get back one fragment of one crystal they've found."

"We don't know how many of these Pantheon's explorations may have turned up," Ellen said. "But just for the sake of argument, let's say that he only has the one and it is intact now. There are but a handful of places on this planet where he could try to establish an energy field strong enough for his purposes."

"Which we still haven't identified," said Connor.

"No, but I think that will become quite clear to us within the next twenty-four hours. I'm simply supposing here. Of all the possible locations, there is only one in England that would suffice."

"But how can we possibly assume that it's in England?" asked Connor with a frown, "You just said there were others."

"Because *we're* here," Ellen replied simply.

"What?"

"We're here, and we are the only ones apparently who know about this. And all of us had a feeling that we are involved in the final outcome. So it's really a simple assumption, given universal law, and the impending date, that we are already where we're supposed to be in order to intervene. Otherwise, we'd all be somewhere else entirely. I know," she said, raising her hand to ward off Connor's logical objections. "It's most definitely a chicken-and-egg thing, but let's save that for another day."

"All right, we'll take on the assumption," said Benjamin. "What is your best guess about Matsumoto's plan?"

"I admittedly can't identify his goal, but whatever the process is, he needs an energy center, a powerful one. And though England is replete with power spots and ley lines and such, there are only two stone circles of any significant power."

"Stonehenge?" ventured Carmen.

Ellen nodded. "Yes, but it's too public and it's too restricted, and most of all, it's probably too young."

"Too young?"

"By cosmic standards, yes. And it wasn't constructed all that long ago, relatively speaking, though I suspect it's another 'visitor' site constructed by races of people perhaps similar to Atlanteans."

"Well, they certainly weren't trying to keep out of the way of the primitives on the planet," said Laura.

"No, they weren't. How do you suppose so many cultures ended up with a complete pantheon of gods? Because visitors would seem very much like gods."

Connor groaned. "Oh, please, not the alien thing. I really hate the alien thing."

Laura shook her head. "We're not talking about Sigourney Weaver movies, darling. The cosmos is inhabited, whether you like it or not. And just because we humans don't manage to get around much doesn't mean other citizens of the universe don't have a booming tourist industry."

"Okay, okay," said Benjamin, well-accustomed to the ongoing argument between his daughter and her lover. "We're not going to settle that question right now. What I would like to know is what Ellen has in mind."

She closed her file of notes. "Avebury."

"You mean the stone circle there?" asked Laura. "I love that place. It feels immensely old to me."

"It is. And yet the standing stones are still highly energized. I feel it whenever I visit there. My theory is that something is feeding them."

"Feeding?" asked Jenny.

"Energy. They're not moribund, like the pillars of Stonehenge.

I think Avebury was constructed for a different purpose entirely, and the stones are still well-grounded to the earth and drawing energy from it, perhaps even from the remains of your culture's crystal formations."

"So if Matsumoto chooses England, and you're quite convinced he already has, then Avebury is the location for his experiment, if indeed that's what it is," said Katy. "But how would someone like that even know what Ellen and William know, or the people in your circle? He's a Japanese businessman with a talent for acquiring money."

"He's more than that, I believe," said Benjamin. "So perhaps this is where I can make my contribution. I did more digging on him. Strangely low-key sort of person, extremely private but, according to a few escapees from his organization, also quite eccentric about certain subjects. I confirmed this with some delicate hacking. His reading tastes are in ancient cultures, especially Greek theology, and he's purchased every book ever written about Atlantis or Lemuria, Easter Island, and the Mayan and Aztec cultures. He is also an expert in geology, archaeology, martial arts, and is rabidly ethnocentric. He believes that the various East Asian cultures represent the height of civilization.

"But our true story has never been written down," protested Jenny. "How could he know any of it?"

"Two possibilities that I see," said William. "He got hold of a copy of this very book that Ellen discovered in our library, and you yourself admit there are startlingly correct details in the drawings."

"And I'll read you parts of it later," said Ellen. "I think you'll be impressed by some other information that is very much aligned with your memories."

"You said there were two possibilities," prompted Laura.

"The other is even simpler. Matsumoto knows because he was there."

"What?" said Benjamin, Connor, and Carmen in unison.

William shrugged. "Why do we assume that Jenny and Carmen are the only individuals currently incarnate on the planet who were part of Atlantis? What if the simple truth is that through some sort of triggering mechanism, Matsumoto has also recovered genetic coding of memory of that time? Then it is easy enough to see why he would behave the way he apparently has."

"But who might he have been?" asked Jenny. "Certainly someone with knowledge of the mysteries, maybe one of the priests from the temple of the Father."

Laura nodded. "And didn't you mention in York that there was someone you didn't trust during that time, someone who was taking advantage of Arkan's death?"

"Yes, his name was…Cantos. He tried to take Arkan's position, but that isn't how it was supposed to work. The priests were required to go the temple of the Mother on the full moon and allow her to select one of them. Then an acolyte, a trainee, sort of, would be chosen to fill the empty seat of that priest. Cantos refused to participate in the ritual. He seized the leadership,"

"Well then, perhaps there's your answer," said William. "At least it's a working theory, and it makes rather more sense than pure coincidence." His eyes twinkled when he said this, for he directed it mostly toward Connor and her arbitrary dislike of coincidence in any form.

Ellen spoke up. "And in this book, I find constant references to the phrase eleven-eleven, and the numbers themselves are used in various contexts. Then there is Jenny's account of the sacred number of priestesses and priests—eleven. I think we're onto something, and I believe that Matsumoto does as well."

"But even if he's attached a significance to November 11, that still wouldn't explain what his goal is. I mean, does he think he can raise an entire city from the dead, restore a lost culture? But why would he even want to?" asked Jenny.

Ellen flipped open her file and pulled out another sketch. "Because of this perhaps. It was also part of the book I had reproduced." She passed it to Jenny, who studied it carefully.

"Of course. You know, it never occurred to me," she said and handed it on to Carmen. Likewise, she treated it with recognition but also puzzlement. Around the group it went until it reached Connor, sitting next to Laura on the small sofa at right angles to the fireplace. She raised an eyebrow. "I think Ellen is on to something." The face looking back at her was a warrior of an unknown era but of unmistakably East Asian appearance. "No wonder Mr. Matsumoto is so fascinated with Atlantis."

Laura turned to Jenny. "This is probably not a question that you or anyone else could answer, but do you suppose there's any chance at all there were survivors of your civilization, that they somehow lived on to propagate an entire race?"

Jenny shook her heard. "No. I don't believe anyone could possibly have survived. Atlantis was an island, a thousand miles or more from any groups of humans and in the midst of an ocean. That was the point—isolation and noninterference. None of us left the island city for any reason. Our stay was to be temporary anyway, no more than a thousand years."

Ellen cleared her throat meaningfully. "That might not be entirely accurate. We didn't restrict our research to books and manuscripts. William and I and the Circle did a little exploration on the astral as well. There's a definite source of concern there, and it is undeniably connected to your lost city. We saw traces of another time stream in which people of your group left the island in small boats and traveled to one or more of the main continents."

"But that just isn't possible," protested Jenny."

"On the other hand," said Connor, "it would explain some rather bizarre anomalies in human evolution that science has never adequately explained—the sudden advancements in technology here and there, the obliteration of one evolutionary branch, and the flourishing of another. Perhaps there was interference of some sort."

Benjamin interrupted the debate. "Again, my friends, we have stumbled upon something so difficult to argue, we might spend hours and get nowhere. I hate to sound like a broken record, but if we could stick to practical matters of what we're going to do about Matsumoto. Do we all agree with Ellen that Avebury is the likeliest location for whatever it is he has planned?"

No one disagreed, so he went on. "I think it's imperative that we be there. Of course, I have absolutely no idea what we are supposed to do or what we'll find. It could turn out to be a colossal waste of time."

"But we do have a chance to lay hands on the man who engineered Katy's kidnapping and quite possibly those responsible for murder of Sister Sonia as well as Dandridge and that Karl fellow," said William. "Not that the latter two were any great loss, but still. I don't like people who go about with the idea that they can murder with impunity if it suits their purposes."

"Nor do I," said Benjamin. "It is only a stroke of fortune really that Katy escaped with her life."

Katy smiled grimly. "Who knew they'd take the batteries out of the PDA, Gramps, and activate the GPS signal without even knowing it? That was a stroke of genius you had, by the way, giving me that."

"Thank your mother. She wouldn't have let you go to York without some way to track you down."

"Okay. Thanks, Mom." She paused, "You haven't planted anything else on me, have you, just to be on the safe side?"

Connor smiled. "No, but it isn't a bad idea. Maybe I'll get one of Dad's wonderboys or wondergirls at the lab in D.C. to cook up something."

"You wouldn't dare!"

"Probably not."

Ellen yawned deeply. "Oh, excuse me, but I'm suddenly exhausted. I vote for a good night's sleep, and we can tackle this again in the morning."

"I'm with you," said Jenny, discovering that Ellen's yawn was highly contagious. She and Carmen said their good-nights, followed closely by Laura and Connor, and then Katy.

The older folk stayed behind for a few moments.

Benjamin eyed the Carlisles with a shrewdly inquisitive expression. "How much risk is there in all this?"

"Risk to what?" asked Ellen.

"This sounds a little odd, but risk to this world. I'm not a believer in all the Armageddon nonsense some of these fringe groups are peddling nowadays, but on the other hand I've seen some of the research our own theoretical physicists have done. Most people don't know that the U.S. government pours money into experiments in things like time travel, for example, though nothing's ever come of it. But it's always worried me that they might stumble onto something and then inadvertently destroy the very world they're trying to improve."

"It isn't out of the realm of possibility, old man," said William kindly. "But don't lose any sleep over it. If everything as we know it on this plane were about to end, I'm fairly sure there would be more indication of it. Don't you, Ellen?"

She looked less convinced but still agreed. "The disturbances in the astral can be explained by a lot of different things, so it's best to reserve judgment. But you are wise to be concerned about humankind's tendency to meddle in things they don't even begin to understand."

Chapter Nineteen

Nature that fram'd us of four elements,
Warring within our breasts for regiment,
Doth teach us all to have aspiring minds;
Or souls, whose faculties can comprehend
The Wondrous architecture of the world:
Still climbing after knowledge infinite,
And always moving as the restless Spheres,
Will us to wear ourselves and never rest...
—Christopher Marlowe,
Conquests of Tamburlaine, Prologue

ELSEWHERE

Within the reaches of the inner temple, young Dante turned to the elder known only as Teacher and asked, "How will we know when it is time?"

"When the there are eleven stars in the eleventh house."

Dante, in the manner of all good novices, pondered the answer quietly, noting as always the significance of the numbers eleven-eleven. He didn't understand, but he was still ashamed of his ignorance. Later he would learn that the hallmark of wisdom was primarily being unafraid to ask what one did not know. Finally, he raised his eyes to the elder once more. "When the great transformation happens, will I be among those who stay in this world, or shift into the next?"

The Teacher smiled. "If I told you the answer to that, you would stop seeking for yourself. Besides, when the end-time is here and the shift occurs, it will be of no consequence to you if you stay in this small world, for you will be unaware of what has happened, and of only passing interest to you if find yourself living the transformation."

Dante sighed softly. Always in riddles they spoke, never an easy answer. But he supposed there were no easy answers. Still, at least he knew that sometime in the future the gateway would appear as it had been foretold. Even though thousands of years must pass before the threads of different realities and existences would mesh in precisely the right configuration, there was a certain inevitability to it that satisfied his human need to know.

♦

Connor felt herself resisting the pull. In her half-sleep, she reached for Laura, who snuggled herself firmly into the curve of Connor's body. Relaxed, sleepy, comfortable, safe…and seconds later she was out of her body and decidedly within the dream plane itself.

"You surprise me, granddaughter."

"How is that possible? You've always said I was very predictable."

"Mostly you are. And impertinent to boot." Gwendolyn's tone was brisk as usual. Connor had become relatively accustomed to these surreal conversations. *"But this time I refer to the restraint of your natural curiosity. You were more anxious to discover the culprit who murdered your acquaintance than you are in discovering an enormous piece of your world's history,"*

"I'm not sure I believe in any of it."

"You have once again rejected the notion of reincarnation. I thought we had finally resolved that debate,"

"No. I'm not saying Jenny and Carmen weren't other people in other lifetimes. But let's face it, Jenny was hospitalized for a mental breakdown, and poor Carmen was victimized for weeks by an irresponsible hypnotist who exercised a lot of influence over her. All of this could be a fantasy,"

"And if I told you it was not a fantasy at all?"

Even in the dream, Connor could feel herself squirming. "Then I suppose I'd have to believe you."

"Well, thank you for that resounding vote of confidence, young lady."

"Sorry, but—"

"I know, and although I don't wish to appear as if I only communicate to nag at you, I must ask that you take your responsibilities to the Circle a little more seriously. You haven't joined with them in some months now. The day after tomorrow would be an excellent time to correct that oversight."

"Why? Is something really going to happen at Avebury."

"Perhaps, and perhaps not, but it is one of those situations where a combination of action on all planes will be required. You must be able to shift into a higher realm if need be. Let your father and your daughter and these two young women anchor your efforts here. And, also, keep in mind that there may be some risk to Alandra and Junela as well. They are closely tied to what happened before and they, like Lady Deirdre, have some interesting karma to work out."

"Grandmother?"

"Yes, child."

"Is the world going to just end one day?"

"Of course."

Connor was stunned at first, but she could almost hear the gentle laughter of her Grandmother Gwendolyn. Obviously, Connor was missing a point. "Everything ends eventually, my dear one. As a matter of fact, on some level, in some reality, the world as you call it, Earth that is, has ended a thousand times and more. And our souls have existed in all of them. But it's best you focus on this particular sliver of reality right now. This time stream is not destined to wind down quite yet. Let's make sure it doesn't."

Before Connor could ask an important follow-up question, she was aware that Gwendolyn was gone. Not gone precisely, but no longer "in touch" with Connor's inner consciousness. She really wished that just once Gwendolyn would inquire if there was anything else Connor needed before flitting off.

◆

Yohiro Matsumoto stood one last time before the magnificent frescoed warrior figure. If he had the privilege of looking upon it again, it would be in a different time, in a different place. He could not predict with any certainty where that would be, only that the magical sensations with which it imbued his very soul would never abandon him.

He closed the drapery and turned back to his children. "All is in readiness, and the prophecies have been fulfilled. You may prepare to leave now. The plane is on the runway." He motioned for Yoshi to stay behind. "As we make the last leg of our journey, I wish to hear more about these two young women from the place in York. You said that the crystal shard ceased to pulsate when it left their proximity."

"Yes, Father. It did."

"You also told me that the man called Karl told you about Sister Sonia's obsession with one of them, that she believed the girl could give her information about some sort of ancient mystery."

"He said that, but I did not particularly believe him. Sister Sonia was nothing more than a cheat and a liar and fraud."

Yohiro looked at his son sternly. "You do not know of what you speak, so hold your tongue on the subject."

He stalked out of the room and Yoshi followed him meekly enough, but only because he had learned to contain anger until it was useful. He had his own ideas about this project, ideas he had shared with no one. The sheer audacity of his father's plan had once held him in thrall. Now he saw greater possibilities for himself, rather than simply on behalf of his father. Once having seen them, the focus of his studies had altered. His plan was no longer in alignment with his father's grand scheme. But the beauty of it was that once Yoshi reached his destination and acted upon his own initiative, there could be no retribution. He could have precisely what he wanted and have to answer to no one at all, especially his father.

Chapter Twenty

Between the idea
And the reality
Between the motion
And the act
Falls the Shadow.
—T.S. Eliot, *The Hollow Men*

Sister Sonia's funeral was as bizarre as the last days of her life had been. It was, quite naturally, given her choice of profession, a media circus. Between the acolytes, the few disciples who remained, the common garden-variety cult members still in residence, and hordes of curiosity seekers, the police were once again faced with serious crowd-control problems.

Alan Durn was there. His face burned with shame as he looked on Sonia's casket and realized what a coward he'd been to simply run away. He'd really loved her—for all her craziness, her arrogance, her unpredictability, he'd loved her. And now she was a lump of flesh in a wooden box. The goddess was indeed dead.

He'd gone straight to the police when he returned to York. He knew they were looking for him to "assist in their enquiries," so it made more sense to show up before they discovered him at the funeral and dragged him off in front of a crowd. A cop named Lindstrom had questioned him off and on for a couple of hours, but finally had to conclude that although Alan certainly was a player in the con game Sonia'd had going, he probably had nothing to do with her murder.

He'd been shown pictures of Karl and a man named Dandridge. They were both obviously dead, and it gave him a bit of a turn to see Karl gray and lifeless on a slab. But at least there was no one left to implicate him in the conspiracy to murder Carmen's sister. That weighed heavily on him still, even though at the time whatever Sonia wanted seemed somehow justified. Now it just seemed incredibly sleazy.

Alan accompanied the casket to the crematorium and watched as it was rolled into the oven. Somehow the sound of the flames made him shudder a little, an old childhood horror of hell, no doubt. As he watched, he began to cry, something so foreign to him he almost didn't know what to make of it. He tried to take his mind off Sonia by worrying at the ragged piece of paper he still carried around in his pocket, the scrap containing the names of the two women Karl was afraid would track down the connection between a murder in Palm Springs and the Children of Artemis 6,000 miles away. He had begun to think that somehow he could atone for all of this if he could at least let someone know that it was Karl who had done it, Karl who had gone too far. But now he didn't know how to find Connor Hawthorne or this other woman, Laura Nez. They had checked out of her hotel in York, and the clerk wouldn't give him a forwarding address. But as he walked out of the crematorium (apparently, it took hours to reduce a human corpse to nothing more than ashes and bits of bone), he had a flash of inspiration, not exactly a common occurrence in his IQ range, which was above room temperature but hardly Mensa level.

He got into his car and started making phone calls. He phoned a bookstore to find out who Connor's publisher was. Then he called that number and asked for the name of the British distributor of her books in England. And he was finally fortunate enough to hook up with a secretary who believed his hastily conceived story about being a chauffeur in York who had Connor's very valuable briefcase in his car, which contained her passport.

Surely she would need to have it immediately, and his car company had authorized him to drive it to London, but he must deliver it personally, of course.

The secretary blithely told him that Ms. Hawthorne was probably at her country house in West Sussex in the village of St. Giles on Wyndle. Alan smiled at his own cleverness and started the car. He'd come back to York for Sonia's ashes and scatter them somewhere. She'd never really indicated a preference, but then toward the end of her life she hadn't really anticipated dying.

◆

One of the problems with hastily conceived plans is the failure to consider all the possible ramifications of one's actions. While Alan started his long drive south, the secretary to whom he'd spoken decided that the kind and courteous thing to do would be to call Connor Hawthorne and relieve her mind over her lost briefcase and passport. Surely she had missed them by now. She flipped through her phone directory and dialed Rosewood Cottage.

"Did you lose your briefcase?" asked Laura, as she returned to the library. The group had reassembled after a late lunch and had been discussing strategy when the phone rang. Laura had been nearest the door to the front hall, where the telephone stood on a little side table.

Connor looked up. "Me? No."

"That was someone in your London publisher's office. Said your driver from York had found your briefcase in his car and your passport was inside it. Said he'd been instructed by the car hire company to deliver it to you." She paused. "You didn't have a driver."

Connor frowned. "And my briefcase is upstairs in our room, and my passport is in my handbag. I just saw it this morning.."

Benjamin interrupted. "Please don't tell me they gave out this address."

Laura nodded. "I asked that exact question. The poor man

got a little flustered. Said he'd thought since it was an obvious emergency he should. I didn't have the heart to give him a royal chewing out, just suggested he check with their clients first before dispensing personal information like that. But the damage has been done."

"Did he get a name?"

"Of course not. But he said the man *sounded* like a chauffeur, if you can believe it. I didn't know they had a specific vocal quality."

"Ours sounds like he's got a throat full of gravel," said Ellen. "And he's got a Scots accent so thick I sometimes have no idea what he's saying. But he's a dear."

"Well, this chauffeur, who isn't a chauffeur, is probably headed in our direction," said Laura. "But he's got a few hours' drive. We'll keep an eye out later."

"Do you suppose it's that man from the farmhouse?" asked Katy, and Connor saw the very real fear in her eyes, though the tone of voice was determinedly nonchalant.

"I doubt it," said Connor. "More likely some tabloid reporter or other. They try all kinds of tricks to get an interview."

No one in the room believed it, but no one contradicted her either.

When the doorbell rang a few minutes later, they all wondered whether the phony chauffeur had somehow sprouted wings. "*I'll go*," said Laura

"No," Benjamin contradicted her with a look that brooked no argument. "I'll go."

In seconds he was back, and he wasn't alone.

♦

Using the long arm of Pantheon, Matsumoto had arranged for delivery of his cargo to a section of the airfield at Gatwick reserved for private aircraft. It had been loaded onto a specially designed lorry and covered in a nondescript gray tarp. The signs on the truck read ATHERTON ART INSTALLATIONS. Not even the most bored or curious of passersby on the road would care about some oversized sculpture no doubt on its way to the estate of some nouveau riche businessman. Matsumoto had planned the journey for the night of the tenth, though the hazards of driving a rig that large over narrow country lanes, especially those near Avebury, grew much greater in the dark. In some places the road passed through villages where the houses actually abutted the very edge of the asphalt. A collision with anything, stationary or moving, would be disastrous because it would draw attention. Still, he wasn't willing to risk the entire trip in the daytime. He wanted the truck to arrive well before dawn, where it would remain parked in the old barn on the piece of farmland he'd leased. The following night, it would be driven out and directly to the location he'd selected.

He had no illusions that his movements on the night of the eleventh would go completely undetected. Avebury was actually a tiny village with a combination pub and bed-and-breakfast plus a few houses. But by then the phone lines to the few homes and the commercial establishments would have been severed, and he had hired three men who would dress as British constables and keep the handful of citizens indoors because of a security alert. If they refused to cooperate, Matsumoto had authorized the fake constables to simply shoot them…with silenced weapons, of course. By the time it was over, none of that would matter in the least. He only needed to buy a few hours' time.

◆

"What on earth are you doing here?" exclaimed Connor.

"That's a nice way to greet people who've spent about eighteen hours traveling by plane, train, and car," said Malcolm Jefferson. Ayalla, standing close beside him, looked a little shell-shocked herself but maintained a pleasant half-smile.

Connor rushed to give him a hug and Ayalla a handshake, their usual method of greeting. Laura, of course, hugged them both. "But I don't get it," she said. "Benjamin never even mentioned—"

"My little surprise. I thought we could use some backup, and who better than these two?"

Laura looked at Benjamin and easily read his thoughts. He was much more concerned about the safety of their little group than he'd let on. But she didn't blame him. From a tactical standpoint, they were not a confidence-inspiring group. Of all of them, only she and Benjamin were experienced fighters, and, she had to admit, he wasn't getting any younger. The Carlisles, for all their magical talent, were Benjamin's age. Katy, Carmen, and Jenny were young, slight, and completely inexperienced at combating the sort of threat Matsumoto could easily present. Connor, of course, was strong and agile, but without training. Basically, Benjamin had called in the cavalry and he couldn't have made a better choice: D.C.'s biggest, strongest, and arguably toughest cop and an FBI agent who, when riled, could make Dirty Harry Callahan look like a school crossing guard.

Benjamin tackled the introductions to Carmen and Jenny. Everyone else, of course, knew Malcolm and Ayalla. The Carlisles and Katy were delighted to hear of the engagement, though Connor showed herself no more enthusiastic than she'd been in D.C. Laura knew she'd come around. It would just take a little time.

"One of your friends met us at the airport," said Malcolm, "and gave me this." He handed over a hard-shell suitcase with such ease that Benjamin didn't realize how heavy it was. He almost dropped it when he caught the full weight. "Sorry," said Malcolm. "Should have warned you."

"That's okay," Benjamin replied a little sheepishly. Laura wondered if he were having any sudden urges to spend more time at the gym. But then, few people could claim the strength of a Malcolm Jefferson.

Connor was still shaking her head. "I can't believe Dad dragged you two all the way to England when we don't even know if anything dastardly is going to happen."

Malcolm grinned. "Doesn't matter. We'd both already put in for our vacation time, and I've been wanting to bring Ayalla here and show her some of the places I've been with you guys. Any strange and bizarre occurrences are just the icing on the cake, for me anyway. I think Ayalla's about as fond of the truly weird as you are, Connor."

"Well, shall we all sit down?" said Ellen. "I'll make us a big"— she looked around—"a really big pot of tea, and we'll strategize."

As everyone got settled, Connor whispered to Laura. "Thank God we've still got another spare room. I suppose they'll stay together."

"Well, of course they will, you goof. And you'd better suck up that attitude, Hawthorne. Your best friend is in love big-time."

"I know, I know. She just better be good enough for him."

◆

Unaware that formidable opposition was coalescing not many miles away, Matsumoto was holding his own strategy session. For what seemed the thousandth time, he put his children through their paces—a recitation of the precise time each of their assigned actions would take place, and the appropriate contingency for each predicted outcome path. This was an exercise in mathematical probabilities of human behavior on a grand scale, much grander in fact than any human had ever envisioned. And Matsumoto, aided by thousands of hours of virtual reality scenarios played again and again, and hundreds of millions of computations by the world's most powerful Cray supercomputers, was confident of success.

He thought time and again of the old adage that those who fail to remember their history are doomed to repeat it. In one simple bold stroke, he would render that claim obsolete. He would do what no one had ever attempted. History would no longer be a completed series of events, its content only altered by the perspective of those who had written it. It would instead become a living, mutable phenomenon, not static, but in motion.

The assignments for each of Matsumoto's brilliant children had one thing in common—an alteration of history itself. His plan would reshape the events of the last few centuries, and that was just the beginning, the test phase. Once he had analyzed the results of relatively minor changes, he would then re-mold the entire face of humanity on a global scale by going back even farther, choosing critical events and altering the outcomes. And he knew what that face would look like. The visage of the warrior came to him once again—proud, fierce, and autocratic.

He did not let himself doubt for even a moment that his plan would work, that the energy of the Atlantis crystal, when supported by the Avebury stones, would open six portals to the past, or more accurately, into a place between various versions of the past, including the one that led to this very day. Once they'd reached the place between time streams, his children had only to watch for the assigned moment and perform a simple task, but one that would have astoundingly far-reaching results. It was the butterfly effect on a time-dimensional scale, and the mathematical model that quantified the theory was Matsumoto's brainchild. It was, in short, flawless.

Yet there was another child, not of the brains but of the loins, whose ambitions had not been factored into the mathematical model. Yohiro's offspring were his only blind spot, and that was because of his single-minded belief in the power of genetic planning. Their mothers had been carefully chosen, mostly on the basis of factors other men would find far less compelling. Physical attributes were well down the list. Instead, factors such as intelligence, perception, intuition, overall health, and childbearing abilities, of course, were of priority. Once each woman's ancestry had been fully documented, the chosen few were handsomely paid to produce one offspring each after signing ironclad nondisclosure agreements. They were never told who had fathered their children through impersonal insemination in a laboratory and had agreed to complete isolation and confinement to a comfortable villa during their pregnancies. What they were, of course, not told was that they would not live to enjoy their million-dollar fees once the child had been born. Each of the women was given a fatal but mercifully quick injection, a solemn ceremony, and a thorough cremation. Their remains were mixed into a marble ossuary in Matsumoto's garden so that he might occasionally honor their contribution to the alteration of history. For all intents and purposes, the six children of Yohiro Matsumoto had no mothers. They were his and his alone.

Perhaps the tests were flawed in some small respect, or perhaps Matsumoto in his arrogance simply overlooked the significance of the human soul—the infinite presence that inhabited each physical body as it emerged into the world. Scientists and sociologists might debate the question of "nature versus nurture" for all time, but few had tackled another more pressing question. Whence did the "nature" emerge? Was it genetics, or was it simply the universe motoring along according to the laws of creation and the inner mysteries of soul journey? Did each soul come with an agenda of its own that could not be entirely sublimated by an external circumstance or internal physical perfection?

Whatever the answers, his son, Yoshi, was not quite the person Matsumoto thought him to be. He had not turned out like the others, but the facade was so perfect that not even the tiniest doubt troubled the father. The main difficulty—he was at least as obsessed as his father and equally as callous to the value of life, but nowhere near as intelligent or analytical in the long run. In practice that combination made him even more dangerous than his father. If Matsumoto Sr. was a megalomaniac xenophobe, Yoshi was simply a sociopath of the worst order, who'd left a trail of bodies, mostly young women, throughout the world and a host of international authorities infuriated at the sheer audacity of a killer who left a calling card at each and every murder—the photocopied image of a demon emerging from gates of a prison that no longer could hold him. That is how Yoshi saw himself, about to break free of the bondage imposed by his own father. No longer would he be a tool of someone else's ambitions. Yoshi had his own and he would enlist his own 'tools' when the time came. In his reckoning, money could, and did, buy anything one wanted.

◆

Having spent sufficient time around the Hawthornes to learn that they tended to take weird impossibilities quite seriously, Ayalla didn't bother to argue the obvious points—that their theories about Yohiro Matsumoto's plans were just that—theories. Nor did she even tackle the entire subject of mythical cities and magical record-keeping crystals capable of manipulating time itself. For once, she didn't feel like arguing, and the sense of peace within her was almost as unsettling as it was welcome. Ayalla was in love. Though she'd fought the temptation with as much logic and determination as she could muster—which was not inconsiderable, given the strength of her character and the challenges life had thrown at her—she'd given in. And then her determination turned in a new and positive direction. She was committed to Malcolm Jefferson with all her heart, and if that meant humoring his dearest friends in their wild escapades, then so be it. Besides, she'd seen them in action and had developed a sincere if grudging respect for the abilities of Benjamin, Connor, and Laura. Even the Carlisles had impressed her with their work in Boston, and she still didn't half believe what they claimed to be able to do.

She'd spent a lovely night with Malcolm and most of the day trying to simply listen and offer mild suggestions. They'd all taken breaks, made lunch together, and then met yet again for more discussion.

Just after lunch she stepped into the garden, needing a little time to breathe and absorb some of the more bizarre aspects of this "mission" she and Malcolm had embarked on. She was expecting to be alone and was startled to hear a voice coming from the far end of the terrace.

"I'll go back in if you'd like some quiet time." It was Connor, seated in one of the wicker chairs and staring out into the garden.

"No," said Ayalla. "I'm the one who's interrupting you." She turned to go, but Connor said, "Please stay."

The last thing Ayalla wanted was a one-on-one encounter with Malcolm's fiercely protective best friend. Connor's less than enthusiastic endorsement of the marriage was painfully obvious, and Ayalla worried, not that Malcolm would change his mind about their engagement, but that any sort of wedge between the two friends would end up hurting all of them in the long run. But she had no idea what to do about it. She, in her own way, was as stubborn as Connor.

"I wanted to talk to you about something."

Ayalla steeled herself for whatever was about to come down on her head, determined not to get into an argument. She took a deep breath and waited.

"I'm sorry."

Ayalla could barely contain the complete surprise she felt. "For what?" she asked lamely, as if she didn't already know.

"For being such a bitch about you and Malcolm. You and I didn't exactly get off to a very good start a couple years ago, and I don't know if we've ever mended fences really, even after what we've all been through together."

"You really don't need to apologize."

"Yes, I really do. And it's not just because Laura gave me a lecture about it last night." The battle between contrition and rebellion at being lectured fought its way across her face. Ayalla kept her smile to herself and waited for Connor to continue.

"She is the only one who usually manages to break through my stubbornness. But I don't want you to think she changed my mind about something. She didn't, because my mind wasn't totally set against this." She paused and added a bit sheepishly. "Though I might have left you with that impression. But Laura made me see that I was being unreasonably overprotective and that I'd let my resentment of you cloud my judgment. When we first met, I could tell how much you disapproved of Laura and me, and that made me angry. It hurt."

Ayalla moved closer and sat down on a chair opposite. "That would be my cue," she said. "I know I can be about as subtle as a bulldozer. I've never really apologized to you either, except in a sort of halfhearted way." She smoothed hair that didn't need smoothing. "Basically, I don't like being wrong. Everything in my life has had to fit into a neat little box—my career, my faith, even my anger at losing my dad the way I did. So I had to cling to this stupidly regimented notion of what was right and wrong. I've never been good at gray areas, no matter what the topic."

"Neither have I," said Connor with a quiet laugh. "I'm like a bull in a china shop sometimes without even realizing it."

"Me, too. And that's been good in some ways. Otherwise, I'd never have made it in the Bureau. All they care about is toughness. So the soft side, if I even have one, got buried along with the anger and the resentment. And I don't get along very well with other people, especially women. Does that sound ridiculous?"

"No, it doesn't. Most women wouldn't have a clue about what you've gone through and what your life has been like...is like. Laura probably understands it better than I do, because of the work she's done for my father over the years. She said it tends to eliminate the possibility of having friends, women or men."

"Thank you for understanding that. So, anyway, that just compounded the problem that I had with you two. I had automatically categorized homosexuality as wrong, and on top of that, I resented two women who could love each other so much, when it didn't seem as if I could love anyone at all—ever."

Ayalla swallowed hard to hold back the tears she absolutely refused to shed in public. "So maybe if you could just see your way clear to forgiving me for all the bullshit I've laid on you about your personal lifestyle and being an 'amateur' who gets mixed up in stuff that's the domain of the so-called professionals like me, I'd appreciate it."

There was a long silence, and Ayalla was about to conclude that her apology had fallen on barren ground when Connor spoke, her voice soft and thoughtful. "Do you love Malcolm, really love him?"

To her credit, Ayalla didn't respond either instantly or glibly. "It took some time to admit it to myself, but yes, I do love him, even though I never thought it would be possible to feel this way, to be this open to anyone."

"And you know how long he's waited to find someone, the right someone to have that place in his life? He didn't want to condemn anyone to living in Marie Louise's shadow."

"You knew her, didn't you?"

"Yes, I did"

"And she was very special, wasn't she?"

"As a matter of fact, she was an extraordinarily kind and loving woman—a good mother and a devoted wife to Malcolm. But you can't worry about that. You can't worry that she's on some pedestal. That's the one of the by-products when people die—and not always a good one for those left behind. The dead get sort of beatified in the process of mourning, and it's easy to forget that they had their faults just like the rest of us. Fortunately, Malcolm's long past the dead-wife worship thing. It just took him quite a while because he's the kind of man who loves well and truly—the same way he'll love again, or else he wouldn't be marrying you."

"He told me that you saved his life and his career after she died."

"He exaggerates," said Connor with a shrug.

"He could be dead from eating his own gun, or in jail for killing the men who murdered his wife."

"Possibly, but we'll never know, will we? He might have made the right decisions all by himself. And besides, the man has returned the favor many times over. He saved my life and Laura's. That's more than enough to even the scales."

"So you're okay with this marriage thing?"

"I am now. It sometimes takes me a while to come around to a sane point of view."

"Kind of like me." Ayalla was smiling now, and she could see Connor's face as the garden lights, operated by timers, winked on one by one.

"I tend to think that people who are alike can end up butting heads more than they really want to."

"And I agree. But I promise you one thing. I do love Malcolm, and I'll always put him first, even above my career, if that's what it takes, and you know how much my job means to me."

"The good thing is, you know he'd never expect you to make that kind of choice. He's a fine man and a wise human being, if a little impulsive sometimes. You are both very lucky to have found each other."

"Thank you," said Ayalla, "although I'm beginning to think luck had nothing do with it. And I should add that I hate it when people make me cry."

"Me, too. So here's a clean tissue, and once you're ready, let's go back in and join the war room gang."

"Friends?" asked Ayalla.

"Growing into being friends," replied Connor, and the answer was precisely what Ayalla would have expected. And she respected it, too. She didn't take friendship lightly and was impressed to realize that Connor felt exactly the same way. It was a process of the heart, not a decision of the mind. Other people might become bosom buddies on a whim. Neither of them were in that category.

When the two women reentered the library, Malcolm and Laura were the first to notice. And they saw what the others didn't see—a peacefulness that hadn't been there before. They looked at each other and shared a mutual understanding—that they were both grateful for the change, whatever had brought it about.

"If Matsumoto's smart, the crystal is already in place, or very nearly so. I did some checking and through a layer of shell corporations, he's leased some land near Avebury. So I think we can at least eliminate the worry that we're going on a wild-goose chase. The only speculation left is whether this is a completely absurd experiment on his part, or a real threat to anyone's well-being."

"The threat is real," said Ellen quietly. "The Circle has met, with Connor in attendance I might add, and we observed great agitation and swirls of angry energy around the Akashic records and around the astral manifestation of Avebury."

"Angry energy?" asked Laura.

"That isn't quite the right term but close enough for comparison with human emotions. Those who are the guardians are in an uproar, including a whole bevy of angels and archangels. I haven't seen such disturbance in my experience."

"Did any of them happen to tell you anything specific?" asked Ayalla in a completely neutral tone, and all of them looked at her in some surprise. They hadn't expected much more from her than polite listening skills and outstanding paramilitary skills if called upon the following night.

"Not exactly," said Ellen. "Direct communication is usually possible, but apparently whatever Matsumoto intends to do is so outside of the expected range of human behavior, the outcome is entirely up in the air. Michael himself was ominously reluctant to even issue one of his usual dire warnings. He simply hovered angrily."

"Do angels really get angry?" asked Ayalla with obvious sincerity.

"Oh, yes, my dear, they do. But not in a human way, or for what we would think of as human reasons. Their responsibilities cover much more than this one little planet. But this incident is drawing their presence away from other duties. They need to try and ameliorate this potential disaster."

"Can't they just…I don't know…take care of Matsumoto?"

Ellen smiled broadly. "Would that it were so easy. But the affairs of humans are left in the hands of humans, for the most part. They will help us, but we must help ourselves. It's that pesky free-will thing that the Creator built into us."

"Okay, so what's the game plan?" said Ayalla. "This map looks like Avebury is pretty spread out."

"It is. The entire Avebury complex covers almost twenty-eight acres. There are actually two main circles within the henge, which is surrounded by a very deep ditch and embankment. Originally, there were at least one hundred stones standing in the inner circle, but they have been destroyed over the centuries by the more rabid Christian elements. There are only twenty-seven of those still upright, but the remaining stones are in some cases hundreds of yards from each other. We're going to have to simply observe in order to figure out where he's going to set up the crystal, although when we get there, William and Connor and I may be able to discern more. We'll be linked with the Circle the entire time. The rest of you will have to take care of more practical matters."

"That's where we come in," said Malcolm, nodding at Laura, Ayalla, and Benjamin. "Matsumoto can't ignore the people who live near there. He's bound to have made arrangements to keep them in their houses—or worse. I suggest we find his guards first and eliminate that threat. In the meantime, the rest of you can approach Matsumoto's setup and do your voodoo number on him."

"Voodoo?" said William. "Really now, Malcolm."

Malcolm laughed. "Only kidding. There is no name I can think of for what you guys do, so you'll just have to live with my bad sense of humor."

"We'll be well-equipped," said Benjamin. "I asked my friend James to send down that case you delivered. It contains firearms and night-vision goggles. Of course, James is itching with curiosity. Thank God he owes me about a hundred favors."

"Cool," said Laura. "I love those things, until some idiot sets off a flare or shines a flashlight in your face."

"This is the latest upgrade," said Benjamin. "They have a split-second override, so your chances of not being blinded are much better than they used to be. The weapons are standard-issue Glocks with optional silencers and some highly effective stun guns. I suggest we keep this as low-key as possible. I'd prefer having the authorities make arrests instead of collecting bodies."

"Agreed," said Laura, as Malcolm and Ayalla nodded.

"I wish there were a way to get the handful of civilians out of there, but we can't do that without arousing suspicion, so they'll be our first priority while Connor and the Carlisles proceed to wherever Matsumoto is basing the crystal."

Katy sat forward on her chair. "You haven't mentioned yet what I'm supposed to do—and Carmen and Jenny."

Benjamin looked both uncomfortable and stubborn. "You three should stay here," he said. "There's no reason to have all of us running around down there."

"Like hell I am," said Katy, then blanched at the look from her mother. "Sorry, I don't mean to be totally disrespectful, but I'm in this, too, and I refuse to be left behind like some child. I can at least be a lookout or something. Give me one of those high-tech radios of yours."

"But—"

"If you don't include us, we'll come anyway. You can't lock us up."

Jenny nodded vigorously. "This is about us, our history, our destiny. We belong there, Carmen and I."

Benjamin sighed and gave his daughter a look that clearly said, "I tried." To his surprise, Connor didn't argue, didn't start a battle with Katy. She calmly sat there studying the map of Avebury, and didn't contribute to the debate at all. Suddenly finding himself without allies, Benjamin sighed and gave in. It seemed they would all be going to Avebury.

◆

Alan Durn had arrived much too late the previous night to try and contact Connor Hawthorne at her home. He'd driven instead to a travel motel just off the motorway and stayed in an antiseptic-smelling, somewhat threadbare room. Lacking courage for the confrontation, however, he didn't go immediately to his destination.

The next afternoon, he drove to the village and had to inquire from a shopkeeper about Rosewood Cottage. He parked his car in the lane, still trying to decide what to say to the two women about Karl, when in his rearview mirror, much to his shock, he saw

Carmen Waters and Jenny Carpenter walking along the lane from the other direction. He immediately slumped down in the seat, and they paid him no attention as they turned into the driveway of the cottage.

Alan was utterly confused. What were those two women doing here? And how did they hook up with the two American women? By now Carmen would certainly have been told of her sister's murder. Would they consider him a suspect? But no. Carmen and Jenny both knew he had never left the compound except for day trips into the city of York. So what was the connection here? And in his usual way he wondered what he might gain from it all. Seeing Jenny Carpenter also reminded him of the crystal. What if she had it? The police had questioned him about Sonia's empty safe, and he hadn't had to pretend to be surprised. It had never occurred to him that it was gone.

He then assumed Karl had taken it, but to what purpose? And now with Karl dead, he'd never know. Suddenly, his mission to see Connor Hawthorne seemed ill-conceived. The only thing he could think to do was keep an eye on them for the time being and see if any police showed up on their doorstep. He turned his car around and parked as far from the cottage as possible while still keeping the driveway in sight. As he passed, he took note of the cars. There were several, which seemed to indicate a large group. Again, the situation baffled him, but that was a normal state of mind for Alan—and one that wasn't likely to improve any time soon.

Chapter Twenty-one

Who shall tempt with wand'ring feet
The dark unbottom'd infinite abyss
And through the palpable obscure find out
His uncouth way.
—John Milton, *Paradise Lost*

A couple of hours before dark, three cars departed Rosewood Cottage. Laura joked that there were enough people in their group to have warranted hiring a small sightseeing bus, but that would hardly have been inconspicuous. First, Malcolm and Ayalla with the Carlisles in the rear seat, then Benjamin with Connor and Laura, and finally, Katy with Carmen and Jenny in the third car. Katy, intent on not being left behind, or losing sight of Benjamin's car, didn't even notice Alan Durn pull out from behind the tree where he'd been sitting, and take up a position as the fourth and uninvited car in the caravan.

For a weekday, traffic was light, and they managed the trip in record time. The plan called for Malcolm and Ayalla, the people least likely to have been identified by Matsumoto as in any way connected with the Children of Artemis compound and the subsequent events in York, to go directly to the parking lot and visit the gift shop and pub and simply act like tourists. They were, of course, trying to identify in advance anyone who looked out of place—less like tourists and more like people waiting for something to happen. For most people, the distinction would be so small as to be undetectable, but Malcolm and Ayalla were both cops, and between them they had years of experience in reading people—call it street smarts, gut instinct, whatever. They'd both developed the one most invaluable tool a cop can have—the ability to know when someone just isn't "right."

The Carlisles immediately started down the path toward the outer edge of the Avebury circle, with cameras slung about their necks and a guidebook in hand. They, too, were playing their parts to perfection. Benjamin drove right past the entrance lane, and drove several hundred yards. As they passed a large stone barn, he pointed it out to them. "That should be the property Matsumoto leased." If they'd hoped to find the crystal immediately and dispense with further risk or drama, they were disappointed. The doors to the barn stood open and it was clearly concealing nothing as large as a twenty-foot crystal. But given the lateness of the season, it was already getting dark. Matsumoto must have had to move his prize while there was still enough light to see. Floodlights would have been foolish under the circumstances.

Knowing that their quarry had moved on to his primary site on the grounds of the Avebury Circle, however, made at least one decision easier. They didn't have to be quite as concerned about where they parked along the road. Benjamin quickly found a lay-by with sufficient room for two cars, and Katy deftly swung around and pulled in behind him. None of them noticed Alan Durn accelerate past them. He didn't find a good place to stop for another quarter mile, and even then his car wasn't entirely off the road. He worked it up onto the verge, groaning as he felt the left wheels sink into the soft earth. The car was very likely stuck, so he might as well leave it there. He'd have to figure something out later. Alan got out, climbed over a low wall and began walking along the edge of a field rather than in the roadway. He couldn't risk being seen by Carmen or Jenny, if for some reason they drove on down the road. As it was, he was concerned they would recognize the car Sonia had always used, which he was still figuring out how to keep without anyone catching on. For now, he had decided during the drive here that he would at the very least find out what happened to the crystal. In his mind it had begun to take on greater and greater significance...and value. All he needed to do was get it back and then figure out how to use it.

♦

"Those three over there," said Ayalla softly. They'd opted not to don the earpieces to their walkie-talkies until it was completely dark out. The cords were too obvious and would mark them instantly as law enforcement. But they carried the small powerful radios in their pockets. At least they wouldn't be reduced to the U.S. Secret Service's somewhat amusing trademark habit of talking into their wrists when the time came to communicate. A microphone on the earpiece cord had a small transmitter switch that would allow them to talk when necessary.

Malcolm slowly let his gaze drift to a table outside the pub occupied by three men. He almost had to laugh at their obviousness: dark-blue pants, dark windbreakers, white shirts, dark ties, as if they hadn't made any effort at all to blend in. That made no sense. Matsumoto didn't sound as if he'd hire help that stupid. Malcolm looked down at his plate and pretended to be engrossed in the Ploughman's Special he'd ordered, and he had a thought. "What do they remind you of?"

Ayalla frowned slightly, glancing at them and back again at Malcolm. "I don't know—the Three Stooges; the Pep Boys: Mannie, Moe, and Jack; Mormon missionaries without their bicycles—what?"

"Uniforms," he said quietly. "Why else would they dress alike? I'd be willing to bet that in that duffel bag under the table they've got the rest of their costumes. In the dark with a cap and belt and nightstick, they could pass for police constables."

Understanding dawned in Ayalla's expression. "I do believe you're right. And it's a perfect ploy. When the main event starts, they could easily convince the people in these cottages and at the B and B to stay inside."

He nodded. "Unlike our more independent countrymen, the Brits, especially out here in the country, tend to show a little more respect for the law. They'd likely do as they're told."

Ayalla nodded. "I daresay they have more than costumes in that bag. It's big enough to carry weapons, too."

"Undoubtedly. Which is why I'm glad we're not relying on our wits and martial arts skills alone." He patted the side of his jacket, feeling the reassuring bulge of the weapon Benjamin had loaned him. Ayalla's was tucked into her shoulder bag in easy reach.

"I think it's time we strolled down the path the Carlisles took. That will probably bother our friends over there since it's supposed to be closing time, but I'm betting they're supposed to stay close to this spot, wait until it's completely dark, and then change into their outfits. They're just going to have to wonder why we don't come back to the car."

◆

There were not enough radios to go around. For one of the few times in his life, Benjamin wasn't entirely prepared. He hadn't planned on there being ten of them on this little adventure, and he had only seven radio sets. Malcolm and Ayalla had both needed radios. The others had been divided with one to the Carlisles to share, one for Benjamin, as the team leader, so to speak, one each for Connor and Laura, and one for the three youngest to share. But since Benjamin had every intention of making Katy, Carmen, and Jenny stay together in the car, one radio for them should suffice to keep them apprised of what was going on. They could hear everything.

This arrangement did not sit well with Benjamin's headstrong granddaughter or with the other two women either. But he remained firm. If they were needed for anything, he would radio. But it was wiser to leave someone on the lookout for new arrivals, and also have someone who could go for help instantly if things turned ugly. Privately, Katy believed this was nothing more than a snow job to keep them in line, but she kept that to herself. This was one of those times when arguing with her grandfather did not seem wise.

Connor naturally approved of the disposition of troops that left her daughter in relative safety, and Laura did not attempt to intervene. So there was no final court of appeals. Katy, however, figured she'd decide for herself if and when her help was needed. She had the feeling Jenny and Carmen felt much the same way as she did. But they all grudgingly agreed and watched Benjamin, Connor, and Laura disappear into the shrubbery alongside the verge.

"We should be there," said Jenny firmly. "Especially me. I'm the one who started all this when I took that crystal shard to Sonia."

"I don't think we can point to any one event as the catalyst for all of this," said Katy. "You didn't invite what happened on that island. I think Matsumoto would have tracked you down eventually and taken the shard away from you no matter what."

"Maybe. Sometimes I can't figure out how life is really supposed to work. There was a time it all seemed so clear."

Carmen reached over the seat and squeezed her shoulder. "But that was more than 10,000 years ago, and we were different people, different beings entirely."

"Maybe not entirely," said Jenny. "I keep thinking there is some part of me that is still very much Alandra. And if that's true, then I know more about how the crystal works than Matsumoto."

"And so do I," said Carmen. "Katy, we've got to go in there. But you stay here, please."

Katy swiveled around in her seat. "Where you go, I go. If anyone tries to raise us on the radio, we'll answer. We just won't mention where we are exactly." She took a flashlight from the glove box, and they all got out of the car, Katy locked it and pocketed the keys. They started through the underbrush and suddenly Jenny yelped. Katy whirled around and there stood Alan Durn, with a vise grip on Jenny's arm.

"What the hell's going on here?" he asked in none too good a mood after falling into a drainage ditch and soaking his trousers up to he knees. "One of you stole the crystal from Sonia's safe, and I want it back."

The Carlisles were the first to locate the spot Matsumoto had chosen as ground zero. Just out of sight of the few village houses, it was situated at the exact center of the inner great ring of stones, spread out as they were over so many acres. He and his six children were using the crane on the transport to lift the crystal and slide it slowly down a ramp. While they watched, the crystal slowly rose upright, and finally settled with a thud. Much thicker at the base than the top, it sat firmly on the level ground Matsumoto had chosen.

William put the microphone close to his lips and quietly told the others the news and the approximate location. "Follow the fence along the perimeter, then on a direct line between the two stones—the two tallest stones nearest the road where you can cross the embankment, you should see them about two hundred meters beyond."

●

"We don't have the crystal, Alan," said Jenny firmly and without a trace of fear in her voice. "We came here to try and get it back from some crazy idiot who thinks he can use it the way Sonia did, only more so."

"What does that mean?" he asked, his eyes narrowing. "And who are you?" he asked Katy.

"My name's Hawthorne," she said unhesitatingly. "Katherine Hawthorne."

"You're related to that woman writer, the one who—"

"Came to investigate my sister's murder? Is that what you were about to say, Alan?" Carmen was instantly furious and pushed past Jenny to look him right in the face. "It was one of you who killed her, wasn't it? Just to get some money. You killed my sister for a stupid inheritance.

Alan backed up and let go of Jenny. He wasn't really sure he could take on all three of them at once. They all looked pissed off. "I didn't have anything to do with that. It was Karl. That's really why I came all the way down here, just to tell you and that Hawthorne woman, that it was Karl. I don't need you getting on my case about it. I didn't do it."

"But you knew! Didn't you?"

"Only after the fact. I had no idea. I thought she was just sending Karl there to have a look around, maybe get your sister to lay off with the threats and cooperate with Sonia's lawyer. But it's over. Karl's dead."

"I know," said Carmen. "You think that makes it any better?"

"No, but…" He seemed to remember his original purpose. "But I want the crystal. I have more right to it than anyone."

Katy gestured toward the grounds of Avebury. "Then be our guest and see if you can get it back. The man who has it had me kidnapped to get it, probably killed your buddy Karl, and I imagine wouldn't think twice about doing the same to you."

"If he's so dangerous, then what are you doing here? Or is that why all those other people came, too? You're all trying to get the crystal back." He looked at Carmen. "First, you take Sonia away from me and now you'd cheat me out of the only valuable thing she had."

Carmen shook her head. "You are such an idiot, Alan. I didn't 'take' Sonia. She only wanted to use me, to pump for information about stuff you wouldn't even understand. There was never anything between Sonia and me, not like what you're thinking. And what would it matter now anyway?"

"It doesn't. But I'm going to get what's mine." He shoved past them and went over the fence.

"He's going to get what's coming to him, more likely," said Jenny.

"I'd better let the others know we've got this moron on the loose. God knows what he'll do."

She quietly radioed Benjamin about Alan Durn, carefully omitting that they were not at their observation post in the car.

◆

"Shit," said Ayalla. "Just what we need to lose the element of surprise is some joker wandering into the middle of this. Who is he anyway?"

"Search me," said Malcolm. "I must have missed that detail of the background briefing. But let's get a move on. I want to take care of our fake boys in blue before they take care of anyone else."

"Three of them, two of us. How do you want to handle this quietly?" Malcolm and Ayalla had circled around behind the pub and the outbuildings and watched the three men hide behind a wall and don their police costumes.

"They'll split up. So we do, too, and take them one at a time."

"I'd rather stay together."

Ayalla touched his cheek. "I'm sure you would, but try not to go all chauvinistic on me. We'll have some quality time later, I promise." She slipped away into the darkness before he could protest further. Now it was his turn to say "Shit!"

The crunch of feet on gravel drew his attention, and he stepped back close to the wall of the old building next to him. Sure enough, the white checkerboard pattern on the cap of the man coming along the path was like a neon sign. With a last prayer that this wasn't some innocent policeman on his nightly rounds, Malcolm waited until he passed and then grabbed him in a painfully effective choke hold. "Not tonight, pal," he said. "Your little job is over." Moments later the man was face down on the ground, secured with his own handcuffs and belt and gagged with his tie and a piece of cloth torn from his shirt. When he started to make noise anyway, Malcolm turned him over and socked him one. The man went limp.

"That's better," said Malcolm rubbing his knuckles.

♦

Ayalla had followed fake cop number two down a narrow passageway between buildings. When he stopped, she waited, wondering if he was suspicious or just taking up a watch post. Then she heard a zipper and the telltale sprinkling sound. *Perfect timing, asshole,* she thought, and within three long strides she had her pistol out and pressed to the back of his neck. His hands being busy, he was at a distinct disadvantage. "Don't let go of your pecker, you jerk, if you want to keep it. Now get on your knees." She slipped the handcuffs out of their case on his belt. "Okay, one hand behind your head." She snapped the cuff around his wrist, fastidiously avoiding his hand since she knew where it had just been. "Okay, now the other one." She swung the first arm down, then the other, and snapped the second cuff. If there was one thing you learned at Quantico, it was how to handcuff a perp before they knew what was happening to them. Now she had to put him out of commission, and for that she used something not exactly taught as official procedure. She tapped him none too gently with the butt of her pistol grip and he was out for the night, or at least an hour or two. Just to be on the safe side, she took his shoes, his fake badge, and his police cap. No risk of anyone thinking he was one of the good guys.

Ayalla radioed Malcolm. "I've got one."

"Me, too. Where's the third one?"

His question was answered in an unpleasant sort of way. He felt a hard barrel pressed into his back. "Just who the fuck are you?" said a voice behind him. And Malcolm was smart enough to leave his mike open. "I'm just looking around, man. I'm just a fuckin' tourist. I thought there was a bathroom behind the pub."

"With a radio? Drop it on the ground."

Behind the pub. Ayalla flew back down the path that led to the parking lot facing the pub. She ran with her heart in her throat and decided this was definitely love. If the guy hurt Malcolm, she'd kill him with her bare hands.

The scales were tipped in her favor simply because the man holding Malcolm at gunpoint was indecisive. He wasn't sure how to safely handle a man as enormous as this one, and he hadn't yet screwed the silencer onto the barrel of his gun. He was under strict orders to make no noises that would alert the residents. He finally decided to get Malcolm down on the ground so he could kneel on his back. That ought to control him long enough. "Face down," he hissed. "Right now." He ground the barrel into the small of Malcolm's back. Slowly Malcolm complied, readying himself to kick hard at the man's legs. As it was, he was saved the risk of being shot in the process. All he heard was, "Hey, jackass," a dull thud, and the man toppled over Malcolm and onto the ground. Ayalla stood there panting from her run. She'd kicked the man square in the face and in the dim light from the pub window, they could see his nose bleeding profusely.

"Thank you," said Malcolm. "I had it under control."

"Yeah. Of course. And you're welcome."

♦

Benjamin tapped Connor's shoulder. "Did you get that? The guards are taken care of."

"Let's hope there were only those three, Dad."

They were gathered together—Connor, Laura, and Benjamin—a mere hundred yards from the site of Matsumoto's great experiment. With their night-vision equipment, they had identified the older man as Matsumoto, but there were six others with him: three men and three women, much younger but remarkably similar in appearance. "I'd swear they were all related," said Laura, peering at the scene. "And Matsumoto looks extremely pissed off."

The crystal remained entirely dark. Other than the reflections of stars and a full moon, no light shimmered from within. They had watched as Matsumoto reverently replaced the last fragment of the crystal in its resting place about four feet up from the base. He'd used some of the compound to secure it, then he stood back and waited. But nothing happened. Perhaps it was only a matter of time before it would activate. Minutes passed and anger rose within him, His children stood quietly, ready to begin, and clearly unwilling to question the delay. That their father's plan would fail was entirely unacceptable, and they knew it. His wrath was the one thing they all feared. All but Yoshi perhaps.

◆

At right angles to where Benjamin, Laura, and Connor were secreted, the three young women who were supposed to be in their car had crept closer and closer to the crystal. They'd seen no sign of Alan Durn, which was a good thing. They only hoped that Malcolm and Ayalla found him first, before he did anything really stupid.

Carmen stared at the obelisk then did something no one expected. She stood up and started walking directly toward it, in plain view of Matsumoto and the others. Laura was the first to spot the movement.

"Oh, no. What on earth is she doing?"

Connor and Benjamin immediately swung their goggles in the direction Laura was looking. To their horror, Jenny came running out of the shrubbery, followed closely by Katy. All three of them were headed straight for the obelisk.

Connor stood up, and Benjamin yanked her down. "Wait! We've got to get everyone else here so we can be sure they're surrounded." He keyed his radio.

"Malcolm, Ayalla, I don't know why, but Jenny, Carmen, and Katy just walked right into the middle of this. Matsumoto can already see them. We need you fast!"

Nearby, William and Ellen were just as shocked, but Ellen's reaction was not to move in, but rather to settle herself quickly on the ground and go into deep meditation with more haste than she'd ever attempted. This was her way of helping. William realized it, too. Within seconds, he joined her, dropping his radio and goggles. Modern technology wasn't really their style anyway.

◆

Matsumoto was on the verge of ordering the intruders shot when something remarkable happened. The crystal came to life, not just in a small way but in a very big way. Bolts of light shimmered upward from base to tip. Its insides turned to molten gold and silver, and the entire crystal shuddered and rocked slightly, as if gaining its footing on the ground beneath. The glow from the obelisk lit up the ground in a 100-foot diameter, and it was Yoshi who recognized them first—the two women from the hotel, the ones who'd been guarding the crystal.

"It's them, Father. The two I told you about."

It was then that Matsumoto knew the gods had smiled upon him. They had brought him the only ones who could activate the giant obelisk, ones who must be connected to his precious warrior.

"Who is the other woman behind them?"

"The one Dandridge kidnapped."

"Ah, I begin to see. I think it is reasonable to assume that we are not alone here, that she has brought help." He raised his voice. "Aim your gun directly at the Hawthorne girl. If her associates do not appear within ten seconds, kill her."

Connor tore off her goggles, no longer necessary in any event, and was tearing across the clearing at a dead run before anyone could stop her. Benjamin ripped off his goggles and radio and said to Laura. "You stay put. He can't possibly know how many of us there are." He ran after his daughter shouting, "Don't shoot. We're right here."

Matsumoto turned. "I think I can guess who you are: Benjamin Hawthorne and, of course, your daughter, who is the mother of his meddlesome girl. But how can I be sure that there are not more spies huddled nearby?"

"Look," said Benjamin. "We didn't even believe these two girls, Carmen and Jenny. We were just humoring them when they said someone would try to set up this huge crystal thing at Avebury. We drove down here just to prove to them there was nothing to it."

"And you thought that if there were something to it, you might pull off a great coup, no doubt."

"Well, there is that," said Benjamin trying to look a little sheepish. "It seemed worth the time."

Matsumoto peered past them. "I tend not to believe you. And I will kill you all anyway, so that question is moot."

At that moment, the crystal began to hum, and the ground trembled slightly. The sky grew lighter in the immediate vicinity, something that should have been impossible, yet it was happening. Small ovals of light appeared, the very portals that Matsumoto had yearned to create.

"You won't kill anyone," said Carmen in a voice no one had heard before. It was resonant, strong, clear, and demanded the attention of those who heard it. "If you harm anyone, I will destroy the crystal."

Matsumoto sneered. "You cannot do such a thing. It is restored. Look, even the cracks are healing themselves." It was true. Every mark of where patches had been applied dissolved before their eyes. Within less than two minutes, the crystal obelisk was as it had been the day it was polished and placed for the first time in the temple of the Mother.

"But you cannot control it, Arkan."

He whirled to face her, "What did you call me?"

"Arkan. That is your name. It *was* your name. I didn't know the truth until just a few minutes ago. It was not Lady Deirdre who destroyed us; it was you."

"You're insane," he snarled at her.

"Am I? Then touch the crystal. Don't worry, it won't harm you. Just touch it, and you will know the truth. Are you afraid to know?"

Matsumoto could not stand this challenge, particularly with his children looking on. He moved close to the obelisk and gingerly placed his hand on it. As they watched, his expression changed, and then for a moment it even seemed his face had changed. Yoshi, closest to his father, was shocked to recognize for a few seconds that warrior of the fresco. And then it was Yohiro Matsumoto again, but changed somehow.

He smiled at Carmen, though it was by no means an expression of friendly recognition. "You are Junela, first priestess, and my wife's successor."

"And you did not want anyone to succeed her at all. For that matter, you wanted to control the Temple of the Mother yourself. You thought that by pretending to be dead, you could hide in the temple and learn the secrets that had been denied you. But you could not have predicted the depth of her grief over losing you."

"She was unwise in many ways."

"Unwise in love, certainly. She dared the wrath of those who created us and sent us to this planet. She dared to break the laws of the very cosmos to bring you back. But you were not where she sought for you. That is the irony, Arkan. Had you actually been in the place between time, she would have joined with you, and the balance might have been restored. I did not understand that then, but I see it now. It was your lie and your ambition that destroyed our civilization, our culture, our people."

"It doesn't matter now," he replied. "I am living this life, and I am going to change this world to suit me. You have just given me even more knowledge. Now I cannot fail. Prepare yourselves, my children."

♦

Though all of her attention should have been on saving her daughter, Connor was involuntarily and forcefully drawn into the Circle. *No*, she protested. *Not now. I need to stay in my human consciousness.*

You are needed here, Ellen reminded her sharply, and instantly Connor could perceive all of them, her Circle of Light, gathered in the astral—only a heartbeat, a shimmering veil from the world in which her body stood. And, thankfully, near her left shoulder, she could feel the presence of her grandmother. *Listen to Lady Ellen,* said Gwendolyn. *This is not the time to let personal feelings override your spiritual judgment. Your task is right here, right now. Others will look after Katy.*

The Circle became one with Connor's acquiescence to its calling. She didn't know what to do. Ellen, who had already devised a plan, sent her thoughts through the group. They were not as strong as when they all gathered physically and then went into the astral as a group, but she knew Connor's strength could hold them together. *Focus on those portals of light appearing on the physical plane. They're beginning to extrude into the astral. We must create dead-end corridors so that anyone stepping into a portal cannot enter another time stream. The only destination they can be allowed is the gray chamber.*

Connor felt a collective shudder go through the Circle, and in her mind she saw the place of which Ellen was speaking. It was not a chamber really, but a place so vast that one might never reach its edges. And within it wandered souls, pathetic souls condemned by their own fear and ignorance to a very long sojourn in nothingness. Eventually they would be led from the place by a Guardian, but not until they themselves were willing to look into the mirror of Truth. For most such lost souls, this was a process of aeons.

She focused entirely on supporting the efforts of her Circle, and one by one the portals were capped with a silvery energy. And as each portal was thus treated, a luminescent figure of almost indistinguishable form came to stand beside it, as if on guard.

♦

"Now what do we do?" whispered Malcolm as he and Ayalla knelt beside Laura. All three of them felt numbly useless at the moment, because charging into the middle of it could put every single one of their friends at risk.

"Matsumoto is getting more and more focused on Carmen. I think he's stopped worrying about whether there are more of us out here, or he figures his hired help will have taken care of that problem. We need to split up and work our way around so we can get them in a cross fire if we have to. And don't forget about Alan Durn. He's here somewhere."

♦

Alan was indeed somewhere. But he was very confused, and not because he didn't understand what Carmen and the Japanese guy were talking about, but because for some reason he did understand. He felt as if he had fallen asleep and was dreaming. But he wasn't dreaming. This was real. And yet someone was talking in his head: someone he knew, someone he respected. He looked upward toward the sky and saw a constellation he knew did not exist—eleven stars in an arc overhead. It meant something important, but what? Just a few feet away from him, a glowing doorway had opened. Was he supposed to go through it? But that was crazy. There was no door. It was just…air.

◆

Two more to go, came the message from Ellen, rippling through the collective consciousness of the Circle. Connor felt as if she were being torn apart. Her precious daughter was in danger, and she was helpless. *Laura,* she whispered in her mind. *Keep her safe, please keep her safe.*

The connection between the two lovers was so strong, the message reached Laura in an instant. She heard Connor as if she were crouched right beside her. And yet Connor was yards away, standing in the full light of the shimmering crystal. Ayalla and Malcolm had carefully crawled through the trees and shrubs to take up better positions, but none of them was close yet to Katy. Laura moved—and quickly.

◆

Junela was fully her former self now, and she felt power coursing through her. In the back of her awareness, she also felt the work of the Celtic Circle gradually closing down the portals from the inside out. But the danger was still present, for now there were seven portals, not six. She murmured something in a language none of them understood, and the crystal began to pulsate wildly.

"Arkan, you will only make the same mistake that Deirdre made. You cannot meddle with the sacred balance. And I will not let you misuse the wisdom of our creators and our ancestors."

"You lie," he snapped. "My children can pass through and into the other time streams. They will do as I have instructed them, and this world will change."

"But you are a fool, Arkan. Even if you succeeded, you would create chaos. For if a single calculation is wrong, then you will not exist in this time and place. We will not exist. This crystal will not be here. Don't you see. You will create a distortion in the fabric of time, a paradox that cannot be undone."

"No!" he shouted. "There is no mistake. Children! Go now!"

Five of them obediently stepped to the portals nearest them and stepped through. Nothing happened, nothing changed. "You see," said Arkan-Matsumoto triumphantly. "You were wrong, or you were lying." Then he saw that Yoshi had not moved. "Go, my son. Quickly now."

"No, Father, I don't think I will."

"What! How dare you disobey?"

"And what will you do? Shoot me? I think I would prefer not to risk my life on your speculations. You will notice that my brothers and sisters have not returned as they were supposed to."

His father looked wildly about him. The five portals were fading, but his children had indeed not reappeared. Their absence should have been but a matter of seconds.

"Where do you suppose they are, Father? Perhaps you yourself should go and find out." Yoshi raised the pistol he'd been holding close to his side. "I will stay here, and as your eldest and only remaining son, I will take over your empire and run it as well as you would have, perhaps even better."

"I don't understand."

Alandra spoke. "This is the consequence of betrayal, Arkan. Your falsehoods and the pain they caused have come back to you. That is the way of the universe."

"No," he screamed, spittle flying from his mouth. "You won't cheat me again." He ran for the sixth portal, the one nearest him, and was through it.

◆

On the astral, the Circle shivered. The sixth portal had not been 'cordoned off,' completely; no guardian of the gray place had been posted. *He's getting through!* cried Ellen. *He's going to reach one of the time streams.* And then they all saw it, at least those in the Circle saw it. From the unsealed end of the corridor came a tall, stately figure— a woman, the form of a goddess both ancient and powerful, clad all in white and gold, her hair shimmering in contrast to the dull gun metal grayness all around them.

"Arkan stopped in his tracks. She smiled at him sadly. "So it has come to this, my love. And now we are both in for a long wait until we can return to the world.

"Deirdre," he whispered. "But how?"

"Deirdre, Sonia. Does it matter? I am here now. It was written down long ago, but neither of us bothered to look."

He tried to push past her. Just beyond he could see dazzling lights, shadow images of other beings in other worlds, other lives, the murmur of their voices, the glow of their living energies. He reached out, grasping, and she caught him around the waist and drew him to her. He could not fight her off. Her strength was inhuman. The opening to another life closed even as he watched, and behind him the portal through which he'd entered blinked out. And suddenly he was alone in a vast gray place where nothing touched him—not Deirdre, not anyone.

◆

"I guess that means my father was entirely wrong," said Yoshi, his gun aimed now at the small group of bystanders. Alandra was out in front of them, but his marksmanship was excellent, and his machine pistol packed a double magazine. A mere half-dozen people presented little challenge. It would make a lot of noise but he would be long gone before anyone in this sleepy little hamlet got around to doing anything. He raised the gun, swinging it in Katy's direction. She could go first so that her mother and grandfather could grieve for a few moments. The added cruelty pleased him. Three shots rang out, but none of them came from his gun or even all from the same direction. Yoshi fell to the ground, groaning, the pistol flying from his hand. Laura rose from behind her cover, gun barrel smoking. She walked to Yoshi and kicked his weapon well out of reach before turning to the others. "Are you all right?"

"We are now," said Katy. "But what's wrong with my mom?" She hasn't said a word, and that's so not like her."

"She'll explain it to you when she gets back."

"Back from where?"

"She'll explain that, too."

◆

Connor's attention was now fully on closing down the last portal. They had all been distracted by the appearance of the Lady Deirdre and had watched with fascination her brief struggle with Arkan. They all knew that the laws of karma had reached their fulfillment in that moment between the two former lovers. Arkan was alone now, and Deirdre, having done her part to atone for past misjudgments, had gone...elsewhere. But she had been correct when she said that it would be a very long time before she chose to become incarnate again. Her life as Sonia would have to be examined in some detail. But her death as Sonia had already proved its meaning.

With Katy and the others safe, the Circle's work was almost done.

◆

Malcolm and Ayalla emerged from their hiding places. "Good shooting," said Laura. "I only fired one shot, and I think it was a little low."

"I think we all hit him," said Ayalla graciously. And in point of fact, they had—all center torso shots.

"Does he still have a pulse?"

"Didn't check yet," said Laura turning around just in time to see Yoshi up and running. "What the hell?"

Yoshi was pleased with himself for having predicted the usefulness of a Kevlar vest, and his patience in waiting until their attention was no longer focused on him. As he lay there, his eyes were drawn to the last remaining portal. Even if he couldn't get back, what did it matter? Here he'd lose everything anyway and spend his life in prison. The unknown sounded like a better risk.

Malcolm raised his gun, but Yoshi was almost at the portal. Juncla shouted at Malcolm, "No, wait. Don't fire into it."

And from out of nowhere came Alan Durn. Not knowing precisely why he was choosing this particular moment in his life to demonstrate an ounce of courage, he stepped right between Yoshi and the fading portal. He didn't feel exactly himself anymore.

"Out of my way!" screamed the desperate son of Yohiro Matsumoto, but Alan smiled at him. "No. I don't think so. You have to stay here now. That's how it's supposed to be." Yoshi aimed a vicious kick at Alan's head, but Alan ducked instantly, and Yoshi tried to get around him. His motion only shoved Alan backward...and into the portal. And then it blinked out of sight. Yoshi lay on the ground and began to sob with frustration and fury until Malcolm picked him by the back of his jacket and yanked his arms behind him. "Kevlar vest," he announced to the others. "Who'd a thought?"

Alan fell, seemingly forever. But when he landed, he was feeling more himself.

Now, said the Teacher, *do you still have a question about the eleven stars that appear on the eleventh day of the eleventh month—and your role in the transition?*

No, Master. I begin to understand.

◆

With a brief but passionate prayer of thanks to the Mother, the Circle dissolved its presence on the astral. Connor blinked once or twice, then took the opportunity to hug the daylights out of her daughter, her father, her lover, and her friends, except for Malcolm who had Yoshi in tow and wasn't about to let him go, despite having tied his hands securely with Laura's belt.

The Carlisles joined them, and they stood there waiting, looking at the crystal. "So what will become of it now?" asked Katy. "We can't really leave it here."

"No," said Carmen. "It isn't supposed to be here at all." She took Jenny's hand and together they walked to within a few feet of the beautiful gem that towered over them. They began to speak once again in that language that had no parallel to any dialect still extant in the world. But even without understanding the meaning, the sounds were so beautiful that each of the onlookers was moved to tears.

Brighter and brighter the crystal glowed, until the moon itself was hardly visible in the sky. It even seemed to grow larger as it pulsated faster and faster. And then it began to dissolve. With each moment it grew more transparent, its shape no longer fully discernible. Alandra and Junela continued to speak, to sing, to chant, and within minutes the crystal simply was no more. It faded away as if it had never existed. They had sung it back into the earth, deep within the Mother.

Epilogue

All other things, to their destruction draw,
Only our love hath no decay;
This, no tomorrow hath, nor yesterday,
Running it never runs from us away,
But truly keeps its first, last, everlasting day.
—John Donne, "The Anniversary"

"What will you do now?" asked Connor as she sat in the kitchen with Jenny and Carmen.

"I don't know," replied Jenny. "I need some time to think about all this. I wonder if the memory will fade. Already, I can't speak that language anymore. It's gone, like a dream you can't quite hold on to."

Carmen nodded. "Funny how you start wondering if it only was a dream. But at least it's over."

Connor looked from one to the other. "I was wondering if maybe you two wouldn't mind staying on at Rosewood Cottage."

"We couldn't keep imposing," said Jenny."

"No, we couldn't," Carmen agreed. "We'll go back to the States, sell the house I have in Palm Springs, and..."

"It's entirely up to you," said Connor. "I imagine your family lawyer, Geri Vale, could manage your affairs there. And I really would like to have someone living here year-round to look after the place. I don't get down here very much at all, and it worries me that no one is taking care of things the way my grandmother would like. I get to visit maybe two or three times a year. And if you'd agree to be the caretakers, I could pay you a salary, and you'd have room and board."

Jenny's eyes filled with tears. "I have to admit I really do love it here, but you're just doing this to be nice."

"She's not really *that* nice," said Laura from the doorway.

"Gee, thanks, sweetheart," replied Connor.

"You know I'm only kidding," she said, giving Connor a quick kiss on the top of the head. "But in all seriousness, Jenny, she's telling you the truth. Much as we both like it here, our lives keep us pretty busy stateside. It would be a big load off Connor's mind to have people here full-time who really cared about this house and the gardens—people she can trust."

"I love the garden," exclaimed Carmen. "I always wanted to have one, but Palm Springs isn't really the place to plant the things I like."

"Then it's settled," said Connor. "I'll let the property manager know that you'll be staying on as the official caretakers and all questions should go to you. And I'll set up an account with the bank for household expenses."

Jenny came around the table to give Connor an enormous hug. "Hey, it's no big deal," said Connor, with the sort of gruffness that Laura knew was a cover for embarrassment. Connor hated being thanked for her good deeds. "Now you two get settled in. You're not guests anymore."

They scurried off to do just that. And Laura put her arms around Connor. "You're really a pretty nice person, you know that?"

"Why?"

"You know perfectly well this place doesn't really *need* a caretaker."

"Yeah, but they do need a home, and Carmen doesn't need to be reminded of Bettina right now. Jenny will help her get through that process of mourning when she's ready."

"I love you."

"And I love you. Which reminds me." Connor grabbed her by the arm.

"Where are we going?"

"Outside, where no one is going to interrupt me."

Laura allowed herself to be propelled out the door and all the way to the back of the garden where Mrs. Broadhurst had created a wonderful sitting area for her private moments. This time it was Connor who needed a private moment.

"Okay, now what is it that can't be interrupted?" said Laura. "If it's a kiss you want, darling, our room might have been a better idea, in case it led to bigger and better things."

"No, it isn't a kiss. Well, I always want a kiss, but not right this minute. What I want is…well, what I want to ask you is…"

"Spit it out, darling"

"You remember the other day when we were getting off the plane and you said, 'It's not like we're married?'"

"Oh," said Laura, blushing a bit. "That was just an offhanded comment. I didn't mean anything in particular. Don't worry about it."

"I'm not worried at all."

"Good."

"So, the deal is…" she took Laura's hand in hers. "I love you. Will you marry me?" Laura stared at her long enough that Connor started to look worried. "You don't want to?"

Laura laughed. "No, darling. Of course I want to. I just never really thought you'd ask. It seems so old-fashioned somehow."

"Then I guess I'm an old-fashioned girl, though I didn't get down on one knee. But you still haven't said the actual words."

"What actual words?"

"You know. The 'Yes, I'll marry you' words."

This time Laura flung her arms around Connor's neck and whispered in her ear. "Yes, I'll marry you, and yes, I love you, and yes, I'll spend the rest of my life with you. Does that cover it?"

She stepped back a bit so she could look in Connor's eyes, "Oh, sweetheart, you're crying."

"I cry at the oddest times, don't I?" said Connor.

"No, you cry at all the right times, which is why I love you so much. So, do we set a date or what? These things take some kind of planning."

"How about tomorrow?" said Connor. "I sort of counted on you saying yes."

"But that's so soon. What about—"

"What? Please don't say you need to get a designer wedding gown."

"Don't be absurd. But I do have to find something perfect to wear."

"You will…by tomorrow evening at seven P.M."

"But tomorrow's Friday the thirteenth."

"And a more auspicious date I couldn't imagine. Don't forget, I'm a witch. We like the number thirteen.

◆

At 7:05 the following evening, Laura Nez and Lydia Connor Hawthorne were married in the village church by Connor's old friend, the vicar Philip Janks. In attendance were Benjamin Hawthorne, Katherine VanDevere (in the process of officially changing her name to Hawthorne), the Lord and Lady Carlisle, Carmen Waters, and Jenny Carpenter. Malcolm Jefferson and Ayalla Franklin served in the capacity of best man and maid of honor for the couple. Connor wore a white silk tunic of Asian design with black silk trousers. Laura, after a frantic morning of shopping in the nearest town large enough to have clothing stores, had chosen a black silk shirt and a long white silk skirt. Around her neck she wore the stunning miniature version of a squash blossom necklace, handcrafted in silver, lapis lazuli, and gold that had belonged to her grandmother. Her long dark and shining hair swirled around her shoulders.

The Carlisles, through some magic of their own had provided the rings, two gold bands of intertwined Celtic love knots that miraculously fit Connor and Laura perfectly.

They said traditional vows from the old Book of Common

Prayer, with a few appropriate alterations here and there as provided by the accommodating vicar. He'd loved Mrs. Broadhurst, and was quite fond of Connor and Laura.

As the ceremony proceeded, there was no doubt in anyone's mind that two hearts and two souls were acknowledging something that had been a simple truth for lifetimes. These were two beings who, regardless of the form they took in this lifetime, were soul mates, twin flames, and deeply in love. So focused was Connor, so attuned to the silence between the words, so aware of the lingering scent of incense, and the beauty of the woman who stood before her, that when it was her turn, she said the words almost in unison with the vicar: "To have and to hold from this day forward, for better for worse, for richer for poorer, in sickness and in health, to love and to cherish, till death us do part according to the Mother's holy ordinance, and thereto I plight thee my troth... With this ring I thee wed, with my body I thee worship, and with all my worldly goods I thee endow."

Just before the vicar was about to make his solemn pronouncement, Connor added a vow of her own devising. "Even after death, my love, when we leave this earth, my soul will seek yours out again, and our journey will last through eternity. This I promise you."

Laura, her eyes glistening with tears, said simply, "And I will be waiting when you come for me."

Mr. Janks smiled, and said. "Those whom the Creator of all Things hath joined together in sacred union, let none dare to put asunder. I now pronounce you wedded partners."

The organist began to play, and Carmen sang a lovely old ballad in a sweet, clear voice. Even the stoic Malcolm looked suspiciously teary-eyed before all was said and done, although before the ceremony, he'd jokingly accused Connor of trying to beat him to the altar.

Laura and Connor walked out of the church together hand in hand, toward the next great adventure, even if that adventure was just about discovering how much two people could love each other, and what effect that depth of love would have in the world.

A sudden gust of wind rippled through the trees in the churchyard, flinging leaves in every direction.

Well done, my child, and Goddess keep you both, Gwendolyn whispered into the wind. And her message arrived on the wings of angels.

"Did you just hear something?" asked Laura.

Connor smiled. "Yes, I did...and I agree."